NEW YORK REVIEW BOOKS
CLASSICS

THE ROAD

VASILY SEMYONOVICH GROSSMAN was born on December 12, 1905, in Berdichev, a Ukrainian town that was home to one of Europe's largest Jewish communities. In 1934 he published both "In the Town of Berdichev"—a short story that won the admiration of such diverse writers as Isaak Babel, Maksim Gorky, and Boris Pilnyak—and a novel, *Glyukauf*, about the life of the Donbass miners. During the Second World War, Grossman worked as a war correspondent for the army newspaper *Red Star*, covering nearly all of the most important battles from the defense of Moscow to the fall of Berlin. His vivid yet sober "The Hell of Treblinka" (late 1944), one of the first articles in any language about a Nazi death camp, was translated and used as testimony in the Nuremberg Trials. His novel *Stalingrad* was published in 1952 and then fiercely attacked. A new wave of purges—directed against the Jews—was about to begin; if not for Stalin's death, in March 1953, Grossman would almost certainly have been arrested. During the next few years Grossman, while enjoying public success, worked on his two masterpieces, neither of which was to be published in Russia until the late 1980s: *Life and Fate* and *Everything Flows*. The KGB confiscated the manuscript of *Life and Fate* in February 1961. Grossman was able, however, to continue working on *Everything Flows*, a novel even more critical of Soviet society than *Life and Fate*, until his last days in the hospital. He died on September 14, 1964, on the eve of the twenty-third anniversary of the massacre of the Jews of Berdichev, in which his mother had died.

OTHER BOOKS BY VASILY GROSSMAN
PUBLISHED BY NYRB CLASSICS

An Armenian Sketchbook
Translated by Robert and Elizabeth Chandler
Introduction by Robert Chandler and Yury Bit-Yunan

Everything Flows
Translated by Robert and Elizabeth Chandler and Anna Aslanyan
Introduction by Robert Chandler

Life and Fate
Translated and with an introduction by Robert Chandler

Stalingrad
Translated by Robert and Elizabeth Chandler

THE ROAD
Stories, Journalism, and Essays

VASILY GROSSMAN

Translated from the Russian by
ROBERT AND ELIZABETH CHANDLER
with OLGA MUKOVNIKOVA

Commentary and notes by
ROBERT CHANDLER
with YURY BIT-YUNAN

Afterword by
FYODOR GUBER

NEW YORK REVIEW BOOKS

New York

THIS IS A NEW YORK REVIEW BOOK
PUBLISHED BY THE NEW YORK REVIEW OF BOOKS
435 Hudson Street, New York, NY 10014
www.nyrb.com

Most of the pieces in this volume are translated from the texts published in
Sobranie sochinenii v 4-h tomakh (Moscow: Agraf, 1998). "A Small Life" and
"The Old Man" are included in *V gorode Berdicheve* (Yekaterinburg: U–Faktoriya,
2005). "The Old Teacher" is available at http://www.lib.ru. Grossman's two
letters to his mother are included in Fyodor Guber, *Pamyat' i pis'ma* (Moscow:
Probel, 2007), p. 78–79.

Earlier versions of some of these translations appeared in *Chtenia* ("The Road"),
The New Yorker ("In Kislovodsk"), and *Prospect* ("The Dog").

Library of Congress Cataloging-in-Publication Data
Grossman, Vasilii Semenovich.
 The road / by Vasily Grossman ; introduction by Robert Chandler ; translated
by Robert Chandler, Elizabeth Chandler, and Olga Mukovnikova.
   p. cm. — (New York Review Books classics)
Includes bibliographical references.
ISBN 978-1-59017-361-9 (alk. paper)
 I. Chandler, Robert, 1953– II. Chandler, Elizabeth, 1947– III. Mukovnikova,
Olga. IV. Title.
PG3476.G7R56 2010
891.73'42—dc22

                         2010023048

ISBN 978-1-59017-361-9

Printed in the United States of America on acid-free paper.
10 9 8 7 6 5 4 3

CONTENTS

Vasily Grossman in Magnitogorsk, July 1934

PART ONE

The 1930s

VASILY Semyonovich Grossman was born on December 12, 1905, in Berdichev, a Ukrainian town that was home to one of Europe's largest Jewish communities. In 1897, not long before Grossman's birth, the overall population had been nearly fifty-four thousand, of whom more than forty-one thousand were Jews. At one time there had been eighty synagogues, and in the first half of the nineteenth century, before being supplanted by Odessa, Berdichev had been the most important banking center in the Russian empire.

Both of Grossman's parents were Jewish and they originally named their son Iosif. Being highly Russified, however, they usually called him Vasily or Vasya—and this is how he has always been known. Grossman himself once said to his daughter, Yekaterina Korotkova, "We were not like the poor shtetl Jews described by Sholem Aleichem, the type that lived in hovels and slept side by side on the floor packed like sardines. No, our family comes from a quite different Jewish background. They had their own carriages and trotters. Their women wore diamonds, and they sent their children abroad to study." It is unlikely that Grossman knew Yiddish.

According to Yekaterina Korotkova, Grossman's parents met in Switzerland, where they were both students. Like many Jewish students living abroad, Semyon Osipovich was active in the revolutionary movement. He joined the Russian Social Democratic Labor Party (as the Communist Party was then called) in 1902. When the Party split in 1903, he joined the Menshevik faction, which was opposed to Lenin and the Bolsheviks. We also know that Semyon

Osipovich played an active role in the 1905 Revolution, helping to organize an uprising in Sebastopol.

At some point in his early childhood Vasily's parents separated, though they seem to have remained on friendly terms throughout their lives. Vasily was brought up by his mother, Yekaterina Save-lievna; they were helped by David Sherentsis, the wealthy husband of his mother's sister. From 1910 to 1912 Vasily and his mother lived in Geneva; they then returned to Berdichev, to live with the Sheren-tsis family. His mother worked as a French teacher, and Vasily would retain a good knowledge of French throughout his life; his stepson Fyodor Guber remembers that the family copy of *War and Peace* did not include any Russian translation of the passages writ-ten in French. From 1914 to 1919 Vasily attended secondary school in Kiev. Between 1921 and 1923 he attended the Kiev Higher Insti-tute of Soviet Education, sharing an apartment in Kiev with his fa-ther, and from 1923 to 1929 he studied chemistry at Moscow State University, while also working part-time in a home for street chil-dren. He soon realized that his true vocation was literature, but he had to continue studying for his degree. His father, a chemical engi-neer himself, had worked hard to support him, and he wanted his son to be properly qualified. The family's financial difficulties were compounded by Vasily's marriage, in January 1928, to Anna Mat-suk and the birth of Yekaterina, his only child, in January 1930.

After graduating from the university, Grossman spent two years in the coal-mining area of the Ukraine known as the Donbass, or Donets Basin, working first as a safety engineer in a mine and then as a chemistry teacher in a medical institute. In 1931, after being di-agnosed with tuberculosis, he managed to obtain permission to re-turn to Moscow; it seems likely that he was misdiagnosed, although his daughter believes that he had *incipient* tuberculosis and that this was successfully treated. For two years he worked as an engi-neer in a factory—with a strange appropriateness, it was a pencil factory—but after that he managed to make his living as a profes-sional writer. He never, however, lost his interest in science.

On returning to Moscow, Grossman went to live with Nadya

Almaz, a first cousin on his mother's side. Five years older than Grossman, she was intelligent and ambitious, a woman of strong moral and political convictions. By the late 1920s, she was working as the personal assistant to Solomon Lozovsky, the head of the Profintern (Trade Union International), an organization whose role was to liaise with trade unions in other countries. For Grossman, Nadya Almaz was both an inspiration and a source of crucial practical help. She encouraged him to write about mines and industrial projects, and she arranged for his manuscripts to be typed. With her many connections in Party circles, she enabled Grossman to join a group of young activists on a trip to Uzbekistan in May and June 1928, and she also helped him to get two of his first articles published, one of them in *Pravda*—the Communist Party's main newspaper.

In April 1933, however, Nadya Almaz was arrested, charged with "anti-Soviet activities." She was expelled from the Party and exiled to Astrakhan. Like many other members of internationalist organizations such as the Profintern and the Comintern (Communist International), she was accused of being in contact with foreign Trotskyists. Later in the 1930s such charges were made all too often and were usually false; Nadya Almaz, however, truly had remained in contact with Trotskyists. She was certainly in communication with Viktor Kibal'chich (the writer and former associate of Trotsky better known by his pseudonym of Victor Serge); her OGPU file records that two "extremely counterrevolutionary letters from Viktor Kibal'chich were found in her possession." Grossman was still living with Nadya at this time, and he was questioned during the search of her room. He does not appear to have said anything in her defense either then or during the period of her detainment; he did, however, write to her and send her money, and in September 1934 he visited her in Astrakhan.

The years immediately after this seem to have gone well for Grossman—at least in regard to practical and professional matters. In April 1933, after a long struggle, he obtained a permanent Moscow residence permit, and in the summer of 1933 his first novel,

Glyukauf, about the life of the Donbass miners, was recommended for publication; this led to his being able to join two important organizations: the Moscow Writers Friendship Society and the Literary Fund. Around this time Grossman also became friends with three former members of the literary group Pereval. Aleksandr Voronsky, the group's leading figure, had been a supporter of Trotsky, and Pereval had been officially disbanded in 1932. Nevertheless, its members were still playing an active role in Moscow literary life, and these three writers—Boris Guber, Ivan Kataev, and Nikolay Zarudin—were able to offer Grossman both practical help and encouragement. It was Kataev and Zarudin who, in 1934, took Grossman's story "In the Town of Berdichev" to the editors of the prestigious *Literaturnaya gazeta*. The story was published promptly, and it won the admiration of such diverse writers as Isaak Babel, Maksim Gorky, and Boris Pilnyak. *Glyukauf* was also published in 1934. In the following three years Grossman published three small collections of short stories: *Happiness* (1935), *Four Days* (1936), and *Stories* (1937). In 1937 he was admitted to the recently established Union of Soviet Writers, and he also published the first volume of his long novel *Stepan Kolchugin*. Set in the early twentieth century, it is about a young coal miner who becomes a revolutionary. Grossman's own experience of the Donbass mines, along with the stories he had heard from his father about the revolutionary movement, enabled him to write about this world from the inside. Like Grossman's later, more famous novels, this is fiction with a firm basis in fact and imbued with a deep concern for both public and private morality.

In 1937 Boris Guber was arrested and shot—as were Kataev, Zarudin, and several other former members of Pereval. Grossman's first marriage had ended in 1933 and in the summer of 1935 he had begun an affair with Guber's wife, Olga Mikhailovna. Grossman and Olga Mikhailovna had begun living together in October 1935, and they had married in May 1936, a few days after Olga Mikhailovna and Boris Guber had divorced. Grossman was clearly in danger himself; 1936–37 was the peak of the Great Terror. In 1938 Olga Mikhailovna was arrested for failing to denounce her previous husband, an "enemy of the people." Grossman quickly had himself registered as the official guardian of Olga's two sons by Boris Guber, thus saving them from being sent to orphanages or camps. He then wrote to Nikolay Yezhov, the head of the NKVD, pointing out that Olga Mikhailovna was now *his* wife, not Guber's, and that she should not be held responsible for a man from whom she had separated long before his arrest. Grossman's friend, Semyon Lipkin, has commented, "In 1937 only a very brave man would have dared to write a letter like this to the State's chief executioner." Later that year—astonishingly—Olga Mikhailovna was released.

The true nature of Grossman's, or anyone else's, political beliefs in the 1930s is almost impossible to ascertain; no evidence—no letter, diary, or even report by an NKVD informer—can ever be considered entirely reliable. It is likely, however, that Grossman felt pulled in different directions. On the one hand, many people close to him were arrested or executed in the 1930s, and his father, with whom he had lived for two years when he was in his late teens, had been a committed member of the Menshevik Party, most of whose members had ended up in prison or exile. And it seems that Grossman had at least some sense, at the time it was happening, of the magnitude of the Terror Famine in the Ukraine in 1932–33. On the other hand, he was an ambitious young writer; he wanted to make his mark in the world and he was, therefore, dependent on the Soviet regime. Under the tsars, even in the absence of pogroms, Jews had been the object of discrimination; in the early Soviet Union, by contrast, they constituted a disproportionately large part of the political, professional, and intellectual elite. Whatever his innermost thoughts as he was writing it, this sentence from Grossman's 1937 letter to Yezhov is objectively true: "All that I possess—my education, my success as a writer, the high privilege of sharing my thoughts and feelings with Soviet readers—I owe to the Soviet government."

And Grossman retained at least some degree of revolutionary romanticism until his last days. It is possible that—like many other members of the intelligentsia—he may have continued, throughout the 1930s, to hope that the Soviet system might, in time, fulfill its revolutionary promise.

All that can be said with certainty is that the distinction between the "establishment" writer of the 1930s and 1940s and the "dissident" who wrote *Life and Fate* and *Everything Flows* in the last fifteen years of his life is essentially one of degree. There is no single moment—or even year—that can be seen as having marked a political "conversion." Even Grossman's first novel, *Glyukauf*, little read today, evidently once had some power to shock; in 1932 Gorky criticized a draft for "naturalism"—a Soviet code word for presenting too much unpalatable reality. At the end of his report Gorky suggested that the author should ask himself: "Why am I writing? Which truth am I confirming? Which truth do I wish to triumph?" What Gorky meant by this is that Grossman was showing too little concern for ideology and too much concern for reality. It is hard not to be impressed by Gorky's intuition; he seems to have sensed where Grossman's love of truth might lead him.

Grossman wrote better with each decade, and it is his last stories that are his greatest. From the twenty or so stories he wrote during the 1930s we have included only one story that was published at the time and two that were first published in the 1960s.

"In the Town of Berdichev" is set at the time of the Polish-Soviet War (February 1919 to March 1921), a war fought against Poland by Soviet Russia and Soviet Ukraine. It is not difficult to see why this story was received so enthusiastically. Grossman writes vividly, and he performs a skillful balancing act, neither praising nor damning his heroine, Vavilova, a commissar who has to choose between deserting her newborn baby and deserting her Red Army comrades.

In both style and subject matter the story owes much to Isaak

Babel, whose story cycle *Red Cavalry* is set against the background of the same war. In some respects Grossman seems to be trying to outdo Babel, to show that he is no less inventive than him in finding ways to startle the reader: "At first she had blamed everything [i.e., her pregnancy] on *him*—on the sad, taciturn man who had proved stronger than her and had found a way through her thick leather jacket and the coarse cloth of her tunic and into her woman's heart." At a deeper level, however, the story can be read as a profound criticism of Babel. Many of the finest stories in *Red Cavalry* are about initiations into a world of male violence. Fascinated as he is by violence, Babel does, on the whole, appear to see this initiation as something to be desired. "In the Town of Berdichev," on the other hand, is about a woman being initiated, or almost initiated, into a feminine world—a world she rejects, then accepts, then rejects again.

Babel was ten years older than Grossman, and he came to fame not long after Grossman began his studies at Moscow State University. Like Grossman, Babel was a Ukrainian Jew, an intellectual with a good knowledge of French literature and a love of Maupassant. It is not surprising that Grossman, as an aspiring writer, should have measured himself against Babel. More important, however, is the degree to which he seems to have defined himself by opposition to Babel. Like Babel, Grossman wrote a great deal about violence. Unlike Babel, he was in no way fascinated by it; he wrote about violence simply because he was thrown up against a number of the most terrible acts of violence of the last century. The theme that fascinated Grossman, the theme to which he repeatedly returns, often in the most unexpected of contexts, is that of maternal love.

"A Small Life," written only two years later, in 1936, is immediately recognizable as the work of the mature Grossman; it is as low-key, as unshowy as "In the Town of Berdichev" is showy. Here too, however, Grossman takes risks—though we do not know whether he tried to publish the story at the time. The hero, Lev Orlov, is timid and depressive; even though his first name means "Lion" and his last name means "Eagle," he is the antithesis of the positive hero of socialist realist doctrine. In November 1935 Stalin had declared that "Life has become better, life has become merrier," and these words were repeated again and again—on banners and posters, in radio programs and newspaper articles, and in speeches at May Day parades and other public events. Against this background, Grossman's use of the words "merrily" and "merriment" and Orlov's lack of interest in May Day festivities are provocative. During the 1930s the radio was the most important medium for State propaganda; Orlov's lack of a radio demonstrates his alienation from Soviet life. Grossman does not, of course, overtly sympathize with Orlov, nor does he explicitly condemn him.

With its delicate irony and apparent inconsequentiality, "A Small Life" owes much to Chekhov, who was evidently of central importance to Grossman at least from the beginning of his professional career. "A Young Woman and an Old Woman" is no less Chekhovian. There is painful irony in the contrast between some of our first glimpses of Gagareva, the older of the two women. First we hear her mouthing wooden platitudes about the attention being given by the authorities to "maintaining the health of the country's citizens"; soon afterward we hear her sobbing, loudly and hoarsely, because her daughter is in the Gulag. Grossman does, admittedly, make a concession to Soviet orthodoxy by allowing a series of arrests on a State farm to end positively, with the triumph of justice, but the story's Chekhovian musical structure—the various repeated words and images, the way the story both begins and ends with a description of speeding cars—leads the reader to a very different understanding. As Goryacheva is being driven to her dacha in the first scene, she is struck "by this troubling swiftness, by the ease with which objects, people, and animals appeared, grew bigger, and then disappeared in a flash." In the story's last lines, Gagareva looks down from the window of her Moscow office at the city below:

"Precipitately, as if out of nowhere, [bright automobile headlights] arose out of the fog and gloom, then swiftly traversed the square." The impression left by the story is of the randomness of Soviet life in the 1930s, the "precipitateness" (this word and its cognates are repeated even more times in the original) with which people are elevated to positions of great authority or cast out into darkness.

IN THE TOWN OF BERDICHEV

VAVILOVA'S face was dark and weather-beaten, and it was odd to see it blush.

"Why are you laughing?" she said finally. "It's all so stupid."

Kozyrev took the paper from the table, looked at it, and, shaking his head, burst out laughing again.

"No, it's just too ridiculous," he said through his laughter. "Application for leave...from the commissar of the First Battalion... for forty days for reasons of pregnancy." Then he turned serious. "So what should I do? Who's going to take your place? Perelmuter from the Divisional Political Section?"

"Perelmuter's a sound Communist," said Vavilova.

"You're all sound Communists," said Kozyrev. Lowering his voice, as though he were talking about something shameful, he asked, "Is it due soon, Klavdiya?"

"Yes," said Vavilova. She took off her sheepskin hat and wiped the sweat from her brow.

"I'd have got rid of it," she said in her deep voice, "but I wasn't quick enough. You know what it was like—down by Grubeshov there were three whole months when I was hardly out of the saddle. And when I got to the hospital, the doctor said no." She screwed up her nose, as if about to cry. "I even threatened the bastard with my Mauser," she went on, "but he still wouldn't do anything. He said it was too late."

She left the room. Kozyrev went on staring at her application. "Well, well, well," he said to himself. "Who'd have thought it? She

15

hardly seems like a woman at all. Always with her Mauser, always in leather trousers. She's led the battalion into the attack any number of times. She doesn't even have the voice of a woman... But it seems you can't fight Nature..."

And for some reason he felt hurt, and a little sad.

He wrote on the application, "The bearer..." And he sat there and frowned, irresolutely circling his pen nib over the paper. How should he word it? Eventually he went on: "to be granted forty days of leave from the present date..." He stopped to think, added "for reasons of health," then inserted the word "female," and then, with an oath, deleted the word "female."

"Fine comrades *they* make!" he said, and called his orderly. "Heard about our Vavilova?" he asked loudly and angrily. "Who'd have thought it!"

"Yes," said the orderly. He shook his head and spat.

Together they damned Vavilova and all other women. After a few dirty jokes and a little laughter, Kozyrev called for his chief of staff and said to him, "You must go around tomorrow, I suppose. Find out where she wants to have it—in a hospital or in a billet— and make sure everything's generally all right."

The two men then sat there till morning, poring over the one-inch-to-a-mile map and jabbing their fingers at it. The Poles were advancing.

A room was requisitioned for Vavilova. The little house was in the Yatki—as the marketplace was called—and it belonged to Haim-Abram Leibovich-Magazanik, known to his neighbors and even his own wife as Haim Tuter, that is, Haim the Tatar.

Vavilova's arrival caused an uproar. She was brought there by a clerk from the Communal Department, a thin boy wearing a leather jacket and a pointed Budyonny helmet. Magazanik cursed him in Yiddish; the clerk shrugged his shoulders and said nothing.

Magazanik then switched to Russian. "The cheek of these snotty little bastards!" he shouted to Vavilova, apparently expecting her to share his indignation. "Whose clever idea was this? As if there weren't a single bourgeois left in the whole town! As if there weren't a single room left for the Soviet authorities except where Magazanik lives! As if there weren't a spare room anywhere except one belonging to a worker with seven children! What about Litvak the grocer? What about Khodorov the cloth maker? What about Ashkenazy, our number-one millionaire?"

Magazanik's children were standing around them in a circle—seven curly-headed angels in ragged clothes, all watching Vavilova through eyes black as night. She was as big as a house, she was twice the height of their father. All this was frightening and funny and very interesting indeed.

In the end Magazanik was pushed out of the way, and Vavilova went through to her room.

From the sideboard, from the chairs with gaping holes and sagging seats, from bedclothes now as flat and dark and flaccid as the breasts of the old women who had once received these blankets as part of their wedding dowries, there came such an overpowering smell of human life that Vavilova found herself taking a deep breath, as if about to dive deep into a pond.

That night she was unable to sleep. Behind the partition wall—as if they formed a complete orchestra, with everything from high-pitched flutes and violins to the low drone of the double bass—the Magazanik family was snoring. The heaviness of the summer night, the dense smells—everything seemed to be stifling her.

There was nothing the room did not smell of.

Paraffin, garlic, sweat, fried goose fat, unwashed linen—the smell of human life, of human habitation.

Now and then she touched her swollen, ripening belly; the living being there inside her was kicking and moving about.

For many months, honorably and obstinately, she had struggled against this being. She had jumped down heavily from her horse. During voluntary working Saturdays in the towns she had heaved huge pine logs about with silent fury. In villages she had drunk every kind of herbal potion and infusion. In bathhouses, she had scalded herself until she broke out in blisters. And she had demanded so much iodine from the regimental pharmacy that the medical assistant had been on the point of penning a complaint to the brigade medical department.

But the child had obstinately gone on growing, making it hard for her to move, making it hard for her to ride. She had felt nauseous. She had vomited. She had felt dragged down, dragged toward the earth.

At first she had blamed everything on *him*—on the sad, taciturn man who had proved stronger than her and had found a way through her thick leather jacket and the coarse cloth of her tunic and into her woman's heart. She had remembered him at the head of his men, leading them at a run across a small and terrifyingly simple wooden bridge. There had been a burst of Polish machine-gun fire—and it was as if he had vanished. An empty greatcoat had flung up its arms, fallen, and then hung there over the stream.

She had galloped over him on her maddened stallion and, behind her, as if pushing her on, the battalion had hurtled forward.

What had remained was *it*. It, now, was to blame for everything. And Vavilova was lying there defeated, while *it* kicked its little hoofs victoriously. It was living inside her.

Before Magazanik went out to work in the morning, when his wife was serving him breakfast and at the same time trying to drive away the flies, the children, and the cat, he said quietly, with a sideways glance at the wall of the requisitioned room, "Give her some tea—damn her!"

It was as though he were bathing in the sunlit pillars of dust, in all the smells and sounds—the cries of the children, the mewing of the cat, the muttering of the samovar. He had no wish to go off to the workshop. He loved his wife, his children, and his old mother; he loved his home.

Sighing, he went on his way, and there remained in the house only women and children.

The cauldron of the Yatki went on bubbling all through the day. Peasant men traded birch logs as white as chalk; peasant women rustled strings of onions; old Jewish women sat above downy hillocks of geese tied together by their legs. Every now and then a seller would pluck from one of these splendid white flowers a living petal with a snaking, twisting neck—and the buyer would blow on the tender down between its legs and feel the fat that showed yellow beneath the soft warm skin.

Dark-legged lasses in colorful kerchiefs carried tall red pots brimming with wild strawberries; as if about to run away, they cast frightened looks at the buyers. People on carts sold golden, sweating balls of butter wrapped in plump burdock leaves.

A blind beggar with the white beard of a wizard was stretching out his hands and weeping tragically and imploringly, but no one was touched by his terrible grief. Everyone passed by indifferently. One woman, tearing the very smallest onion off her string, threw it into the old man's tin bowl. He felt it, stopped praying, and said angrily, "May your children be as generous to you in your old age!" And he again began intoning a prayer as ancient as the Jewish nation.

People bought and sold, poked and prodded, raising their eyes as if expecting someone from the tender blue sky to offer them counsel: Should they buy the pike or might they be better off with a carp? And all the time they went on cursing, screeching, scolding one another, and laughing.

Vavilova tidied and swept her room. She put away her greatcoat, her sheepskin hat, and her riding boots. The noise outside was making her head thump, while inside the apartment the little Tuters were all shouting and screaming, and she felt as though she were asleep and dreaming somebody else's bad dream.

In the evening, when he came back home from work, Magazanik stopped in the doorway. He was astounded: his wife, Beila, was sitting at the table—and beside her was a large woman in an ample dress, with loose slippers on her bare feet and a bright-colored kerchief around her head. The two women were laughing quietly, talking to each other, raising and lowering their large broad hands as they sorted through a heap of tiny undershirts.

Beila had gone into Vavilova's room during the afternoon. Vavilova had been standing by the window, and Beila's sharp feminine eye had made out the swollen belly partly concealed by Vavilova's height.

"Begging your pardon," Beila had said resolutely, "but it seems to me that you're pregnant."

And Beila had begun fussing around her, waving her hands about, laughing and lamenting.

"Children," she said, "children—do you have any idea what misery they bring with them?" And she squeezed the youngest of the Tuters against her bosom. "Children are such a grief, such a calamity, such never-ending trouble. Every day they want to eat, and not a week passes by but one of them gets a rash and another gets a boil or comes down with a fever. And Doctor Baraban—may God grant him health—expects ten pounds of the best flour for every visit he makes."

She stroked little Sonya's head. "And every one of my lot is still living. Not one of them's going to die."

Vavilova had turned out to know nothing at all; she did not understand anything, nor did she know how to do anything. She had immediately subordinated herself to Beila's great knowledge. She had listened, and she had asked questions, and Beila, laughing with pleasure at the ignorance of this woman commissar, had told her everything she needed to know.

How to feed a baby; how to wash and powder a baby; how to stop a baby crying at night; how many diapers and babies' shirts she was going to need; the way newborn babies can scream and scream until they're quite beside themselves; the way they turn blue and your heart almost bursts from fear that your child is about to die; the best way to cure the runs; what causes diaper rash; how one day a teaspoon will make a knocking sound against a child's gums and you know that it's started to teethe.

A complex world with its own laws and customs, its own joys and sorrows.

It was a world about which Vavilova knew nothing—and Beila indulgently, like an elder sister, had initiated her into it.

"Get out from under our feet!" she had yelled at the children.

"Out you go into the yard—quick march!" The moment they were alone in the room, Beila had lowered her voice to a mysterious whisper and begun telling Vavilova about giving birth. Oh no, childbirth was no simple matter—far from it. And like an old soldier talking to a new recruit, Beila had told Vavilova about the great joys and torments of labor.

"Childbirth," she had said. "You think it's child's play, like war. Bang, bang—and there's an end to it. No, I'm sorry, but that's not how it is at all."

Vavilova had listened to her. This was the first time in all the months of her pregnancy that she had met someone who spoke of the unfortunate accident that had befallen her as if it were a happy event, as if it were the most important and necessary thing in her life.

Discussions, now including Magazanik, continued into the evening. There was no time to lose. Immediately after supper, Magazanik took a candle, went up into the attic, and with much clattering brought down a metal cradle and a little tub for bathing the new person.

"Have no fears, comrade Commissar," he said. He was laughing and his eyes were shining. "You're joining a thriving business."

"Shut your mouth, you rascal!" said his wife. "No wonder they call you an ignorant Tatar."

That night Vavilova lay in her bed. The dense smells no longer felt stifling, as they had during the previous night. She was used to them now; she was not even aware of them. She no longer wanted to have to think about anything.

It seemed to her that there were horses nearby and that she could hear them neighing. She glimpsed a long row of horses' heads; the horses were all chestnut and each had a white blaze on its forehead. The horses were constantly moving, nodding, snorting, baring their teeth. She remembered the battalion; she remembered Kirpichov, the political officer of the Second Company. There was a lull in the fighting at present. Who would give the soldiers their political talks? Who would tell them about the July days? The quartermaster should be hauled over the coals for this delay in the issue of boots. Once they had boots, the soldiers could make themselves foot-cloths. There were a lot of malcontents in the second company, especially that curly-headed fellow who was always singing songs about the Don. Vavilova yawned and closed her eyes. The battalion had gone somewhere far, far away, into the pink corridor of the dawn, between damp ricks of hay. And her thoughts about it were somehow unreal.

It gave an impatient push with its little hoofs. Vavilova opened her eyes and sat up in bed.

"A boy or a girl?" she asked out loud.

And all of a sudden her heart felt large and warm. Her heart-beats were loud and resonant.

"A boy or a girl?"

In the afternoon she went into labor.

"Oy!" she screamed hoarsely, sounding more like a peasant woman than a commissar. The pain was sharp, and it penetrated everywhere.

Beila helped her back to her bed. Little Syoma ran off merrily to fetch the midwife.

Vavilova was clutching Beila's hand. She was speaking quickly and quietly: "It's started, Beila. I'd thought it would be another ten days. It's started, Beila."

Then the pains stopped, and she thought she'd been wrong to send for the midwife.

But half an hour later the pains began again. Vavilova's tan now seemed separate from her, like a mask; underneath it her face had gone white. She lay there with her teeth clenched. It was as if she were thinking about something tormenting and shameful, as if, any minute now, she would jump up and scream, "What have I done! What have I gone and done!" And then, in her despair, she would hide her face in her hands.

The children kept peeping into the room. Their blind grand-mother was by the stove, boiling a large saucepan of water. Alarmed by the look of anguish on Vavilova's face, Beila kept looking toward the street door. At last the midwife arrived. Her name was Rosalia Samoilovna. She was a stocky woman with a red face and close-cropped hair. Soon the whole house was filled by her piercing, cantankerous voice. She shouted at Beila, at the children, at the old grandmother. Everyone began bustling about. The Primus stove in the kitchen began to hum. The children began dragging the table and chairs out of the room. Looking as if she were trying to put out a fire, Beila was hurriedly mopping the floor. Rosalia Samoilovna was driving the flies away with a towel. Vavilova watched her and for a moment thought they were in the divisonal headquarters and that the army commander had just arrived. He too was stocky, red-faced, and cantankerous, and he used to show up at times when the Poles had suddenly broken through the front line, when everyone was reading communiqués, whispering, and exchanging anxious looks as though a dead body or someone mortally ill were lying in the room with them. And the army commander would slash through this web of mystery and silence. He would curse, laugh, and shout out orders: What did he care about supply trains that had been cut off or entire regiments that had been surrounded?

Vavilova subordinated herself to Rosalia Samoilovna's powerful voice. She answered her questions; she turned onto her back or her side; she did everything she was told. Now and then her mind clouded. The walls and the ceiling lost their outlines; they were breaking up and moving in on her like waves. The midwife's loud voice would bring her back to herself. Once again she would see Rosalia Samoilovna's red, sweating face and the ends of the white kerchief tied over her hair. Her mind was empty of thoughts. She wanted to howl like a wolf; she wanted to bite the pillow. Her bones were cracking and breaking apart. Her forehead was covered by a sticky, sickly sweat. But she did not cry out; she just ground her teeth and, convulsively jerking her head, gasped in air.

Sometimes the pain went away, as if it had never been there at all, and she would look around in amazement, listening to the noise of the market, astonished by a glass on a stool or a picture on the wall.

When the child, desperate for life, once again began fighting its way out, she felt not only terror of the pain to come but also an uncertain joy: there was no getting away from this, so let it be quick.

Rosalia Samoilovna said quietly to Beila, "If you think I'd wish it upon myself to be having my first child at the age of thirty-six, then you're wrong, Beila."

Vavilova had not been able to make out the words, but it frightened her that Rosalia Samoilovna was speaking so quietly.

"What?" she asked. "Am I going to die?"

She did not hear Rosalia Samoilovna's answer. As for Beila, she was looking pale and lost. Standing in the doorway, shrugging her shoulders, she was saying, "Oy, oy, who needs all this? Who needs all this suffering? She doesn't need it. Nor does the child. Nor does the father, drat him. Nor does God in his heaven. Whose clever idea was it to torment us like this?"

The birth took many hours.

When he got back from work, Magazanik sat on the front steps, as anxious as if it were not Vavilova but his own Beila who was giving birth. The twilight thickened; lights appeared in the windows. Jews were coming back from the synagogue, their prayer garments rolled up under their arms. In the moonlight the empty marketplace and the little streets and houses seemed beautiful and mysterious. Red Army men in riding breeches, their spurs jingling, were walking along the brick pavements. Young girls were nibbling sunflower seeds, laughing as they looked at the soldiers. One of them was gabbling: "And I was eating sweets and throwing the wrappers at him, eating sweets and tossing the wrappers at him ..."

"Yes," Magazanik said to himself. "It's like in the old tale ... So little work to do in the house that she had to go and buy herself a clutch of piglets. So few cares of my own that I have to have a whole partisan brigade giving birth in my house." All of a sudden he pricked up his ears and stood up. Inside the house he had heard a hoarse male voice. The oaths and curses this voice was shouting were so foul that Magazanik could only shake his head and spit. The voice was Vavilova's. Crazed with pain, and in the last throes of labor, she was wrestling with God, with woman's accursed lot.

"Yes," said Magazanik. "You can tell it's a commissar giving birth. The strongest words I've ever heard from my own dear Beila are 'Oy, Mama! Oy, Mama! Oy, dearest Mama of mine!' "

Rosalia Samoilovna smacked the newborn on its damp, wrinkled bottom and declared, "It's a boy!"

"What did I say!" cried Beila. Half opening the door, she cried out triumphantly, "Haim, children, it's a boy!"

And the entire family clustered in the doorway, excitedly talking to Beila. Even the blind grandmother had managed to find her way over to her son and was smiling at the great miracle. She was moving her lips; her head was shaking and trembling as she ran her numb hands over her black kerchief. She was smiling and whispering something no one could hear. The children were pushing her back from the door, but she was pressing forward, craning her neck. She wanted to hear the voice of ever-victorious life.

Vavilova was looking at the baby. She was astonished that this insignificant ball of red-and-blue flesh could have caused her such suffering.

She had imagined that her baby would be large, snub-nosed, and freckled, that he would have a shock of red hair and that he would immediately be getting up to mischief, struggling to get somewhere, calling out in a piercing voice. Instead, he was as puny as an oat stalk that had grown in a cellar. His head wouldn't stay upright; his bent little legs looked quite withered as they twitched about; his pale blue eyes seemed quite blind; and his squeals were barely audible. If you opened the door too suddenly, he might be extinguished—like the thin, bent little candle that Beila had placed above the edge of the cupboard.

And although the room was as hot as a bathhouse, she stretched out her arms and said, "But he's cold—give him to me!" The little person was chirping, moving his head from side to side. Vavilova watched him through narrowed eyes, barely daring to move. "Eat,

eat, my little son," she said, and she began to cry. "My son, my little son," she murmured—and the tears welled up in her eyes and, one after another, ran down her tanned cheeks until they disappeared into the pillow.

She remembered *him*, the taciturn one, and she felt a sharp maternal ache—a deep pity for both father and son. For the first time, she wept for the man who had died in combat near Korosten: never would this man see his own son.

And this little one, this helpless one, had been born without a father. Afraid he might die of cold, she covered him with the blanket.

Or maybe she was weeping for some other reason. Rosalia Samoilovna, at least, seemed to think so. After lighting a cigarette and letting the smoke out through the little ventilation pane, she said, "Let her cry, let her cry. It calms the nerves better than any bromide. All my mothers cry after giving birth."

Two days after the birth, Vavilova got up from her bed. Her strength was returning to her; she walked about a lot and helped Beila with the housework. When there was no one around, she quietly sang songs to the little person. This little person was now called Alyosha, Alyoshenka, Alyosha...

"You wouldn't believe it," Beila said to her husband. "That Russian woman's gone off her head. She's already rushed to the doctor with him three times. I can't so much as open a door in the house: he might catch a cold, or he's got a fever, or we might wake him up. In a word, she's turned into a good Jewish mother."

"What do you expect?" replied Magazanik. "Is a woman going to turn into a man just because she wears a pair of leather breeches?" And he shrugged his shoulders and closed his eyes.

A week later, Kozyrev and his chief of staff came to visit Vavilova. They smelled of leather, tobacco, and horse sweat. Alyosha was sleeping in his cradle, protected from the flies by a length of gauze. Creaking deafeningly, like a pair of brand-new leather boots, the two men approached the cradle and looked at the sleeper's thin little face. It was twitching. The movements it made—although no more than little movements of skin—imparted to it a whole range of different expressions: sorrow, anger, and then a smile.

The soldiers exchanged glances.

"Yes," said Kozyrev.

"No doubt about it," said the chief of staff.

And they sat down on two chairs and began to talk. The Poles had gone on the offensive. Our forces were retreating. Temporarily, of course. The Fourteenth Army was regrouping at Zhmerinka. Divisions were coming up from the Urals. The Ukraine would soon be ours. In a month or so there would be a breakthrough, but right now the Poles were causing trouble.

Kozyrev swore.

"Sh!" said Vavilova. "Don't shout or you'll wake him."

"Yes, we've been given a bloody nose," said the chief of staff.

"You do talk in a silly way," said Vavilova. In a pained voice she added, "I wish you'd stop smoking. You're puffing away like a steam engine."

The soldiers suddenly began to feel bored. Kozyrev yawned. The chief of staff looked at his watch and said, "It's time we were on our way to Bald Hill. We don't want to be late."

"I wonder where that gold watch came from," Vavilova thought crossly.

"Well, Klavdiya, we must say goodbye to you!" said Kozyrev. He got to his feet and went on: "I've given orders for you to be delivered a sack of flour, some sugar, and some fatback. A cart will come around later today."

The two men went out into the street. The little Magazaniks were all standing around the horses. Kozyrev grunted heavily as he clambered up. The chief of staff clicked his tongue and leaped into the saddle.

When they got to the corner, the two men abruptly, as though by prior agreement, pulled on the reins and stopped.

"Yes," said Kozyrev.

"No doubt about it," said the chief of staff. They burst into laughter. Whipping their horses, they galloped off to Bald Hill.

The two-wheeled cart arrived in the evening. After dragging the provisions inside, Magazanik went into Vavilova's room and said in a conspiratorial whisper, "What do you make of this, comrade Vavilova? We've got news—the brother-in-law of Tsesarsky the cobbler has just come to the workshop." He looked around and, as if apologizing for something, said in a tone of disbelief, "The Poles are in Chudnov, and Chudnov's only twenty-five miles away."

Beila came in. She had overheard some of this, and she said resolutely, "There's no two ways about it—the Poles will be here tomorrow. Or maybe it'll be the Austrians or the Galicians. Anyway, whoever it is, you can stay here with us. And they've brought you enough food—may the Lord be praised—for the next three months."

Vavilova said nothing. For once in her life she did not know what to do.

"Beila," she began, and fell silent.

"I'm not afraid," said Beila. "Why would I be afraid? I can manage five like Alyosha—no trouble at all. But whoever heard of a mother abandoning a ten-day-old baby?"

All through the night there were noises outside the window: the neighing of horses, the knocking of wheels, loud exclamations, angry voices. The supply carts were moving from Shepetovka to Kazatin.

Vavilova sat by the cradle. Her child was asleep. She looked at his little yellow face. Really, nothing very much was going to happen. Kozyrev had said that they would be back in a month. That was exactly the length of time she was expecting to be on leave. But what if she were cut off for longer? No, that didn't frighten her, either.

Once Alyosha was a bit stronger, they'd find their way across the front line.

Who was going to harm them—a peasant woman with a babe in arms? And Vavilova imagined herself walking through the countryside early on a summer's morning. She had a colored kerchief on her head, and Alyosha was looking all around and stretching out his little hands. How good it all felt! In a thin voice she began to sing, "Sleep, my little son, sleep!" And, as she was rocking the cradle, she dozed off.

In the morning the market was as busy as ever. The people, though, seemed especially excited. Some of them, watching the unbroken chain of supply carts, were laughing joyfully. But then the carts came to an end. Now there were only people. Standing by the town gates were just ordinary townsfolk—the "civilian population" of decrees issued by commandants. Everybody was looking around all the time, exchanging excited whispers. Apparently the Poles had already taken Pyatka, a shtetl only ten miles away. Magazanik had not gone out to work. Instead, he was sitting in Vavilova's room, philosophizing for all he was worth.

An armored car rumbled past in the direction of the railway station. It was covered in a thick layer of dust—as if the steel had gone gray from exhaustion and too many sleepless nights.

"To be honest with you," Magazanik was saying, "this is the best time of all for us townsfolk. One lot has left—and the next has yet to arrive. No requisitions, no 'voluntary contributions,' no pogroms."

"It's only in the daytime that he's so smart," said Beila. "At night, when there are bandits on every street and the whole town's in uproar, he sits there looking like death. All he can do is shake with terror."

"Don't interrupt," Magazanik said crossly, "when I'm talking to someone."

Every now and then he would slip out to the street and come back with the latest news. The Revolutionary Committee had been evacuated during the night, the district Party Committee had gone next, and the military headquarters had left in the morning. The station was empty. The last army train had already gone.

Vavilova heard shouts from the street. An airplane in the sky! She went to the window. The plane was high up, but she could see the white-and-red roundels on its wings. It was a Polish reconnaissance plane. It made a circle over the town and flew off toward the station. And then, from the direction of Bald Hill, cannons began firing.

The first sound they heard was that of the shells; they howled by like a whirlwind. Next came the long sigh of the cannons. And then, a few seconds later, from beyond the level crossing—a joyful peal of explosions. It was the Bolsheviks—they were trying to slow the Polish advance. Soon the Poles were responding in kind; shells began to land in the town.

The air was torn by deafening explosions. Bricks were crumbling. Smoke and dust were dancing over the flattened wall of a building. The streets were silent, severe, and deserted—now no more substantial than sketches. The quiet after each shell burst was terrifying. And from high in a cloudless sky the sun shone gaily down on a town that was like a spread-eagled corpse.

The townsfolk were all in their cellars and basements. Their eyes closed, barely conscious, they were holding their breath or letting out low moans of fear.

Everyone, even the little children, knew that this bombardment was what is known as an "artillery preparation" and that there would be another forty or fifty explosions before the soldiers entered the town. And then—as everyone knew—it would become unbelievably quiet until, all of a sudden, clattering along the broad street from the level crossing, a reconnaissance patrol galloped up. And, dying of fear and curiosity, everyone would be peeping out from behind their gates, peering through gaps in shutters and curtains. Drenched in sweat, they would begin to tiptoe out to the street.

The patrol would enter the main square. The horses would prance and snort; the riders would call out to one another in a marvelously simple human language, and their leader, delighted by the humility of this conquered town now lying flat on its back, would yell out in a drunken voice, fire a revolver shot into the maw of the silence, and get his horse to rear.

And then, pouring in from all sides, would come cavalry and infantry. From one house to another would rush tired dusty men in blue greatcoats—thrifty peasants, good-natured enough yet capable of murder and greedy for the town's hens, boots, and towels.

Everybody knew all this, because the town had already changed hands fourteen times. It had been held by Petlyura, by Denikin, by the Bolsheviks, by Galicians and Poles, by Tyutyunik's brigands and Marusya's brigands, and by the crazy Ninth Regiment that was a law unto itself. And it was the same story each time.

"They're singing!" shouted Magazanik. "They're singing!"

And, forgetting his fear, he ran out onto the front steps. Vavilova followed him. After the stuffiness of the dark room, it was a joy to breathe in the light and warmth of the summer day. She had been feeling the same about the Poles as she had felt about the pains of labor: they were bound to come, so let them come quick. If the explosions scared her, it was only because she was afraid they would wake Alyosha; the whistling shells troubled her no more than flies—she just brushed them aside.

"Hush now, hush now," she had sung over the cradle. "Don't go waking Alyosha."

She was trying not to think. Everything, after all, had been decided. In a month's time, either the Bolsheviks would be back or she and Alyosha would cross the front line to join them.

"What on earth's going on?" said Magazanik. "Look at that!"

Marching along the broad empty street, toward the level crossing from which the Poles should be about to appear, was a column of young Bolshevik cadets. They were wearing white canvas trousers and tunics.

"Ma-ay the re-ed banner embo-ody the workers' ide-e-als," they sang, drawing out the words almost mournfully.

They were marching toward the Poles.

Why? Whatever for?

Vavilova gazed at them. And suddenly it came back to her: Red Square, vast as ever, and several thousand workers who had volunteered for the front, thronging around a wooden platform that had been knocked together in a hurry. A bald man, gesticulating with his cloth cap, was addressing them. Vavilova was standing not far from him.

She was so agitated that she could not take in half of what he said, even though, apart from not quite being able to roll his r's, he had a clear voice. The people standing beside her were almost gasping as they listened. An old man in a padded jacket was crying.

Just what had happened to her on that square, beneath the dark walls, she did not know. Once, at night, she had wanted to talk about it to *him*, to her taciturn one. She had felt he would understand. But she had been unable to get the words out...And as the men made their way from the square to the Bryansk Station, *this* was the song they had been singing.

Looking at the faces of the singing cadets, she lived through once again what she had lived through two years before.

The Magazaniks saw a woman in a sheepskin hat and a greatcoat running down the street after the cadets, slipping a cartridge clip into her large gray Mauser as she ran.

Not taking his eyes off her, Magazanik said, "Once there were people like that in the Bund. Real human beings, Beila. Call us human beings? No, we're just manure."

Alyosha had woken up. He was crying and kicking about, trying to kick off his swaddling clothes. Coming back to herself, Beila said to her husband, "Listen, the baby's woken up. You'd better light the Primus—we must heat up some milk."

The cadets disappeared around a turn in the road.

A SMALL LIFE

Moscow spends the last ten days of April preparing for May Day. The cornices of buildings and the little iron railings along boulevards are repainted, and in the evenings mothers throw up their hands in despair at the sight of their sons' trousers and coats. On all the city's squares carpenters merrily saw up planks that still smell of pine resin and the damp of the forest. Supplies managers use their directors' cars to collect great heaps of red cloth.

Visitors to different government institutions find that their requests all meet with the same answer: "Yes, but let's leave this until after the holiday!"

Lev Sergeyevich Orlov was standing on a street corner with his colleague Timofeyev. Timofeyev was saying, "You're being an old woman, Lev Sergeyevich. We could go to a beer hall or a restaurant. We could just wander about and watch the crowds. So what if it upsets your wife? You're an old woman, the most complete and utter old woman!"

But Lev Sergeyevich said goodbye and went on his way. Morose by nature, he used to say of himself, "I'm made in such a way that I see what is tragic, even when it's covered by rose petals."

And Lev Sergeyevich truly did see tragedy everywhere.

Even now as he made his way through the crowds he was thinking how awful it must feel to be stuck in a hospital during these days of merriment, how miserable these days must be for pharmacists, engine drivers, and train crews—people who have to work on the First of May.

When he got home, he said all this to his wife. She began to laugh at him, but he just shook his head and carried on being upset.

Still turning over the same thoughts, he continued to let out loud sighs until late into the night. His wife said angrily, "Lyova, why do you have to feel so sorry for the pharmacists? Why not feel sorry for me for a change and let me sleep? You know I've got to be at work by eight o'clock."

And, the next day, she did indeed leave for work while Lev Sergeyevich was still asleep.

In the mornings he was usually in a good mood at the office, but by two in the afternoon he would be missing his wife, feeling anxious and fidgety and constantly watching the clock. His colleagues understood all this and used to make fun of him.

"Lev Sergeyevich is already looking at the clock," someone would say—and everyone would laugh except for Agnessa Petrovna, the elderly head accountant, who would pronounce with a sigh: "Orlov's wife is the luckiest woman in all Moscow."

This day was no different. As the afternoon wore on, he grew fidgety, shrugging his shoulders in disbelief as he watched the minute hand of the clock.

"Someone to speak to you, Lev Sergeyevich," a voice called from the adjoining room. It turned out to be his wife—phoning to say that she would have to stay on at work for an extra hour and a half to retype the director's report.

"All right then," Lev Sergeyevich replied in a hurt voice, and he hung up.

He did not hurry home. The city was buzzing, and the buildings, streets, and sidewalks all seemed somehow special, not like themselves at all. And this intangible something, born of the May Day sense of community, took many forms. It could be sensed even in the way a policeman was dragging away a drunk. It was as though all the men wandering about the street were related—as though they were all cousins, or uncles and nephews.

Today he would have been only too glad to saunter about with Timofeyev. It was unpleasant being the first to get back home. The room always seems empty and unwelcoming, and there is no getting away from frightening thoughts: What if something had happened to Vera Ignatyevna? What if she had twisted her ankle jumping off a tram?

Lev Sergeyevich would start to imagine that some hulking trolley car had knocked Vera Ignatyevna down, that people were crowding around her body, that an ambulance was tearing along, wailing ominously. He would be seized with terror; he would want to phone friends and family; he would want to rush to the Emergency First-Aid Institute or to the police.

Every time his wife was ten or fifteen minutes late it was the same. He would feel the same panic.

What a lot of people there were on the street now! Why were they all sauntering up and down the boulevard, sitting idly on benches, stopping in front of every illuminated shop window? But then he came to his own building, and his heart leaped for joy. The little ventilation pane was open—his wife was already back.

He kissed Vera Ignatyevna several times. He looked into her eyes and stroked her hair.

"What a strange one you are!" she said. "It's the same every time. Anyone would think I've come back from Australia, not from the Central Rubber Office."

"If I don't see you all day," he replied, "you might just as well be in Australia."

"You and your eternal Australia!" said Vera Ignatyevna. "They ask me to help type the wall newspaper—and I refuse. I skip Air-Chem Defense Society meetings and come rushing back home. Kazakova has two little children—but Kazakova has no trouble at all staying behind. And that's not all—she's a member of the automobile club as well!"

"What a silly darling goose you are!" said Lev Sergeyevich. "Who ever heard of a wife giving her husband a hard time for being too much of a stay-at-home?"

Vera Ignatyevna wanted to answer back, but instead she said in an excited voice, "I've got a surprise for you! The Party committee's been asking people to take in orphanage children for a few days over the holiday. I volunteered—I said we'd like a little girl. You won't be cross with me, will you?"

Lev Sergeyevich gave his wife a hug.

"How could I be cross with my clever girl?" he said. "It scares me even to think about what I'd be doing and how I'd be living now if chance hadn't brought us together at that birthday party at the Kotelkovs."

On the evening of April 29, Vera Ignatyevna was brought back home in a Ford. As she went up the stairs, pink with pleasure, she said to the little girl who had come with her, "What a treat to go for a ride in a car. I could have carried on riding around for the rest of my life!"

It was the second time Vera Ignatyevna had been in a car. Two years before, when her mother-in-law had come to visit, they had taken a taxi from the station. True, that first ride had not been all it might have been—the driver had never stopped cursing, saying his tires would probably collapse and that, with such a mountain of luggage, they should have taken a three-ton truck.

Vera Ignatyevna and her little guest had barely entered the room when the doorbell rang.

"Ah, it must be Uncle Lyova," said Vera Ignatyevna. She took the little girl by the hand and led her toward the door.

"Let me introduce you," she said. "This is Ksenya Mayorova, and this is comrade Orlov, Uncle Lyova, my husband."

"Greetings, my child!" said Orlov, and patted the little girl on the head.

He felt disappointed. He had imagined the little girl would be tiny and pretty, with sad eyes like the eyes of a grown-up woman. Ksenya Mayorova, however, was plain and stocky, with fat red cheeks, lips that stuck out a little, and eyes that were gray and narrow.

"We came by car," she boasted in a deep voice.

While Vera Ignatyevna was preparing supper, Ksenya wandered about the room examining everything.

"Auntie, have you got a radio?" she asked.

"No, darling. But come here—there's something we have to do."

Vera Ignatyevna took her into the bathroom. There they talked about the zoo and the planetarium.

During supper Ksenya looked at Lev Sergeyevich, laughed, and said pointedly, "Uncle didn't wash his hands!"

She had a deep voice, but her laugh was thin and giggly.

Vera Ignatyevna asked Ksenya how much seven and eight came to, and what was the German word for a door. She asked her if she knew how to skate. They argued about what was the capital of Belgium; Vera Ignatyevna thought it was Antwerp. "No, it's Geneva," Ksenya insisted, pouting and stubbornly shaking her head.

Lev Sergeyevich took his wife aside and whispered, "Put her to bed. Then I'll sit with her and tell her a story—she doesn't feel at home with us yet."

"Why don't you go out into the corridor and have a smoke?" answered his wife. "In the meantime we can air the room."

Lev Sergeyevich walked up and down the corridor and struggled to recall a fairy tale. Little Red Riding Hood? No, she probably knew it already. Maybe he should just tell her about the quiet little town of Kasimov, about the forests there, about going for walks on the bank of the Oka—about his grandmother, about his brother, about his sisters?

When his wife called him back, Ksenya was already in bed. Lev Sergeyevich sat down beside her and patted her on the head.

"Well," he asked, "how do you like it here?"

Ksenya yawned convulsively and rubbed her eyes with one fist.

"It's all right," she said. "But it must be very hard for you without a radio."

Lev Sergeyevich began recounting stories from his childhood. Ksenya yawned three times in quick succession and said, "You shouldn't sit on someone's bed if you're wearing clothes. Microbes can crawl off you."

Her eyes closed. Half asleep, she began mumbling incoherently, telling some crazy story.

"Yes," she whined. "They didn't let me go on the excursion. Lidka saw when we were still in the garden...Why didn't she say anything...? And I carried it twice in my pocket...I've been pricked all over...but it wasn't me who told them about the glass, she's a sneak..."

She fell asleep. Lev Sergeyevich and his wife went on looking at her face in silence. She was sleeping very quietly, her lips sticking out more than ever, her reddish pigtails moving very slightly against the pillow.

Where was she from? The Ukraine, the north Caucasus, the Volga? Who had her father been? Perhaps he had died doing some glorious work in a mine or in the smoke of some huge furnace? Perhaps he had drowned while floating timber down a river? Who had he been? A mechanic? A porter? A housepainter? A shopkeeper? There was something magnificent and touching about this peacefully sleeping little girl.

In the morning Vera Ignatyevna went off to do some shopping. She needed to stock up for the three days of the holiday. She also wanted to go to the Mostorg Department Store and buy some silk for a summer dress. Lev Sergeyevich and Ksenya stayed behind.

"Listen, *mein liebes Kind*," he said. "We're not going out anywhere today, we're going to stay at home."

He sat Ksenya down on his knee, put an arm around her shoulder, and began telling her stories.

"Sit still now, be a good girl," he would say every time she tried to get down. In the end Ksenya sat still, snuffling occasionally as she watched this talking uncle.

By the time Vera Ignatyevna got back, it was already four o'clock. There had been a lot of people in the shops.

"Why are you looking so sulky, Ksenya?" she asked in a startled voice.

"Why shouldn't I look sulky?" Ksenya answered. "Maybe I'm hungry."

Vera Ignatyevna hurried into the kitchen to prepare supper; Lev Sergeyevich carried on entertaining their little guest.

After supper, Ksenya asked for a pencil and some paper, so she could write a letter. "But I don't need a stamp," she added. "I'll give it to Lidka myself."

While Ksenya was writing, Vera Ignatyevna suggested to her husband that they all go out to the cinema, but Lev Sergeyevich did not like this idea. "What on earth are you thinking of, Vera? The crowds tonight will be terrible. In the first place we won't be able to get tickets. In the second place, it's the kind of evening one wants to spend at home."

"It's our good fortune to spend all our evenings at home," retorted Vera Ignatyevna.

"Please don't start an argument," snapped Lev Sergeyevich.

"The girl's bored. She's used to being with other people all the time. She's used to being with her friends."

"Oh, Vera, Vera," he replied.

Later in the evening they all had tea with cornel jam, and they ate a cake and some pastries. Ksenya enjoyed the cake very much indeed; Vera Ignatyevna felt worried, put her hand on the little girl's tummy, and shook her head. Soon afterward the girl's tummy did indeed start to ache. She turned very sullen and stood for a long time by the window, pressing her nose to the cold glass. When the glass became warm, she moved along a little and began to warm another patch of glass with her nose.

Lev Sergeyevich went up to her and asked, "What are you thinking about?"

"Everything," the girl answered crossly, and went back to squashing her nose into the glass.

In the orphanage they were probably about to have supper. There hadn't been time for her to receive her present, and she was sure to be left something boring, like a book about animals. She already had one of those. Still, she'd be able to do a swap. This Auntie Vera was really nice. A pity she wasn't one of the staff. The girls who'd stayed behind in the orphanage were going to spend all day riding about in a truck. As for herself, she was going to become a pilot and drop a gas bomb on this strange Uncle Lyova ... There were some quite big girls out in the yard...they were probably from group seven.

She dozed off on her feet and banged her forehead against the glass.

"Go to bed, Ksenka!" said Vera Ignatyevna.

"I butted the glass just like a ram," said Ksenya.

Lev Sergeyevich woke up in the night. He put out a hand to touch his wife's shoulder, but she wasn't there.

"What's up? Where's my darling Verochka?" he thought in alarm.

He could hear a quiet voice coming from the sofa, and sobs.

"Calm down now, you silly thing," Vera Ignatyevna was saying. "How can I take you back at night? There aren't any trams, and we'd have to walk all the way across Moscow."

"I kno-o-o-w," answered a deep voice, in between sobs. "But he's so very dismable."

"Never mind, never mind. He's kind, he's good. You can see *I'm* not crying!"

Lev Sergeyevich covered his head with the blanket, so as not to hear any more. Pretending he was asleep, he began quietly snoring.

A YOUNG WOMAN
AND AN OLD WOMAN

STEPANIDA Yegorovna Goryacheva, head of a department of an All-Union People's Commissariat, was leaving for the Crimea that evening. Her vacation began on August 1, but since July 30 was a Saturday, she had decided to leave early, on the evening of the twenty-ninth.

First, however, she had to hurry straight from her office to her dacha in Kuntsevo. Her car was being serviced; afraid of being late, she telephoned her old comrade Cheryomushkin. In 1932 they had worked in the same brigade on a State grain farm; they had both been assistants to the operator of the combine harvester. Cheryomushkin immediately sent over a car—an M-1.

Now she was being driven down the broad new highway to Kuntsevo.

"What's that knocking?" Goryacheva asked the driver.

The driver gave her a sideways look, licked his upper lip, and by way of reply, asked a question himself: "Will you be needing me long?"

"I shall be needing you for as long as I need you."

"The car should have gone in for a service today. I told Cheryomushkin."

"I have to be at the station by eleven. I can't let you go until then."

Goryacheva glanced at the driver several times, but she did not say any more to him; he really did look very sullen. They continued along the road. Coming from the opposite direction were other M-1s, their paintwork gleaming, and long ZIS's—beige, green, or black. At intervals along the highway, which was delineated by a broken white line, were benches with awnings, so that people could wait for buses in comfort, and smart, brightly colored little bridges at places where pedestrians needed to cross over. There were also policemen in white gloves, patrolling the highway with the unhurried calm of men aware of their power. None of the cars was traveling at a speed of less than seventy kilometers an hour—barely had Goryacheva noticed a black point on the gray, matte roadway than this point began to increase in size with precipitate swiftness. And only a few seconds later she glimpsed people's faces, shining glass, and then the oncoming car was gone—as if it had never been there at all, as if she had simply imagined a forage cap, a heap of wildflowers, a woman's head below a broad hat. Equally swift, equally precipitate in their appearance and disappearance were a wooden shelter, little wooden houses with little windows crowded with flowerpots, and a woman in a black dress who was grazing a goat.

Goryacheva had driven to the dacha many times, and she was still always struck by this troubling swiftness, by the ease with which objects, people, and animals appeared, grew bigger, and then disappeared in a flash. In the dacha lived her mother, Marya Ivanovna, and her two nieces—Vera and Natashka, the daughters of her late sister. It was a big luxurious dacha, and she and her family shared the eight rooms with the family of another senior official. Until 1937 a certain Yezhegulsky, a man without any children, had lived there with his wife and his old father. Yezhegulsky had been arrested as an enemy of the people; it was over a year now since Goryacheva had moved in, and there was nothing left to recall Yezhegulsky's existence except for the yellow lilies his father had planted outside the windows. And her fellow occupant, Senyatin—a director of the People's Commissariat of State Farms—had once shown her a large chest he had found in a shed. It was filled with pinecones, each one wrapped in its own piece of white paper and surrounded by cotton wool. Some of the cones were huge, like strange birds whose wooden feathers, adorned with drops of amber resin, were all standing on end; some were tiny, smaller than acorns. There were pinecones from the Mediterranean and pinecones from the far north of Siberia. These hundreds of pinecones had been collected by the former occupant of their dacha. There was something comical about all these pinecones of different sizes, all so decorous and self-important, all of them wrapped like little dolls in paper and cotton wool. Goryacheva and Senyatin had looked at each other, shaken their heads, and smiled.

"We'll just have to burn them in the stove," she had said. "We can't even use them for the samovar—hand grenades like these are too big!"

"What do you mean, comrade Goryacheva?" Senyatin had answered. "You're lacking in consciousness. To a botanist they could be of real value. I'll take the box to the Young Naturalists—or else to a museum."

The car drew up outside the dacha. While Goryacheva was still talking to the driver, discussing what time they'd need to leave for the station, Vera and Natashka came running to meet her. Their grandmother, Marya Ivanovna, followed them out of the house. The driver parked the car in the shade, on some grass near the gate, as if it were nicer and more fun for the car to stand on fresh grass and in the shade of tall trees. He walked slowly around the car, admired the pneumatic tires, kicked one of them with his boot—not to check its condition but simply for his own satisfaction—wiped the windscreen with his sleeve, shook his head a little, walked over toward the fence, and lay down on the grass. The car smelled of gasoline and hot oil. He breathed this in with delight and thought, "She's had a good run, she's worked up a sweat."

He was dozing off when old Marya Ivanovna walked by with a bucket.

"Our water's no good, it's stagnant," she said, stopping beside him. "We can't even use it for cooking." He did not say anything himself, but she began telling him how their water would be fine too if it weren't for their neighbor's vicious dog. The dog didn't let anyone near the well, so the water stagnated. "The well is sick," she said, "it's like a cow that isn't being milked."

"Why are you having to fetch water yourself?" he said, with a blend of mockery and reproach. Looking at her thin brown face and her gray hair, he went on: "Sending an old woman out to fetch water—important cadres ought to know better! You must be about sixty, yes?"

The old woman could not remember her age. When she wanted the women in the neighboring dachas to express surprise at her readiness to fetch water, scrub floors, and do the laundry, she would say that she was seventy-one. In the polyclinic, however, she had registered herself as being fifty-nine, and that was what she had said to her daughter. She wanted her daughter to feel sorry for her when she died, not to be saying, "Oh well, she had a good long life." She sighed and said to the driver, "I'm into my seventies. Yes, my dear, well into my seventies."

"Your daughter should be fetching the water herself," said the driver. "Or she should send the girls. No, an old woman like you shouldn't be having to fetch water."

"You don't understand," said Marya Ivanovna. "It's only today she's here so early. It's because she's going on leave. Normally she doesn't get back here until nighttime. The girl's completely worn out. It's getting better now, she's calming down, but last winter, when she'd only just started working in Moscow, she'd get back here in her car—and burst into tears. 'What's the matter, darling?' I'd ask. 'Has someone upset you?' 'No,' she'd reply, 'it's just that everything's so new and strange.' No, she's certainly not going to start fetching water! As for the little girls, to be honest with you, they're bitches, right little bitches. Yes, they tell lies and they use foul words. The older one's not too bad—she just lies there and reads—but Natashka's a horror. This morning she said to me, 'Granny, you've guzzled all the sweets that my auntie left me. I'm going to punch you in the teeth.' Yes, that's Natashka for you."

"Insulting the aged is a criminal offense. She should be tried in a people's court," said the driver. A moment later, he went on to ask, "So they're not her own daughters?"

"They're her nieces, they're the children of my eldest daughter, Shura. Shura died in 1931, during the famine. Yes, she just swelled up and died. And my old man—he was such a hard worker—he died the same year. He was so swollen his heart could barely keep beating, but all he could think about was the house and the yard. I wanted to bake some flatbreads from thorn apple and I needed wood for the fire, but he wouldn't let me break up the fence. Then Stepanida took charge of us all. Her State farm gave her eight hundred grams of bread a day and so the four of us stayed alive. At the time she was just a little scrap of a girl—but look where she's got now!"

"So everything's all right now?" said the driver, pointing at the dacha and its tall windows.

"Yes, of course," said the old woman. "Only I feel sad, there are things I'll never forget. Shura, my eldest one, went out of her mind. She kept wailing, 'Mama, the whole world's on fire! Mama, our wheat's all burning!' No, I won't be forgetting that. My old man was so gentle...Heavens!" she exclaimed all of a sudden. "I've been talking and talking, but who's going to give Stepanida her tea? She's got a train to catch. And she's still got to call at her apartment in town."

"There's time enough," said the driver. "After all, we do have a car."

Goryacheva was glad to be going away.

For the first time in her life she was going for a holiday by the sea. She still had not got used to how precipitately life had changed. After finishing school, when she was just a fun-loving seventeen-year-old, she had gotten a job on the State farm, as a cleaner in the workers' hostel. The other girls in the hostel had talked her into going on a nine-month course to become a combine-harvester operator. She had graduated without the least difficulty; she was one of the best students. She had absorbed technical information with extraordinary ease—an ease she herself found surprising—and her technical drawings were outstanding. It took her only a moment to memorize a complex diagram—and then she could dismantle an entire motor. In less than a year she became a senior combine-harvester operator. In 1935 her work had been named the best in the region. In 1937 the agronomist, the head of the repair workshops, and the director of the State farm had all been arrested. A new director was appointed, Semidolenko. Goryacheva did not like him; she was rather afraid of him. If anything went wrong on the farm, Semidolenko always made out it was because of sabotage. The slightest mechanical breakdown, the least delay in a workshop, and Semidolenko would be writing denunciations to the district representative. As a result, there were twelve arrests, one after the other. At public meetings, Semidolenko referred to those who had been arrested as saboteurs and provocateurs. At a meeting after the arrest of Nevraev—a severe, taciturn old man who was an instructor in the repair workshop and who had won everyone's respect by always working until late into the night and not taking any leave for five years on end, refusing all financial compensation—Semidolenko had said, "This fellow deceived us all. Behind the mask of a shock worker was hidden a sworn enemy of the people, an adept spy, working for a foreign State, who managed to penetrate to the very heart of our State farm."

Then the director's secretary had taken the floor: only now, he declared, had he understood why Nevraev had stayed on alone at night in the repair-workshop office and why he had ordered photographic apparatus from Moscow. Then Goryacheva had stood up. In a loud, clear voice she had said, "He had nothing whatsoever to do with any foreign State. He was sent here by the district Party committee, and he's from Puzyri. It's not far away. His sister and younger brother still live there."

Semidolenko had turned on her, saying that the district Party secretary who had appointed Nevraev had turned out to be an enemy of the people and that Goryacheva too had evidently succumbed to enemy influence and that there were one or two more things he had recently learned. A few days after this, Semidolenko's typist informed Goryacheva, after swearing her to secrecy, that she had just typed out a statement by Semidolenko, addressed to the district representative, to the effect that Goryacheva (a Komsomol member) had been cohabiting with Nevraev (an enemy of the people) and had regularly been receiving gifts of money from him. At that moment it had seemed the truth would never come out—everything was just a tangle of lies. Soon afterward, however, everything had changed. Semidolenko himself had been arrested—along with the district representative and a number of provincial officials. And then, suddenly, it had all begun. Goryacheva had been summoned before the secretary of the provincial Party Committee, a man with a broad face who wore a calico shirt and blue canvas shoes with rubber soles.

"We have decided to appoint you director of the State farm," he told her.

This both frightened Goryacheva and made her angry. "What on earth do you mean? You must be joking. I'm twenty-four. I'm from a village. This is only the third time in my life I've been in a train."

"And I'm twenty-seven," said the Party secretary. "What can we do about it?"

Two years passed. Goryacheva was transferred to Moscow. She worked and studied at the same time. Often she had the feeling that everything was a dream—the telephones, the secretaries, the meetings of the Presidium, the cars, her Moscow apartment, her dacha. And there were nights when she really did dream that she was walking down the village street with her friends after work, singing songs to the accompaniment of a squeezebox. She would be smiling in these dreams, feeling how nice it was to walk barefoot over the soft cool grass on the little square in front of the village soviet. And only when she was being driven to the dacha and buildings were appearing from nowhere, then vanishing in front of her eyes, did she feel that there wasn't really anything so extraordinary about her existence; it was just that her life too had subordinated itself to this precipitate movement, to this swiftness that took one's breath away.

———

Goryacheva would not be traveling alone that evening; Gagareva, the deputy director of the planning department, was going with her, to the same resort on the Black Sea. Gagareva—who was not a

Party member—was a stout old woman with gray hair and a pince-nez on her fleshy nose. Just before ten o'clock Goryacheva called by to collect her. Gagareva was ready and waiting. They did not talk in the car. Goryacheva just looked out of the window, and Gagareva polished her pince-nez. Then they got to the train and found their two-berth compartment.

"I'll go on top," said Goryacheva. "I'm young."

"But it's not difficult with these little steps," said Gagareva. "If you'd rather, I can easily go on top myself."

"Don't even think of it," said Goryacheva, looking at Gagareva and laughing.

"I may be big," said Gagareva, also laughing, "but that's neither here nor there. I've been doing my gymnastics right up to the last minute."

The attendant brought them some tea, and they decided to have their supper there in the compartment rather than go to the restaurant car. They quickly struck up a rapport. They were smiling, offering each other tastes of their food.

"This will be the first time I've ever seen the sea," said Goryacheva. She went on: "The resort network's growing so fast now."

"Yes," said Gagareva, "a great deal of thought is going into maintaining the health of the country's citizens. Our commissariat alone has planned eight centers on the shores of the Black Sea."

"Foreigners are very attracted to our wealth, too," said Goryacheva. "The Japanese have quite lost their heads over it. And one can understand them. Our seas, our rivers, our forests—there's such beauty everywhere!"

"The Red Army will soon knock that out of them. This will be the last time they try to get their hands on our Motherland!" said Gagareva.

"Yes, on May Day I couldn't take my eyes off our tanks. Iron mountains—but they move fast!"

"I didn't have the good fortune to be there on Red Square myself, but I know anyway that the strength of our army lies not only in its equipment but also in its Socialist ideology."

"You've hit the nail on the head, comrade Gagareva," Goryacheva agreed. "Our whole country will want to fight."

They carried on chatting for a while, then went to bed. Goryacheva woke up during the night. It was comfortable on the upper bunk, like being in a cradle. The train was going at a good speed, but the heavy first-class carriage was barely swaying. Goryacheva looked down. Gagareva was wearing a flannel nightgown and her gray hair was hanging loose on her shoulders; propped up on one elbow, she was looking out of the dark window and crying. Rather than weeping silently, as old women often do, she was sobbing loudly and hoarsely, her fleshy shoulders quivering with each sob. Goryacheva wanted to ask her what was the matter; she wanted to comfort her. Instead, however, she said nothing and very quietly, without Gagareva hearing, lay down again and closed her eyes. She had realized why Gagareva was crying. Eight or nine months before, she had been called to the deputy of the People's Commissar to discuss Gagareva. Gagareva held an important position, and she was a good worker who knew her job well. But one day she had handed in a statement saying that she considered it her duty to report that in the autumn of 1937 her son-in-law, an important official at the People's Commissariat of Heavy Industry, had been arrested; soon after this, her daughter had been arrested too.

"What do you make of it all?" the deputy had asked Goryacheva. "Kozhuro, you know, has handed me a carefully argued summary of the reasons why she should be removed from her post."

Goryacheva and the deputy had both laughed; Kozhuro, the head of the planning department, was known as the most cautious and fearful of all the heads of department. He had dismissed a huge number of people and had even been reprimanded for this by the Moscow Party Committee: he was too ready, apparently, to dismiss his staff at the merest hint of suspicion. Once he had dismissed a young woman, the wife of a cost accountant, merely because the cost accountant's sister was married to a professor who had been excluded from the Party "for links to enemies of the people." All this had only come to light when the professor was reinstated in the

Party and Kozhuro could not decide whether or not to bring back the cost accountant's wife.

In reply to the deputy's question, Goryacheva had said, "Kozhuro's the one who should be dismissed—he over-insures his every move. If Gagareva's fired, I'm going straight to the Central Committee. She's an old woman I really admire!"

The deputy had replied, "It's not for you and me to make decisions about Kozhuro—that's not our concern. And there will be no need for you to appeal to the Central Committee, since Gagareva is not being dismissed."

Goryacheva had thought to herself, "This fellow's pretty careful too," but she had said nothing.

And just now, in the train, she had understood: Gagareva was crying because she was on her way to a holiday resort, in a comfortable train compartment—while her daughter was in a camp barrack, sleeping on bed boards.

In the morning Gagareva asked, "How was your night, comrade Goryacheva? These last few years I've been sleeping badly on trains. I wake up feeling battered, like after a serious illness." Her face looked puffy, and her eyelids were red.

"Do you receive letters from your daughter?" Goryacheva asked suddenly.

Gagareva was taken aback. "How can I put it?" she began. "Really I have no official contact with her. She and I have nothing in common. But I happen to know that she's working in Kazakhstan, and that she's petitioning for a review of her case."

It was stuffy in the compartment, but they had to close the window because of the dust. All around them were fields of ripe grain. In the evening, after Kharkov, they came to places where the harvest had already started, where there were trucks and combine harvesters waiting in the fields. "I used to work on those," said Goryacheva, her heart beating faster.

The house of recreation for senior cadres was small but very comfortable. Each of the visitors had their own room. There was a choice of dishes for lunch, and there was always wine—proper wine made from grapes. There would even be a choice of desserts—ice cream, custard, blintzes with jam. Goryacheva did not see a lot of Gagareva; not only were they on different floors but there were also days when Gagareva felt unwell and had her meals brought to her room. In the evenings, when it was cooler, Gagareva would wrap a shawl around her shoulders and go for a walk, book in hand, along the avenue of cypress trees above the sea; she took short steps, often pausing to get her breath back, and sometimes she would sit on one of the low stone benches. She had no regular companions. The only person who visited her in her room was Kotova, an old doctor who worked there; she and Gagareva would talk together for a long time. And sometimes, after supper, Gagareva would call on Kotova.

"I feel I'm in a kindergarten here," Gagareva would complain. "I've got no one to talk to."

"Yes," said Kotova. "It really is like a kindergarten. Nobody here in August is older than thirty—apart from me, of course."

Gagareva talked about what a good time they had all had in this same house of recreation in 1931. There had always been things going on: evenings of reminiscences, amateur singers and musicians, readings from books, literary debates.

"Yes, there were some interesting people then," said Kotova, "but I sometimes had a hard time of it myself. There was one man I remember—a handsome man with a blond beard. He had heart problems—an accumulation of fat around the heart, some degree of metabolic disturbance, and symptoms of gout in the joints of his left arm. I've forgotten his name and where he worked. None of his illnesses was serious, but he didn't half give me a lot of trouble. He was so capricious, so very used to getting whatever he wanted. I even ended up writing to the Health Department, asking to be relieved from my post."

"Oh, I know the man you mean," said Gagareva. "He isn't around anymore. During collectivization he was head of the regional land department. We used to talk about him a lot in our activist group."

"Well," said Kotova, "all I can say is that he was unbearable when he was here. Once I was woken up in the middle of the night. He'd called me. He was sitting on his bed, and all he could say was, 'Doctor, I feel sick.' At that point I lost all patience. 'You should be ashamed of yourself,' I snapped, 'waking an old woman in the middle of the night just because you ate too much supper.' "

"Yes," said Gagareva, "people are strange..."

Kotova lived on her own, and Gagareva liked her white clean room and her little "private" garden outside the window. She preferred this small plot to the large and splendid park, and she liked to sit on the little step with a book, beside the pot with the pink oleander.

The visitors spent most of their time on the beach. But not even the keenest swimmers and sunbathers could match Goryacheva in their enthusiasm. She was mesmerized by the sea; it was as if she had fallen in love. In the morning she would quickly eat her breakfast, wrap some pears and some grapes in a shaggy towel, and walk down the narrow path to the beach.

"Wait a moment, Goryacheva!" jokers would call out. "Give us a moment to have a smoke—then we can go down together. Or are you afraid of being twenty-one minutes late? Don't worry! There are enough rocks for everyone—there's no shortage of tickets!"

She hurriedly undressed, then threw herself into the sea and began to swim—the way village girls swim, thrashing her legs, sticking her head right out of the water and screwing up her eyes, and choking on the spray she churned up with her powerful but clumsy arms. There was a childish pleasure on her face that verged on bewilderment; it was as if she were unable to believe it was possible to feel so good. She would swim for hours on end; often she would not even return for lunch. She particularly enjoyed her lunch hours by the sea. The beach would empty; the waves would gradually take hold of the grape skins and cigarette butts, and the remains of apples and pears, and carry them away. Goryacheva would help the water to clean the beach. When the rubbish had all gone and the waves were left with only the sand and shingle to play with, she would lie on her stomach and prop herself up on her elbows, her cheekbones cupped in her palms. Obstinately, as if waiting for something, she would gaze at the gleaming, pliant water and the deserted, rocky shore. She wanted it to remain deserted for longer, and she was upset when she heard the bell that marked the end of the quiet hour after lunch and the voices of people on their way down to the beach. But just why she should feel upset she could not understand; many of the other visitors, after all, were people she knew, pleasant, straightforward people with a sense of fun. There was Ivan Mikheyevich, a deputy to the Supreme Soviet, who had once been a brigade leader on the collective farm where Goryacheva had operated a combine harvester. There were two Ukrainian women whom she had once met at a conference in Moscow, in the days when they too were still working on a collective farm. Now one of them was about to graduate from the Industrial Academy, and the other—Stanyuk—was working in the Supreme Court of the Ukrainian Republic. And there was the director of the Donetsk Coal Trust, a man who, only a few years ago, had been working at the pit face, hewing coal. Goryacheva recognized him. The two of them had been in the Kremlin on the same day; they had both gone there to receive awards. These were all people she liked; she felt close to them and enjoyed their company. Nevertheless, it was a relief to be alone on the beach. She would listen to the noise of the water and remember how, as a little girl, she had used to run to the river, not far from the mill, and swim across, her shirt ballooning out of the water. Then she would gaze at the sea and go into the water again and again.

The other visitors all began teasing her straightaway; they did not waste a moment.

Ivan Mikheyevich said, "Well, madam combine harvester, shouldn't you be telegraphing home to say you're about to combine with a husband?"

Stanyuk grinned and said, "Careful, Goryacheva. You might find you suddenly lose all your holiday weight!"

By the evening, even Gagareva, who never went down to the beach, had heard the news. Meeting Goryacheva in the glass-walled corridor, she said, "Doctor Kotova worries that too many hours in the sun might bring about a cardiac neurosis, but I think you need to be careful not to spend too long in the moonlight."

"What do you mean?" asked Goryacheva, who was not used to Black Sea wit.

Goryacheva had got to know a certain Colonel Karmaleyev who was staying next door, in the house of recreation for senior Red Army commanders. They had chatted a little and then gone into the water together. He had told Goryacheva that he had been wounded in August 1938—only now were the doctors allowing him to go swimming again. Goryacheva had been terrified as she watched him strike out; she thought that his swift, powerful arm movements were going to reopen the wound on his chest, which was now covered by pink, fresh skin. And there had been moments when his face had looked not tanned but pale. When they went for walks together, she sometimes asked, "You're not getting tired, are you?"

"What do you mean?" he would reply, a little affronted.

He was four years older than her, but their life stories had much in common. Until 1926, he too had lived in a village and been a member of the Komsomol. Then he had gone to the Far East to serve in the frontier forces. After his military service, he had joined a military-command training course and remained in the Far East. He seemed to be someone very calm; he spoke slowly, articulating each word clearly. Even though his movements were quick and effortless, their measure and precision somehow added to this general impression of slowness. Goryacheva thought he spoke to her like a teacher; this amused her, and on one occasion she commented on it. He was embarrassed and said it was a habit he had slipped into; it was because he had to spend a lot of time dinning things into the soldiers and junior commanders.

"So I'm like a junior commander, am I?" said Goryacheva. It was now her turn to feel affronted. "I'll have you know that a departmental head in an All-Union People's Commissariat is superior to a colonel!"

"Yes, you'd be a corps commander at the very least!" Karmaleyev replied with a smile. His teeth were so straight and even that they seemed like a single white strip. He had fair hair that looked soft, and his eyes were pale, serious, and sad.

The two houses of recreation watched the growth of their relationship with interest, laughing and joking, but from the very first day everything between Goryacheva and Karmaleyev was so utterly clear and straightforward that neither of them ever felt the least embarrassment. In the evenings they carried on going out for walks, hand in hand, around the park or down to the sea. Karmaleyev would bring some special kind of grapes to the dining room for Goryacheva, and in the morning he would go to the post office for the newspaper and then give it to her before he had so much as glanced at it.

His comrades continued to make jokes. "So, Aleksandr Nikiforovich, you're going to be the husband of a deputy people's commissar. One word from her, and they'll transfer you to Moscow, to the General Staff Academy. You'll have quite a life!"

He smiled calmly and said nothing.

Gagareva was moved by this development, which really, of course, concerned only Goryacheva and Karmaleyev. She observed Goryacheva benevolently, with sadness and resignation. There seemed to be some law governing the fates of different generations. "So now it's their turn to be happy," she would say to herself. "Well then, may they be happy!" And she would recall her own youth—political debates, trips to Sparrow Hills, and years in exile after her husband had escaped from a tsarist prison colony and she had abandoned her studies to join him in France. She even felt proud that she had come to a philosophical understanding of time and of Russian life, that she had grasped the meaning of all the sacrifices, the meaning of movement itself. "Yes, yes," she thought. "It's true, we didn't struggle and suffer in vain. Whole generations didn't sacrifice themselves for nothing." She did a great deal of thinking, and she was so taken up with her thoughts that she stopped visiting Kotova, preferring to spend all her time on her own. To have reached this universal understanding was no mean achievement—and Gagareva looked at the young people around her with a kindly but condescending smile.

During the last week of August it began unexpectedly to rain; this, apparently, was very unusual—something that happened only once every ten or fifteen years. The mountains were hidden by clouds, a cold wind was blowing off the sea, and it rained several times every day. Many of the visitors left. Goryacheva left on the twenty-sixth. She might have stayed longer, but Karmaleyev had received a telegram recalling him to the Far East. He had to set off on the twenty-sixth, and Goryacheva had decided to go with him as far as Moscow. Gagareva, however, stayed in the house of recreation; she did not mind the bad weather. She had brought her galoshes and raincoat with her and, unless it was raining particularly hard, she carried on going out for walks down the graveled paths. She even liked this kind of weather. It was more in keeping with her mood; her mind worked better during these gray sad days.

———

Late one November afternoon Gagareva called on Goryacheva in her office. She found her in conversation with a visiting instructor, a man who worked in the provinces.

"Is this going to take long?" Goryacheva asked her.

"No, no, it's all right, I'll wait, it's about something very particular," said Gagareva, smiling and sitting herself down on the sofa. She looked at Goryacheva's face, which was lit by the lamp on her desk, and thought, "She's lost her tan, and she looks very thin. She never stops, she works day and night—she must be missing her husband."

The instructor left. With an embarrassed little laugh, Gagareva said, "Comrade Goryacheva, there's something I want to say to you. I do, after all, know the stand you took last year, when there was a possibility of my being dismissed. Well, now I want to share some good news with you: my daughter's case is to be reviewed. She may soon be back here in Moscow."

They chatted for a few minutes. Then Goryacheva remembered that she had a meeting. She left the room. Gagareva went to the secretariat and said to Goryacheva's secretary, "Lydia Ivanovna, do you know what? It may not be long till my daughter comes back."

The usually stern secretary looked Gagareva straight in the eye, laughed joyfully, and shook her hand.

"But tell me—is everything all right with Goryacheva? She's not ill, is she?" asked Gagareva. "She seemed a little strange just now."

Glancing at the door, the secretary said quietly, "She's been having a terrible time. It's been one tragedy after another for her. In October her mother died of a heart attack. She was doing the laundry—and she just dropped dead. And then, only a few days ago, she was told that her husband had been killed in action, on the Far East border. They were married the day they got back from the Crimea, and he had to leave that same evening."

Gagareva walked across to the window and watched the bright automobile headlights down below. Precipitately, as if out of nowhere, they arose out of the fog and gloom, then swiftly traversed the square. "No, it's not like I thought," she said to herself. "I don't understand anything at all about the laws of life."

But she was feeling happy, and so she no longer wanted to think. She no longer wanted to understand the laws of life.

PART TWO

The War, the Shoah

IN THE early hours of June 22, 1941, Hitler invaded the Soviet Union. Stalin had refused to believe more than eighty intelligence warnings of Hitler's intentions, and Soviet forces were taken by surprise. More than two thousand Soviet aircraft were destroyed within twenty-four hours. The Germans repeatedly encircled entire Soviet armies. By the end of the year the Wehrmacht had reached the outskirts of Moscow and more than three million Soviet soldiers had been captured or killed.

Before the German invasion, Grossman appears to have been depressed. He was overweight and, though only in his mid-thirties, he walked with a stick. In spite of this—and his poor eyesight—he volunteered to serve in the ranks. Assigned instead to *Red Star* (*Krasnaya zvezda*), the Red Army newspaper, he quickly became one of the best-known Soviet war correspondents, astonishing everyone with his courage, tenacity, and physical endurance; he even proved to be an excellent shot with a pistol.

David Ortenberg, the chief editor of *Red Star*, was evidently impressed by the articles and stories that Grossman contributed. In May 1942 he allowed Grossman a three-month leave to work on a novel about a Soviet military unit that breaks out of German encirclement. Grossman worked fast, and *The People Immortal*—the first Soviet novel about the war—was serialized in *Red Star* in July and August. Today much of it seems propagandistic, but at the time it was admired for its realism. As always, Grossman not only has a fine eye for a vivid detail but also the ability to make unexpected use of this detail. One memorable passage ends with a political commissar glimpsing the burning ruins of the town of Gomel as reflected in the eye of a dying horse: "The horse's dark, weeping, torment-filled pupil, like a crystal mirror, absorbed the fire of the burning buildings, the smoke swirling through the air, the luminous, incandescent ruins and this forest of thin, tall chimneys now growing in the place of the buildings which had vanished in flames. And Bogaryov suddenly had the thought that he too had taken into himself all this destruction—this nighttime destruction of an ancient and peaceful town."

In the autumn of 1942, Grossman was posted to Stalingrad. Unlike other Soviet journalists, who stayed in relative safety on the left bank of the Volga, Grossman spent nearly three months on the right bank. Earlier, before crossing the Volga, he had said to a group of colleagues, "To write about the Stalingrad battle one needs to have been on the right bank of the Volga, among those who are fighting in the ruins and on the bank of the river. Until I have been there I do not have the moral right to write about the defenders of Stalingrad." Once on the right bank, he shared the soldiers' lives and won their trust. In the words of his fellow war correspondent Ilya Ehrenburg, "The soldiers at Stalingrad did not consider Grossman a journalist, but rather one of their comrades in arms."

Grossman achieved particular renown for his reports from Stalingrad, but he covered all the main battles of the war, from the defense of Moscow to the vast tank battle of Kursk and the fall of Berlin, and his articles were valued by ordinary soldiers and generals alike. Groups of frontline soldiers would gather to listen while one of them read aloud from a single copy of *Red Star*; the writer Viktor Nekrasov, who fought at Stalingrad as a young man, remembers how "the papers with [Grossman's] and Ehrenburg's articles were read and reread by us till they were in tatters." And it was not only Soviet citizens who valued Grossman's articles. *The Years of War*, a collection of Grossman's reports from Stalingrad and elsewhere, was translated into a number of languages, including English, French, Dutch, and—in 1945—German. According to the historian Jochen Hellbeck, "a German Stalingrad veteran, Wilhelm Raimund Beyer, a young soldier during the war and later a noted philosopher and Hegel scholar, writes with great admiration about Grossman's war stories [...] as coming very close to his own experience of the battle."

Yekaterina Korotkova has written that "A Stalingrad veteran once told me that he witnessed my father drawing an entire platoon—every last man of them—into a general conversation. And I myself often saw him in conversation with yardmen or listening attentively to a little woman we all despised and whom we had nicknamed Zhuchka." Grossman had a remarkable gift for listening and no less a gift for evoking—even in the space of only a few lines—the uniqueness of an individual life. Ortenberg records that Grossman was always interested in someone's life as a whole, not merely in his or her wartime experiences, and he suggests that this may have been one of the reasons why otherwise inarticulate people were often so very ready to talk to him. This concern for the individual, perhaps not surprisingly, also sometimes brought Grossman into conflict with the authorities. For all his wholehearted commitment to the Soviet cause, he was no less wholeheartedly opposed to the unnecessary sacrifice of individual lives for the apparent good of this cause. Korotkova has summarized Grossman's own account of a meeting at the editorial office of *Red Star*: "Ortenberg once summoned three correspondents—Aleksey Tolstoy, Vasily Grossman, and Pyotr Pavlenko—and suggested that one of them write an article to illustrate the necessity for the new decree about the execution of deserters. My father responded sharply, 'I'm not going to write such a piece.' Pavlenko somehow 'wriggled up to my father and, hissing like a snake,' said, 'You're a proud man, Vasily Semyonovich, a very proud man.' Only one man remained silent—Aleksey Tolstoy. It was he who then wrote the required article."

After encircling the German Sixth Army at Stalingrad, the Red Army began its long march westward. The liberation of the Ukraine, however, almost certainly brought Grossman more bitterness than joy. In the autumn of 1943 he learned about the massacre at Babi

Yar, a ravine on the outskirts of Kiev, where a hundred thousand people, nearly all Jews, were shot in the course of six months, more than thirty-three thousand of them during the first two days, September 29 and 30. Soon afterward, in Berdichev, he learned the details of the death of his mother, Yekaterina Savelievna, in what was probably the first of the Einsatzgruppen massacres carried out in the Ukraine in September 1941. This knowledge must have been all the harder to bear because Grossman blamed himself for failing to fetch Yekaterina Savelievna from Berdichev while this was still possible during the first weeks of the war.

One of the most striking of Grossman's wartime works is "The Ukraine Without Jews"—an article that combines factual detail and moving lament. It also includes a remarkable passage in which Grossman not only analyzes the appeal of Nazism but also, through the use of incantatory, almost folkloric repetition, forces the reader to feel this appeal:

> "You fear proletarian revolution," the National Socialists said to the German industrialists. "You fear Communism, which is a hundred times more terrible for us than any Versailles treaty. We too fear proletarian revolution—so let us fight together against the Jews. They, after all, are an eternal source of sedition and bloody rebellion. They know how to incite the masses. They are orators and authors of revolutionary books. It is they who gave birth to the ideas of class struggle and proletarian revolution!"
>
> "You are suffering from the consequences of the Versailles treaty," the National Socialists said to the laboring masses of Germany. "You are hungry, you are without work. The heavy millstone of the reparations is crushing your exhausted shoulders. But look whose hands are turning the wheel that moves this stone. It is the hands of the Jewish plutocracy, the hands of Jewish bankers—the uncrowned kings of America, France, and England. Your enemies are our enemies—let us fight shoulder to shoulder against them!"

"You have been insulted—and your ideals desecrated," the National Socialists said to the German intelligentsia. "Your enemies write contemptuously about Germany, examining with cold skepticism the history of a great nation. Your thought has been castrated, your pride crucified. There is no one who needs your talents and knowledge. You, the salt of the earth, are doomed to become waiters and taxi drivers. Can you not see the cold eyes looking out of the fog that now surrounds Germany? Can you not see the cold merciless eyes of the world's Jews—of the Jew who is the eternal, hate-filled enemy of the national hearth; the Jew who is without country; the Jew who hates and despises your poor nation; the Jew who now excitedly awaits the triumph of his age-old dream of dominion? Let us fight shoulder to shoulder for our national honor, for a dignity that has been vilified. Let us cleanse the world, let us cauterize it of Jewry."

Grossman's original text was refused by *Red Star* and remained unpublished until 1988. The first two sections were published, in Yiddish translation, in consecutive issues of *Eynikayt* (the journal of the Jewish Anti-Fascist Committee, an organization established in 1942 to gather international political and material support for the fight against Nazi Germany), but the last two sections never appeared—and no explanation was given for this. An article titled "The Ukraine" was published in the monthly journal *Znamya*, but this is an entirely separate article and it contains only a single—albeit powerfully worded—mention of the massacre at Babi Yar. These details are significant. Grossman was one of the first journalists to write about what is now being called the "Shoah by bullets," the massacres of Jews in the western Soviet Union; he was also one of the first journalists to write about the death camps in Poland, the "Shoah by gas." His moral and imaginative courage appears still more remarkable if we bear in mind that he was doing this at a time when the Soviet authorities were moving toward a policy of what would now be called Holocaust denial. There was not yet an outright ban on all mention of the mass murders of Jews, but there was no doubt as to what was the authorities' preferred line: that all nationalities had suffered equally under Hitler. A frequently used slogan—all the more effective, no doubt, because of its apparent nobility—was "Do not divide the dead!"

From 1943 to 1946, along with Ilya Ehrenburg, Grossman worked for the Jewish Anti-Fascist Committee on *The Black Book*, a documentary account of the massacres of Jews on both Soviet and Polish soil. As well as editing the testimonies of others, Grossman also intended to include two articles he had written himself. "The Murder of the Jews in Berdichev" is a soberly written account of life in the Berdichev ghetto and the massacre of September 15, 1941, at an airfield just outside the town; Grossman does not mention that one of the twelve thousand victims was his mother. Dated November 4, 1944, this too remained unpublished until long after Grossman's death. The other article, "The Hell of Treblinka," though probably refused by *Red Star*, was published in *Znamya* in November 1944; it was republished in 1945, in the form of a very small hardback book. It seems to have been impossible, at this date, to publish a substantial article about the extermination of Jews in the Soviet Union, but it was evidently at least a little easier to write about what had happened in Poland.

The Black Book was ready for production in 1946; all that was needed was for the authorities to confirm their final approval. No such confirmation was forthcoming. On February 3, 1947, Georgy Aleksandrov, the head of the Agitprop Department of the Central Committee, wrote that "the book presents a distorted picture of the real nature of Fascism [since the impression it gave was that] the Germans fought against the Soviets only in order to annihilate the Jews." A final decision was announced on August 20, 1947: *The Black Book* was not to be published. And in 1948, after yet another year had passed, the plates were destroyed. Now that the war had been won, now that there was no longer any need to solicit international support against Hitler, no amount of compromises by the editors could render *The Black Book* acceptable. Admitting that

Jews constituted the overwhelming majority of the dead would have entailed admitting that members of other Soviet nationalities had been accomplices in the genocide; in any case, Stalin appears to have understood that anti-Semitism was a force that he could exploit in order to unite the majority of the population behind his regime.

Grossman had devoted himself to *The Black Book* for much of the preceding four years, and in late spring 1945 he had taken over from Ilya Ehrenburg as head of the editorial board. What he must have felt when *The Black Book* was finally aborted is hard to imagine.

In 1943, Grossman had begun work not only on *The Black Book* but also on the first of his two epic novels centered on the battle of Stalingrad. Six years later, in August 1949, Grossman submitted this novel, then titled *Stalingrad* but soon to be retitled *For a Just Cause*, to the journal *Novy mir.* In what seems strangely like a literary reenactment of the battle, Grossman appears to have had to fight with his editors over every chapter, if not every paragraph, of his novel.

The battle lines are laid out in an exchange in December 1948 between Grossman and Boris Agapov, one of the members of the editorial board:

Agapov: "I want to render the novel safe, to make it impossible for anyone to criticize it."

Grossman: "Boris Nikolaevich, I don't want to render my novel safe."

Even though Konstantin Simonov (chief editor of *Novy mir* until February 1950), Aleksandr Tvardovsky (chief editor of *Novy mir* from February 1950), and Aleksandr Fadeyev (general secretary of the Writers Union for most of the period from 1937 until 1954) seem genuinely to have admired *For a Just Cause*, its publication was repeatedly postponed. The Russian State Archives now contain no less than twelve different typed versions. The first six are Grossman's own early versions; the last six were produced, between 1949 and 1952, in response to editorial "suggestions." These suggestions range from the most trivial to the most sweeping; one of the more extraordinary was that Grossman should remove from the novel the central figure of Viktor Shtrum—because he was Jewish. At one point Tvardovsky suggested that Grossman should make Shtrum the head of a military commissariat rather than an important physicist; in reply, Grossman asked what post he should give Einstein. On another occasion Grossman was asked to remove all the "civilian" chapters; the editors appear to have thought that a documentary, or near-documentary, account of the fighting would be "safer" than a work of fiction. The novel was set in type three times, but on each occasion the decision to publish was countermanded and the type broken up—although it seems that, at least on two of these occasions, a very few copies were, in fact, printed. The April 30, 1951, entry in Grossman's "Diary of the Journey of the Novel *For a Just Cause* through Publishing Houses" reads, "Thanks to the splendid, comradely attitude of the technical editors and printing-press workers, the new typesetting was carried out with fabulous speed. I now have in my hands a new copy: second edition; print run—6 copies."

The reason for the anxiety shown by Grossman's editors is that the Soviet victory at Stalingrad had acquired the status of a sacred myth—a myth that legitimized Stalin's rule. With regard to a matter of such importance, there could be no room for even the slightest political error. Tvardovsky and Fadeyev found it necessary, even when they themselves were satisfied with the novel, to ask for approval from a variety of different bodies: the Writers Union; the Historical Section of the General Staff; the Institute of Marx, Engels, and Lenin; the Central Committee of the Communist Party. They were afraid of offending Nikita Khrushchev, who is portrayed in the novel in his role as a senior political commissar at Stalingrad, and they were, no doubt, still more concerned about Stalin's reaction; they could not have forgotten that Grossman had twice been nominated for a Stalin Prize—for his novel about the Revolution, *Stepan Kolchugin*, in 1941, and for *The People Immortal*, his novel about the first year of the war, in 1943—and that his candidacy had been vetoed both times, almost certainly at the instigation of Stalin himself. Grossman evidently understood the need for Stalin's explicit approval, and in December 1950 he sent him a letter which ends, "The number of pages of reviews, stenograms, conclusions, and responses is already approaching the number of pages taken up by the novel itself, and although all are in favor of publication, there has not yet been a final decision. I passionately ask you to help me by deciding the fate of the book I consider more important than anything else I have written."

Stalin, it seems, did not reply. Nor did Molotov, to whom Grossman wrote in October 1951. Nevertheless, after a last flurry of new suggestions for the title, the novel was finally published in 1952, in the July through October issues of *Novy mir*. In a letter to Fadeyev, Grossman wrote, "Dear Aleksandr Aleksandrovich [...] Even after being published and republished for so many years, I felt more deeply and intensely moved, on seeing the July issue of the journal, than when I saw my very first story ['In the Town of Berdichev'] in *Literaturnaya gazeta*."

Initial reviews were enthusiastic and on October 13 the Prose Section of the Union of Soviet Writers nominated the novel for a Stalin Prize. On January 13, 1953, however, an article appeared in *Pravda* titled "Vicious Spies and Killers Passing Themselves off as Doctors and Professors." A group of the country's most eminent doctors—all of them Jewish—had allegedly been plotting to poison Stalin and other members of the political and military leadership. These accusations were intended to serve as a prelude to a vast purge of Soviet Jews.

A month after this, on February 13, Mikhail Bubyonnov, who in 1948 had won a State Prize for *The White Birch*—a novel, like Grossman's *The People Immortal*, about the first year of the war—published a denunciatory review of *For a Just Cause*. A new campaign against Grossman quickly gathered momentum. Major newspapers printed articles with such titles as "A Novel That Distorts the Image of Soviet People," "On a False Path," and "In a Distorting Mirror." In response, Tvardovsky and the editorial board of

Novy mir duly acknowledged that publication of the novel had been a grave mistake. What seems to have hurt Grossman most was being betrayed by Tvardovsky; Tvardovsky was a true writer, not merely a literary functionary, and he probably genuinely liked and admired Grossman. When Grossman called in at *Novy mir* and—it would seem—spoke his mind, Tvardovsky retorted, "What, do you think I should have returned my Party membership card?" "Yes, I do," said Grossman. Still more angrily, Tvardovsky said, "I know where you're going now. Go on then, get going. There's obviously a lot you haven't understood yet. It'll be explained to you there."

Earlier that day Grossman had received a telephone call asking him to go to the head office of *Pravda*; he had called in at *Novy mir* on his way there. Grossman probably did not know the exact reason for his summons to *Pravda*; he had been told only that it was "in connection with the fate of the Jewish people." Tvardovsky, however, evidently knew that Grossman was among the Jewish writers and journalists who were being asked to sign a letter calling for the execution of the "Killer Doctors."

Not long before this, Grossman had stood firm when Fadeyev begged him to renounce his novel and make a show of public repentance. Uncharacteristically, however, Grossman agreed to sign the letter about the "Killer Doctors." He was, no doubt, feeling lost and confused after quarreling with Tvardovsky. He may have thought— reasonably enough—that the doctors were certain to be executed anyway and that the letter was worth signing because it affirmed that the Jewish people *as a whole* was innocent. Whatever his reasons, Grossman at once regretted what he had done. He drank vodka on the street and, by the time he got back home, he was feeling badly sick. This act of betrayal—as he himself soon saw it— haunted Grossman for the rest of his life; a passage in *Life and Fate* based on this incident ends with Viktor Shtrum (who has just signed a similar letter) praying to his dead mother to help him never to show such weakness again.

Rather than being corroded by guilt, Grossman seems to have been able to find a way to draw strength from it. Most important of all, he was able to put his sense of guilt to creative use. Few writers have written more subtly about so many forms of personal and political betrayal, and it is possible that no one has articulated more clearly how hard it is for an individual to withstand the pressure of a totalitarian State. Several years later, in *Life and Fate*, Grossman was to write,

> But an invisible force was crushing him. He could feel its weight, its hypnotic power; it was forcing him to think as it wanted, to write as it dictated. This force was inside him; it could dissolve his will and cause his heart to stop beating [...] Only people who have never felt such a force themselves can be surprised that others submit to it. Those who have felt it, on the other hand, feel astonished that a man can rebel against it even for a moment—with one sudden word of anger, one timid gesture of protest.

At the time, however, Grossman's act of betrayal did nothing to ease his position. The campaign against him continued to intensify. At a meeting of the Writers Union, Bubyonnov quoted Mikhail Sholokhov: "Grossman's novel is spittle in the face of the Russian people." Fadeyev published an article full of what Grossman described in his "Diary" as "mercilessly severe political accusations." Voenizdat, the military publishing house that had agreed to publish *For a Just Cause* in book form, asked Grossman to return his advance—in view of what Grossman caustically referred to as "the now unexpectedly discovered anti-Soviet essence of the book."

All this happened in less than six weeks. The viciousness of the campaign, and its suddenness, is remarkable even by Soviet standards. David Fel'dman—a researcher into Soviet literary politics—has provided a striking explanation. Grossman was a central figure in what were probably the two most important postwar Soviet ideological projects. One was the creation of an internal enemy; now that the war was over, Stalin needed a new enemy in order to justify his continued dictatorship. The other was the creation of a "Red"

Leo Tolstoy. The choice of internal enemy was simple enough—it could only be the Jews. The choice of a Soviet Tolstoy, however, was more complicated. There had always been rivalry between the Writers Union and the Agitprop Department (the Department of Agitation and Propaganda) of the Communist Party's Central Committee. In this instance the Agitprop Department was backing Bubyonnov, while Fadeyev, Tvardovsky, and the Writers Union were backing Grossman, who was by far the greater writer. The two projects, inevitably, collided. Fadeyev and Tvardovsky had, for all their political acumen, underestimated how fiercely the anti-Jewish campaign would intensify. They began publishing *For a Just Cause* during the very month—July 1952—when most of the leading members of the Jewish Anti-Fascist Committee were undergoing secret trial.

During the war, Grossman was sometimes called "Lucky Grossman" because of the number of times he narrowly escaped death. On one occasion a grenade landed between his feet—and failed to explode. What happened in February and March 1953 was of the same order; Grossman was fortunate that Stalin died on March 5, 1953.

Denunciations of Grossman and his novel continued for another few weeks, but by April the campaign had petered out, and in mid-June Grossman received a letter from Voenizdat, repeating their original offer to publish *For a Just Cause*. The final, laconic entry in Grossman's "Diary" reads, "26 October, 1954. The book is on sale on the Arbat, in the shop the Military Book."

———

The period covered by this section begins with Grossman, after the Nazi invasion, feeling a renewed commitment to the Soviet cause, and ends with him, in the early 1950s, breaking with this cause irrevocably. The first of the stories, "The Old Man," is based on accounts of the German occupation he had heard from Russian villagers. No less vivid for being entirely Soviet in both matter and manner, it was published in *Red Star* in February 1942.

The second and much longer story, "The Old Teacher," is set in an unnamed town that seems like a smaller Berdichev. It represents Grossman's first attempt to address the fate of his mother. Soviet troops had not yet liberated the western Ukraine, but Grossman had evidently already learned a great deal about the massacres the Einsatzgruppen had carried out there. Published in the September and October 1943 issues of *Znamya*, "The Old Teacher" is among the first works of fiction about the Shoah in any language.

The story's main character is male but, like Grossman's mother, Yekaterina Savelievna, he is a retired schoolteacher. The final scene, during which a small child shows great kindness to this teacher just before they are both shot, is one of several scenes in Grossman's work that show a Jewish parent—or parent figure—and a child affirming their love during the last minutes of their lives. In a memorable chapter from *Life and Fate*, Sofya Levinton, an unmarried doctor, befriends a child on the way to the gas chamber and feels that she has, at last, become a mother. In "The Old Teacher," however, it is the bachelor teacher who feels like an abandoned child and the little girl who unexpectedly takes upon herself the role of mother.

The next piece in this section, "The Hell of Treblinka"—one of the first publications in any language about a Nazi death camp—was quickly translated into a number of European languages. Grossman presents a clear overall picture of the camp's organizational structure, and he writes with insight about the satanically astute understanding of human psychology that made it possible for so few SS guards to murder such a vast number of people. There are, however, both major errors and minor inaccuracies, and there is no doubt that Grossman would have corrected these had he been granted the opportunity. We have therefore provided both detailed notes and a separate appendix.

The final work in this section, "The Sistine Madonna," was inspired by a Raphael Madonna from Dresden that the Soviet authorities had taken to Moscow in 1945. Grossman saw it in 1955, when it was exhibited in the Pushkin Museum before being returned to the

Dresden Art Gallery. For nearly 150 years *The Sistine Madonna* had been the object of something approaching a special cult in Russia. Dostoevsky, for example, saw the painting as a symbol of the faith and beauty that would save the world, and a large reproduction of it hung over his writing desk. Grossman's article has a twofold importance. It too is a statement of faith, and its highly personal structure provides a transition to the freer, less genre-bound work of Grossman's last years: the short novel *Everything Flows*, the travel sketch *Good Wishes*, the essay "Eternal Rest," and the last short stories. Grossman is wrestling, in "The Sistine Madonna," with huge questions. He is addressing such vast tragedies as collectivization and the Terror Famine; he is also—at a time when humanity's very survival has become threatened as never before—questioning the nature and purpose of art.

Grossman wrote "The Sistine Madonna" in the second half of 1955—probably, given the number of times he mentions the hydrogen bomb, in November or December; the first American thermonuclear bomb had been tested in 1952, and the first Soviet test was carried out in November 1955. There are moments in the first section when Grossman's prose cracks under this pressure, when he slips into sententiousness or sentimentality. But in the second section, and above all in his evocation of Christ as a thirty-year-old kulak deported to the taiga, he fuses poetry, religion, and fact to achieve a Dantesque intensity: "He was walking along a path through a bog. A huge cloud of midges was hanging above him, but he was unable to drive them away; he was unable to remove this living, flickering halo because he needed both his hands to steady the damp heavy log on his shoulder."

THE OLD MAN

OLD Semyon Mikheich—everyone said—was the quietest man in the village. He did not drink; he did not smoke; and he never complained to his neighbors. He was never heard to quarrel with his old woman. His voice was quiet and gentle; his movements were no less quiet and gentle.

As the Germans drew near, several of his neighbors got ready to join partisan groups.

"Granddad, are you going to come too?" they would ask jokingly.

He would reply, "Shooting and killing—I just don't have it in me."

"On the side of the Germans, are you?" Fedka once asked.

"On the side of the Germans!" answered Semyon Mikheich. "What truth do the Germans bring? But I'm still no warrior. It's just not in my nature. I can't even bear to strike a horse with a whip. I'm tenderhearted."

Wanting to defend her husband, old Filippovna joined in. "He's with his bees all the time. That's why he's so quiet. Bees don't like a man who gets angry."

"Too true," said the old man. "Take our chairman, Prokofy. The bees can't stand him. He's always in a hurry, and he makes a lot of noise."

Just then Prokofy himself came along. He had two hand grenades hanging from his belt and a rifle on his shoulder.

"What are you talking about?" he asked.

"I'm saying that you're a stern man," said Semyon Mikheich. "But in my family we've never shed blood. My mother was afraid to slaughter a chicken—she used to ask a neighbor to do it for her."

"Well," said Prokofy, "don't you be too kind to the Germans. Or you'll have to answer for it before the people."

And he strode off down the village street.

The old man just shook his head, but his wife was upset. She spat on the ground.

———

The Germans had been in the village for nearly three months. First the forward units had gone through. The village had been plundered. When the women went into the dark, empty sheds, they wept. All they could think about was the cows that were no longer there. Everything from their huts was vanishing: sheepskin coats, embroidered towels, quilted jerkins, pillows, and blankets. In the afternoons the old men and women would get together and curse the Germans, reciting long lists of grievances.

Semyon Mikheich would say nothing; he just listened to all the furious words and sighed. He himself had suffered as much as anyone at the hands of the Germans. They had ravaged his beloved hives; they had seized his stores of honey and wheat. Even the old bed, on which he had slept for long decades, had been taken off on the back of a truck by some corporal with bloodshot eyes.

In the evenings, in the dark empty hut, the old couple would kneel by the icons and pray to God. At night Filippovna would weep; Semyon Mikheich would try to comfort her.

"What's the good of tears?" he would say. "Everyone's grieving now. The whole people is suffering. We're old, there's just the two of us, we'll get by somehow."

In December the village became the headquarters of a German division. The billeting officers chose the best house, the one with an iron roof, for the generals. Then they made the men lay a red-brick pavement in front of the house while the women cleaned the floors and whitewashed the walls. Old Semyon Mikheich was ordered to lay a long brick path from the yard to the outhouse in the kitchen garden. The corporal got cross with him for not making the path straight enough. He made him redo it twice. For the first time in his life Semyon Mikheich used foul language.

The old couple's hut was requisitioned for a doctor, a thin man with a small bald head. The old couple had to move into the entrance room, which was so cold at night that they were unable to sleep. Instead, they heard *der Arzt* shouting down the telephone in a rasping voice, "Kamyshevakha! Kamyshevakha!"

The doctor was demanding coaches for the evacuation of the wounded. There were many soldiers suffering from wounds and frostbite, and very few trains indeed, since the partisans were destroying the tracks. "That must be Prokofy's doing," the old man said to himself. "He's hard at it!"

Der Arzt shouted hoarsely at everyone who came in to see him. Every now and then he called the orderly and sent him on some errand. The orderly was scared to death of him. The look on the orderly's face when he entered the room was always so pale and anguished that Semyon Mikheich couldn't help but feel sorry for him.

Der Arzt had ordered Semyon Mikheich to chop wood for the stove. He liked listening to the sound of the ax. Sometimes he summoned the orderly during the night and told him to send Semyon Mikheich out to chop wood.

"Why is the Russian not working? The Russian sleeps too much."

And so Semyon Mikheich would chop wood beneath the German's window. He turned gloomy and taciturn, sometimes not saying a word for days on end. He even stopped sighing. Silently, as if made of stone, he would just stand and stare. His old woman would look at him in fear: Had he lost his mind?

One night he said to her, "You know, Filippovna, a wild beast will devour what it needs. It may slaughter a cow or destroy a hive—and that's life. But these...these ones have been spitting on my soul—and beasts don't do that. I used to think that these ones are not people. But now I can see they're not even beasts. They're worse than beasts."

"Pray to God," said Filippovna. "That will help."

"No," said the old man. "It won't help."

In the morning one of their neighbors, Galya Yakimenko, came by. She was in tears. In a whisper, looking around all the time at the door—on the other side of which was sitting the terrible *Arzt*—she began talking about the five staff officers now quartered in her hut. "They're like bears. They eat and drink all day and all night. They get drunk, they shout, and they throw up. They have no shame. They walk about naked in front of me. And now, now it's turned cold, no, you wouldn't believe it . . . They've begun soiling their beds. Until now, at least, they used to do it on the floor, but now they don't even get out of bed. Then they pull the fouled sheets off the bed and tell me to wash them. I say, no, I'm not going to, not even if you beat me to death. So they beat me. You can do what you like, I say, but it'll make no difference. I'm not going to shame myself. And off I went. What are they—people or beasts?"

Semyon Mikheich said nothing. A dark cloud of shame and suffering was hanging over the village. It seemed as if life had come to an end, as if the sun had stopped shining, as if there were no air left to breathe. Most terrible of all, worse than the cold nights in cellars and dugouts, were the humiliations to the soul.

Deep in the soul of the old beekeeper something was changing. Any time at night that *der Arzt* wanted to hear the sound of the ax, the old man had to get up, put on his hat, and go out to chop wood. His ax resounded against the frozen logs. Sometimes the old man would stop for a moment to straighten up and get his breath back. At once the division's senior doctor would go to the window. He would look out into the yard, wondering why the ax had gone silent. A moment later the orderly would dart out. In a terrified voice, he would shout, "Chop wood, Russki! Chop, Russki, chop wood!"

On one occasion the orderly whispered excitedly to the old man, "General—kaput! Fly front line. Russkies—Tara-tara! General—kaput!"

And the Germans never saw their divisional commander again.

Then a black marketeer from Kharkov passed through. He told them what the prices were for *makhorka*, bread, and peas. He told them about an outbreak of typhus among the German soldiers. Then he bent down and whispered in the old man's ear, "I've seen it in leaflets and I've heard it on the radio: the Reds are on their way back. They've already recaptured thirty towns. They'll be here any day."

In response, the old man went to a secret place, dug a jar of honey out of the earth, and gave it to the black marketeer. "There!" he said. "For your good news!"

Then came an evening when the orderly rushed in and hurriedly began packing.

"*Zurück, zurück*," he explained, gesticulating in the direction of Poltava.

Some signalers came and quickly removed the telephone. There was no sound of shooting, but the Germans were in such a rush you would have thought that they were under fire already. They were running down the street with armfuls of all kinds of stuff, falling down in the snow and shouting. The village women saw several orderlies weeping. They were gasping for breath. Their frozen fingers kept losing their grip on the officers' heavy cases. They were worn out before they had even reached the edge of the village—but they had to keep going on foot, across the steppe. Their vehicles were stuck in the snow, with no fuel; the officers had already taken the last sledges.

The old men, who had served in the militia during the First World War, explained to the women, "Looks like our boys are back on the offensive!"

The divisional staff left while it was still dark. They were replaced by retreating machine gunners. With unkempt red-and-black beards, their noses peeling, their cheeks burned by the frost, they talked in loud barks. When they went out into the street, they kept firing random bursts into the air. And every night they pestered the young women and girls.

The fighting started early one morning. The villagers crept down into their cellars. There was the sound of machine-gun fire and of shell bursts. The women screamed and the children cried, while the old men said calmly, "All right, all right. There's no need to make such a racket. It's our own boys, with their fifteen-pounders."

Semyon Mikheich was sitting on an upturned bucket, saying nothing at all. He was thinking.

"Well, Mikheich," said old Kondrat, who had won a George Cross back in 1905, during the Japanese war, "it seems no one can escape the sound of fighting—not even a quiet soul like you."

Mikheich did not reply.

The fighting grew fiercer. The pounding grew so loud that the old women wrapped shawls around the little children. And then, not far away, they heard a muffled voice.

"It's our boys, it's our own boys!" shouted Galya Yakimenko. "Who'll come up with me?"

"I will!" replied Semyon Mikheich.

They climbed up out of the cellar. Evening was already drawing in. A vast sun was sinking into snow made pink by blazing fires. In the middle of the yard stood a Red Army soldier with a rifle.

"Good people," he said quietly, "help me. I'm wounded."

"My darling boy!" Galya shouted, and rushed to the soldier. She embraced him and led him quickly toward the hut. Semyon Mikheich just walked on.

"My darlings," said Galya, "you boys have been shedding your blood for us! Now it's our turn to do something. Soon we'll have you lying down in the warm!"

From somewhere near the well came the sound of shooting. A German submachine gunner came running toward the hut. He saw a wounded Red Army soldier and a woman with her arms around him. Still running, he fired a shot. The wounded soldier, suddenly heavy, began to sink to the ground, slipping out of the arms of the woman, who was still struggling to keep him upright. The German fired a second shot. Galya Yakimenko fell to the ground.

Semyon Mikheich could never remember how it was that he had come to be holding a heavy cudgel. For the first time in his life he was in the grip of a terrible rage, a rage that was burning away the humiliations of the previous months, a rage that he felt both on his own behalf and on behalf of others—on behalf of thousands and thousands of old men, children, young girls, and women, a rage on behalf of the earth herself, abused as she had been by the enemy. He raised the cudgel high above his head and advanced on the German. Tall and majestic, with snow-white curls, this old beekeeper was the living embodiment of the Great Patriotic War.

"Halt!" shouted the German, raising his submachine gun high into the air. But the old man smashed down his cudgel.

Just then a group of Red Army soldiers appeared. Leading them was a man in a black sheepskin coat, with a grenade in his hand. It was Prokofy, the chairman of the collective farm. What he saw was a terrifying picture: dead bodies lying outside a hut, a German lying beside a doorway and—brilliantly lit by the flames—the quiet beekeeper, cudgel in hand.

Lozovenka Village, Kharkov Province,
1942

THE OLD TEACHER

I.

DURING the last few years, Boris Isaakovich Rosenthal had left the house only on warm still days. When it rained, or if there was fog or a heavy frost, his head would spin. Doctor Weintraub believed that the vertigo was caused by sclerosis; he prescribed a small glass of milk with fifteen drops of iodine before meals.

On warm days Rosenthal would go out into the yard. He did not take philosophy books with him: the noise of the children, and the women's laughter and cursing, were entertainment enough. He would sit on the bench near the well with a small volume of Chekhov. Resting the open book on his knees, he would keep looking at one and the same page, half closing his eyes and smiling a dreamy smile like that of a blind man listening to the noise of life. He was not reading, but he was so used to having a book with him that he felt it necessary to stroke the rough binding and to check with his trembling fingers the thickness of the pages. The women sitting nearby would say, "Look—the teacher's fallen asleep," and go on talking about women's matters as if he were not there. But he was not asleep. He was breathing in the smell of onions and sunflower-seed oil and enjoying the warmth of the sun-warmed stone; he was listening to the old women's conversations about their sons- and daughters-in-law, and he was also aware of the ruthless, frenzied excitement of the little boys at their games. Sometimes the heavy wet sheets on the clotheslines would flap in the wind like sails, spraying fine drops of water onto his face. Once again, for a moment, he was a young student—sailing across the sea in a small boat.

He loved books—and books were not a barrier between him and life. His God was Life. And he learned about this God—a living, earthly, sinful God—by reading historians and philosophers, by reading the works of both greater and lesser writers. All of them, as best they could, celebrated, justified, blamed, and cursed Man on this splendid earth.

Sitting there in the yard, he could hear the children's shrill voices:

"Quick, butterfly overhead—fire!"

"Got her! Finish her off with stones!"

Rosenthal was not horrified by this cruelty—he had known it all through his eighty-two years of life and he was not afraid of it.

Then six-year-old Katya, the daughter of Weissman, the lieutenant who had been killed, came up to him in her torn dress, shuffling along in galoshes that were falling off her dirty, scratched little feet. Offering him a cold, sour pancake, she said, "Eat, teacher!"

He took the pancake and began to eat it, looking at the little girl's thin face. As he ate, there was a sudden hush in the yard. Everyone—the old women, the big-breasted young women who could no longer remember their husbands, the one-legged lieutenant Voronenko lying on a mattress under a tree—was looking at the old man and the little girl. Rosenthal dropped his book and did not try to pick it up—he was looking at the little girl's huge eyes, which were intently, even greedily, watching him as he ate. Once again he felt the urge to understand a wonder that never ceased to amaze him: human kindness. Perhaps the answer was there in the child's eyes. But her eyes must have been too dark, or maybe what got in the way were his own tears—once again he saw nothing and understood nothing.

The women were always surprised at the people who came to see this old man who lived on a pension of just 112 rubles a month and who did not possess even a paraffin stove or a kettle. There was the director of the teacher training college, and there was the chief engineer from the sugar refinery. Once there was even an officer with two medals who arrived in an automobile.

"My former pupils," the old teacher would explain. And on days when the postman brought him two or three letters at once, he would say the same thing: "My former pupils."

They remembered him, these former pupils.

And so here he was, on the morning of June 5, 1942, sitting out in the yard. Sitting beside him, on a mattress someone had carried out from the house for him, was Lieutenant Voronenko, whose leg had been amputated above the knee. Voronenko's wife, the young and beautiful Darya Semyonovna, was cooking lunch on her summer stove, bending down over the saucepans and crying. Voronenko was teasing her, wrinkling his white face and saying, "Why are you crying, Dasha? Just wait—my leg will grow back again!"

"No, it's not that. That's not why I'm crying at all," said Darya Semyonovna, still crying. "All that matters is that you stay alive."

At one in the afternoon, there was an air-raid alert; a German airplane was approaching. Snatching up their children, the women ran to the slit trenches, looking back now and then to see if some thief was about to make off with the food they had left on the little tables and stools. Only Voronenko and Rosenthal remained in the yard. From out on the street a young boy shouted, "There's a tanker nearby—it's stopped on the road. It's an easy target. The driver's run away—he's hiding in one of the trenches!"

The dogs had already seen many air raids. Tails between their legs, they would follow the women into the trenches at the very first distant sounds of a German plane.

There was a moment of silence, and then the boys announced in their shrill voices, "Overhead...Now he's banking...Now he's diving, the swine!"

The little town shook from the blow; smoke and dust rose up; there was shouting and loud weeping from the trenches. Then it was quiet again, and the women were climbing out of the earth. Shaking themselves, laughing at one another, straightening their dresses, and brushing the dust and dirt off their children, they hurried back to their stoves.

"He's put out the fire—damn him!" the old women grumbled. Puffing at the embers, tears in their eyes from the smoke, they went on muttering away: "May he find no peace—neither in this world nor in the next!"

Voronenko explained that it had been a two-hundred-kilogram bomb and that the antiaircraft guns had been five hundred meters off target. Old Mikhailyuchka muttered, "If only the Germans would get a move on and bring an end to this misery. During yesterday's alert someone made off with a whole pot of borshch I was cooking."

The neighbors all knew that her son, Yashka, had deserted and was hiding away in her attic, coming out only at night. Mikhailyuchka said that if anyone snitched, she'd have them executed when the Germans arrived. And the women were afraid to say anything—the Germans were very close now.

Koryako the agronomist, instead of letting himself be evacuated with the district soviet agricultural section, had boasted that he would stay in the town until the very last moment and only leave when the troops left. As soon as an alert sounded, he would run to his room on the ground floor, knock back a glass of home-distilled vodka—which he referred to as "anti-bombine"—and then go down into the cellar. After the all clear, he would walk up and down the yard, saying, "You can't deny it—our town's im-impregnable! Jusht one little hut—all the Jerries could do was shmash up one little hut!"

The boys were the first to bring back precise information: "It fell just opposite the Zabolotskys. It killed Rabinovichka's goat. Old Miroshenko had her leg blown off. She was taken away on a cart and she died on her way to the hospital. Her daughter's making such a hullabaloo you can hear her four whole blocks away."

That evening Doctor Weintraub called on Rosenthal. Weintraub was sixty-eight years old. He was wearing a light jacket made from tussah silk. His Russian shirt was unbuttoned, showing a plump chest covered with gray hair.

"How are you doing, young man?" asked Rosenthal.

But, after climbing the stairs to the first floor, the young man was breathing heavily. He pointed to his chest and sighed. Then he said, "It's time to go. They say the last trainload of workers from the sugar refinery will be leaving tomorrow. I've reminded Shevchenko the engineer—he's promised to send a cart to pick you up."

"Shevchenko was once a pupil of mine. He was brilliant at geometry," said Rosenthal. "We must ask him to take Voronenko. He's wounded. His wife found him five days ago in the hospital and now he's convalescing at home. And Weissman and her little girl. Her husband's been killed—she's received an official letter."

"There may not be room—there'll be several hundred workers," said Weintraub. Then he began speaking more quickly, his breath still hot and heavy. "Just think—I came here on June 16, 1901." He smiled. "It's quite a coincidence. I came here forty-one years ago to see my first patient. Mikhailyuk had got food poisoning—from some fish he'd eaten. Since then I've treated everybody in this house; I've treated him and I've treated his wife. I treated their son, Yashka, with his never-ending diarrhea. I treated Dasha Tkachuk before she married young Vitya Voronenko. I've treated Dasha's father, and I've treated Vitya himself. And I've done the same in every house. Who'd have thought it? Who'd have thought that one day I'd have to run away from here? And to be honest with you—the nearer that day comes, the less certain I feel. I keep thinking I'll stay behind. Let fate take its course!"

"Well, *I* feel all the more determined to leave," said the teacher. "I'm eighty-two years old. Don't think I don't know how hard it will be for me—an endless journey in a crowded freight wagon. I have no relatives in the Urals. I haven't got a kopeck to my name. More than that," he went on with a shrug of the shoulders, "I know, I'm as sure as sure can be, that I won't even get as far as the Urals. But it's still a better way out—if I have to die anyway, I'd rather die with dignity on the dirty floor of a dirty freight wagon. I'd rather die in a country where I'm seen as a human being."

"I'm not so sure," said Weintraub. "I don't think it'll be so terrible as all that. They're going to need people like us—surely you can see that they're going to need doctors and teachers?"

"You're a naive young man," said Rosenthal.

"I don't know, I don't know," said the doctor. "I can't make up my mind. Many of my patients keep telling me to stay. But there are others who say I absolutely must leave." Then he jumped to his feet and shouted, "What's happening? Tell me! I've come here, Boris Isaakovich, so that you can give me an explanation! You're a philosopher and a mathematician. Please explain to me—a doctor—what on earth is happening! Some kind of delirium? How can a cultured European people, a people that has built such fine clinics, a people that has engendered such luminaries of advanced medicine—how can such a people now be spreading medieval darkness and the philosophy of the Black Hundreds? Where has this infection of the soul come from? What is it? A mass psychosis? Mass insanity? Some evil spell? Or could things really be a little bit different? Have the colors all been piled on a bit thick?"

From out on the staircase came the sound of crutches. It was Voronenko.

"Permission to report, comrade Colonel?" he asked with a wry smile.

Weintraub immediately calmed down and asked, "So, young Vitya, how are you doing?" He used the familiar *Ty*, rather than the more formal *Vy*, to address nearly the entire population of the town. All the men now in their thirties and forties had, after all, once been little boys he had treated.

"One of my legs has deserted," Voronenko answered wryly. Embarrassed by his loss, he always spoke about it with a smile.

"Well?" asked Rosenthal. "Have you finished that little book yet?"

"What little book?" Voronenko repeated, still smiling. "Wait till you see the book that's going to be written now!"

And Voronenko bent down toward them, his face now calm and still. In a quiet, steady voice he said, "German tanks have crossed the railway and taken the village of Malye Nizgurtsy. That's about twenty kilometers east of here."

"Eighteen and a half," said the doctor. "So there'll be no train evacuating the sugar-refinery workers?"

"That goes without saying," said the old teacher.

"We're trapped now," said Voronenko. He went silent for a moment, then added, "Well and truly in the bag."

"Well," said Weintraub, "fate's fate. We'll see what happens. I'm off home now."

Rosenthal looked at him. "As you know, I've never been one for medicines, but now you must give me the one medicine that can help."

"What? What can save us now?" Weintraub asked quickly.

"Poison."

"Never!" said Weintraub, raising his voice. "Never in all my life have I given anyone poison!"

"You're a naive young man," said Rosenthal. "Epicurus taught that, if his sufferings become unbearable, a wise man can kill himself out of love of life. Well, I love life no less than Epicurus did."

He rose to his full height. His hair, his face, his trembling fingers, his thin neck—everything had been dried out and made colorless by time. Everything about him looked transparent, light, weightless. Only in his eyes was there something not subject to time: the power of thought.

"No, no!" Weintraub moved toward the door. "You'll see—one way or another we'll get through all this."

And he left.

"There's one thing I fear more than anything," said the teacher. "That the people among whom I have lived my whole life, the people I love and trust—that this people will be taken in by a vile, cheap lie."

"No," said Voronenko. "It won't be like that."

The night was dark because heavy clouds had covered the sky and shut out the light of the stars. And it was dark from the darkness of the earth. The Nazis were a great falsehood, life's greatest falsehood. Wherever they passed, up from the depths rose cowardice, treachery, murderousness, and violence against the weak. The

Nazis drew everything dark up to the surface, just as a black spell in an old tale calls up the spirits of evil. That night the little town lay stifling, gripped by something foul and dark. Something vile had awoken; stirred by the Nazis' arrival, it was now reaching toward them. The treacherous and the weak-spirited had emerged from their cellars and gullies and were ripping up letters, Party cards, and books by Lenin; they were tearing down portraits of their own brothers from the walls of their rooms. Fawning speeches of disavowal were taking shape in the hearts of the poor in spirit. Thoughts of revenge—for some chance word or for some marketplace quarrel—were being conceived. Hearts were being infected by callousness, pride, and indifference. Cowards, fearing for their own lives, were thinking how to save themselves by denouncing a neighbor. And so it was in every town large and small, in every country large and small where the Nazis set foot. Murk rose from the beds of lakes and rivers; toads swam to the surface; thistles sprang up where wheat had been planted.

Rosenthal did not sleep that night. It seemed as if the sun would not rise in the morning, as if darkness had spread over the town forever. But the sun rose at its predetermined hour, and the sky turned blue and cloudless, and the birds began to sing.

Not far above them was a German bomber. It was flying slowly, as if it too had been exhausted by a sleepless night. There was not a shot from the antiaircraft guns; the town and the sky over the town had become German.

The house was now waking. Yashka Mikhailyuk had come down from his attic and was strolling about the yard. He was sitting on the bench where the old teacher had been sitting only the day before. He said to Dasha Voronenko, who was lighting her little stove, "So what's he going to do now—your defender of the Motherland? The Reds have run away, have they? Left him behind, have they?"

And the beautiful Dasha, smiling a pathetic smile, said, "Don't report him, Yashka. He was conscripted, the same as everyone else."

After being confined for a long time in the dark, Yashka had come out into the warmth of the sun. He was breathing the morning air, looking at the green onions in the vegetable patch. He had shaved and put on an embroidered shirt.

"All right," he said lazily. "But I could do with a drink. D'you know where I can find something?"

"I'll get you some moonshine," said Dasha. "I know a woman who's got some. But I'm begging you! Poor Vitya's a cripple now. Don't snitch on him."

Then Koryako the agronomist came out into the yard. The women whispered to one another, "Look at him now—anyone would think it was Easter Sunday!"

Koryako went up to Yashka and whispered a few words in his ear. They both laughed.

The two men went to Koryako's home and began to drink. Yashka's mother, old Mikhailyuchka, brought them some fatback and pickled tomatoes. Varvara Andreyevna, who had five sons in the Red Army and the most vicious tongue of all the old women in the yard, said, "Well, Mikhailyuchka, the Germans have arrived—you're going to be quite somebody now! A deserter for a son and a husband in a labor camp for anti-Soviet agitation—yes, soon this house will be all yours again. The Germans will be putting you in charge of the whole town!"

The highway lay five kilometers to the east, and the German troops had simply bypassed the little town. It was midday before the first motorcyclists rode down the main street. They were wearing only forage caps, underpants, and gym shoes, and they were heavily tanned. Each had a watch on his wrist.

"Dear God! Naked on the main street!" said the old women. "They know no shame."

The motorcyclists rummaged about the yards. They took the priest's turkey, which had come out to investigate some horse manure. They guzzled down two and a half kilos of the church elder's honey, drank a bucket of milk, and went on their way, promising that the commandant would arrive in a couple of hours. In the afternoon Yashka was joined by two more deserter friends. All very

drunk, they sang together, "Three tank men, three merry chums."
Probably they would have been glad to sing German songs, except
that they didn't know any. Koryako walked up and down the yard
and, with a sly grin, asked the women, "So what's happened to our
Jews? Children, old men—I haven't glimpsed a Jew all day. It's as if
they'd never existed. And only yesterday they were all coming back
from the market with eighty-kilo baskets!"

But the women shrugged their shoulders and said nothing. Koryako felt surprised. He had expected them to respond differently.

Then the drunken Yashka decided to purge his apartment: until
1936, after all, the entire lower floor had belonged to his family. After Yashka's father had been sent into exile, Voronenko and his wife
had taken two of the rooms. And during the war the town soviet
had installed Sublieutenant Weissman's family in the third room;
they had been evacuated from Zhitomir.

Yashka's friends were helping him clear the rooms. Katya Weissman and little Vitaly Voronenko were sitting outside crying. Katya's
granny was carrying out dishes and cooking pots. As she walked
past the crying children, she said in a whisper, "There, there, children, you mustn't cry."

But there was something so terrifying about her sweating face
and the gray strands of hair plastered to her temples and cheeks that
the children only cried all the more.

Dasha reminded Yashka about their conversation that morning,
but he answered, "You can't buy Yashka with a half liter of vodka.
Do you think people here have forgotten how that Vitya of yours
went around dispossessing whoever he said was a kulak?"

Lida Weissman, the sublieutenant's widow, was a little out of her
mind. She had never quite recovered from receiving notification of
the deaths of her husband and brother on the same day. She looked
at little Katya and said, "There's not a drop of milk at the market
today. Cry all you like—there isn't a single drop."

And Viktor Voronenko was smiling, lying there on an empty
sack and tapping the ground with one crutch.

Tall, gray-haired, and bright-eyed, old Mikhailyuchka stood there without saying a word. She was looking at the crying children, at her bustling son, at old Granny Weissman, at the smiling cripple.

"What's up, Mama?" asked Yashka. "You're standing there as if you've been struck dumb."

Only when he repeated this a third time did she reply. "So here we are—our day's dawned at last!"

The evicted families sat silently on their bundles until it began to grow dark. Then the teacher came out and said, "Please all come to my room."

The women, who had seemed turned to stone, burst out sobbing.

Picking up two small bundles, the teacher went back to his room. Soon the room was heaped with bundles, pots and pans, and suitcases tied shut with pieces of string and wire. The children fell asleep on the bed, the women on the floor; Rosenthal and Voronenko went on talking in low voices.

"I've dreamed of many things in my life," said Voronenko. "I've wanted the Order of Lenin. I've wanted a motorcycle with a sidecar, so my wife and I could go to Donetsk on our days off. While I was at the front, I dreamed of seeing my family, of bringing an Iron Cross and some condensed milk back for my son. But now I've only got one dream: to get hold of some hand grenades. Then I'd show those Fritzes a thing or two!"

The teacher replied, "The more you think about life, the less you understand it. Very soon, when they've smashed my skull in, I'll stop thinking altogether. But for now the German tanks are powerless to stop me thinking—and what I'm thinking about is peace!"

"Why think about anything?" said Voronenko. "What I want is a few hand grenades—to put the wind up Hitler while I still can!"

2.

Koryako the agronomist was waiting to see the town commandant.

He had heard that the commandant was middle-aged and that

he knew Russian. Apparently he had studied a long time ago in Riga.

The commandant knew that Koryako was here, and Koryako was pacing anxiously up and down the waiting room, glancing now and then at a huge portrait of Hitler talking to some children. Hitler was smiling; the children, smartly dressed, with tense, serious faces, were looking up at him from the lowly height of their childish stature.

Koryako was troubled. It was he who had drawn up the collectivization plan for the district: What if this had been reported to the Germans? And he was troubled because this was the first time in his life he would be talking to the Fascists. He was also troubled because this had once been the agricultural college; he himself, only a year ago, had taught field husbandry in this very building. He understood that he was taking an irrevocable step, that he would never be able to return to his former life. And he tried to stifle all his anxieties with a single phrase, which he repeated again and again: "I must play my trump card. I must play my trump card."

From the commandant's office came a hoarse, stifled, tormented scream.

Koryako began to walk toward the street door. "What am I doing, sticking my nose in? I should have just lain low and kept out of trouble," he thought with sudden melancholy. Then the office door flew open and out rushed the Ukrainian *Polizei* chief, who had recently arrived from Vinnitsa, and the commandant's pale young adjutant, who had spent the last market day rounding up partisans. The adjutant shouted something to the clerk, and the clerk jumped up and rushed to the telephone. The *Polizei* chief, seeing Koryako, shouted, "Quick, quick! Where's there a doctor? The commandant's had a heart attack!"

"There—in the house across the road," said Koryako, looking out of the window and pointing. "He's the best doctor in town. Only his name—forgive me—is Weintraub. He's a Jew."

"*Was? Was?*" the adjutant asked in German.

The *Polizei* chief, who had already picked up a few words of German, said, "*Hier, ein gut Doktor, aber er ist Jud.*"

The adjutant gestured dismissively and rushed toward the door. Catching up with him, Koryako pointed him in the right direction: "There—that little house there!"

Major Werner had had a severe attack of angina. The doctor understood this quickly, after asking only a few questions. He ran into the other room. He embraced his wife and daughter in farewell. Then he snatched up a syringe and a few capsules of camphor and hurried after the young officer. "Just a moment," he said. "I must put on my armband."

"Quick," said the adjutant. "Come as you are."

As they went into the office, the adjutant said, "I must warn you. Our own doctor will be here soon. A car's been sent for him. He'll be checking both your medicines and your methods."

Weintraub smiled ruefully and said, "Young man, you're speaking to a doctor. But if you don't trust me, I can leave."

"Quick! Don't waste time!" shouted the adjutant.

Werner, a thin man with gray hair, was lying on a sofa. His face was pale and covered in sweat. His eyes looked terrible, full of deathly anguish. Slowly he said, "Doctor, for the sake of my poor mother, for the sake of my sick wife. It . . . it would be the death of them." And he stretched out toward Weintraub a powerless hand with white, bloodless fingernails. The clerk and the adjutant both gave a sob.

"At such a moment he remembers his mother," the clerk said reverently.

"Doctor, I can't breathe. My eyes are going dark," the commandant moaned, his eyes pleading for help.

And the doctor saved him.

The sweet feeling of life returned to Werner. Free now from spasms, his coronary arteries were now freely sending his blood on its way. Werner was free again; he could breathe. As Weintraub got ready to leave, Werner seized him by the hand. "No, no, don't go— I'm afraid it might happen again."

Werner went on quietly complaining. "It's a fearful illness. This is my fourth attack. The moment it starts, I sense all the darkness of impending death. Nothing in the world is darker, more terrifying, and more awful than death. How unjust it is that we're mortal! Don't you agree?"

They were alone in the room.

Weintraub bent down over the commandant and—not knowing why, as if being pushed by someone—said, "I'm a Jew, Herr Major. You are right. Death is terrifying."

For a moment their eyes met. And in the eyes of the commandant the gray-haired doctor saw a sense of confusion. The German depended on him; he was afraid of another attack, and the old doctor with the calm, assured movements was defending him from death. The doctor stood between him and the terrible darkness that lay so close to him, that lived right beside him, there in his sclerotic heart.

Soon they heard the sound of a car drawing up.

The adjutant came in and said, "Herr Major, the head doctor from the therapeutic hospital has arrived. You can let this man go now."

The old man went on his way through the waiting room. Seeing a uniformed doctor with an Iron Cross, he said with a smile, "Good day, colleague. The patient is in good condition now."

The doctor looked at him silently and without moving.

On the way home, Weintraub said in a loud singsong voice, "There's only one thing I want now: I want a patrol to come the other way and shoot me outside the commandant's window, right in front of his eyes. This is my one and only wish. Don't go out without your armband. Don't go out without your armband."

He was laughing, waving his arms about as if he were drunk.

His wife ran out to meet him. "Did everything go all right?" she asked.

"Yes, yes, the life of our dear commandant is now out of danger," he said with a smile. Then he went inside, dropped to the ground, and began to weep, beating his large bald head against the floor.

"The teacher is right," he said, "the teacher is right. And may the day I became a doctor be accursed."

Time passed. Koryako was appointed block warden. Yashka was now working in the *Polizei*. Marusya Varaponova, the most beautiful young woman in the town, was playing the piano in the officers' café and living with the young adjutant.

The women went to the villages to exchange old clothes and other bits and pieces for wheat, millet, and potatoes; they complained about the huge sums charged by the German drivers. The labor exchanges sent out hundreds of notices—and young men and women went to the station, with knapsacks and bundles, to be packed into freight cars. A German cinema opened—and a brothel for soldiers and officers. A large brick toilet was built on the main square. On it, in both Russian and German, was written FOR GERMANS ONLY.

In the school Klara Franzevna gave the first class the following problem: "Two Messerschmitts brought down eight Red fighters and twelve Red bombers, while the antiaircraft guns destroyed eleven Bolshevik attack aircraft. How many Red airplanes were destroyed altogether?" The other teachers were afraid of talking about their own affairs in front of her; they waited until she left the common room.

Ragged, staggering from hunger, prisoners of war were herded through the town—and women ran out to them with boiled potatoes and pieces of bread. The prisoners were so exhausted by hunger and thirst and so infested with lice that they seemed to have lost all human likeness. Some of them had swollen faces, while others had sunken cheeks covered by dark, dusty stubble. But for all their terrible sufferings, they bore their cross bravely, and they looked with hate at the well-dressed and well-fed *Polizei*, and at the traitors in German uniforms. And their hatred was so great that, had they been offered the choice, their hands would have reached out not toward a warm loaf of bread but to grip the throat of one of these traitors.

Every morning, under the supervision of soldiers and *Polizei*, the women went out to build aerodromes and bridges, to repair roads and railway embankments. Trains of tanks and munitions passed by on their way east, and long lines of freight cars full of cattle and wheat passed by on their way west; some of the cars, packed with young boys and girls, were boarded up.

Women, old men, little children—everyone understood what was happening. Everyone clearly understood what lay in store for them and why the Germans were fighting this appalling war. One day, old Varvara Andreyevna went up to Rosenthal in the yard. Weeping, she said to him, "What's happening in the world, grandfather?"

The old teacher went back to his room in silence. "In a day or two," he said to Voronenko, "there's probably going to be a mass execution of Jews—the life to which they've condemned the Ukraine is just too terrible."

"But what have the Jews got to do with it?" asked Voronenko.

"What do you mean? The whole system is founded on them. The Fascists have created an all-European system of forced labor and, to keep the prisoners obedient, they have constructed a huge ladder of oppression. The Dutch are worse off than the Danes; the French are worse off than the Dutch; the Czechs are worse off than the French. Things are still worse for the Greeks and the Serbs, worse still for the Poles, and last of all come the Ukrainians and Russians. These are the rungs of the ladder of forced labor. The farther down you go, the more blood, the more sweat, the more slavery. And then, at the very bottom of this huge, many-storied prison is the abyss to which the Germans have condemned the Jews. Their fate has to terrify all the forced laborers of Europe, so that even the most terrible fate will seem happiness in comparison with that of the Jews. Well, it seems to me that the sufferings of the Russians and Ukrainians are so great that the time has come to demonstrate that there is a fate still more awful, still more terrible. The Germans will say, 'Don't grumble! Be happy and proud, be glad that you are not Jews!' It's not a matter of elemental hatred. It's simple arithmetic—the simple arithmetic of brutality."

3.

During the last month there had been a number of changes in the house where the teacher lived. Koryako the agronomist had put on weight and become uncommonly self-important. Women with bottles of home-distilled vodka were always coming to ask things of him; every evening he got drunk, put on the gramophone, and sang, "There in the mist my campfire shines." Words of German began to appear in his speech. He would say, "Please don't bother me with requests when I'm on my way to *nach Haus* or for to *spazier*." Yashka Mikhailyuk was seldom to be seen; most of the time he was driving around the district, tracking down partisans. When he came back, it was usually with a cart laden with fatback, eggs, and home-distilled vodka.

Yashka's old mother, who adored him, prepared fine suppers. Once, after some Gestapo corporal or sergeant had come to one of these suppers, she said to Dasha Voronenko, "You made the wrong choice, you fool. See what kind of people visit us now—while you live with your one-legged cripple in a room that belongs to a Yid!"

She had never forgiven the beautiful Dasha. In 1936 Dasha had refused Yashka and married Voronenko instead.

Yashka made a strange little joke: "Soon you'll be able to breathe more freely. Yes, I've seen some towns that have already been purged—purged root and branch!"

Dasha repeated what Yashka had said. Old Granny Weissman began lamenting over her little granddaughter.

"Dasha," she said after a while, "I'll leave you my wedding ring. And there'll be more than five hundredweight of potatoes from our vegetable patch, along with some pumpkin and beetroot. One way or another there'll be enough to feed the child until spring. And I've got a roll of woolen cloth for a lady's coat—you can exchange it for bread. And anyway the child has no appetite—she hardly eats anything at all."

"She'll be all right with us," Dasha replied. "And once she's grown up, she can marry our young Vitalik."

That same day Doctor Weintraub came to see the teacher. He held out to him a little vial, with a close-fitting glass stopper.

"A concentrated solution," he said. "My views have changed. During the last few days I've come to see this substance as a useful and necessary medicament."

The teacher slowly shook his head. "Thank you," he said sadly. "But my views have also changed. I've decided not to resort to this medicine."

"Why?" Weintraub asked in surprise. "You were right, and I was wrong. I've had all I can bear. I'm not allowed to walk down any of the main streets. My wife is forbidden to go to the market—on pain of death. We all have to wear this armband. When I go out on the street now, I feel as if my arm's weighed down by a band of red-hot steel. This is no way to live, you're right. And it seems that even forced labor in Germany is considered too good for us Jews. I'm sure you've heard about unfortunate young boys and girls being taken to work there. But Jewish young boys and girls aren't being taken—so what awaits them, what awaits all of us, must be something many times worse than this terrible forced labor. What it will be I don't know. Why should I wait for it? You're right. If it weren't for my bronchial asthma, I'd go and join the partisans."

"Well, I myself," said the teacher, "have become an optimist during the terrible weeks since we last met."

"What!" exclaimed Weintraub. "An optimist? Forgive me—but you've gone out of your mind. Don't you know what these people are like? Yesterday I went to the commandant's office to ask for my daughter to be released from work for one day after being beaten up. I was thrown out—and I'm glad they didn't do anything worse."

"That's not what I mean," said the teacher. "There was one thing that truly terrified me. The mere thought of it used to bring me out in a cold sweat. I was afraid that the Fascists might turn out to have calculated correctly. I talked about this to Voronenko. I was terrified, I didn't want to live to see that day. I didn't want to live to see that hour. Surely you don't think that the Fascists embarked on this vast persecution, this destruction of a nation of millions, just for the sake of it? Behind what they're doing lies a cold, mathematical calculation. They awake what is dark. They incite hatred. They resurrect prejudices. In this lies their power. Divide, persecute, and rule! The resurrection of darkness! Set each nation against some neighboring nation, set enslaved nations against nations that have retained their freedom, set nations from across the ocean against nations living on this side of the ocean—and set every nation in the world against the Jewish nation. Divide and rule! After all, there is more than enough cruelty and darkness in the world, more than enough superstition and prejudice. But the Fascists miscalculated. They meant to unleash hatred, but what has been born is compassion. They wanted to call up malice and schadenfreude; they wanted to eclipse the reason of great nations. But I've seen with my own eyes that the fate of the Jews has evoked only grief and compassion. I've seen that the Ukrainians and Russians, having suffered under the weight of the German terror, are ready to help the Jews in any way they can. They forbid us to buy bread or to go to the market for milk—and so our neighbors offer to buy things for us. Dozens of people have come around and given me advice about where to hide. I have seen much compassion. I have, of course, also seen indifference. But I have not often seen malicious joy at our destruction—only three or four times. The Germans got it wrong. They miscalculated. My optimism is triumphing. And I never had any illusions—I've always known that life is cruel."

"That's all true," said Weintraub. He looked at his watch and went on: "But I must go now. It's half-past three, the Jewish day is coming to an end . . . We probably won't be seeing each other again." He went up close to the teacher and said, "Allow me to say farewell to you. We've known each other for nearly fifty years. It's not for me to be your teacher at a time like this."

They embraced and kissed. And the women, watching them say farewell, began to cry.

A lot happened that day. Voronenko had managed, the previous evening, to get hold of two F-1 hand grenades. Some boys had given them to him in exchange for a tumbler of beans and two tumblers of sunflower seeds. "What can I do?" he said to the teacher. He was standing under a tree and watching his little son, Vitalik, bullying little Katya Weissman. "What can I do? I've come back home, but it's brought me no joy—though God knows how often I dreamed of home while I was in the trenches and in the hospital. What have I come back to? The occupation: the labor exchanges, people being packed off to work in Germany. Hunger, depravity, German faces, *Polizei* faces, filthy traitors ..."

Then Voronenko shouted angrily to his son, "What are you doing to the girl, you Fascist? You'll break every bone in her body. Why? Her father died fighting for the Motherland, he was posthumously awarded the Order of Lenin—and you have to beat her up mercilessly from morning till night! Though God knows what's the matter with the girl ... She just stands there like a sheep, eyes wide open and not even crying. If only she'd run away from the fool, instead of just standing there patiently."

No one saw Voronenko leave, his crutches quietly tapping against the ground. He stood for a while on the corner, looking back at the house where he had left his wife and son, and then set off toward the commandant's office. He never saw his wife and son again. Nor did Koryako the agronomist ever return home. The grenade thrown by the one-legged lieutenant exploded in the commandant's waiting room, where the town's block wardens were awaiting new instructions. The commandant himself was at that moment going for a stroll in the garden; the doctor with the Iron Cross had advised a daily forty-minute walk in the orchard, followed by a brief rest on the little bench.

The following morning crazy Lida Weissman was sent by a policeman to clear away the corpses of Doctor Weintraub and his wife and daughter. They had taken poison during the night.

A few benighted people tried to get into the doctor's apartment. His wife had a coat made from Astrakhan fur, and they had a lot of other good things: carpets, silver spoons, crystal glasses they used only when their son, a Leningrad professor, came to visit them. But the Germans had left a guard there, and no one got anything at all—not even Doctor Ageyev, who begged for the Big Medical Encyclopedia and repeated heatedly that its many volumes were all in Russian and could therefore be of no use at all to the Germans.

The bodies were driven around the town. The thin, wretched horse stopped at every corner, as if the dead passengers kept asking to stop and look—at the boarded-up houses, at the blue-and-yellow windowpanes of the Lyubimenkos' porch, at the fire observation tower.

Standing by windows, gates, and doors, the doctor's former patients watched his last journey. No one, of course, wept, took their hat off, or came out to say farewell. No one during this terrible time was moved by blood, suffering, and death; what surprised and shook people was kindness and love. The town no longer needed the doctor. Who needed treatment at a time when health was a punishment in itself? Paralysis, crippling hernias, dangerous heart attacks, coughing up blood, malignant tumors—these things saved people from exhausting work, from forced labor in Germany. People dreamed of illnesses, summoned them up, prayed for them. The dead doctor was seen off with gloomy, silent looks. The only person who wept when the cart passed her house was old Granny Weissman; the previous day, when he came to take his leave of the teacher, the doctor had brought a kilo of rice, a small paper bag of cocoa, and twelve lumps of sugar for little Katya. Doctor Weintraub had been a good doctor, but he had not liked to treat people free of charge; never had he given anyone such a generous present.

As for Lida Weissman, she did not come back until evening. She said that the doctor and his wife had been heavy, that the ground was hard and stony, but that she had not, fortunately, had to dig them a deep grave. She also complained that she had broken the heel of one of her shoes with the spade and torn her skirt on a nail as she got down from the cart. She had enough good sense—or perhaps the sly intuition that often goes with insanity—not to tell Dasha that Viktor Voronenko was hanging from one of the main gates into the town.

But after Dasha left, she said in a quiet, matter-of-fact voice,

"Viktor's hanging there. He looks terribly thirsty—his mouth is wide open and his lips are quite dry."

Later in the afternoon old Mikhailyuchka told Dasha about Viktor. Dasha went silently into the back of the yard, where the cucumbers grew, and sat down in between the rows. At first the boys kept a careful watch on her, thinking she was about to steal their food, but then they realized that she was lost in thought. She was biting her lip and thinking terrible thoughts, punishing herself remorselessly. She remembered the first day of her life with Viktor, and she remembered their last day. She remembered an army doctor. She had made sweet coffee for him. While they drank it, they had listened to records. She remembered how her husband had asked her at night, in a whisper, "You don't find it disgusting to be sleeping with a one-legged cripple?" She had answered, "I'll just have to get used to it." Yes, she had sinned against him—in every possible way. What she wanted now was to run away from people. But the world had turned cruel, and there was no one who could show her compassion—she had to get herself up off the ground and go and be with people again. It was her turn that evening to fetch the water.

There was a German soldier living next door. He ran to the outhouse, pulling his belt off as he went by. On his way back he saw Dasha sitting there, and he went up to the fence. He stood there without a word, admiring her beauty, her white neck, her hair, her breasts. She sensed his look and wondered why God had punished her—on top of all her other miseries—with such beauty. It was impossible, during this vile, terrible time, for a beautiful woman to live cleanly and without sin.

Then Rosenthal came up to her and said, "Dasha, you want to be on your own. I'll go to the well instead of you. You sit here as long as your soul needs. I've already given Vitalik some cold millet porridge."

She nodded silently, looked at him, and let out a sob. He was probably the only person in the town who had not changed. He was still as polite and considerate as ever. He went on reading his books, saying, "I won't be disturbing you, will I?" and wishing people good health if they sneezed. Everyone else had lost every quality she most loved in people: politeness, delicacy, and responsiveness. This old man seemed to be the only person left in the town who still asked, "How are you feeling today?," who still said, "You look very pale this morning" or "Have something to eat—you didn't eat anything at all last night."

Everyone else in the world was living their life as if nothing mattered: what with the war and the Germans, everything seemed to have become worthless. And that was how she herself had lived, carelessly, giving no thought to things of the soul.

Using a little stick as a trowel, she quickly began digging between the cucumber runners and then carefully filling the pits, until the ground was quite level again. And when it was dark, she cried a little—she was breathing more easily now, and she wanted some tea and something to eat. She wanted to go up to mad Lida Weissman and say, "Well, now we're both of us widows!" And then she'd go off and become a nun.

In the twilight Rosenthal put a candlestick on the table and took two candles from the cupboard. He had been keeping them for a long time. Each had been wrapped in blue paper. He lit the two candles, opened a drawer he never opened, and took out some bundles of old letters and photographs. He sat at the table, put on his glasses, and began intently studying the photographs and rereading the letters; the letters were written on blue and pink paper that had faded with time.

Old Granny Weissman went quietly up to him. "What will happen to my children?" she asked.

She did not know how to write. In all her life she had not read a single book. She was an ignorant old woman—except that, instead of book learning, she had learned to observe, and she had acquired a worldly wisdom that could penetrate to the heart of many things.

"How long will those candles last you?" she asked.

"Two nights, I think," said the teacher.

"Today and tomorrow?"

"Yes, tomorrow as well."

"And the day after tomorrow it will be dark?"

"Yes, I think it will be dark the day after tomorrow."

She trusted few people. But Rosenthal could be trusted, and she trusted him. Grief welled up in her heart. She looked for a long time at the face of her sleeping granddaughter and said sternly, "Tell me—what is the child guilty of?"

But Rosenthal did not hear her; he was reading his old letters.

During the night he went through his vast store of memories. He remembered the hundreds of people who had passed through his life. He remembered pupils and teachers, friends and enemies. He remembered books and student discussions; he remembered the cruel, unhappy love he had lived through sixty years before and which had cast a cold shadow over his whole life. He remembered years of wandering and years of labor. He remembered his spiritual vacillations—from a passionate, frenzied religiosity to a cold, clear atheism. He remembered heated, fanatical arguments in which no one would yield.

All that now lay far in the past. He had, of course, lived an unsuccessful life. He had thought a lot but achieved little. For fifty years he had worked as a schoolteacher in a boring little town. Once he had taught in a Jewish trade school; later he had taught geometry and algebra in a Soviet school. He should have lived in the capital. He should have written books, published articles in newspapers, and argued with the whole world.

But he was not, now, feeling sad because his life had been a failure. Nor was he mourning those who had long ago departed this life; they, for the first time, were no longer of any concern to him. Now he only desired a single thing; he passionately wanted the miracle he could not understand: love. He had never known it. He had lost his mother when he was a little child, and he had been brought up in the family of his uncle; as a young man, he had known the bitterness of being betrayed by a woman. The whole of his life had been lived in a world of noble thoughts and rational actions.

He wanted someone to come up to him and say, "Put a shawl

over your legs. There's a cold draft, it'll be bad for your rheumatism." He wanted someone to say, "Why are you fetching water from the well today? What about your sclerosis?" He was hoping one of the women lying on the floor would come up to him and say, "Go to bed now. You shouldn't be sitting at your desk so late at night—it's not good for you." Never had anyone come up to his bed, pulled up his blanket for him, and tucked him in with the words, "Have my blanket too—or you'll get cold." He knew that he was going to die soon, at a time when life was ruled by the laws of evil—and the laws of this brutal force, in the name of which unprecedented crimes were being committed, were determining the actions not only of the victors but also of those who had fallen into their power. Life was at the mercy of indifference and apathy. It was during this terrible time that he was fated to die.

It was announced the following morning that all the town's Jews were to report at 6:00 AM the next day to the *Platz* by the steam mill. They would then be transported to the western part of the occupied Ukraine, where the Reich authorities were setting up a special ghetto for them. They were to take not more than fifteen kilograms of belongings. There was no need to take food, since dry rations and hot water would be provided throughout the journey by the military command.

4.

All day long neighbors kept calling to ask for advice, to ask the teacher what he thought of this decree. First there was Borukh, the witty, foul-mouthed old cobbler who crafted such fashionable shoes; then came Mendel, the stove maker and taciturn philosopher; then Leiba, the tinsmith and father of nine children; and Haim Kulish, the broad-shouldered, gray-whiskered blacksmith. All of them had heard that similar announcements had been made in many other towns, but nowhere had anyone seen any trainloads of Jews—nor had anyone seen any columns of Jews on the highways, nor had anyone heard anything about life in these ghettoes. All of them had heard that Jews were being taken not to railway stations, nor along the main highways, but to gullies and ravines, to marshes and old quarries on the outskirts of towns. All of them had heard that, a few days after the Jews had left, German soldiers had been going to the markets and bartering shoes, women's coats, and children's pullovers for honey, eggs, and sour cream. People had come back home and said quietly, "A soldier was trying to barter a woolen jumper—the one Sonya from next door was wearing the morning the Germans marched them out of the town." Or, "A German was trading the sandals belonging to that boy who was evacuated from Riga." Or, "A German wanted three kilos of honey in exchange for the suit that belonged to our friend Kugel the engineer." All of the Jews knew what was in store for them; they were all able to guess. But in their heart of hearts they did not believe it. The murder of a whole nation was something too terrible. Nobody could believe it.

And so old Borukh said, "How can they kill a man who makes shoes like I do? The shoes I make could be shown at an exhibition in Paris."

"The Germans are capable of anything," said Mendel, the stove maker. "Anything at all."

"Very well," said Leiba the tinsmith. "Let's say they don't need my kettles and saucepans and samovar flues. But why should they want to kill my nine children?"

And Rosenthal, the old teacher, said nothing. He listened to them and thought that he had been right not to take poison. He had lived all his life with these people; he should live his last bitter hour with them too.

"I'd slip off into the forest," said Haim Kulish the blacksmith. "But how? The *Polizei* keep following us. The block warden's been around three times since this morning. I sent one of my boys to my father-in-law—and my landlord followed him. He's an honest man. He told me absolutely straightforwardly, 'I've had a warning from the police. "You're the man of the house," they said to me. "If even just one little boy doesn't show up at the *Platz*, you'll be paying for it with your life.'"

"What can we do?" said Mendel the stove maker. "Fate's fate. A neighbor said to my son, 'Yashka, you don't look like a Jew. Run away to some village or other.' And my little Yashka replied, 'But I want to look like a Jew. Wherever they take my father—that's where I'm going too.'"

"I can say one thing," muttered the blacksmith. "Whatever happens, I'm not going to die like a sheep."

"Well said, Kulish!" said the old teacher. "You're a fine man!"

In the evening Major Werner had a meeting in his office with Gestapo officer Becker.

"Tomorrow's operation must go without a hitch," said Becker. "Then we'll be able to breathe freely. I've had enough of these Jews. Every day there are outrages: five Jews escaping, apparently to join the partisans; a whole family committing suicide; three Jews walking about without armbands; a Jewish woman found buying eggs in the market in spite of being categorically forbidden to go there; two Jews arrested on Berlinerstrasse, even though they know that they're forbidden to walk down any of the main streets; eight of them wandering about the town after four o'clock in the afternoon; two girls shot for trying to escape into the forest while being marched to work. Now these incidents may all be trifling—a great deal less serious, of course, than some of the problems encountered by our frontline troops—but they get on one's nerves nevertheless. They all occurred during a single day, and other days are no different."

"What is the operational procedure?" asked Werner.

Becker wiped his pince-nez with a piece of chamois. "It's not us who determine the operational procedure. In Poland, of course, we have had broader possibilities to apply more energetic measures—and these, when it comes down to it, are essential. We are, after all, talking statistics with an impressive number of zeros. Here, of course, we're having to work in field conditions—we are, after all, near the front line. The latest orders allow us to deviate from the procedures laid down and make adaptations for local conditions."

"How many men do you need?" asked Werner.

Becker's manner during this conversation was authoritative, a great deal more so than usual. Talking to him, Werner felt an inner timidity.

"The procedure is as follows," said Becker. "There will be two squads—the execution squad and the guard squad. The execution squad should be fifteen or twenty men, all volunteers. The guard squad must be relatively large—one soldier to every fifteen Jews."

"Why?" asked the commandant.

"Experience shows that, when a column realizes that it is not heading toward a railway line or a highway, hysteria and panic set in and there will be attempts at escape. Also, the use of machine guns has recently been prohibited—the percentage of shots resulting in mortality is too low. We have to use handheld weapons, and this greatly slows down the work. And then the recommendation is that the execution squad should be as small as possible—not more than twenty men for a thousand Jews. While the work is in progress, the guard squad has a fair amount to do. As you know, quite a high proportion of the Jews are men."

"How long will this take?" asked Werner.

"With an experienced organizer, not longer than two and a half hours for a thousand people. The main thing is clarity in the assignation of roles, proper organization of the column, and correct timing. The operation itself does not take long."

"But how many men do you need?"

"At least a hundred," said Becker emphatically. He looked out through the window and added: "Weather conditions are also a factor. I've spoken to a meteorologist. Tomorrow morning is likely to be calm and sunny. There may be rain in the evening, but that's neither here nor there."

"And so..." Werner said hesitantly.

"The procedure is as follows. You yourself choose an officer—a member of the National Socialist Party, of course. It is his role to draw up a list for the execution squad. He begins by announcing, 'Now then, I'm going to need a few men with strong nerves.' This will have to be done this evening, in the barracks. The officer must collect at least thirty names—experience indicates that ten percent always drop out. Then he must talk to each man individually: 'Are you afraid of blood? Can you endure a considerable degree of nervous strain?' At this point there's no need for any further explanation. The members of the guard squad must be chosen at the same time—and the Unteroffiziere must be given their instructions. Weapons must be checked. The execution squad must report, wearing helmets, outside the commandant's office, by 5:00 AM. The officer will then explain the task in detail, after which he must speak to each of the volunteers again. Each volunteer is then issued three hundred cartridges, and by 6:00 AM they must be present on the assembly square. The Jews are then escorted to their destination, the execution squad proceeding thirty meters ahead of the column. Behind the column follow two carts, since there is always a certain number of women—the old, the pregnant, and the hysterical—who lose consciousness on the way."

Becker said all this slowly, in order that the major should take in every detail. "Well then, that's it for now," he continued. "All further instructions will be given by my officers on-site."

Major Werner looked at Becker and suddenly asked, "And what about the children?"

Becker cleared his throat disapprovingly. In an official conversation a question like this was inappropriate.

"You must understand," he said very seriously, looking intently into the commandant's eyes, "that the recommendation is to remove them from their parents and to work with them separately, but I prefer not to do that. I'm sure you can see how difficult it is to tear a child away from its mother at such a sad moment."

When Becker took his leave, the commandant summoned his adjutant, repeated the instructions to him in detail, and said quietly, "All the same, I'm glad that that old doctor did away with himself in advance. Otherwise I'd have felt pangs of conscience. Like it or not, he helped me a great deal. Without him I don't know if I'd have survived till the army doctor arrived ... And during these last few days I've been feeling excellent. I've been sleeping a lot better, and my digestion's improved. Two people have told me that I've got more color in my face now. It's quite possible that all this is because of my daily stroll in the orchard. And the air in this little town is exceptional. Before the war, apparently, there were sanatoriums here for lung and heart patients."

The sky was deep blue, and the sun was shining, and the birds were singing.

When the column of Jews crossed the railway and, leaving the highway, headed off toward the ravine, Haim Kulish the blacksmith took in a lungful of air and, above the hubbub of hundreds of voices, shouted in Yiddish, "Oy, friends, I've had my day!"

Landing a punch on the temple of the soldier walking beside him, he knocked him down and snatched his submachine gun out of his hands. There was no time to work out what to do with an alien, unfamiliar weapon, and so, just as he had used to swing his hammer, he took a swing with this heavy gun and smashed it into the face of an Unteroffizier who had come running up from one side.

In the commotion that followed, little Katya Weissman lost her mother and her grandmother. She was clutching at the hem of old Rosenthal's jacket; with some difficulty he picked her up, turned his head to bring his mouth close to her ear, and said, "Don't cry, Katya, don't cry!"

Holding on to his neck with one hand, the girl answered, "I'm not crying, teacher."

It was difficult for him to keep holding her: his head was spinning, his ears were ringing, his legs were shaking from not being used to walking so far, from the agonizing tension of these last hours.

People were backing away from the ravine. Some were refusing to move forward; some were falling to the ground, trying to crawl back. Soon Rosenthal was close to the front of the crowd.

Fifteen men were led to the edge of the ravine. Rosenthal knew some of them: Mendel, the taciturn stove maker; Meyerovich, the dental technician; Apelfeld, that good-natured old rogue of an electrician. Apelfeld's son was now a teacher in the Kiev Conservatory; when he was a boy, Rosenthal had taught him math. His breathing became labored, but the old man went on holding the little girl in his arms. Thinking about her was a distraction.

"How can I comfort her? How can I deceive her?" the old man wondered, gripped by a feeling of infinite sorrow. At this last minute too, there would be no one to support him, no one to say what he had longed all his life to hear—the words he had desired more than all the wisdom of books about the great thoughts and labors of man.

The little girl turned toward him. Her face was calm; it was the pale face of an adult, a face full of tolerant compassion. And in a sudden silence he heard her voice.

"Teacher," she said, "don't look that way, it will frighten you." And, like a mother, she covered his eyes with the palms of her hands.

The Gestapo boss was wrong. The execution of the Jews did not enable him to breathe freely. In the evening he received a report that a large armed group had appeared near the town. It was led by Shevchenko, the chief engineer from the sugar refinery. He and 140 workers, whom there had not been time to evacuate, had joined the partisans. That night they blew up the steam mill, which had been commandeered by the German commissariat. They also set fire to a huge store of hay that the foragers of a Hungarian cavalry division had collected in a building just behind the station. No one in the town slept that night—the wind was blowing toward the town and the fire might have spread to people's houses and sheds. Swaying this way and that way, the heavy, brick-red flames crept farther and farther. Black smoke eclipsed the stars and the moon; the clear summer sky was full of menace and flame.

Standing in their yards, people watched the huge fire slowly spread. The wind carried with it the staccato sound of machine guns and the blasts of hand grenades.

That evening Yashka Mikhailyuk came back home in a hurry, without his cap and without any vodka or fatback. As he went past the women standing silently in the yard, he said to Dasha, "Well, I was right, wasn't I? You've got more living space now—a whole room to yourself!"

"More than enough living space," said Dasha. "More than enough. My Vitya and a six-year-old little girl and the old teacher have all been laid in a single grave. I'm mourning all of them—all of them." Then she shouted, "Go away, don't look at me with your filthy eyes. I'll stab you with a blunt knife, I'll hack you to pieces with my meat ax."

Yashka ran off to his room and sat there in silence. When his mother wanted to put up the shutters, he said to her, "No, don't go out. Don't even open the door. They're all there, damn them, and they've gone crazy—they'll throw boiling water in your face."

"Yashenka," she said, "you'd better go to your attic. The bed's made up. I'll lock you in there."

In the light of the flames, soldiers were slipping past like shadows. The alarm had been sounded, and they had been called to the commandant's office. Old Varvara Andreyevna was standing in the middle of the yard. Lit by the blaze, her disheveled gray hair looked rose pink.

"Well?" she shouted, "do you think we're scared of you? Just look at those flames! I'm not afraid of any Fritzes. They fight old men and children. Dasha, the day will come when we'll be burning the whole lot of them."

The sky grew deeper and deeper crimson, more and more incandescent, and it seemed to the people standing outside in their yards that the dark smoky flames were burning away everything bad, everything impure and evil with which the Germans had tried to poison the human soul.

THE HELL OF TREBLINKA

I.

TO THE east of Warsaw, along the Western Bug, lie sands and swamps, and thick evergreen and deciduous forests. These places are gloomy and deserted; there are few villages. Travelers try to avoid the narrow roads, where walking is difficult and cartwheels sink up to the axle in the deep sand.

Here, on the branch line to Siedlce, stands the remote station of Treblinka. It is a little over sixty kilometers from Warsaw and not far from the junction station of Małkinia, where the lines from Warsaw, Białystok, Siedlce, and Łomza all meet.

Many of those who were brought to Treblinka in 1942 may have had reason to pass this way in peaceful times. Gazing abstractedly at the dull landscape—pines, sand, sand and more pines, heather and dry shrubs, dismal station buildings and the intersections of tracks— bored passengers may have let their gaze settle for a moment on a single-track line running from the station into the middle of the dense pine forest around it. This spur led to a quarry where gravel was extracted for industrial and municipal construction projects.

This quarry is about four kilometers from the station, in a stretch of wilderness surrounded on all sides by pine forest. The soil here is poor and barren, and the peasants do not cultivate it. And so the wilderness has remained wilderness. The ground is partly covered by moss, with thin pines here and there. Now and then a jackdaw flies by, or a brightly colored crested hoopoe. This miserable wilderness was the place chosen by some official, and approved by SS

Reichsführer Himmler, for the construction of a vast executioner's block—an executioner's block such as the human race has never seen, from the time of primitive barbarism to our own cruel days. An executioner's block, probably, such as the entire universe has never seen. This was the site of the SS's main killing ground, which surpassed those of Sobibor, Majdanek, Bełzec, and Auschwitz.*

There were two camps at Treblinka: Treblinka I, a penal camp for prisoners of various nationalities, chiefly Poles; and Treblinka II, the Jewish camp.

Treblinka I, a labor or penal camp, was located next to the quarry, not far from the edge of the forest. It was an ordinary camp, one of the hundreds and thousands of such camps that the Gestapo established in the occupied territories of Eastern Europe. It appeared in 1941. Many different traits of the German character, distorted by the terrible mirror of Hitler's regime, find expression in this camp. Thus the delirious ravings occasioned by fever are an ugly, distorted reflection of what the patient thought and felt before he was ill. Thus the acts and thoughts of a madman are a distorted reflection of the acts and thoughts of a normal person. Thus a criminal commits an act of violence; his hammer blow to the bridge of his victim's nose requires not only a subhuman cold-bloodedness but also the keen eye and firm grip of an experienced foundry worker.

Thrift, precision, calculation, and pedantic cleanliness are qualities common to many Germans, and they are not bad qualities in themselves. They yield valuable results when applied to agriculture or industry. Hitler's regime, however, harnessed these qualities for a crime against humanity. In this Polish labor camp the SS acted as if they were doing something no more out of the ordinary than growing cauliflowers or potatoes.

The camp was laid out in neat uniform rectangles; the barracks were built in straight rows; birch trees lined the sand-covered paths.

---

*Grossman mistakenly estimated that around three million people were murdered in Treblinka; the true figure was probably less than 800,000. This compares with a death toll of 1,100,000 at Auschwitz-Birkenau. See note on page 335.

Asters and dahlias grew in the fertilized soil. There were concrete ponds for the ducks and geese; there were small pools, with convenient steps, where the staff could do their laundry. There were services for the German personnel: an excellent bakery, a barber, a garage, a gasoline pump with a glass ball on top, stores. The Majdanek camp outside Lublin was organized along the same principles—as were dozens of other labor camps in eastern Poland where the SS and the Gestapo intended to settle in for a long time; there were the same little gardens, the same drinking fountains, the same concrete roads. Efficiency, precise calculation, a pedantic concern for order, a love of detailed charts and schedules—all these German qualities were reflected in the layout and organization of these camps.

People were sent to the labor camp for various periods of time, sometimes as little as four to six months. There were Poles who had infringed the laws of the General Government—usually this was a matter of minor infringements, since the penalty for major infringements was immediate death. A slip of the tongue, a word overheard on the street, a failure to make some delivery, someone else's random denunciation, a refusal to hand over a cart or a horse to a German, a young girl being so bold as to refuse the advances of a member of the SS, the merest unproven hint of suspicion of being involved in some act of sabotage at a factory, these were the offenses that brought thousands of Polish workers, peasants, and intellectuals—the old and the young, mothers, men, and young girls—to this penal camp. Altogether, about fifty thousand people passed through its gates. Jews ended up in this camp only if they were unusually skilled craftsmen: bakers, cobblers, cabinetmakers, stonemasons, tailors. There were all kinds of workshops in the camp, including a substantial furniture workshop that supplied the headquarters of German armies with tables, straight-backed chairs, and armchairs.

Treblinka I existed from the autumn of 1941 until July 23, 1944. By the time it had been fully destroyed, the prisoners could already hear the distant rumble of Soviet artillery. Early in the morning of July 23, the SS men and the Wachmänner fortified themselves with a stiff schnapps and set to work to wipe out every last trace of the camp. By nightfall all the prisoners had been killed and buried. Max Levit, a Warsaw carpenter, managed to survive; he lay wounded beneath the corpses of his comrades until it grew dark, and then he crawled off into the forest. He told us how, as he lay in the pit, he heard thirty boys from the camp singing "Broad Is My Motherland!" just before they were shot. He heard one of the boys shout, "Stalin will avenge us!" He told us how the redheaded Leib—one of the most popular of the prisoners and the leader of this group of boys—fell down on top of him after the first volley, raised his head a little, and called out, "*Panie Wachman*, you didn't kill me. Shoot again, please! Shoot again!"

It is now possible to describe the regimen of this labor camp in some detail; we have testimonies from dozens of Polish men and women who escaped or were released at one time or another. We know about work in the quarry; we know how those who failed to fulfill their work quota were thrown over the edge of a cliff into an abyss below. We know about the daily food ration: 170 to 200 grams of bread and half a liter of some slop that passed for soup. We know about the deaths from starvation, about the hunger-swollen wretches who were taken outside the camp in wheelbarrows and shot. We know about the wild orgies; we know how the Germans raped young women and shot them immediately afterward. We know how people were thrown from a window six meters high. We know that a group of drunken Germans would sometimes take ten or fifteen prisoners from a barrack at night and calmly demonstrate different killing methods on them, shooting them in the heart, the back of the neck, the eyes, the mouth, and the temple. We know the names of the SS men in the camp; we know their characters and idiosyncrasies. We know that the head of the camp was a Dutch German named van Euppen, an insatiable murderer and sexual pervert with a passion for good horses and fast riding. We know about a huge young man named Stumpfe who broke out into uncontrollable laughter every time he murdered a prisoner or when one was executed in his presence. He was known as "Laughing Death." The last person to hear him laugh was Max Levit, on July 23 of this year, when thirty boys were shot on Stumpfe's orders and Levit was lying at the bottom of the pit. We know about Svidersky, a one-eyed German from Odessa who was known as "Master Hammer" because of his supreme expertise in "cold murder"—that is, killing without firearms. It took him only a few minutes—with no weapon but a hammer—to kill fifteen children, aged eight to thirteen, who had been declared unfit for work. We know about Preifi, a skinny SS man who looked like a Gypsy and whose nickname was "the Old One." He was sullen and taciturn. He would relieve his melancholy by sitting on the camp rubbish dump and waiting for a prisoner to sneak up in search of potato peelings; he would then shoot the prisoner in the mouth, having forced him or her to hold their mouth open.

We know the names of the professional killers Schwarz and Ledeke. They used to amuse themselves by shooting at prisoners returning from work in the twilight. They killed twenty, thirty, or forty every evening.

None of these beings was in any way human. Their distorted brains, hearts, and souls, their words, acts, and habits were like a caricature—a terrible caricature of the qualities, thoughts, feelings, habits, and acts of normal Germans. The orderliness of the camp; the documentation of the murders; the love of monstrous practical jokes that recall the jokes of drunken German students; the sentimental songs that the guards sang in unison amid pools of blood; the speeches they were constantly delivering to their victims; the exhortations and pious sayings printed neatly on special pieces of paper—all these monstrous dragons and reptiles were the progeny of traditional German chauvinism. They had sprung from arrogance, conceit, and egotism, from a pedantic obsession with one's own little nest, from a steely indifference to the fate of everything living, from a ferocious, blind conviction that German science, German music, poetry, language, lawns, toilets, skies, beer, and homes were the finest in the entire universe. These people's vices and crimes were born of the vices of the German national character, and of the German State.

Such was life in this camp, which was like a lesser Majdanek, and one might have thought that nothing in the world could be more terrible. But those who lived in Treblinka I knew very well that there was indeed something more terrible—a hundred times more terrible—than this camp. In May 1942, three kilometers away from the labor camp, the Germans had begun the construction of a Jewish camp, a camp that was, in effect, one vast executioner's block. Construction proceeded rapidly, with more than a thousand workers involved. Nothing in this camp was adapted for life; everything was adapted for death. Himmler intended the existence of this camp to remain a profound secret; not a single person was to leave it alive. And not a single person—not even a field marshal—was allowed near it. Anyone who happened to come within a kilometer of the camp was shot without warning. German planes were forbidden to fly over the area. The victims brought by train along the spur from Treblinka village did not know what lay in wait for them until the very last moment. The guards who had accompanied the prisoners during the journey were not allowed into the camp; they were not allowed even to cross its outer perimeter. When the trains arrived, SS men took over from the previous guards. The trains, which were usually made up of sixty freight wagons, were divided into three sections while they were still in the forest, and the locomotive would push twenty wagons at a time up to the camp platform. The locomotive always pushed from behind and stopped by the perimeter fence, and so neither the driver nor the fireman ever crossed the camp boundary. When the wagons had been unloaded, the SS Unteroffizier on duty would signal for the next twenty wagons, which would be waiting two hundred meters down the line. When all sixty wagons had been fully unloaded, the camp Kommandantur would phone the station to say they were ready for the next transport. The empty train then went on to the quarry, where the wagons were loaded with gravel before returning to Treblinka and then on to Małkinia.

Treblinka was well located; it was possible to bring transports from all four points of the compass: north, south, east, and west.

Trains came from the Polish cities of Warsaw, Międzyrzecze, Częstochowa, Siedlce, and Radom; from Łomza, Białystok, Grodno, and other Belorussian cities; from Germany, Czechoslovakia, and Austria; and from Bulgaria and Bessarabia.

Every day for thirteen months the trains brought people to the camp. In each train there were sixty wagons, and a number chalked on the side of each wagon—150, 180, 200—indicated the number of people inside. Railway workers and peasants secretly kept count of these trains. Kazimierz Skarzuński, a sixty-two-year-old peasant from the village of Wólka (the nearest inhabited point to the camp), told me that there were days when as many as six trains went by from Siedlce alone, and that there was barely a day during these thirteen months without at least one train. And the line from Siedlce was only one of the four lines that supplied the camp. Lucjan Żukowa, who was enlisted by the Germans to work on the spur from Treblinka village, said that throughout the time he worked on this line, from June 15, 1942 until August 1943, one to three trains went to the camp each day. There were sixty wagons in each train, and at least 150 people in each wagon. We have collected dozens of similar testimonies. Even if we were to halve the figures provided by these observers, we would still find that around two-and-a-half to three million people were brought to Treblinka during these thirteen months. We shall, however, return to this figure.

The fenced-off area of the camp proper, including the station platform, storerooms for the executed people's belongings, and other auxiliary premises, is extremely small: 780 by 600 meters. If for a moment one were to entertain the least doubt as to the fate of the millions transported here, if one were to suppose for a moment that the Germans did not murder them immediately after their arrival, then one would have to ask what has happened to them all. There were, after all, enough of them to populate a small state or a large European capital. The area of the camp is so small that, had the new arrivals stayed alive for even a few days, it would have been only a week and a half before there was no more space behind the barbed wire for this tide of people flowing in from Poland, from

Belorussia, from the whole of Europe. For thirteen months—396 days—the trains left either empty or loaded with gravel. Not a single person brought by train to Treblinka II ever made the return journey. The terrible question has to be asked: "Cain, where are they? Where are the people you brought here?"

Fascism did not succeed in concealing its greatest crime—but this is not simply because there were thousands of involuntary witnesses to it. It was during the summer of 1942 that Hitler made the decision to exterminate millions of innocent people; the Wehrmacht was enjoying its greatest successes and Hitler was confident that he could act with impunity. We can see now that it was during this year that the Germans carried out their greatest number of murders. Certain that they would escape punishment, the Fascists showed what they were capable of. And had Hitler won, he would have succeeded in covering up every trace of his crimes. He would have forced every witness to keep silent. Even if there had been not just thousands but tens of thousands of witnesses, not one of them would have said a word. And once again one cannot but pay homage to the men who—at a time of universal silence, when a world now so full of the clamor of victory was saying not a word— battled on in Stalingrad, by the steep bank of the Volga, against a German army to the rear of which lay gurgling, smoking rivers of innocent blood. It is the Red Army that stopped Himmler from keeping the secret of Treblinka.

Today the witnesses have spoken; the stones and the earth have cried out aloud. And today, before the eyes of humanity, before the conscience of the whole world, we can walk step by step around each circle of the Hell of Treblinka, in comparison with which Dante's Hell seems no more than an innocent game on the part of Satan.

Everything written below has been compiled from the accounts of living witnesses; from the testimony of people who worked in Treblinka from the first day of the camp's existence until August 2, 1943, when the condemned rose up, burned down the camp, and escaped into the forest; from the testimony of Wachmänner who have been taken prisoner and who have confirmed the witnesses' accounts and often filled in the gaps. I have seen these people myself and have heard their stories, and their written testimonies lie on my desk before me. These many testimonies from a variety of sources are consistent in every detail—from the habits of Barry, the commandant's dog, to the technology used for the conveyor-belt executioner's block.

Let us walk through the circles of the Hell of Treblinka.

Who were the people brought here in trainloads? For the main part, Jews. Also some Poles and Gypsies. By the spring of 1942 almost the entire Jewish population of Poland, Germany, and the western regions of Belorussia had been rounded up into ghettoes. Millions of Jewish people—workers, craftsmen, doctors, professors, architects, engineers, teachers, artists, and members of other professions, along with their wives, daughters, sons, mothers, and fathers—had been rounded up into the ghettoes of Warsaw, Radom, Częstochowa, Lublin, Białystok, Grodno, and dozens of smaller towns. In the Warsaw ghetto alone there were around half a million Jews. Confinement to the ghetto was evidently the first, preparatory stage of Hitler's plan for the extermination of the Jews.

The summer of 1942, the time of Fascism's greatest military success, was chosen as the time to put into effect the second stage of this plan: physical extermination. We know that Himmler came to Warsaw at this time and issued the necessary orders. Work on the construction of the vast executioner's block proceeded day and night. By July the first transports were already on their way to Treblinka from Warsaw and Częstochowa. People were told that they were being taken to the Ukraine, to work on farms there; they were allowed to take food and twenty kilograms of luggage. In many cases the Germans forced their victims to buy train tickets for the station of "Ober-Majdan," a code word for Treblinka. Rumors about Treblinka had quickly spread through the whole of Poland, and so the SS had to stop using the name when they were herding people onto the transports. Nevertheless, people were treated in such a way as to be left with little doubt about what lay in store for them. At least 150 people, but more often 180 to 200, were crowded into each freight wagon. Throughout the journey, which sometimes lasted two or three days, they were given nothing to drink. People's thirst was so terrible that they would drink their own urine. The guards would offer a mouthful of water for a hundred zloty, but they usually just pocketed the money. People were packed so tightly together that sometimes they only had room to stand. In each wagon, especially during the stifling days of summer, a number of the old or those with weak hearts would die. Since the doors were kept shut throughout the journey, the corpses would begin to decompose, poisoning the air inside. And someone had only to light a match during the night for guards to start shooting through the walls. A barber by the name of Abram Kon states that in his wagon alone five people died as a result of such incidents, and a large number of people were wounded.

The conditions on the trains arriving from Western Europe were very different. The people in these trains had never heard of Treblinka, and they believed until the last minute that they were being taken somewhere to work. The Germans told them charming stories of the pleasures and comforts of the new life awaiting them once they had been resettled. Some trains brought people who were convinced that they were being taken to a neutral country; they had, after all, paid the German authorities large sums of money for the necessary visas.

Once a train arrived in Treblinka bringing citizens of Canada, America, and Australia who had been stranded in Western Europe and Poland when the war broke out. After prolonged negotiations and the payment of huge bribes, they were allowed to travel to neutral countries. All the trains from Western Europe were without guards; they had the usual staff, along with sleeping and dining cars. The passengers brought large trunks and cases, as well as ample supplies of food. When trains stopped at stations, children would run out and ask how much farther it was to Ober-Majdan.

There were a few transports of Gypsies from Bessarabia and

elsewhere. There were also a number of transports of young Polish workers and peasants who had taken part in uprisings or joined partisan units.

It is hard to say which is the more terrible: to go to your death in agony, knowing that the end is near, or to be glancing unsuspectingly out of the window of a comfortable coach just as someone from Treblinka village is phoning the camp with details of your recently arrived train and the number of people on it.

In order to maintain until the very end the deception of the Western European passengers, the railhead at the death camp was made up to look like an ordinary railway station. On the platform where a batch of twenty carriages was being unloaded stood what seemed like a station building with a ticket office, a left-luggage office, and a restaurant. There were arrows everywhere, with signs reading TO BIAŁYSTOCK, TO BARANOWICZE, TO WOŁKOWICE, etc. An orchestra played in the station building to greet the new arrivals, and the musicians were well dressed. A station guard in railway uniform collected tickets and let the passengers through onto a large square.

Soon the square would be filled by three to four thousand people, laden with bags and suitcases. Some were supporting the old and the sick. Mothers were holding little children in their arms; older children clung to their parents as they looked around inquisitively. There was something sinister and terrifying about this square that had been trodden by millions of human feet. People's sharp eyes were quick to notice alarming little signs. Lying here and there on the ground—which had evidently been swept only a few minutes before their arrival—were all kinds of abandoned objects: a bundle of clothing, some open suitcases, a few shaving brushes, some enameled saucepans. How had they got there? And why did the railway line end just beyond the station? Why was there only yellow grass and three-meter-high barbed wire? Where were the lines to Białystok, Siedlce, Warsaw, and Wołkowice? And why was there such an odd smile on the faces of the new guards as they looked at the men adjusting their ties, at the respectable old ladies, at the boys in sailor suits, at the slim young girls still managing to look neat and tidy after the journey, at the young mothers lovingly adjusting the blankets wrapped around babies who were wrinkling their little faces?

All these Wachmänner in black uniforms and SS Unteroffiziere were similar, in their behavior and psychology, to cattle drivers at the entrance to a slaughterhouse. The SS and the Wachmänner did not see the newly arrived transport as being made up of living human beings, and they could not help smiling at the sight of manifestations of embarrassment, love, fear, and concern for the safety of loved ones or possessions. It amused them to see mothers straightening their children's jackets or scolding them for running a few yards away, to see men wiping their brows with a handkerchief and then lighting a cigarette, to see young girls tidying their hair, looking in pocket mirrors, and anxiously holding down their skirts if there was a gust of wind. They thought it funny that the old men should try to squat down on their little suitcases, that some should be carrying books under their arms, that the sick should moan and groan and have scarves tied around their necks.

Up to twenty thousand people passed through Treblinka every day. Days when only six or seven thousand people passed through the station building were considered quiet. The square would fill with people four or five times each day. And all these thousands, all these tens and hundreds of thousands of people, of frightened, questioning eyes, all these young and old faces, all these dark- and fair-haired beauties, these bald and hunchbacked old men, and these timid adolescents—all were caught up in a single flood, a flood that swallowed up reason, and splendid human science, and maidenly love, and childish wonder, and the coughing of the old, and the human heart.

And the new arrivals trembled as they sensed the strangeness of the look on the faces of the watching Wachmänner—a cool, sated, mocking look, the look of superiority with which a living beast surveys a dead human being.

And once again during these brief moments the people who had come out into the square found themselves noticing all kinds of alarming and incomprehensible trifles.

What lay behind that huge six-meter-high wall covered with blankets and yellowing pine branches? Even the blankets were somehow frightening. Quilted, many-colored, silken or with calico covers, they looked all too similar to the blankets the newcomers had brought with them. How had these blankets got here? Who had brought them? And who were their owners? And why didn't they need their blankets any longer? And who were these men wearing light-blue armbands? Troubling suspicions came back to mind, frightening rumors that had been passed on in a whisper. But no, no, this was impossible. And the terrible thought was dismissed.

This sense of alarm always lasted a little while, perhaps two or three minutes, until everyone had made their way to the square. There was always a slight delay at this point; there were always cripples, the old, the sick, and the lame, people who could barely move their legs. But soon everybody was present.

An SS Unteroffizier instructs the newcomers in a loud, clear voice to leave their things in the square and make their way to the bathhouse, taking with them only identity documents, valuables, and toiletries. They want to ask all kinds of questions: Should they take their underwear? Is it really all right to undo their bundles? Aren't all their belongings going to get mixed up? Might they not disappear altogether? But some strange force makes them hurry on in silence, not looking back, not asking questions, toward an opening—an opening in a barbed-wire wall, six meters high, that has been threaded with branches. They walk past antitank hedgehogs, past thickets of barbed wire three times the height of a human being, past an antitank ditch three meters deep, past thin coils of steel wire strewn on the ground to trip a fugitive and catch him like a fly in a spiderweb, past another wall of barbed wire many meters high. And everyone is overwhelmed by a sense of helplessness, a sense of doom. There is no way to escape, no way to turn back, no way to fight back: staring down at them from low squat wooden towers are the muzzles of heavy machine guns. Should they call out for help?

But all around them are SS men and Wachmänner armed with sub-machine guns, hand grenades, and pistols. These men are power; they are power itself. Tanks, aircraft, lands, cities and sky, railways, the law, newspapers, radio—everything is in their hands. The whole world is silent, crushed, enslaved by a gang of bandits who have seized all power. London is silent, and so is New York. And only somewhere thousands of kilometers distant, on the banks of the Volga, is the Soviet artillery pounding away, obstinately proclaiming the determination of the Russian people to fight to the death for liberty, calling upon every nation to join in the battle.

Back on the square by the station two hundred workers with light-blue armbands ("the blue squad") were silently, swiftly, and deftly untying bundles, opening baskets and suitcases, removing straps from bedrolls. The belongings of the new arrivals are being sorted out and appraised. Onto the ground tumble neatly packed darning kits, spools of thread, children's underwear, shirts, sheets, pullovers, little knives, shaving kits, bundles of letters, photographs, thimbles, scent bottles, mirrors, bonnets, shoes, homemade boots made from quilted blankets (to protect against extreme cold), ladies' slippers, stockings, lace, pajamas, packs of butter, coffee, tins of cocoa, prayer shawls, candlesticks, books, dry biscuits, violins, children's toy building blocks. It requires real skill to sort out, in the course of only a few minutes, all these thousands of objects. Everything of value is to be sent to Germany; everything old, shabby, and valueless is to be burned. And God help the unfortunate worker who puts an old wicker suitcase into a pile of leather cases destined for Germany, or who throws a new pair of stockings from Paris, still bearing their factory stamp, onto a heap of worn-out socks. Workers were not given the chance to make more than one mistake. Usually there were forty SS men and sixty Wachmänner "on transport duty," as they called this first stage of the work: meeting the trains, escorting people out from the "railway station" and into the square, and then supervising the workers with the light-blue armbands as they sorted through the things left behind on the square. These workers often infringed the regulations by slipping into their mouths little pieces of bread, sugar, or sweets that they found. They were, however, allowed to wash their hands and faces with eau de cologne and perfume, given that there was a shortage of water at Treblinka and only Wachmänner and the SS were allowed to wash with it. And while the still-living people who had left all these things were preparing to enter the "bathhouse," the work of the blue squad was nearing completion. Items of value were already being taken away to the storerooms, while the letters, the yellowed wedding announcements, the photographs of newborn babies, brothers, and brides, all the thousands of little things that were so infinitely precious to their owners yet the merest trash to the masters of Treblinka were being gathered into heaps and taken away to vast pits already containing hundreds of thousands of similar letters, postcards, visiting cards, photographs, and sheets of paper covered in children's scribbles or children's first clumsy drawings in crayon. The square was then hurriedly swept and made ready to receive a new contingent of the doomed.

Not always, however, did things go so smoothly. Sometimes, when the prisoners knew where they were being taken, there were rebellions. Skrzeminski, a local peasant, twice saw people smash their way out of trains, knock down the guards, and run for the forest. On both occasions every last person was killed by machine-gun fire. The men had been carrying four children, aged four to six; they were shot too. Another peasant, Marianna Kobus, has described similar attempts at escape. Once, when she was working in the fields, she saw sixty people break out of a train and run toward the forest; all were shot before her eyes.

But the contingent of new arrivals has now reached a second square, inside the inner camp fence. On one side of this square stands a single huge barrack, and there are three more barracks to the right. Two of these are used for storing clothes, the third for storing footwear. Farther on, in the western section of the camp, are barracks for the SS, barracks for the Wachmänner, food stores, and a small farmyard. There are cars, trucks, and an armored vehicle. All in all, this seems like an ordinary camp, like Treblinka I.

In the southeastern corner of the compound is an area fenced off with tree branches; toward the front of this area is a booth bearing the sign LAZARETT. The very old and the decrepit are separated from the crowd waiting for the "bathhouse" and taken on stretchers to this so-called infirmary. A man in a doctor's white coat, with a Red Cross armband on his left arm, comes out to meet them. Precisely what happened in the *Lazarett*—how the Germans used their Walther automatic pistols to spare old people from the burden of all possible diseases—I shall describe later.

The main thing in the next stage of processing the new arrivals was to break their will. There was a never-ending sequence of abrupt commands—bellowed out in a manner in which the German army takes pride, a manner that is proof in itself of the Germans being a master race. Simultaneously hard and guttural, the letter *r* sounded like the crack of a whip.

"Achtung!"

After this, in the leaden silence, the crowd would hear words that the Scharführer repeated several times a day for month after month: "Men are to remain where they are. Women and children must go to the barracks on the left and undress."

This, according to the accounts of eyewitnesses, marked the start of heartrending scenes. Love—maternal, conjugal, or filial love— told people that they were seeing one another for the last time. Handshakes, kisses, blessings, tears, brief hurried words into which people put all their love, all their pain, all their tenderness, all their despair...The SS psychiatrists of death knew that all this must be cut short, that these feelings must be stifled at once. The psychiatrists of death knew the simple laws that operate in slaughterhouses all over the world, laws which, in Treblinka, were exploited by brute beasts in order to deal with human beings. This was a critical moment: the moment when daughters were separated from fathers, mothers from sons, grandmothers from grandsons, husbands from wives.

Once again, echoing over the square: *"Achtung! Achtung!"* Once again people's minds must be confused with hope; once again the regulations of death must be passed off as the regulations of life.

The same voice barks out word after word: "Women and children are to remove their footwear on entering the barrack. Stockings are to be put into shoes. The children's little stockings into their sandals, boots, and shoes. Be tidy!"

And straight after this: "As you proceed to the bathhouse, take with you your valuables, documents, money, towel, and soap. I repeat…"

Inside the women's barrack was a hairdresser. The hair of the naked women was cut with clippers; old women had their wigs removed. This had a strange psychological effect: the hairdressers testify that this haircut of death did more than anything to convince the women that they really were going to the bathhouse. Young women would sometimes stroke their heads and say, "It's uneven here. Please make it smoother." Most of the women calmed down after their haircut; nearly all of them left the barrack carrying their piece of soap and a folded towel. Some young women wept over the loss of their beautiful plaits.

Why did the Germans shave women's hair? To deceive them better? No, Germany needed this hair. It was a raw material. I have asked many people what the Germans did with the hair that they removed from the heads of the living departed. Every witness said that the vast heaps of hair—black, red-gold, and fair, straight, curly, and wavy—were first disinfected, then packed into sacks and sent off to Germany. All the witnesses confirmed that the sacks bore German addresses. How was the hair used? No one could answer. There is just one written deposition, from a certain Kohn, to the effect that the hair was used by the navy to fill mattresses and for such things as making hawsers for submarines. Other witnesses claim that the hair was used to pad saddles for the cavalry.

This testimony, in my view, requires further confirmation. In due course, this will be given to humanity by Grossadmiral Raeder, who in 1942 was in charge of the German navy.

The men undressed outside, in the yard. One hundred and fifty to three hundred strong men from the first contingent of the day would be chosen to bury the corpses; they themselves were usually killed the following day. The men had to undress quickly but in an orderly manner, leaving their shoes, socks, underwear, jackets, and trousers in neat piles. These were then sorted out by a second work squad, known as "the reds" because of the red armbands they wore to distinguish them from the squad " on transport duty." Items considered worth sending to Germany were taken to the store; first, though, any metal or cloth labels had to be carefully removed from them. All other items were burned or buried in pits.

Everyone was feeling more and more anxious. There was a terrible stench, intermingled with the smell of lime chloride. There were fat and persistent flies—an extraordinary number of them. What were they doing here, among pine trees, on dry well-trodden ground? Everyone was breathing heavily now, shaking and trembling, staring at every little trifle that might give them some understanding, at anything that might lift the curtain of mystery and let them glimpse the fate that awaited them. And what were those gigantic excavators doing, rumbling away in the southern part of the camp?

Next, though, came another procedure. The naked people had to stand in line at a "ticket window" to hand over their documents and valuables. And again they heard that terrible, hypnotizing voice: "*Achtung! Achtung!*" The penalty for concealing valuables is death. "*Achtung! Achtung!*"

The Scharführer sat in a small wooden booth. Other SS men and Wachmänner stood nearby. On the ground were a number of wooden boxes into which they threw valuables. One was for paper money; one was for coins; a third was for watches, rings, earrings, and brooches with precious stones and bracelets. Documents were just thrown on the ground, since no one had any use for the documents of the living dead who, within an hour, would be lying crushed in a pit. Gold and valuables, however, were carefully sorted; dozens of jewelers were engaged in ascertaining the quality of the metal, the value of the stones, the clarity of the diamonds.

Astonishingly, the brute beasts were able to make use of everything. Leather, paper, cloth—everything of use to man was of use to these beasts. It was only the most precious valuable in the world—human life—that they trampled beneath their boots. Powerful minds, honorable souls, glorious childish eyes, sweet faces of old women, proudly beautiful girlish heads that nature had toiled age after age to fashion—all this, in a vast silent flood, was condemned to the abyss of nonbeing. A few seconds was enough to destroy what nature and the world had slowly shaped in life's vast and tortuous creative process.

This booth with its small "ticket window" was a turning point. It marked the end of the process of torture by deception, the end of the lie that held people in a trance of ignorance, in a fever that hurled them between hope and despair, between visions of life and visions of death. This torture by deception aided the SS men in their work; it was an essential feature of the conveyor-belt executioner's block. Now, however, the final act had begun; the process of plundering the living dead was nearly completed, and the Germans changed their style of behavior. They tore off rings and broke women's fingers; earlobes were ripped off along with earrings.

At this point a new principle had to be implemented if the conveyor-belt executioner's block was to continue to function smoothly. The word *"Achtung"* was replaced by the hissing sounds of *"Schneller! Schneller! Schneller!* Faster! Faster! Faster! Faster into nonexistence!"

We know from the cruel reality of recent years that a naked man immediately loses his powers of resistance. He ceases to struggle. Having lost his clothes, he loses his instinct of self-preservation and starts to accept whatever happens to him as his inevitable fate. Someone with an unquenchable thirst for life becomes passive and apathetic. Nevertheless, to make doubly sure that there were no mishaps, the SS found a way to stun their victims during this last stage of the conveyor belt's work, to reduce them to a state of complete psychic paralysis.

How did they achieve this?

Through a sudden recourse to pointless, alogical brutality. The naked people—people who had lost everything but who obstinately persisted in remaining human, a thousand times more so than the creatures around them wearing the uniforms of the German army—were still breathing, still looking, still thinking; their hearts were still beating. All of a sudden their towels and pieces of soap were knocked out of their hands. They were lined up in rows of five.

"*Händer hoch! Marsch! Schneller! Schneller!*"

They were then marched down a straight alley, 120 meters long and two meters wide, bordered by flowers and fir trees. This led to the place of execution. There was barbed wire on either side of the alley, which was lined by SS men and Wachmänner standing shoulder to shoulder, the former in gray uniforms, the latter in black. The path was sprinkled with white sand, and those who were walking in front with their hands in the air could see on this loose sand the fresh imprint of bare feet: the small footprints of women, the tiny footprints of children, the heavy footprints of the old. This faint trace in the sand was all that remained of the thousands of people who had not long ago passed this way, who had walked down this path just as the present contingent of four thousand people was now walking down it, just as another contingent of thousands, already waiting on the railway spur in the forest, would walk down it in two hours' time. Those whose footprints could be seen on the sand had walked down this path just as people had walked down it the day before, just as people had walked down it ten days before, just as people would walk down it the next day and in fifty days' time, just as people walked down it throughout the thirteen months of the existence of the Hell that was Treblinka.

The Germans referred to this alley as "The Road of No Return." A smirking, grimacing creature by the name of Suchomel used to shout out, deliberately garbling the German words: "Children, children, *schneller, schneller*, the water's getting cold in the bathhouse! *Schneller*, children, *schneller*!" This creature would then burst out laughing; he would squat down and dance about. Hands above their heads, the people walked on in silence between the two rows of guards, who beat them with sticks, submachine-gun butts, and rubber truncheons. The children had to run to keep up with the adults.

Everyone who witnessed this last sorrowful procession has commented on the savagery of one particular member of the SS: Sepp. This creature specialized in the killing of children. Evidently endowed with unusual strength, it would suddenly snatch a child out of the crowd, swing him or her about like a cudgel, and then either smash their head against the ground or simply tear them in half.

When I first heard about this creature—supposedly human, supposedly born of a woman—I could not believe the unthinkable things I was told. But when I heard these stories repeated by eyewitnesses, when I realized that these witnesses saw them as mere details, entirely in keeping with everything else about the hellish regime of Treblinka, then I came to believe that what I had heard was true.

Sepp's actions were necessary. They helped to reduce people to a state of psychic shock. They were an expression of the senseless cruelty that crushed both will and consciousness. He was a useful, necessary screw in the vast machine of the Fascist State.

What should appall us is not that nature gives birth to such monsters—there are, after all, any number of monsters in the physical world. There are Cyclops, and creatures with two heads, and there are corresponding psychic monstrosities and perversions. What is appalling is that creatures which should have been isolated and studied as psychiatric phenomena were allowed to live active lives, to be active citizens of a particular State. Their diseased ideology, their pathological psyches, their extraordinary crimes are, however, a necessary element of the Fascist State. Thousands, tens of thousands, hundreds of thousands of such creatures are pillars of German Fascism, the mainstay and foundation of Hitler's Germany. Dressed in uniforms and carrying weapons, decorated with imperial orders, these creatures lorded it for years over the peoples of Europe. It is not they that should appall us but the State that summoned them out of their holes, out of their underground darkness—the State that found them useful, necessary, and even irreplaceable in Treblinka near Warsaw, in Majdanek near Lublin, in

Bełzec, Sobibor, and Auschwitz, in Babi Yar, in Domanevka and Bogdanovka near Odessa, in Trostyanets near Minsk, in Ponary in Lithuania, and in hundreds of other prisons, labor camps, penal camps, and camps for the destruction of life.

A particular kind of State does not appear out of nowhere. What engenders a particular regime is the material and ideological relations existing among a country's citizens. It is to these material and ideological relations that we need to devote serious thought; the nature of these relations is what should appall us.

The walk from the "ticket window" to the place of execution took only sixty to seventy seconds. Urged on by blows and deafened by shouts of "*Schneller! Schneller!*," the people came out into a third square and, for a moment, stopped in astonishment.

Before them stood a handsome stone building, decorated with wooden fretwork and built in the style of an ancient temple. Five wide concrete steps led up to the low but very wide, massive, beautifully ornate doors. By the entrance there were flowers in large pots. Everything nearby, however, was in chaos; everywhere you looked there were mountains of freshly dug earth. Grinding its steel jaws, a huge excavator was digging up tons of sandy yellow soil, raising a dust cloud that stood between the earth and the sun. The roar of the vast machine, which was digging mass graves from morning till night, mingled with the fierce barks of dozens of Alsatian dogs.

On either side of the house of death ran narrow-gauge tracks along which men in baggy overalls were pushing small self-tipping trolleys.

The wide doors of the house of death slowly opened, and in the entrance appeared two of the assistants to Schmidt, who was in charge of the complex. Both were sadists and maniacs. One, aged about thirty, was tall, with massive shoulders, black hair, and a swarthy, laughing, animated face. The other, slightly younger, was short, with brown hair and pale yellow cheeks, as if he had just taken a strong dose of quinacrine. The names of these men who betrayed humanity, their Motherland, and their oaths of loyalty are known.

The tall man was holding a whip and a piece of heavy gas piping, about a meter long. The other man was holding a saber.

Then the SS men would unleash their well-trained dogs, who would throw themselves into the crowd and tear with their teeth at the naked bodies of the doomed people. At the same time the SS men would beat people with submachine-gun butts, urging on petrified women with wild shouts of "*Schneller! Schneller!*"

Other assistants to Schmidt were inside the building, driving people through the wide-open doors of the chambers.

At this point Kurt Franz, one of the camp commandants, would appear, leading on a leash his dog, Barry. He had specially trained this dog to leap up at the doomed people and tear out their sexual organs. Franz had done well for himself in the camp, starting as a junior SS Unteroffizier and attaining the fairly high rank of Untersturmführer. This tall, thin, thirty-five-year-old member of the SS was not only a gifted organizer who adored his work and could not imagine any better life for himself than his life at Treblinka, where nothing escaped his tireless vigilance; he was also something of a theoretician. He loved to explain the true significance of his work. Really, only one thing was missing during these last terrible moments by the doors of the chambers: the pope himself, and Mr. Brailsford, and other such humane defenders of Hitlerism should have put in an appearance, in the capacity, it goes without saying, of spectators. Then they would have learned new arguments with which to enrich their humanitarian preachings, books, and articles. And while he was about it, the pope, who kept so reverently silent while Himmler was settling accounts with the human race, could have worked out how many batches his staff would have constituted, how long it would have taken the Treblinka SS to process the entire staff of his Vatican.

Great is the power of true humanity. Humanity does not die until man dies. And when we see a brief but terrifying period of history, a period during which beasts triumph over human beings, the man being killed by the beast retains to his last breath his strength of spirit, clarity of thought, and passionate love. And the beast that triumphantly kills the man remains a beast. This immortality of spiritual strength is a somber martyrdom—the triumph of a dying man over a living beast. It was this, during the darkest days of 1942, that brought about the beginning of reason's victory over bestial madness, the victory of good over evil, of light over darkness, of the forces of progress over the forces of reaction. A terrible dawn over a field of blood and tears, over an ocean of suffering—a dawn breaking amid the cries of dying mothers and infants, amid the death rattles of the aged.

The beasts and the beasts' philosophy seemed to portend the sunset of Europe, the sunset of the world, but the red was not the red of a sunset, it was the red blood of humanity—a humanity that was dying yet achieving victory through its death. People remained people. They did not accept the morality and laws of Fascism. They fought it in all ways they could; they fought it by dying as human beings.

To hear how the living dead of Treblinka preserved until the last moment not only the image and likeness of human beings but also the souls of human beings is to be shaken to one's very core; it is to be unable to find sleep or any peace of mind. We heard stories of women trying to save their sons and thus accomplishing feats of hopeless bravery. We heard of women trying to hide their little babies in heaps of blankets and trying to shield them with their own bodies. Nobody knows, and nobody ever will know, the names of these mothers. We heard of ten-year-old girls comforting their sobbing parents with divine wisdom; we heard of a young boy shouting out by the entrance to the gas chamber, "Don't cry, Mama—the Russians will avenge us!" Nobody knows, and nobody ever will know, what these children were called. We heard about dozens of doomed people, fighting alone against a band of SS men armed with machine guns and hand grenades—and dying on their feet, their breasts riddled with bullets. We heard about a young man stabbing an SS officer, about a youth who had taken part in the uprising in the Warsaw ghetto and who by some miracle managed to hide a hand grenade from the Germans; already naked, he threw it into a group of executioners. We heard about a battle that lasted all through the night between a group of the doomed and units of SS and Wachmänner. All night long there were shots and explosions—and when the sun rose the next morning, the whole square was covered with the fighters' bodies. Beside each lay a weapon: a knife, a razor, a stake torn from a fence. However long the earth lasts, we will never know the names of the fallen. We heard about a tall young woman who, on "The Road of No Return," tore a carbine from the hands of a Wachmann and fought back against dozens of SS. Two of the beasts were killed in this struggle, and a third had his hand shattered. He returned to Treblinka with only one arm. She was subjected to terrible tortures and to a terrible execution. No one knows her name; no one can honor it.

Yet is that really so? Hitlerism took from these people their homes and their lives; it wanted to erase their names from the world's memory. But all of them—the mothers who tried to shield their children with their own bodies, the children who wiped away the tears in their fathers' eyes, those who fought with knives and flung hand grenades, and the naked young woman who, like a goddess from a Greek myth, fought alone against dozens—all these people, though they are no longer among the living, have preserved forever the very finest name of all, a name that no pack of Hitlers and Himmlers has been able to trample into the ground, the name: Human Being. The epitaph History will write for them is: "Here Lies a Human Being."

The inhabitants of Wólka, the nearest village to the camp, say that there were occasions when they could not endure the screams of the women being killed. They would all disappear deep into the forest—anything not to hear those screams that penetrated wooden walls, that pierced the earth and the sky. Sometimes the screams would suddenly fall silent, only to break out again equally suddenly, as all-penetrating as before, piercing bones, boring through skulls and souls . . . And this was repeated three or four times a day.

I questioned one of the executioners whom we had taken prisoner. He explained that the women began to scream when the dogs were set on them and the entire contingent of doomed people was being driven into the house of death: "They could see death. Besides, it was very crowded in there, and the dogs were tearing at them, and they were being badly beaten by the Wachmänner."

The sudden silence was when the doors of the gas chamber were closed. And the screams began again when a new contingent was brought there. This was repeated three, four, sometimes five times each day. After all, the Treblinka executioner's block was no ordinary executioner's block. It was a conveyor-belt executioner's block; it was run according to the same principles as any other large-scale modern industrial enterprise.

Like any other industrial enterprise, Treblinka grew gradually, developing and acquiring new production areas; it was not always as I have described it above. In the beginning there were three small gas chambers. While these were still under construction, a number of transports arrived, and the people they brought were murdered with "cold" weapons: axes, hammers, and clubs. The Germans did not want to use guns, since this would have revealed the true purpose of Treblinka to the surrounding population. The first three concrete chambers were relatively small, five meters by five meters and 190 centimeters high. Each chamber had two doors: one through which the living were admitted, one through which the corpses of the gassed were dragged out. The second door was very wide, about two and a half meters. The three chambers stood side by side on a single foundation.

These three chambers lacked capacity; they could not generate the conveyor-belt power required by Berlin.

The construction of a larger building was begun straightaway. The officials in charge of Treblinka took pride and joy in the fact that, in terms of power, handling capacity, and production floor space, this would far surpass the other SS death factories: Majdanek, Sobibor, and Bełzec.

Seven hundred prisoners worked for five weeks on the construction of the new death facility. When the work was in full swing, an engineer arrived from Germany with a team of workers and began to install the equipment. The new gas chambers, ten in all, were symmetrically located on either side of a broad concrete corridor. Each chamber—like the three earlier chambers—had two doors: one from the corridor, for the admission of the living, the other in the opposite wall, so that the corpses of the gassed could be dragged out. These doors opened onto special platforms on either side of the building. Alongside these platforms were narrow-gauge tracks. The corpses were thrown out onto the platforms, loaded onto trolleys, and then taken away to the mass graves that the vast excavators were digging day and night. The floor of each chamber sloped down from the central corridor toward the platform outside, and this greatly facilitated the work of unloading the chambers. In the earlier chambers the unloading methods had been primitive—the corpses had been carried out on stretchers or dragged out with the help of straps. Each new gas chamber was seven meters by eight meters. The floor area of the ten new chambers totaled 560 square meters. Including the three old chambers, which went on being used for smaller contingents, there was thus a total death-producing area of 635 square meters. From four hundred to six hundred people were loaded into each gas chamber; working at full capacity, the ten new chambers were therefore able to destroy four thousand to six thousand lives at once. The chambers of the Treblinka Hell were loaded at least two or three times a day (there were days when they were loaded six times). A conservative estimate indicates that a twice-daily operation of the new gas chambers alone would have meant the death of ten thousand people a day, three hundred thousand a month. Treblinka was functioning every day for thirteen months on end. But even if we allow ninety days for stoppages and repairs, and for delays on the railway, this still leaves us with ten months of uninterrupted operation. If the average number of deaths a month was three hundred thousand, then the number of deaths in ten months would have been three million. Once again we have come to the same figure: three million—the figure we arrived at before through a deliberately low estimate of the number of people brought to Treblinka by train. We will return to this figure a third time.*

The death process in the gas chambers took from ten to twenty-five minutes. When the new chambers were first put into operation and the executioners were still determining how best to administer the gas and which poisons to use, the victims sometimes remained alive for two to three hours, undergoing terrible agony. During the very first days there were serious problems with the delivery and exhaust systems, and the victims were in torment for anything up to nine or ten hours. Various means were employed to effect death. One was to force into the chambers the exhaust fumes from the engine, taken from a heavy tank, that was used to generate electricity for the camp. Such fumes contain two to three percent of carbon monoxide, which combines with the hemoglobin in the blood to form a stable compound known as carboxyhemoglobin. Carboxyhemoglobin is far more stable than the compound of oxygen and hemoglobin that is formed in the alveoli during the respiratory process. Within fifteen minutes all the hemoglobin in the blood has combined with carbon monoxide, and breathing ceases to have any real effect. A person is gasping for air, but no oxygen reaches their organism and they begin to suffocate; the heart races frenziedly, driving blood into the lungs, but this blood, poisoned as it is with carbon monoxide, is unable to absorb any oxygen. Breathing becomes hoarse and labored, and consciousness dims. People show all the agonizing symptoms of suffocation, and they die just as if they were being strangled.

A second method, and the one most generally employed at Treblinka, was the use of special pumps to remove the air from the chambers. As with the first method, death resulted from oxygen deprivation. A third method, employed less often, was the use of

---

*Grossman is also mistaken with regard to the number of people killed during a single operation of the gas chambers. The true figure was probably between two thousand and three thousand.

steam. This too brought about death from oxygen deprivation, since the steam had the effect of expelling the air from the chambers. Various poisons were also employed, but only on an experimental basis; it was the first and second of these methods that were employed for murder on an industrial scale.

The conveyor belt of Treblinka functioned in such a way that beasts were able methodically to deprive human beings of everything to which they have been entitled, since the beginning of time, by the holy law of life.

First people were robbed of their freedom, their home, and their Motherland; they were transported to a nameless wilderness in the forest. Then, on the square by the station, they were robbed of their belongings, of their personal letters, and of photographs of their loved ones. After going through the fence, a man was robbed of his mother, his wife, and his child. After he had been stripped naked, his papers were thrown onto a fire; he had been robbed of his name. He was driven into a corridor with a low stone ceiling; now he had been robbed of the sky, the stars, the wind, and the sun.

Then came the last act of the human tragedy—a human being was now in the last circle of the Hell that was Treblinka.

The door of the concrete chamber slammed shut. The door was secured by every possible kind of fastening: by locks, by hooks, by a massive bolt. It was not a door that could be broken down.

Can we find within us the strength to imagine what the people in these chambers felt, what they experienced during their last minutes of life? All we know is that they cannot speak now…Covered by a last clammy mortal sweat, packed so tight that their bones cracked and their crushed rib cages were barely able to breathe, they stood pressed against one another; they stood as if they were a single human being. Someone, perhaps some wise old man, makes the effort to say, "Patience now—this is the end." Someone shouts out some terrible curse. A holy curse—surely this curse must be fulfilled? With a superhuman effort a mother tries to make a little more space for her child: may her child's dying breaths be eased, however infinitesimally, by a last act of maternal care. A young woman, her tongue going numb, asks, "Why am I being suffocated? Why can't I love and have children?" Heads spin. Throats choke. What are the pictures now passing before people's glassy dying eyes? Pictures of childhood? Of the happy days of peace? Of the last terrible journey? Of the mocking face of the SS man in that first square by the station: "Ah, so that's why he was laughing..." Consciousness dims. It is the moment of the last agony... No, what happened in that chamber cannot be imagined. The dead bodies stand there, gradually turning cold. It was the children, according to witnesses, who kept on breathing for longest. After twenty to twenty-five minutes Schmidt's assistants would glance through the peepholes. It was time to open the second doors, the doors to the platforms. Urged on by shouting SS men, prisoners in overalls set about unloading the chambers. Because of the sloping floor, many of the bodies simply tumbled out of their own accord. People who carried out this task have told me that the faces of the dead were very yellow and that around seventy percent of them were bleeding slightly from the nose and mouth; physiologists, no doubt, can explain this.

SS men examined the bodies, talking to one another as they did so. If anyone turned out to be still alive, if anyone groaned or stirred, they were finished off with a pistol shot. Then a team of men armed with dental pliers would extract all the platinum and gold teeth from the mouths of the murdered people waiting to be loaded onto the trolleys. The teeth were then sorted according to value, packed into boxes, and sent off to Germany. Had the SS found it in any way more convenient or advantageous to extract people's teeth while they were still alive, they would, of course, have done this without hesitation, just as they removed women's hair while they were still alive. But it was evidently easier and more convenient to extract people's teeth when they were dead.

The corpses were then loaded on the trolleys and pushed along the narrow-gauge tracks toward long grave pits. There they were laid out in rows, packed closely together. The huge pit was not filled in; it was still waiting. In the meantime, as soon as the work of unloading the chambers had begun, the Scharführer "on transport duty" would have received a short order by telephone. The Scharführer would then blow his whistle—a signal to the engine driver—and another twenty wagons would slowly be brought up to the platform of a make-believe railway station called Ober-Majdan. Another three or four thousand people carrying suitcases, bundles, and bags of food would get out and walk to the station square. Mothers were holding little children in their arms; elder children clung to their parents as they looked intently around. There was something sinister and terrifying about this square that had been trodden by millions of feet. And why did the railway line end just beyond the station? Why was there only yellow grass and three-meter-high barbed wire?

The processing of the new contingent was carefully timed; they set out along "The Road of No Return" just as the last corpses from the gas chambers were being taken toward the grave pits. The pit had not been filled in; it was still waiting.

A little later, the Scharführer would blow his whistle again—and another twenty wagons would slowly be brought up to the station platform. More thousands of people carrying suitcases, bundles, and bags of food would get out and walk to the station square and look around. There was something sinister and terrifying about this square that had been trodden by millions of feet.

And the camp commandant, sitting in his office amid heaps of papers and charts, would telephone the station in Treblinka village—and another sixty-car train escorted by SS men with submachine guns and automatic rifles would pull heavily out of a siding and crawl along a single track between rows of pines.

The vast excavators worked day and night, digging vast new pits, pits that were many hundreds of meters long and many dark meters deep. And the pits were waiting. Waiting—though not for long.

2.

As the winter of 1942–43 was drawing to an end, Himmler came to Treblinka, along with a group of important Gestapo officials. Himmler's party flew to a landing strip in the area and was then taken in two cars to the camp, which they entered by the main gate. Most of the visitors were in army uniform; some—perhaps the various scientific experts—seemed like civilians, in fur coats and hats. Himmler inspected the camp in person, and one of the people who saw him has told us that the minister of death walked up to a huge grave pit and, for a long time, stared silently into it. His retinue waited at a respectful distance as Heinrich Himmler contemplated the colossal grave, already half full of corpses. Treblinka was the most important of all the factories in Himmler's empire. Later that same day the SS Reichsführer flew back. Before leaving Treblinka, he issued an order that dumbfounded the three members of the camp command: Hauptsturmführer Baron von Pfein, his deputy Karol, and Captain Franz Stangl. They were to start work immediately on digging up the corpses and burning every last one of them; the ashes and cinders were to be removed from the camps and scattered over fields and roads. Since there were already millions of corpses in the ground, this would be an extraordinarily complex and difficult task. In addition, the newly gassed were to be burned at once, instead of being buried.

What was the reason for Himmler's visit and his personal categorical order? The answer is very simple: the Red Army had just defeated the Germans at Stalingrad. This must have been a terrifying blow for the Germans. Within a matter of days men in Berlin were, for the first time, showing concern about being held to account, about possible retribution, about the revenge to which they might be subjected; within a matter of days Himmler had flown to Treblinka and issued urgent orders calculated to hide the traces of crimes committed within sixty kilometers of Warsaw. Himmler's orders were an echo, a direct repercussion of the mighty blow that the Red Army had just struck against the Germans, far away on the Volga.

At first there was real difficulty with the process of cremation; the corpses would not burn. There was, admittedly, an attempt to use the women's bodies, which burned better, to help burn the men's bodies. And the Germans tried dousing the bodies with gasoline and fuel oil, but this was expensive and turned out to make only a slight difference. There seemed to be no way around this problem, but then a thickset man of about fifty arrived from Germany, a member of the SS and a master of his trade. Hitler's regime, after all, had the capacity to produce experts of all kinds: experts in the use of a hammer to murder small children, expert stranglers, expert designers of gas chambers, experts in the scientifically planned destruction of large cities in the course of a single day. The regime was also able to find an expert in the exhumation and cremation of millions of human corpses.

And so, under this man's direction, furnaces were constructed. Furnaces of a special kind, since neither the furnaces at Majdanek nor those of any of the largest crematoria in the world would have been able to burn so vast a number of corpses in so short a time.

The excavator dug a pit 250 to 300 meters long, 20 to 25 meters wide, and 6 meters deep. Three rows of evenly spaced reinforced-concrete pillars, 100 to 120 centimeters in height, served as a support for giant steel beams that ran the entire length of the pit. Rails about five to seven centimeters apart were then laid across these beams. All this constituted a gigantic grill. A new narrow-gauge track was laid from the burial pits to the grill pit. Two more grill pits of the same dimensions were constructed soon afterward; each took 3,500 to 4,000 corpses at once.

Another giant excavator arrived, followed soon by a third. The work continued day and night. People who took part in the work of burning the corpses say that these grill pits were like giant volcanoes. The heat seared the workers' faces. Flames erupted eight or ten meters into the air. Pillars of thick black greasy smoke reached up into the sky and stood there, heavy and motionless. At night, people from villages thirty or forty kilometers away could see these flames curling above the pine forest that surrounded the camp. The smell of burned human flesh filled the whole area. If there was a wind, and if it blew in the direction of the labor camp three kilometers away, the people there almost suffocated from the stench. More than eight hundred prisoners—more than the number of workers employed in the furnaces of even the largest iron and steel plants—were engaged in the work of burning the bodies. This monstrous workshop operated day and night for eight months, without interruption, yet it still could not cope with the millions of human bodies. Trains were, of course, delivering new contingents to the gas chambers all the time, which added to the work of the grill pits.

Transports sometimes arrived from Bulgaria. These were a particular joy to the SS and the Wachmänner, since the Bulgarian Jews, who had been hoodwinked both by the Germans and by the Fascist Bulgarian government of the time, had no idea of the fate that awaited them and brought with them large quantities of valuables and plenty of tasty food, including white bread. Then there were transports from Grodno and Białystok, and—after the uprising—from the Warsaw ghetto. There was a transport of rebels from other parts of Poland—peasants, workers, and soldiers. There was a contingent of Bessarabian Gypsies: around two hundred men, with eight hundred women and children. They had come on foot, a string of horses and carts trailing behind them. They too had been hoodwinked; they were escorted by only two guards—and even these guards had no idea that they were leading these people to their death. I have been told that the Gypsy women clapped their hands in delight when they saw the handsome exterior of the gas chamber, and that they had no inkling until the very last minute of what lay in store for them. This greatly amused the Germans.

The SS singled out for particular torment those who had participated in the uprising in the Warsaw ghetto. The women and children were taken not to the gas chambers but to where the corpses were being burned. Mothers crazed with horror were forced to lead their children onto the red-hot grid where thousands of dead bodies were writhing in the flames and smoke, where corpses tossed and turned as if they had come back to life again, where the bellies of women who had been pregnant burst from the heat and babies killed before birth were burning in open wombs. Such a spectacle was enough to rob the most hardened man of his reason, but its effect—as the Germans well knew—was a hundred times greater on a mother struggling to keep her children from seeing it. The children clung to their mothers and shrieked, "Mama, what are they going to do to us? Are they going to burn us?" Not even Dante, in *his* Hell, saw scenes like this.

After amusing themselves for a while with this spectacle, the Germans burned the children.

It is infinitely painful to read this. The reader must believe me when I say that it is equally hard to write it. "Why write about it then?" someone may well ask. "Why recall such things?"

It is the writer's duty to tell the terrible truth, and it is a reader's civic duty to learn this truth. To turn away, to close one's eyes and walk past is to insult the memory of those who have perished. Only those who have learned the whole truth can ever understand against what kind of monster our great and holy Red Army has entered into mortal combat.

The SS had begun to feel bored in Treblinka. The procession of the doomed to the gas chambers had ceased to excite them. It had become routine. When the cremation of the corpses began, the SS men spent hours by the grill pits; this new sight amused them. The expert who had just come from Germany used to stroll around between the grill pits from morning till night, always animated and talkative. People say they never saw him frown or even look serious; he was always smiling. When the corpses were thrown down onto the bars of the grill, he would repeat: "Innocent, innocent." This was his favorite word.

Sometimes the SS organized a kind of picnic by the grill pits; they would sit upwind from them, drink wine, eat, and watch the flames. The "infirmary" was also reequipped. During the first months the sick and the aged had been taken to a space screened off by branches—and murdered there by a so-called doctor. Their bodies had then been carried on stretchers to the mass graves. Now a round pit was dug. Around this pit, as if the infirmary were a stadium, was a circle of low benches, all so close to the edge that anyone sitting on them was almost dangling over the pit. On the bottom of the pit was a grill, and on it corpses were burning. After being carried into the "infirmary," sick and decrepit old people were taken by "nurses" to these benches and made to sit facing the bonfire of human bodies. After enjoying this sight for a while, the Nazi barbarians shot the old people in the back, or in the backs of their gray heads. Dead or wounded, the old people fell into the bonfire.

German humor has never been highly valued; we have all heard people speak of it as heavy-handed. But who on earth could have imagined the humor, the jokes, the entertainments of the SS at Treblinka? They organized football matches between teams of the doomed, they made the doomed play tag, they organized a choir of the doomed. A small zoo was set up near the Germans' sleeping quarters. Innocent beasts from the forest—wolves and foxes—were kept in cages, while the vilest and cruelest predators ever seen on earth walked about in freedom, sat down for a rest on little benches made of birch wood, and listened to music. Someone even wrote a special anthem for the doomed, which included the words:

Für uns giebt heute nur Treblinka,
Das unser Schiksal ist . . .

A few minutes before their death, wounded, bleeding people were forced to learn idiotic, sentimental German songs and sing them in unison:

. . . Ich brach das Blumelein
Und schenkte es dem Schönste
Geliebte Mädelein . . .

The chief commandant selected a few children from one contingent. He killed their parents, dressed the children up in fine clothes, gave them lots of sweets, and played with them. A few days later, when he had had enough of this amusement, he gave orders for them to be killed.

The Germans posted one old man in a prayer shawl and phylacteries next to the outhouse and ordered him not to allow people to stay inside for more than three minutes. An alarm clock was hung from his chest. The Germans would look at his prayer shawl and laugh. Sometimes the Germans would force elderly Jewish men to recite prayers or to arrange funerals for those who had been murdered, observing all the traditional rites. They would even have to go and fetch gravestones—but after a while they were made to open the graves, dig up the bodies, and destroy the gravestones.

One of the main entertainments was to rape and torment the beautiful young women whom the SS selected from each contingent. In the morning the rapists would personally accompany them to the gas chambers. Thus the SS—the bulwark of Hitler's regime and the pride of Fascist Germany—entertained themselves at Treblinka.

It needs to be emphasized that these creatures were far from being mere robots that mechanically carried out the wishes of their superiors. Every witness attests to their shared love of philosophizing. The SS loved to deliver speeches to the doomed; they loved to discuss what was happening at Treblinka and its profound significance for the future. They were all deeply and sincerely convinced that what they were doing was right and necessary. They explained at length how their race was superior to all other races; they delivered tirades about German blood, the German character, and the mission of the German race. These beliefs have been expounded in books by Hitler and Rosenberg, in pamphlets and articles by Goebbels.

After they had finished work for the day, and after amusements such as those described above, they would sleep the sleep of the just, not disturbed by dreams or nightmares. They were not tormented by conscience, if only because not one of them possessed a conscience. They did gymnastics, drank milk every morning, and generally took good care of their health. They showed no less concern with regard to their living conditions and personal comforts, surrounding their living quarters with tidy gardens, sumptuous flower beds, and summerhouses. Several times a year they went on leave to Germany, since their bosses considered work in this "factory" detrimental to health and were determined to look after their workers. Back at home they walked about with their heads held high. If they said nothing about their work, this was not because they were ashamed of it but simply because, well disciplined as they were, they did not dare to violate their solemn pledge of silence. And when, in the evening, they went arm in arm with their wives to the cinema and burst into loud laughter, stamping their hobnailed boots on the floor, it would have been hard to tell them apart from the most ordinary man in the street. Nevertheless, they were beasts—vile beasts, SS beasts.

The summer of 1943 was exceptionally hot. For weeks on end there was no rain, no clouds, and no wind. The work of burning the corpses was in full swing. Day and night for six months the grill pits had been blazing, but only a little more than half of the corpses had been burned.

The moral and physical torment began to tell on the prisoners charged with this task; every day fifteen to twenty prisoners committed suicide. Many sought death by deliberately infringing the regulations.

"To get a bullet was a luxury," I heard from a baker by the name of Kosow, who had escaped from the camp. In Treblinka, evidently, it was far more terrible to be doomed to live than to be doomed to die.

Cinders and ashes were taken outside the camp grounds. Peasants from the village of Wólka were ordered to load them on their carts and scatter them along the road leading from the death camp to the labor camp. Child prisoners with spades then spread the ashes more evenly. Sometimes these children found melted gold coins or dental crowns. The ashes made the road black, like a mourning ribbon, and so the children were known as "the children from the black road." Car wheels make a peculiar swishing sound on this road, and, when I was taken along it, I kept hearing a sad whisper from beneath the wheels, like a timid complaint.

This black mourning-ribbon of ashes, lying between woods and fields, from the death camp to the labor camp, was like a tragic symbol of the terrible fate uniting the nations that had fallen beneath the ax of Hitler's Germany.

The peasants began carting out the cinders and ashes in the spring of 1943, and they continued until the summer of 1944. Each day twenty carts made from six to eight trips; during each trip they scattered 120 to 130 kilos of ash.

"Treblinka"—the song that eight hundred people were made to sing while they cremated corpses—included words exhorting the prisoners to humility and obedience; their reward would be "a little, little happiness, that would flash by in a single moment." Astonishingly, there really was one happy day in the living Hell of Treblinka. The Germans, however, were mistaken: what brought the condemned this gift was not humility and obedience. On the contrary, this happy day dawned thanks to insane audacity—thanks to the insane audacity of people who had nothing to lose. All were expecting to die, and every day of their life was a day of suffering and torment. All had witnessed terrible crimes, and the Germans would have spared none of them; the gas chambers awaited them all. Most, in fact, were sent to the gas chambers after only a few days of work and were replaced by people from new contingents. Only a few dozen people lived for weeks and months, rather than for days and hours; these were skilled workers, carpenters, and stonemasons, and the bakers, tailors, and barbers who ministered to the Germans' everyday needs. These people created an organizing committee for an uprising. It was, of course, only the already condemned, only people possessed by an all-consuming hatred and a fierce thirst for revenge, who could have conceived such an insane plan. They did not want to escape until they had destroyed Treblinka. And they destroyed it. Weapons—axes, knives, and truncheons—began to appear in the prisoners' barracks. The risk they incurred, the price they paid to obtain each ax or knife, is hard to imagine. What cunning and skill, what astonishing patience, were required to hide these things in the barracks! Stocks of gasoline were laid in—to douse the camp buildings and set them ablaze. How did the conspirators achieve this? How did gasoline disappear, as if it had evaporated, from the camp stores? How indeed? Through superhuman effort—through great mental ingenuity, through determination and a terrifying audacity. A large tunnel was dug beneath the ammunition store. Audacity worked miracles; standing beside the conspirators was the God of courage. They took twenty hand grenades, a machine gun, rifles, and pistols and hid them in secret places. Every detail in their complex plan was carefully worked out. Each group of five had its specific assignment. Each mathematically precise assignment called for insane daring. One group was to storm the watchtowers, where the Wachmänner sat with their machine guns. A second group was to attack the sentries who patrolled the paths between the various camp squares. A third group was to attack the armored vehicles. A fourth was to cut the telephone lines. A fifth was to seize control of the barracks. A sixth would cut passages through the barbed wire. A seventh was to lay bridges across the antitank ditches. An eighth was to pour gasoline on the camp buildings and set them on fire. A ninth group would destroy whatever else could be destroyed.

There were even arrangements to provide the escapees with money. There was one moment, however, when the Warsaw doctor who was collecting this money nearly ruined the whole plan. A Scharführer noticed a wad of banknotes sticking out of his pocket; the doctor had only just collected the notes and had been about to hide them away. The Scharführer pretended not to have seen anything and reported the matter to Kurt Franz. Something extraordinary was clearly going on—what use, after all, was money to a man condemned to death?—and Franz immediately went off to interrogate the doctor. He began the interrogation with calm confidence; there may well, after all, have been no more skilled torturer in the world. And there was certainly no one at all in the world— Franz believed—who could withstand the tortures he practiced. But the Warsaw doctor outwitted the SS captain. He took poison. One of the participants in the uprising told me that never before in Treblinka had such efforts been made to save a man's life. Evidently Franz sensed that the doctor would be slipping away with an important secret. But the German poison did its job, and the secret remained a secret.

Toward the end of June it turned suffocatingly hot. When graves were opened, steam billowed up from them as if from gigantic boilers. The heat of the grills—together with the monstrous stench—was killing even the workers who were moving the corpses; they were dropping dead onto the bars of the grills. Billions of overfed flies were crawling along the ground and buzzing about in the air. The last hundred thousand corpses were now being burned.

The uprising was planned for August 2. It began with a revolver shot. The banner of success fluttered over the holy cause. New flames soared into the sky—not the heavy flames and grease-laden smoke of burning corpses but bright wild flames of life. The camp buildings were ablaze, and to the rebels it seemed that a second sun was burning over Treblinka, that the sun had rent its body in two in celebration of the triumph of freedom and honor.

Shots rang out; machine-gun fire crackled from the watchtowers that the rebels had captured. Hand grenades rang out as triumphantly as if they were the bells of truth. The air shook from crashes and detonations; buildings collapsed; the buzzing of corpse flies was drowned out by the whistle of bullets. In the pure, clear air flashed axes red with blood. On August 2 the evil blood of the SS flowed onto the ground of the Hell that was Treblinka, and a radiant blue sky celebrated the moment of revenge. And a story as old as the world was repeated once more: creatures who had behaved as if they were representatives of a higher race; creatures who had shouted *"Achtung! Mützen ab!"* to make people take off their hats; creatures who had bellowed, in their masterful voices *"Alle r-r-r-raus unter-r-r-r!"* to compel the inhabitants of Warsaw to leave their homes and walk to their deaths—these conquering beings, so confident of their own might when it had been a matter of slaughtering millions of women and children, turned out to be despicable, cringing reptiles as soon as it came to a life-and-death struggle. They begged for mercy. They lost their heads. They ran this way and that way like rats. They forgot about Treblinka's diabolically contrived defense system. They forgot about their all-annihilating firepower. They forgot their own weapons. But need I say more? Need anyone be in the least surprised by these things?

Two and a half months later, on October 14, 1943, there was an uprising in the Sobibor death factory; it was organized by a Soviet prisoner of war, a political commissar from Rostov by the name of Sashko Pechersky. The same thing happened as in Treblinka: people half dead from hunger managed to get the better of several hundred SS beasts who were bloated from the blood of the innocent. With the help of crude axes that they themselves had forged in the camp smithies, the rebels overpowered their executioners. Many of the rebels had no weapon except sand. Pechersky had told them to fill their pockets with fine sand and throw it in the guards' eyes. But need we be surprised by any of this?

As Treblinka blazed and the rebels, saying a silent farewell to the ashes of their fellows, were escaping through the barbed wire, SS and police units were rushed in from all directions to track them down. Hundreds of police dogs were sent after them. Airplanes were summoned. There was fighting in the forests, fighting in the marshes—and few of those who took part in the uprising are still alive. But what does that matter? They died fighting, with guns in their hands.

After August 2, Treblinka ceased to exist. The Germans burned the remaining corpses, dismantled the stone buildings, removed the barbed wire, and torched the wooden barracks not already burned down by the rebels. Part of the equipment of the house of death was blown up; part was taken away by train. The grills were destroyed, the excavators taken away, the vast pits filled in with earth. The station building was razed; last of all, the track was dismantled and the crossties removed. Lupines were sown on the site of the camp, and a settler by the name of Streben built himself a little house there. Now this house has gone; it too was burned down. What were the Germans trying to do? To hide the traces of the murder of millions in the Hell that was Treblinka? Did they really imagine this to be possible? Can silence be imposed on thousands of people who have witnessed transports bringing the condemned from every corner of

Europe to a place of conveyor-belt execution? Did the Germans really think that they could hide the dead, the heavy flames, and the smoke that hung in the sky for eight months, visible day and night to the inhabitants of dozens of villages and hamlets? Did they really think that they could force the peasants of Wólka to forget the screams of the women and children—those terrible screams that continued for thirteen months and that ring in their ears to this day? Can the memory of such screams be torn from the heart? Did they really think they could force silence upon the peasants who for a whole year had been transporting human ash from the camp and scattering it on the roads?

Did they really think they could silence the still-living witnesses who had seen the Treblinka executioner's block in operation from its first days until August 2, 1943, the last day of its existence? Witnesses whose descriptions of each SS man and each of the Wachmänner precisely corroborate one another? Witnesses whose step by step, hour by hour accounts of life in Treblinka have made it possible to create a kind of Treblinka diary? It is no longer possible to shout *"Mützen ab!"* at these witnesses; it is no longer possible to lead them into a gas chamber. And Himmler no longer has any power over his minions. Their heads bowed, their trembling fingers tugging nervously at the hems of their jackets, their voices dull and expressionless, Himmler's minions are now telling the story of their crimes—a story so unreal that it seems like the product of insanity and delirium. A Soviet officer, wearing the green ribbon of the Defense of Stalingrad medal, takes down page after page of the murderers' testimonies. At the door stands a sentry, wearing the same green Stalingrad ribbon on his chest. His lips are pressed tight together and there is a stern look on his gaunt weather-beaten face. This face is the face of justice—the people's justice. And is it not a remarkable symbol that one of the victorious armies from Stalingrad should have come to Treblinka, near Warsaw? It was not without reason that Himmler began to panic in February 1943; it was not without reason that he flew to Treblinka and gave orders for the construction of the grill pits followed by the obliteration of all traces of the camp. It was not without reason—but it was to no avail. The defenders of Stalingrad have now reached Treblinka; from the Volga to the Vistula turned out to be no distance at all. And now the very earth of Treblinka refuses to be an accomplice to the crimes the monsters committed. It is casting up the bones and belongings of those who were murdered; it is casting up everything that Hitler's people tried to bury within it.

————

We arrived in Treblinka in early September 1944, thirteen months after the day of the uprising. For thirteen months from July 1942 the executioner's block had been at work—and for thirteen months from August 1943, the Germans had been trying to obliterate every trace of this work.

It is quiet. The tops of the pine trees on either side of the railway line are barely stirring. It is these pines, this sand, this old tree stump that millions of human eyes saw as their freight wagons came slowly up to the platform. With true German neatness, white-washed stones have been laid along the borders of the black road. The ashes and crushed cinders swish softly. We enter the camp. We tread the earth of Treblinka. The lupine pods split open at the least touch; they split with a faint ping and millions of tiny peas scatter over the earth. The sounds of the falling peas and the bursting pods come together to form a single soft, sad melody. It is as if a funeral knell—a barely audible, sad, broad, peaceful tolling—is being carried to us from the very depths of the earth. And, rich and swollen as if saturated with flax oil, the earth sways beneath our feet—earth of Treblinka, bottomless earth, earth as unsteady as the sea. This wilderness behind a barbed-wire fence has swallowed more human lives than all the earth's oceans and seas have swallowed since the birth of mankind.

The earth is casting up fragments of bone, teeth, sheets of paper, clothes, things of all kinds. The earth does not want to keep secrets.

And from the earth's unhealing wounds, from this earth that is splitting apart, things are escaping of their own accord. Here they are: the half-rotted shirts of those who were murdered, their trousers and shoes, their cigarette cases that have turned green, along with little cogwheels from watches, penknives, shaving brushes, candlesticks, a child's shoes with red pompoms, embroidered towels from the Ukraine, lace underwear, scissors, thimbles, corsets, and bandages. Out of another fissure in the earth have escaped heaps of utensils: frying pans, aluminum mugs, cups, pots and pans of all sizes, jars, little dishes, children's plastic mugs. In yet another place—as if all that the Germans had buried was being pushed up out of the swollen, bottomless earth, as if someone's hand were pushing it all out into the light of day: half-rotted Soviet passports, notebooks with Bulgarian writing, photographs of children from Warsaw and Vienna, letters penciled in a childish scrawl, a small volume of poetry, a yellowed sheet of paper on which someone had copied a prayer, ration cards from Germany... And everywhere there are hundreds of perfume bottles of all shapes and sizes— green, pink, blue... And over all this reigns a terrible smell of decay, a smell that neither fire, nor sun, nor rain, nor snow, nor wind have been able to overcome. And thousands of little forest flies are crawling about over all these half-rotted bits and pieces, over all these papers and photographs.

We walk on over the swaying, bottomless earth of Treblinka and suddenly come to a stop. Thick wavy hair, gleaming like burnished copper, the delicate lovely hair of a young woman, trampled into the ground; and beside it, some equally fine blond hair; and then some heavy black plaits on the bright sand; and then more and more... Evidently these are the contents of a sack, just a single sack that somehow got left behind. Yes, it is all true. The last hope, the last wild hope that it was all just a terrible dream, has gone. And the lupine pods keep popping open, and the tiny peas keep pattering down—and this really does all sound like a funeral knell rung by countless little bells from under the earth. And it feels as if your heart must come to a stop now, gripped by more sorrow, more grief, more anguish than any human being can endure...

Scholars, sociologists, criminologists, psychiatrists, and philosophers—everyone is asking how all this can have happened. How indeed? Was it something organic? Was it a matter of heredity, upbringing, environment, or external conditions? Was it a matter of historical fate, or the criminality of the German leaders? Somehow the embryonic traits of a racial theory that sounded simply comic when expounded by the second-rate charlatan professors or pathetic provincial theoreticians of nineteenth-century Germany—the contempt in which the German philistine held "Russian pigs," "Polish cattle," "Jews reeking of garlic," "debauched Frenchmen," "English shopkeepers," "hypocritical Greeks," and "Czech blockheads"; all the nonsense about the superiority of the Germans to every other race on earth, all the cheap nonsense that seemed so comical, such an easy target for journalists and humorists—all this, in the course of only a few years, ceased to seem merely infantile and was transformed into a threat to mankind. It became a deadly threat to human life and freedom and a source of unparalleled crime, bloodshed, and suffering. There is much now to think about, much that we must try to understand.

Wars like the present war are terrible indeed. A vast amount of innocent blood has been spilled by the Germans. But it is not enough now to speak about Germany's responsibility for what has happened. Today we need to speak about the responsibility of every nation in the world; we need to speak about the responsibility of every nation and every citizen for the future.

Every man and woman today is duty-bound to his or her conscience, to his or her son and to his or her mother, to their motherland and to humanity as a whole to devote all the powers of their heart and mind to answering these questions: What is it that has given birth to racism? What can be done to prevent Nazism from ever rising again, either on this side or on the far side of the ocean? What can be done to make sure that Hitlerism is never, never in all eternity resurrected?

What led Hitler and his followers to construct Majdanek, Sobibor, Bełzec, Auschwitz, and Treblinka is the imperialist idea of exceptionalism—of racial, national, and every other kind of exceptionalism.

We must remember that Fascism and racism will emerge from this war not only with the bitterness of defeat but also with sweet memories of the ease with which it is possible to commit mass murder. It has turned out that it is really not so very difficult to kill entire nations. Ten small chambers—hardly enough space, if properly furnished, to stable a hundred horses—ten such chambers turned out to be enough to kill three million people.

Killing turned out to be supremely easy—it does not entail any uncommon expenditure.

It is possible to build five hundred such chambers in only a few days. This is no more difficult than constructing a five-story building.

It is possible to demonstrate with nothing more than a pencil that any large construction company with experience in the use of reinforced concrete can, in the course of six months and with a properly organized labor force, construct more than enough chambers to gas the entire population of the earth.

This must be unflinchingly borne in mind by everyone who truly values honor, freedom, and the life of all nations, the life of humanity.

THE SISTINE MADONNA

I.

THE VICTORIOUS Soviet forces, after annihilating the army of Fascist Germany, removed paintings from the collection of the Dresden Art Gallery and took them to Moscow. These paintings were then locked away for ten years.

In the spring of 1955 the Soviet government decided to return these paintings to Dresden. First, though, they were to be exhibited in Moscow for three months.

And so, on the cold morning of May 30, 1955, I walked along the Volkhonka, past the lines of policemen controlling the huge crowds who wanted to see the works of the Old Masters. I entered the Pushkin Museum, climbed the stairs to the first floor, and went up to *The Sistine Madonna*.

As soon as you set eyes on this painting, you immediately realize one thing, one thing above all: that it is immortal.

I realized that I had, until this moment, been careless in my use of this awesome word "immortal." I had confused the powerful life of some particularly great human achievements with immortality. Now, however, it came home to me that—for all the admiration I feel for Rembrandt, Beethoven, and Tolstoy—there was no work of art other than *The Sistine Madonna*, no other work created by brush, chisel, or pen, no other work that had conquered my heart and mind, that would continue to live for as long as people continued to live. And should people die, then whatever other creatures

might replace them on earth—wolves, rats, bears, or swallows—would also walk or wing their way to look at this Madonna.

This painting has been seen by twelve generations of people—a fifth of the generations that have lived on earth since the beginning of recorded history.

Old beggar women have looked at this painting—as have European emperors and students, American millionaires, popes, Russian princes. Young virgins, prostitutes, colonels from the general staff, thieves, geniuses, weavers, bomber pilots, and schoolteachers have looked at it. Good and evil people have looked at it.

During the centuries this painting has existed, European and colonial empires have risen and fallen, the American nation has come into being, the factories of Pittsburgh and Detroit have gone into production, revolutions have taken place, and the world's social structure has changed. During these centuries humanity has left behind it the superstitions of the alchemists, just as it has abandoned hand-driven spinning wheels, muskets and halberds, sailing ships and horse-drawn mail-coaches. Humanity has entered the age of electric generators, electric motors, and turbines; it has entered the age of atomic reactors and hydrogen bombs. During these centuries great scientists have shaped a new understanding of the universe: Galileo has written his *Dialogue*, Newton his *Principia*, Einstein his *On the Electrodynamics of Moving Bodies*. During these centuries Rembrandt, Goethe, Beethoven, Dostoevsky, and Tolstoy have enriched our souls and made our lives more beautiful.

What I saw was a young mother holding a child in her arms.

How is one to convey the grace of a slender apple tree bearing its first pale heavy apple, the grace of a young bird raising its first fledglings, the grace of a young roe deer that has just borne a fawn? The helplessness—the new motherhood—of a girl, of a little girl, still almost a child.

After *The Sistine Madonna* one can no longer refer to this special grace as ineffable or mysterious.

In his Madonna, Raphael has revealed the mystery of maternal beauty. But the secret of the painting's inexhaustible life lies elsewhere. The secret of the painting's life, of the Madonna's great beauty, is that the young woman's body and face are—in fact—her soul. In this visual representation of a mother's soul lies something inaccessible to human consciousness.

We know about thermonuclear reactions during which matter is transformed into an enormous quantity of energy, but we cannot as yet conceive of a reverse process—the transformation of energy into matter. Here, though, a spiritual force—motherhood—has been crystallized, transmuted into a meek and gentle Madonna.

The Madonna's beauty is closely tied to earthly life. It is a democratic, human, and humane beauty. It is a beauty that lives in every woman: in the cross-eyed, in hunchbacks with long pale noses, in golden-skinned Asians, in black-skinned Africans with curly hair and full lips. It is a universal beauty. This Madonna is the soul and mirror of all human beings, and everyone who looks at her can see her humanity. She is the image of the maternal soul. That is why her beauty is forever interwoven and fused with the beauty that lies hidden, deep down, indestructible, wherever life is being born—be it in cellars, attics, pits, or palaces.

I believe that this Madonna is a purely atheistic expression of life and humanity, without divine participation.

There have been moments when I have felt that this Madonna expresses not only all that is human but also something that is a part of earthly life in a still broader sense, something that is present in the animal world as a whole. I have felt that the Madonna's miraculous shadow can be glimpsed in the brown eyes of a horse, dog, or cow that is feeding its young.

The child in the Madonna's arms seems more earthly still. His face is more adult than that of his mother.

His gaze is sad and serious, focused both ahead and within. It is the kind of gaze that allows one to glimpse one's fate.

Both faces are calm and sad. Perhaps they can see Golgotha, and the dusty rocky road up the hill, and the hideous, short, heavy, rough-hewn cross lying on a shoulder that is now only little and that now feels only the warmth of the maternal breast.

Yet neither anxiety nor pain grips our hearts. Instead, we feel something new, something we have never experienced. It is a human feeling, a new feeling, and it seems as if it has just arisen from the salty and bitter depths of the sea. Here it is—and its newness and unfamiliarity make your heart beat faster.

Here lies yet another unique quality of the painting.

It engenders something new, as if an eighth color has been added to the seven colors of the spectrum that we already know.

Why is there no fear on the mother's face? Why have her fingers not fastened around her son's body so tightly that even death cannot untwine them? Why does she not wish to keep her son from his fate?

Rather than hiding her child, she holds him forward to meet his fate.

And the child is not hiding his face in his mother's breast. Any moment now he will climb down from her arms and walk forward on his own little bare feet to meet his fate.

How are we to explain this? How are we to understand it?

They are one—and they are separate. They see, feel, and think together. They are fused, yet everything says that they will separate from each other, that they cannot not separate, that the essence of their communion, of their fusion, lies in their coming separation.

There are bitter and painful moments when it is children who amaze adults with their good sense, their composure, and their acceptance of fate. Peasant children dying in years of famine have shown these qualities—as did the children of Jewish craftsmen and shopkeepers during the Kishinyov pogrom, as have the children of coal miners when a wailing siren proclaims to a panic-stricken settlement that there has been an explosion in the mine.

What is human in man goes to meet its fate, and in every epoch this fate is peculiar, distinct from the characteristic fate of the preceding epoch. What these various fates have in common is that all are painful and difficult.

But even when a man was crucified on a cross or tortured in a prison, what is human in him continued to exist.

What is human in man survived in quarries, in lumber camps in the taiga where the temperature was fifty degrees below freezing, in the flooded trenches of Przemyśl and Verdun. What is human in man continued to live on in the monotonous existence of clerks, in the joyless labor of women factory workers, in the wretched lives of cleaners and washerwomen, in their hopeless and exhausting struggle against poverty.

The Madonna with the child in her arms represents what is human in man. This is why she is immortal.

Looking at *The Sistine Madonna*, our own epoch glimpses its own fate. Every epoch contemplates this woman with a child in her arms, and a tender, moving, and sorrowful sense of brotherhood comes into being between people of different generations, nations, races, and eras. Conscious now of themselves and the cross they must bear, people suddenly understand the miraculous links between different ages, the way everything that ever has lived and ever will live is linked to what is living now.

2.

Afterward, as I was walking back down the street, stunned and confused by these sudden and powerful impressions, I made no attempt to unravel my various feelings and thoughts.

My confusion of feeling was nothing like the days of tears and joy I had known when I first read *War and Peace* at the age of fifteen, nor did it resemble what I had felt when I listened to Beethoven during a particularly somber and difficult time of my life.

And then I realized that the vision of a young mother with a child in her arms had taken me back not to a book, not to a piece of music, but to Treblinka:

It is these pines, this sand, this old tree stump that millions of human eyes saw as their freight wagons came slowly up to the platform ... We enter the camp. We tread the earth of Treblinka. The lupine pods split open at the least touch; they split with a faint ping ... The sounds of the falling peas and the bursting pods come together to form a single soft, sad melody. It is as if a funeral knell—a barely audible, sad, broad, peaceful tolling—is being carried to us from the very depths of the earth . . . Here they are: the half-rotted shirts of those who were murdered, their shoes, little cogwheels from watches, penknives, candlesticks, a child's shoes with red pompoms, an embroidered towel from the Ukraine, lace underwear, pots, jars, children's plastic mugs, letters penciled in a childish scrawl, small volumes of poetry . . .

We walk on over the swaying, bottomless earth of Treblinka and suddenly come to a stop. Thick wavy hair, gleaming like burnished copper, the delicate lovely hair of a young woman, trampled into the ground; and beside it, some equally fine blond hair; and then some heavy black plaits on the bright sand; and then more and more . . .

And the lupine pods keep popping open, and the tiny peas keep pattering down—and this really does all sound like a funeral knell rung by countless little bells from under the earth.

And it feels as if your heart must come to a stop now, gripped by more sorrow, more grief, more anguish than any human being can endure . . .

What had surfaced in my soul was the memory of Treblinka, though at first I had failed to realize this . . .

It was she, treading lightly on her little bare feet, who had walked over the swaying earth of Treblinka; it was she who had walked from the "station," from where the transports were unloaded, to the gas chambers. I knew her by the expression on her face, by the look in her eyes. I saw her son and recognized him by the strange, unchildlike look on his own face. This was how mothers and children looked, this was how they were in their souls when they saw, against the dark green of the pine trees, the white walls of the Treblinka gas chambers.

How many times had I stared through darkness at the people getting out of the freight wagons, but their faces had never been clear to me. Sometimes their faces had seemed distorted by extreme horror, and everything had dissolved in a terrible scream. Sometimes despair and exhaustion, physical and spiritual, had obscured their faces with a look of blank, sullen indifference. Sometimes the carefree smile of insanity had veiled their faces as they left the transport and walked toward the gas chambers.

And now at last I had seen these faces truly and clearly. Raphael had painted them four centuries earlier. This is how someone goes to meet their fate. The Sistine Chapel...The Treblinka gas chambers...In our days a young woman brings a child into the world. It is terrifying to be holding a child against one's heart and hear the roar of the crowds welcoming Adolf Hitler. The mother gazes into the face of her newborn son and hears the ringing and crunching of breaking glass, and the howling of car horns. On the streets of Berlin a wolfish choir is singing the Horst Wessel song. From the Moabit prison comes the dull thud of an ax.

The mother breast-feeds her baby, and thousands of thousands of men build walls, lay barbed wire, and construct barracks. And in quiet offices men design gas chambers, mobile gassing vans, and cremation ovens.

A wolfish time had come, the time of Fascism. It was a time when people led wolfish lives and wolves lived like people.

During this time the young mother was raising her child. And a painter by the name of Adolf Hitler stood before her in the Dresden Art Gallery; he was deciding her fate. But the ruler of Europe could not look into her eyes, nor could he meet the gaze of her son. Both she and her son, after all, were people.

Their human strength triumphed over his violence. The Madonna walked toward the gas chamber, treading lightly on her small bare feet. She carried her son over the swaying earth of Treblinka.

German Fascism was destroyed. The war carried away tens of millions of people. Huge cities were reduced to ruins.

In the spring of 1945 this Madonna first saw our northern sky. She came to us not as a guest, not as a foreign tourist, but in the company of soldiers and drivers, along the smashed roads of the war. She is a part of our life; she is our contemporary.

She has seen everything before: our snow, the cold autumn mud, soldiers' dented mess tins with their murky gruel, a limp onion with a crust of black bread.

She has walked alongside us; she has traveled for six weeks in a screeching train, picking lice out of her son's soft, unwashed hair.

She is a contemporary of the total collectivization of agriculture.

Here she is, barefoot, carrying her little son, boarding a transport train. What a long path lies ahead of her—from Oboyan near Kursk, from the black-earth region of Voronezh, to the taiga, to marshy forests beyond the Urals, to the sands of Kazakhstan.

And where is your father, little one? Where did he perish? In some bomb crater? Felling logs in the taiga? In some dysentery barrack?

Vanya, Vanya, why are you looking so sad? Fate took you away from the hut where you were born, nailing a wooden cross over its windows. What long journey lies ahead of you? Will you reach its end? Or will you come to the end of your strength and die somewhere along the way, in a station on a narrow-gauge railway, on the swampy bank of some little river beyond the Urals?

Yes, it was she. I saw her in 1930, in Konotop, at the station. Swarthy from hunger and illness, she walked toward the express train, looked up at me with her wonderful eyes, and said with her lips, without any voice, "Bread . . ."

I saw her son, already thirty years old. He was wearing worn-out soldiers' boots—so completely worn out that no one would even take the trouble to remove them from the feet of a corpse—and a padded jacket with a large hole exposing his milk-white shoulder. He was walking along a path through a bog. A huge cloud of midges was hanging above him, but he was unable to drive them away; he was unable to remove this living, flickering halo because he needed both of his hands to steady the damp heavy log on his shoulder. At one moment he raised his bowed head. I saw his fair curly beard, covering the whole of his face. I saw his half-open lips. I saw his eyes—and I knew them at once. They were the eyes that look out from Raphael's painting.

We met his mother more than once in 1937. There she was—

holding her son in her arms for the last time, saying goodbye to him, gazing into his face and then going down the deserted staircase of a mute, many-storied building. A black car was waiting for her below; a wax seal had already been affixed to the door of her room. How mute the tall buildings, how strange and watchful the silence of the ash-gray dawn...

And out of the half-light before dawn emerges her new life: a transport train, a transit prison, sentries looking down from wooden watchtowers, barbed wire, night shifts in the workshops, boiled water in place of tea, and bed boards, bed boards, bed boards...

With his slow soft stride, wearing his low-heeled kid-leather boots, Stalin went up to the painting and, stroking his gray mustache, gazed for a long, long time at the faces of mother and son.

Did he recognize her? He had met her during his own years of exile in eastern Siberia, in Novaya Uda, in Turukhansk and Kureisk. He had met her in transit prisons. He had met her when prisoners were being transferred from one place of exile to another. Did he think of her later, during the days of his grandeur?

But we, we people, we recognized her, and we recognized her son too. She is us; their fate is our own fate; mother and son are what is human in man. And if some future time takes the Madonna to China, or to the Sudan, people will recognize her everywhere just as we have recognized her today.

The painting speaks of the joy of being alive on this earth; this too is a source of its calm, miraculous power.

The whole world, the whole vast universe, is the submissive slavery of inanimate matter. Life alone is the miracle of freedom.

And the painting also tells us how precious, how splendid life has to be, and that no force in the world can compel life to change into some other thing that, however it may resemble life, is no longer life.

The power of life, the power of what is human in man, is very great, and even the mightiest and most perfect violence cannot enslave this power; it can only kill it. This is why the faces of the mother and child are so calm: they are invincible. Life's destruction, even in our iron age, is not its defeat.

Young or gray-haired, we who live in Russia stand before Raphael's Madonna. We live in a troubled time. Wounds have not yet healed, burned-out buildings still stand black. The mounds have not yet settled over the shared graves of millions of soldiers, our sons and brothers. Dead, blackened poplars and cherry trees still stand guard over partisan villages that were burned to the ground. Tall dreary grasses and weeds grow over the bodies of people who were burned alive: grandfathers, mothers, young lads and lasses. Over the ditches that contain the bodies of murdered Jewish children and mothers the earth is still shifting, still settling into place. In countless Russian, Belorussian, and Ukrainian huts widows are still weeping at night. The Madonna has suffered all this together with us—for she is us, and her son is us.

And all this is frightening, and shaming, and painful. Why has life been so terrible? Are you and I not to blame? Why are we alive? A difficult and terrible question—only the dead can ask it. Yet the dead are silent; they ask nothing.

Every now and again the postwar silence is disrupted by the thunder of explosions, and a radioactive cloud spreads across the sky.

And then the earth on which we live shudders; the atom bomb has been replaced by the hydrogen bomb. Soon we must see *The Sistine Madonna* on her way. She has lived with us; she has lived our life. Judge us then, judge us all—along with the Madonna and her son. Soon we will leave life; our hair is already white. But she, a young mother carrying her son in her arms, will go forward to meet her fate. Along with a new generation of people, she will see in the sky a blinding, powerful light: the first explosion of a thermonuclear bomb, a superpowerful bomb heralding the start of a new, global war.

What can we, people of the epoch of Fascism, say before the court of the past and the future? Nothing can vindicate us.

We will say, "There has been no time crueler than ours, yet we did not allow what is human in man to perish."

Seeing *The Sistine Madonna* go on her way, we preserve our faith that life and freedom are one, that there is nothing higher than what is human in man.

This will live forever and triumph.

PART THREE

Late Stories

DURING the second half of the 1950s Grossman enjoyed public success. Three separate editions of *For a Just Cause* were published—in 1954, 1955, and 1959—and he was awarded a prestigious decoration, the Red Banner of Labor. Meanwhile he was writing *Life and Fate*—the sequel to *For a Just Cause* and the work usually considered his masterpiece.

Grossman's personal life, however, was troubled. He was growing estranged from his wife, Olga Mikhailovna, and he was deeply in love with Yekaterina Vasilievna Zabolotskaya, the wife of the poet Nikolay Zabolotsky. The Grossmans and the Zabolotksys were neighbors, and the two families—parents and children alike—saw a great deal of each other. The first stages of the relationship between Zabolotskaya and Grossman have been convincingly described by Nikita Zabolotsky, the Zabolotskys' only son. After saying that Grossman's political outspokenness often led him into awkward situations, Nikita Zabolotsky continues: "At such moments [Grossman] was particularly touched by Yekaterina's innate sensitivity and sympathy, her readiness to come to his help every time he needed moral support. Their relations were for a long time limited to family gatherings, but then they sometimes started to take walks together in the Neskuchny Park or on the city streets. Zabolotsky saw that Grossman's friendship with his wife was growing into a deeper feeling."

The story of this relationship is complex. In late 1956 Grossman left Olga Mikhailovna and moved, with Zabolotskaya, first to a room he rented privately and then to a small room—officially "a study"—that he had obtained from the Literary Fund. For around two years Grossman and Zabolotskaya lived together most of the time in this small room in an apartment on Lomonosovsky Prospekt. In early September 1958, they both went back to their partners, probably intending this return to be permanent. On October 14, however, Nikolay Zabolotsky unexpectedly died, of a heart attack, and within a year Grossman and Zabolotskaya were once more living together; Yekaterina Korotkova remembers introducing her future husband to them in 1959, in the room on Lomonosovsky Prospekt. And in 1961 Grossman obtained a small apartment in a new Writers Union block near the Airport Metro Station; Zabolotskaya was a close neighbor, living in the same section of the building, and they saw each other every day for nearly all that remained of Grossman's life.

———

The other sorrow that hung over Grossman's last years was the "arrest"—as Russians still refer to it—of *Life and Fate*. In October 1960, against the advice of both Semyon Lipkin and Zabolotskaya, Grossman delivered the manuscript to the editors of *Znamya*. It was the height of Khrushchev's "thaw" and Grossman seems to have believed that *Life and Fate* could be published, even though one of its central themes is the identity of Nazism and Stalinism. Grossman is generally thought to have behaved naively, but he was evidently clearheaded enough to take precautions. He himself censored about fifteen percent of the text he submitted. He left a copy of the complete typescript with Lipkin, and he entrusted his original manuscript to Lyolya Klestova, a friend from his student days who had no connection with the literary world.

In February 1961, three KGB officers came to Grossman's apartment. They confiscated the typescript and everything bearing any relation to it, even carbon paper and typing ribbons. This is one of only two occasions when the Soviet authorities "arrested" a book while leaving the writer at liberty; no other book, apart from *The*

Gulag Archipelago, was ever considered so dangerous. Grossman refused to sign an undertaking not to speak of this visit. He agreed to take the KGB officers to his two typists and to his cousin Viktor Sherentsis in order for them to confiscate other copies of the typescript, but he may well have done this in the hope of deflecting attention from the copies he had left with Lipkin and Klestova. The KGB, in any case, did not find the remaining copies, even though they evidently made considerable efforts. According to Tatiana Menaker, a distant younger relative of Grossman's, they went to Viktor Sherentsis's dacha and dug up the whole of his vegetable garden.

In 1975, more than ten years after Grossman's death, Lipkin asked the writer Vladimir Voinovich to help get *Life and Fate* published in the West. After making what turned out to be an inadequate microfilm, Voinovich asked Andrey Sakharov to make a second microfilm; Voinovich then sent this abroad. The microfilm reached Vladimir Maksimov, the chief editor of the émigré journal *Kontinent*, but Maksimov published only a few somewhat randomly chosen chapters; his lack of interest probably stemmed from his anti-Semitism. In 1977 Voinovich made a third microfilm, which he entrusted—along with his first, poor-quality microfilm—to an Austrian professor, Rosemarie Ziegler. These two microfilms reached Yefim Etkind, a writer and scholar then living in Paris. With the help of a colleague, Shimon Markish, Etkind established an almost complete text; this was not easy, since both microfilms were flawed. Several émigré publishing houses then turned the novel down. Vladimir Dimitrijevic—a Serb working for the publishers Éditions L'Âge d'Homme in Lausanne—eventually accepted the novel and in 1980 published an almost-complete Russian text. At a conference about Vasily Grossman in 2003 in Turin, Dimitrijevic said how he had sensed at once that Grossman was portraying "a world in three dimensions" and that he was one of those rare writers whose aim was "not to prove something but to make people live something."

Grossman, however, did not live to see any of this; he did not know that his manuscripts would be preserved, let alone published.

According to Lipkin: "Grossman aged before our eyes. His curly hair turned grayer and a bald patch appeared. His asthma [...] returned. His walk became a shuffle." Grossman himself said, "They strangled me in a dark corner."

Menaker has provided us with another glimpse of Grossman during these years—although the first of her memories, in fact, dates back to 1959, two years before the "arrest" of *Life and Fate*:

A mysterious stone wall of unsaid things and secrecy always surrounded him. My first memory of this sadness and secrecy belongs to the year 1959, when I spent a winter vacation in Viktor Sherentsis's house in Moscow. Grossman came to visit every day and I was constantly being kicked out into the corridor stuffed with books. No wonder: as my grandma was always repeating, "Even the cat reports to the OGPU." I knew that Grossman was a famous writer. We had his huge novels, which were published in millions of copies, but the aura of sadness and tragedy was never explained to me in his lifetime. Later I realized that the people who came to our apartment had been sharing with Grossman their prison camp memories. I vividly recall that I felt in their presence the truth of Grossman's observation that these people are "frozen in time."

From late 1961 Grossman was often seriously ill. He did not realize this, but he was suffering from the first stages of cancer. A doctor ascribed his symptoms to eating too much spicy food during his journey to Armenia in November and December 1961. Lipkin also remembers Grossman telling him in late 1962 that there was blood in his urine; he seems to have failed to act on a doctor's advice to visit a urologist. In May 1963 Grossman underwent an operation to remove one of his kidneys—the initial site of his cancer.

Late on September 14, 1964, after a period of several months in the hospital, Grossman died of lung cancer.

For all Grossman's trials, the three and a half years from the "arrest" of *Life and Fate* to his death constitute a remarkably creative period. As well as *Good Wishes*—a vivid account of his two months in Armenia—he wrote the finest of his short stories and around half of *Everything Flows*, including the trial of the four Judases, the account of the Terror Famine, and the chapters about Lenin, Russian history, and the Russian soul that arguably constitute the greatest passage of historico-political writing in the Russian language. This degree of creativity casts doubt on the widely held view that Grossman was severely depressed throughout his last years. Grossman himself wrote to his wife in October 1963, "I'm in good spirits, and I'm working eagerly. This greatly surprises me—where do these good spirits come from? I feel I should have thrown up my hands in despair long ago, but they keep stupidly reaching out for more work."

If *Life and Fate* has something in common with a Shostakovich symphony, *Everything Flows*, *Good Wishes*, and the stories he wrote during his last three years are more like Shostakovich's quartets. Stylistically, structurally, and even philosophically, these works are more daring than *Life and Fate*. Their qualities show up especially clearly if we compare them with two stories from the mid-1950s. "Abel" (1953) is about the crew of the plane that dropped the first atom bomb on Hiroshima; "Tiergarten" (1955) is about a misanthropic Berlin zookeeper during the last days of the war. Important as these stories are in the development of Grossman's political and philosophical thought, both are somewhat labored. A little like the caged animals he describes in "Tiergarten," Grossman repeatedly goes over the same ground, asserting the value of freedom but failing to attain it himself. In his last works, however, Grossman succeeds—as in the second part of "The Sistine Madonna"—in reconciling moral, artistic, and even factual truth. These last works not only extol freedom; they also embody freedom. The subject matter is mostly dark, but the liveliness of Grossman's intelligence makes these works surprisingly heartening.

The first story in this section is "The Elk," which was probably written in 1954 or 1955. In February 1958 Grossman wrote in a letter, "I visited the Petropavlovsk Fortress, I went into the room where Andrey Zhelyabov was confined before his execution. I want to write about him." Zhelyabov was an important figure in the terrorist organization known as The People's Will, and he was executed, in 1881, for his role in the assassination of Tsar Alexander II. Grossman never, in fact, wrote a story in which Zhelyabov plays a central role, but he is an important background presence in "The Elk." Aleksandra Andreyevna, the story's heroine, is obsessed with The People's Will. As an archivist, she studies the various revolutionary organizations of the period, and a picture of Zhelyabov hangs on the wall of the room she shares with her husband. Grossman has even given her a name that brings together the first names of the assassinated tsar and the executed terrorist.

"The Elk" can be read in many ways. It is a truthful evocation of the misery of a terminal illness. It contains an implicit criticism of man's violence against animals—a repeated theme in Grossman's work. And it hints at ways in which violence repeats itself in complex cycles. Just as Zhelyabov helps to assassinate the tsar and is then executed himself, so Dmitry Petrovich watches the cow elk through his rifle sights only to be watched over by the cow elk's glass eyes, many years later, as he himself lies dying. It is also possible that Aleksandra Andreyevna's obsession with The People's Will is about to lead to her own execution; the early Bolsheviks venerated the terrorist revolutionaries of the 1870s, but by the mid-1930s these terrorists had again become suspect figures. Afraid that The People's Will might inspire a new generation of terrorists, and perhaps even alarmed by its mere name, Stalin gradually closed down the journals and museums associated with it and removed all mention of the organization and its members from public places. The renaming of a Volga steamboat—previously the *Sofya Perovskaya* (after a famous revolutionary), the boat is renamed the *Valeriya Barsova* (after a famous singer)—is just one instance of this second silencing of The People's Will. It is characteristic of Aleksandra Andreyevna to complain about the steamboat's new name—and it is significant that a younger colleague, who may well be working for the NKVD, publicly criticizes Aleksandra Andreyevna for her excessive interest in the 1870s. At the end of the story Aleksandra Andreyevna fails to return home when expected. Neither her husband nor the reader ever learn what has happened to her.

———

"Mama"—the next story in this section—is also set in the 1930s. It is based on the true story of an orphaned girl who was adopted by Nikolay Yezhov and his wife, Yevgenia; Yezhov was the head of the NKVD between 1936 and 1938, at the height of the Great Terror. The orphaned girl, Natalya Khayutina, is still alive as we complete this introduction, and during the last twenty years she has given a number of interviews to journalists. Her story is of interest in its own right, independently of Grossman's treatment of it, and is discussed in an appendix. Her own account of her first twenty years, however, diverges little from Grossman's. As with his articles and stories about the war and the Shoah, Grossman seems to have done all he could to ascertain the historical truth, employing his imaginative powers not to create an alternative reality but to enter more deeply into the historical reality.

All the most prominent Soviet politicians of the time, including Stalin, used to visit the Yezhov household—as did many important artists, musicians, filmmakers, and writers, including Isaak Babel. We see these figures, however, only through the eyes of Nadya, as Grossman calls the orphaned girl, or of her good-natured peasant nanny. Grossman leads us into the darkest of worlds, but with compassion and from a perspective of peculiar innocence—the nanny is described as the only person in the apartment "with calm eyes." Grossman's evocation of Babel's ambivalence, his uncertainty as to what world he belongs to, is especially moving. For the main part, Nadya has no difficulty in distinguishing between the politicians who visit her father and the artists who visit her mother. Babel, however, confuses her; on the face of it, he has come to see her mother, but he looks more like her father's guests and Nadya perhaps senses that it is indeed her father who interests Babel more deeply.

Grossman wrote this story nearly twenty-five years after Babel had been shot. Grossman admired Babel, and he would probably have considered it wrong to make any public criticism of such a tragic figure. In conversation, however, Grossman was more forthright. Lipkin remembers telling Grossman how, in 1930, he had heard Babel say, "Believe me [...] I've now learned to watch calmly as people are shot." Lipkin quotes Grossman's response at length: "How I pity him, not because he died so young, not because they killed him, but because he—an intelligent, talented man, a lofty soul—pronounced those insane words. What had happened to his soul? Why did he celebrate the New Year with the Yezhovs? Why do such unusual people—him, Mayakovsky, your friend Bagritsky—feel so drawn to the OGPU? What is it—the lure of strength, of power? [...] This is something we really need to think about. It's no laughing matter, it's a terrible phenomenon." There are no such criticisms in "Mama," but Grossman delicately hints at Babel's extreme curiosity in a sentence he deleted from one of his drafts: "[Marfa Domityevna's] calm, just and straightforward mind noticed many things that the perceptive and sensitive Isaak Babel, who she thought was the kindest of Nikolay Ivanovich's guests, would have been avid to know."

In his earlier "In the Town of Berdichev" Grossman implicitly criticizes Babel; in "Mama" he evokes him with respect and affection. Nevertheless, the two stories have much in common. In "Mama," as in the earlier story, Grossman juxtaposes the world of male violence with the world of motherhood. Korotkova has written with great sensitivity about this aspect of "Mama": "There are so many mothers in the story that one begins to feel that, if one were to look more closely, one would find more, maybe even in the orphanage. The theme of 'Mother' washes through the whole story—sweet faces, kind eyes, seagulls, and the splash of waves that might be from a film or might be from the unknown depths known as the subconscious. It is very strange. A terrifying, hopeless story about loneliness, about talent that is crushed and people who are destroyed, gives off not only a breath of deathly cold but also the warming breath of motherly love."

Several of Grossman's last stories can be read as a response to the work of Andrey Platonov, the one writer among his contemporaries whom Grossman admired wholeheartedly.

Platonov was six years older than Grossman, but Grossman was the more established figure and there was at least one occasion when he succeeded in being of real help to Platonov; in 1942 he asked David Ortenberg, the chief editor of *Red Star*, to take Platonov under his protection, saying that "this good writer" was "defenseless" and "without any settled position." Ortenberg duly took Platonov on as a war correspondent. Later Grossman invited Platonov to collaborate on *The Black Book*; at some point in 1945 Platonov was given responsibility for all the material relating to the Minsk ghetto. During Platonov's final illness, Grossman visited him almost daily, and he gave one of the main speeches at Platonov's funeral. In a 1960 radio broadcast based on this speech, Grossman described Platonov as "a writer who wanted to understand the most complicated—which really means the most simple—foundations of human existence." Lipkin refers to this broadcast as "the first sensible and worthwhile word said in Russia about Platonov."

Platonov and Grossman are in many respects very different. Platonov's prose often moves close to poetry whereas Grossman's is perhaps as close to journalism as great prose can be while remaining great prose. Nevertheless, the two writers evidently found much in common. Ortenberg writes in his wartime memoirs, "Grossman, like his friend Andrey Platonov, was not a talkative person. The two of them sometimes came to *Red Star*, settled on one of the sofas [...] and stayed there for an entire hour without saying a word. They seemed, without words, to be carrying on a conversation known only to them." Lipkin, for his part, describes Platonov as "more independent in his judgments" and Grossman as a "more traditional" writer. He goes on to relate how he used to sit with Platonov and Grossman on the street opposite Platonov's apartment. The three of them would take turns making up stories about passersby. Grossman's were detailed and realistic; Platonov's were "plotless," more focused on the person's inner life, which was "both unusual and simple, like the life of a plant."

Still more interesting, however, is the extent to which Grossman, throughout the period from Platonov's death in 1951 to his own death in 1964, seems to have absorbed something of Platonov's idiosyncratic style and vision—almost as if he were trying to keep Platonov's spirit alive. "The Dog" is about a mongrel by the name of Pestrushka—the first living creature to survive a journey in space. With her capacity for devotion, her past life as a homeless wanderer, and her quick understanding of technology, Pestrushka has much in common with Platonov's peasant heroes. In another story, "The Road," Grossman seems more Platonov-like than Platonov himself. Platonov often shows us uneducated people grappling with difficult philosophical questions; Grossman presents us with a mule who not only resolves Hamlet's dilemma about whether to be or not to be but even arrives at the concept of infinity.

Like Platonov, Grossman moves freely between abstract ideas and an intense physicality. The account at the end of "In Kislovodsk" of a husband kissing his wife's underwear and slippers is reminiscent of a passage from Platonov's *Happy Moscow*: "She gave him her shoes to carry. Without her noticing, he sniffed them and even touched them with his tongue; now neither Moscow Chestnova herself, nor anything about her, however dirty, could have made Sartorius feel in the least squeamish, and he could have looked at the waste products of her body with the greatest of interest, since they too had not long ago formed part of a splendid person." More Platonov-like still is the moment in "Tiergarten" when a misanthropic zookeeper kisses his beloved gorilla on the lips.

Grossman and Platonov share an admiration for simple, unintellectual working people. Lipkin has suggested that in Grossman's case this sprang from the populist beliefs he had imbibed from his parents, whereas in Platonov's case it was simply part of a pantheistic reverence for life in all its manifestations. By the end of Grossman's career, however, this distinction has ceased to operate; his last stories are imbued with a pantheistic reverence very similar to Platonov's.

Like "The Dog," "Living Space" (written in 1960) is a response to an important historical event—in this case, the release of hundreds of thousands of prisoners from the Gulag between 1953 and 1956. In 1956, on the anniversary of Stalin's death, the poet Anna Akhmatova had said, "Now those who have been arrested will return, and two Russias will look each other in the eye—the Russia that sent people to the camps, and the Russia that was sent to the camps." Grossman's elderly heroine, however, returns to Moscow after nineteen years in the camps to meet with nothing more—nor less—than indifference. Soon after moving into a communal apartment with what the other tenants see as absurdly few belongings, she dies. Little is known about her except that she had once been someone important, and she is soon forgotten. One Sunday morning the tenants are playing cards when the postman brings a letter addressed to the old woman. Only one person, a teenage girl, even recognizes her name. It is an important official letter: the woman's late husband, who died in prison in 1938, has been rehabilitated "due to the absence of a body of evidence." At firsts no one knows what to do with this letter, but eventually the tenants agree that it should be handed in to the house management committee.

The story ends with a chilling—and sadly untranslatable—play on words. One of the cardplayers asks, "*Komu sdavat'*?" This can be understood both as "Whose deal?" and as "Who should hand in the document?" The reply, "*Kto ostalsya, tomu i sdavat',*" can be understood either as "Whoever lost/ended up as 'fool' in the last round should deal" or as "Whoever is left alive should hand in the document to the house management committee." Anatoly Bocharov has interpreted this dense bundle of disparate meanings as an expression of concern on Grossman's part that "those who remain alive should not allow themselves to be fooled."

The three last stories in this collection, "The Road," "The Dog," and "In Kislovodsk," all contain pointed repetitions of the phrase "life and fate." The words are like markers—or like tolling bells, telling the reader how much the loss of his novel dominates Grossman's thoughts.

"The Road" (1961–62) can be read as a distillation of *Life and Fate*, a re-creation of it in miniature. It may even represent an attempt on Grossman's part to compensate for the novel's "arrest," to get the better of the despair this had occasioned him. Not even in *Life and Fate* itself does he so powerfully evoke the relentlessness of the long winter campaign that culminated in the Battle of Stalingrad. The evocations of the horror of war and the miracle of love appear all the more universal because of the unexpected point of view from which the story is told—that of a mule from an Italian artillery regiment.

"In Kislovodsk"—the last story Grossman wrote—is also set during the first year of the war. Nikolay Viktorovich, a highly placed Soviet doctor with a perhaps excessive love of comfort and beauty, is not an evil man, nor is he entirely selfish—but he has always been too ready to make compromises. The story ends on a note of redemption. Asked by the Nazis to facilitate the murder of the wounded Soviet soldiers who are his patients, Nikolay commits suicide. His wife joins him. In their last hours the usually impeccably tasteful husband and wife allow themselves to behave "vulgarly," to dance to "vulgar" music, to kiss goodbye to their beloved porcelain and to kiss goodbye to each other as if they were young lovers.

An important source for this story is "The Germans in Kislovodsk," an article in *The Black Book* based on the recollections of an elderly Jew, Moisey Samuilovich Yevenson, who, protected by his Russian wife, survived the German occupation. His recollections were prepared for *The Black Book* by the scholar and literary theorist Viktor Shklovsky. The article includes a brief mention of two Jewish doctors who commit suicide along with their wives—although they, unlike Nikolay Viktorovich, do this simply because they know they are about to be shot anyway. It is interesting that Grossman chose to return, during the last year of his life, to material from *The Black Book*, but it is no less interesting that he chose to excise from his story any reference to Jews and the Shoah. This casts at least some degree of doubt on the view held by Lipkin and John and Carol Garrard that Grossman, during his last years, was obsessed with questions of Jewish suffering and Jewish identity.

In response to the Nazis' demands, Nikolay Viktorovich shows a moral strength he has never shown before. By most people's standards, Grossman himself showed great moral strength throughout his life—but his own standards were severe and there is no doubt that he criticized himself for the various compromises he had made over the decades. Until the "arrest" of *Life and Fate* Grossman had tried to work within the system; only during his last three years did he cease to make compromises. This new intransigence cost him a great deal. In December 1962, for example, he chose not to publish *Good Wishes* in *Novy mir* rather than agree to the omission of a single short paragraph about the Shoah and Russian anti-Semitism. Lipkin, thinking that a new publication would greatly help Grossman, both financially and with regard to his public standing, pleaded with him to yield, but to no avail. Grossman seems to have thought it better to become a nonperson than to betray himself, his people, and his mother's memory.

The intensity of Grossman's determination to behave honorably, and his awareness of how hard it is to not to yield to pressure, are well illustrated by a passage from a memoir by Anna Berzer, the editor from *Novy mir* responsible for publishing several of his stories in the early 1960s. Berzer was one of Grossman's most regular visitors during his last months in the hospital, and one of only four people to whom he showed *Everything Flows.* She relates how, on one occasion, Grossman awoke from sleep in her presence. Still half in the world of dreams, he said, "They took me off for interrogation during the night. I didn't betray anyone, did I?"

THE ELK

As she was leaving for work, Aleksandra Andreyevna would spread a napkin on a chair. On it she would put a glass of milk, along with a white rusk on a saucer. Then she would kiss Dmitry Petrovich on his warm, hollow temple.

On her way back in the evening, she would imagine how lonely the sick man must be feeling. On seeing her, he would prop himself up on one elbow, and his empty eyes would come to life.

One evening he said, "You must see so many people at work and in the metro, while all I ever see is this moth-eaten head." And he pointed a pale finger at a brown elk head hanging on the wall.

Aleksandra Andreyevna's colleagues felt sorry for her. They knew that her husband was seriously ill and that he needed a lot of care, even during the night.

"You, Aleksandra Andreyevna," they would say, "are a true martyr."

"What do you mean? It's really not difficult at all. Far from it."

But a twenty-hour day, at home and at her workplace, was too great a burden for an aging woman who was in poor health herself. After night after night of too little sleep, she was suffering not only from headaches but also from high blood pressure.

Aleksandra Andreyevna said nothing about her poor health to her husband. Sometimes, though, she would come to a sudden standstill as she was walking about the room. As if trying to remember something, she would put her hand over her eyes and the lower part of her forehead.

"You need a rest, Shura," he would say. "Be kind to yourself."

But words like this upset her, and even angered her.

She was on the staff of the archives of the Central Library. When she got to work, she would forget about the difficulties of the night. Fair-haired Zoya, who had been sent there immediately after graduating from her institute, would say, "Sit down now. Take the weight off your poor swollen legs!"

"They're not so bad," Aleksandra Andreyevna would answer with a smile.

Back at home she would tell her husband about the manuscripts and documents she was analyzing at work. She loved the 1870s and 1880s. To her there was something deeply precious about every least trifle to do with the Populists of that era—every least trifle concerning not only the more famous figures such as Osinsky, Kovalsky, Khalturin, Zhelvakov, Zhelyabov, Perovskaya, and Kibal'chich but also dozens of other forgotten revolutionaries in the inner circles or on the outer fringes of the various revolutionary organizations of the time: the Chaikovtsy, the Ishutin circle, the Black Repartition, and The People's Will.

Dmitry Petrovich did not share his wife's enthusiasm, which he put down to her coming from a revolutionary family. Her family photograph album was full of pictures of long-haired students with rugs thrown over their shoulders, of young women with short hair and severe faces, in dresses with narrow waists, long sleeves, and high black collars. Aleksandra Andreyevna remembered all their names. She—and she alone—remembered their sad and noble fates: this man had died, in exile, from tuberculosis; this woman had drowned herself in the Yenisey; another woman had perished while working in the province of Samara during a cholera epidemic; a third woman had lost her mind and died in a prison hospital.

To Dmitry Petrovich, an engineer and turbine specialist, all this seemed very noble and exalted but not exactly necessary. He was quite unable to remember the hyphenated surnames of so many of the populists. He was equally confused by the large number of them who shared the same surname; there were, for example, no less than three Mikhailovs: Adrian, Aleksandr, and Timofey. He also confused Sinegub of the Chaikovets with Lizogub of The People's Will.

Nor could Dmitry Petrovich understand why his wife had once got so upset during a summer cruise down the Volga. After passing through Vasilsursk they had seen a steamer that had once been called the *Sofya Perovskaya* and that, after a refit and a new coat of paint, had been renamed the *Valeriya Barsova*. Valeriya Barsova, after all, was a truly splendid singer.

On another occasion, during a trip to Kiev, he had said to Aleksandra Andreyevna, "Look! There's a huge pharmacy over there—named after your Zhelyabov!"

In answer she had shouted angrily, "It's the main street, the Kreshchatik, that should be named after Zhelyabov, not just a pharmacy."

"Dear, darling Shura!" Dmitry Petrovich had replied. "You *do* get carried away."

He had no sympathy for the asceticism—the almost religious fanaticism—of the members of The People's Will.

Those men and women had passed on; new generations had forgotten them. What Dmitry Petrovich loved was beautiful things. He loved wine and opera; he had enjoyed hunting. Even when he was getting on in years, he still liked wearing a fashionable suit. He liked choosing the right tie; he liked tying the knot the correct way.

One might have imagined that Aleksandra Andreyevna, who was indifferent to clothes, would be irritated by her husband's tastes. In reality, however, there was nothing about him that she disliked. She liked all his weaknesses, all his whims. And so she talked freely to him, sharing all her thoughts about the era that captivated her, about the tragic struggle fought by the members of The People's Will.

Now too, as he lay sick in bed, she would tell him about the things that upset her.

"Do you know what happened today, Mitya? I was criticized at a meeting. Remember that enchanting young Zoya who's been sent to us? Well, she said I burden her with lots of unnecessary work to do with the 1870s and '80s."

Listening to his wife, seeing her cheeks flush with agitation, Dmitry Petrovich thought about how she was the only person in the world who was inseparably joined to him—through thought, feeling, and constant attention. No one else truly kept him in mind. Yes, everyone else, even their own daughter, merely recalled him— merely called him to mind now and then.

It was strange to think about the moments when Aleksandra Andreyevna got carried away by her work and stopped thinking about him. At such moments there was no one at all remembering him—not even the very finest of threads to link him to other people: people in other towns and cities, people in villages, people on trains...

He talked about this to Aleksandra Andreyevna, and she replied, "Your turbines, your methods for calculating the reliability of a blade—these things truly exist. As for Zhenya, she's devoted to you. She doesn't often write to you, but that's neither here nor there. And do you really think your friends have forgotten you? Life's hectic nowadays and they get very tired—but don't forget how caring your colleagues were when you first got ill."

"Yes, darling, I know," he replied, and gave an exhausted nod of the head.

But she too understood that not all of his complaints could be put down to the excessive anxiety of a sick man.

His friends were all getting older now and they did, of course, find it tiring having to travel to work on crowded buses and trolleys. And they had worries and obligations of their own; they had problems at work, and there were tasks to be done at the dacha during the summer. All the same, it was upsetting for him that his old friends seldom asked after him, and that, if they did occasionally pay him a visit, they came neither in order to make him feel better, nor because they truly enjoyed it, but to avoid being nagged by a guilty conscience.

At the start of his illness, his colleagues had brought him presents of sweets and flowers, but it had not been long before they gave up coming. The progress of his illness was of no interest to them, and he himself was no longer interested in the life of the institute.

Their daughter, Zhenya, had married and moved to Kuibyshev, on the banks of the Volga. She had used to send him detailed letters, but now she wrote only to her mother. In her last letter she had written as a postscript, "How's Papa? No change, I suppose."

Zhenya was upset with her mother. It was annoying enough that her mother should devote all her time to people whom no one needed any longer. And now she was wasting her time on a sick man who was every bit as forgotten and useless as those forlorn figures from the 1870s and '80s.

Why was it that Shura was so devoted to him? Maybe it was not simply from love but also from a sense of duty? After all, when she had been sent into exile in 1929, he, a man who adored Moscow, had left everything. He had left his friends, the work he loved, their comfortable room in the center of town—and had gone to spend three years with her in Kazakhstan, living in a little wooden house in Semipalatinsk and working in a small brick factory.

Shura was always saying things like, "Your turbines, your calculation methods—they're still alive." But there had never been any turbines of his design—that was just Shura getting carried away—and as for his methods for calculating turbine-blade reliability, they were no longer in use, they had been replaced by newer methods.

No one could go on and on being one of the ill; one was expected either to get better again or else to join the ranks of the dead. When his colleagues gave him sweets, what they had really been saying was "We're helping you to overcome this illness of yours!" And when his childhood friend Afanasy Mikhailovich—Afonka—had talked about hunting trips, what he had really been saying was "It won't be long, Mitya—soon you and I will be out there again, making our way through bogs and forests!" During the first two weeks of his illness Zhenya too had believed that her father would recover, that he would join her in the summer on the banks of the Volga, that he would help to look after his grandson, and that with his advice—

and his many important contacts—he would be able to help her husband in his work as an engineer. She had believed that he would continue to play many different roles in her life. But time had passed, and Dmitry Petrovich's life remained very different indeed from the lives of healthy people: he did not work, he did not pay court to pretty colleagues, he did not join in arguments at meetings. He did not receive his pay, nor did he receive encouragements or rebukes from his superiors. Nor did he dance at birthday parties, get caught in the rain, or go for a quick glass of beer after work.

Dmitry Petrovich's present concerns were very different: Would the medicine from the pharmacy come as a powder or in capsules? Would the nurse who came to give him his injection be the friendly nurse with the light, delicate touch, or would it be the sullen, slovenly nurse with the blunt needle and cold, heavy hands? What would his next cardiogram show? And these concerns were of no interest to his friends and colleagues.

The day came when all of them—daughter, friends, and colleagues alike—ceased to believe in Dmitry Petrovich's recovery and therefore ceased to be interested in Dmitry Petrovich. If a man cannot get better, he must die. It is cruel. As far as the people around someone terminally ill are concerned, the only thing that can give meaning to his or her existence is death. Death is of interest to healthy people, but the life of someone terminally ill holds no interest for anyone. The interests of the terminally ill can never coincide with the interests of those who are healthy.

His life could no longer lead to actions or events of any kind—neither at work, nor among his fellow hunters, nor among the friends who were used to drinking and arguing with him, nor in the life of his own daughter. His death, on the other hand, could bring about a number of events and changes and even emotional conflicts. This is why news of someone who is terminally ill feeling better is always less interesting than the news that they have taken a turn for the worse.

Dmitry Petrovich's impending death was of interest to a broad circle of people: the other tenants of his communal apartment; the house manager; his daughter, who could not help thinking that her father's death might make it possible for her to return to Moscow; the receptionist at the district polyclinic; his fellow hunters, with their selfless curiosity about what would happen to his unique hunting rifle; and the woman who came every two weeks to clean the communal toilet and bathroom.

His hopeless, terminal existence, on the other hand, was of interest to only one person: Aleksandra Andreyevna. He never had even the least difficulty reading the look on her face; he could see it shift between joy and anxiety depending on whether he said that he had been less short of breath and had suffered no pains in his chest or that he had had spasms that day and had had to take nitroglycerine. Even if he was terminally ill, she still needed him. More than that— it was utterly impossible for her to exist without him. He knew this. She was horrified by the thought of his death, and this horror of hers was his only lifeline, the single thread that still tied him to life.

It was a quiet Saturday evening—a time when the other people in the apartment were usually at their dachas.

Sundays were a joy to Dmitry Petrovich. On Sundays he saw his wife all day long; he could hear her voice and the soft sound of her slippers.

He half opened his eyes and sighed. Aleksandra Andreyevna should have been home by now. But then he remembered: on her way back she was going to go to the pharmacy and the food shop.

He tried to doze off. When he dozed, he was less acutely aware of the agonizing slowness of time—and by evening his need for his wife was overwhelming. It was with a power equal to the power of extreme hunger that he felt the need to hear the familiar sound of the key, and then the sound of his wife's voice, and to see in her eyes something that felt more necessary to him even than camphor: a living interest in a life that no one needed any longer.

"You know," he had said a few days before this, "when you come near, I feel as if my mother were there beside me, as if I'm just a little baby lying in my cradle."

"I've been missing you," Aleksandra Andreyevna had replied.

He opened his eyes. The room was dark, although there was a little light from the streetlamps, and his wife was asleep in the bed beside him. He remembered that she had come back from work and given him some tea, and that he had then gone to sleep.

For a few moments he lay there half asleep, with a dim and anxious awareness that it was very silent. And then he realized. He realized that the silence was coming from Aleksandra Andreyevna's bed.

He was seized with terror. He had been wrong. He had only imagined that his wife had come home, given him a cup of tea, and counted his drops of medicine into the glass. That had been yesterday—and the day before yesterday. It had been every day, but it had not been today.

He broke out into a sweat; his chest and his palms were damp. He had not—as he had previously thought—been the unhappiest being in the world. To be dying, warmed by the love of his wife, now seemed like happiness. But Shura was not there.

His fingers were slow to turn on the switch. Darkness was a defense; in darkness lay hope.

But he turned on the light. He saw the bed that Aleksandra Andreyevna had made up in the morning—and he saw that she was not there. She must have ... she must have died.

What lay behind his last panic? Was it grief for his wife? Was it that her thoughts, her breath, her every look were more precious to him than anything else in the world? Or did his burning despair stem from the fact that he was alone and helpless, and that the only person who loved him had perished?

He tried to climb out of bed. He knocked on the wall with his withered fists. He lay unconscious for a moment. Then he knocked again.

But the apartment was empty. The other tenants would not come back from their dachas until Sunday evening. The nurse from the district polyclinic would not be coming until Monday morning.

Sunday evening…Monday morning…There was an unimaginably long time to get through.

Where was Shura? Had she had a heart attack? Had she been knocked down by a car? Maybe she had breathed her last breath and her body was this moment being carried on a stretcher to the dissecting room.

Dmitry Petrovich no longer had any doubt about his wife's death. He had turned on the light and seen her empty bed—and at that moment he had, it seemed to him, ceased to be of interest to anyone on earth. Continuing to exist, he had become a matter of indifference to everyone.

Shura and the reverence she felt for the members of The People's Will…Some powerful force had drawn her to those young men and women, to their short path that had ended at the executioner's block. But as for him…No, it was not for the sake of her pitying heart, not for the sake of her conscience and purity of soul that she had loved her sick husband. She had simply loved him—she just had. And that was something he had always found impossible to understand.

Thoughts were arising out of the darkness and giving birth to a still greater darkness.

Shura…Shura…

If he had had the strength to get to the window, he would have thrown himself out, down into the street.

But he was not only drawn to death; he was also terrified of it.

Everything around him was keeping silent—the dry electric light, the napkin on the table, Zhelyabov's handsome, thoughtful face.

His heart was aching, burning, pierced by a hot, thick needle. Helpless before the terror of death—though death was something he himself was invoking—Dmitry Petrovich searched with trembling fingers for the pulse on his wrist.

And suddenly Dmitry Petrovich's eyes met someone else's slow, attentive eyes.

For many years now that head had been there on the wall, and he had long ago ceased to notice it.

When he had first brought the head back from the zoological museum taxidermist, it had seemed to fill the whole of space.

Hurrying off in the morning, standing in the doorway in his coat and hat, he had used to look around at the elk's head before leaving the room. He had used suddenly to remember it in the tram.

When people he knew called by, he would tell them how he had come to kill the animal. Aleksandra Andreyevna had found this cruel story utterly unbearable.

The years had gone by. Dust had covered the elk's head and Dmitry Petrovich's eyes had slid over it with ever-increasing indifference. And eventually this long, powerful head, with a thin mouth and a nose that still seemed to be breathing, had once and for all become separate from the half dark of the autumn forest, from the smell of moss and decaying leaves—and Dmitry Petrovich, now remembering the elk only when they were cleaning the apartment, would say, "We must sprinkle DDT on the elk's head. I think it's become a home for bedbugs."

And now, at this moment of terror, his eyes had again met the eyes of the cow elk.

———

He had emerged from the forest on a cold October morning, and he had caught sight of her straightaway. The village where Dmitry Petrovich was staying was very close indeed, and he had felt flustered—it was a startling encounter, in a spot where one would never expect to find a wild animal. From this spot on the margin of the forest, after all, one could see the plumes of smoke over the village huts.

He had been able to see her absolutely clearly. He had been able to make out her brown-black nose with its wide nostrils and her large, broad teeth—teeth accustomed to breaking off small branches and stripping the bark from them—beneath a long, slightly raised upper lip.

She had seen him too—in his leather jacket, Austrian boots, and green puttees, strong and thin, with a rifle in his hands. She was standing by a gray calf. The calf was lying down among the lingonberry bushes.

Dmitry Petrovich had begun to take aim, and for a second everything had disappeared. There was no granite sky, no red lingonberries—nothing but two eyes, turned toward him. The elk was looking at him. He was, after all, the sole witness of the disaster that had that morning befallen her.

And with a sense of strength and happiness, with a hunter's accurate premonition of a fine shot, taking care not to disturb the gossamer-fine thread linking him and his target, he pressed slowly and smoothly on the trigger.

Then, going up to the elk he had shot, Dmitry Petrovich realized what had happened. Her calf had damaged a front leg—it was caught in the split trunk of a fallen alder tree, and the calf was evidently terrified of being abandoned. Even after the shot, even after his mother had fallen to the ground, the calf had gone on trying to persuade her not to abandon him—and she had not abandoned him.

———

Dmitry Petrovich, now calmer, was lying close to the cow elk, just like the injured calf whose throat he had slit on that October morning. The cow elk was looking down intently at a man with a thin neck, a bald head, and a large forehead, his withered legs drawn up under the blanket.

Her glassy eyes were covered by a misty film of blue moisture. It seemed to Dmitry Petrovich that there were now tears in these maternal eyes and that from their corners there now ran dark little paths of matted fur—the very fur that had once been teased out by the taxidermist's tweezers.

He looked at his wife's bed, at his own withered fingers, and at Zhelyabov's stiff, sorrowful face. He gave a wheeze and fell silent.

Still gazing down from above, still turned toward him, were the kind and compassionate maternal eyes.

MAMA

I.

THERE had been a sense of agitation in the orphanage all morning. The director had quarreled with the doctor and shouted at the supply manager. The floors had to be polished, and new sheets and swaddling clothes had to be issued without delay to the ward for infants. The nurses had to put on starched gowns like doctors. Then the director had called the doctor and the senior sister to his office, and they had all set off together to inspect the children.

Soon after the infants' midday feeding, a stout middle-aged man in military uniform was driven up to the orphanage; he was accompanied by two young officers. The middle-aged man glanced casually at the senior members of staff who came out to meet him and walked through to the director's office. He sat down, caught his breath, and asked the doctor if she would allow him to smoke. She nodded and rushed off in search of an ashtray.

He smoked, flicked the ash into the little saucer the doctor had given him, and listened to stories about the orphanage babies—babies whose parents had been arrested as enemies of the people. He heard about babies who couldn't stop scratching, about babies who were always crying, and babies who were always sleeping, about baby gluttons and babies who showed no interest in their bottles at all—and about who preferred to adopt little boys and who preferred to adopt little girls. Meanwhile, the young officers, now also wearing doctors' gowns, were striding up and down the orphanage corridors, looking into duty rooms and storerooms. The gowns were too short and their blue twill cavalry trousers poked out underneath. The look in their eyes and their persistent questioning sent a chill through the nurses' hearts. And there was no end to their questions. "Where does this door lead?" they would ask. Or "Where's the key to the attic?"

Taking off their gowns, the young men entered the director's office. "Permission to report, comrade Commissar?" said one of them, addressing the stout middle-aged man.

The middle-aged NKVD officer—an army commissar, second grade—nodded.

A few minutes later the commissar flung a white gown over his shoulders and, accompanied by both the doctor and the director, made his way to the infants' ward.

"Here she is," said the director, pointing to a cot standing between two windows.

"Yes, yes, I'm entirely confident about this girl," said the doctor, quick and anxious, just as when she had been looking for an ashtray. "She's entirely normal, she's developing absolutely correctly. She's normal, correct and normal, normal in every respect."

Soon after this, the sisters and nurses were pressing their faces to the windows as they watched the stout NKVD commissar drive off in his car. The two young officers, however, stayed in the orphanage and began reading the newspapers.

And out on the little street—a side street beyond the Moscow River—that led to the orphanage, some other young men in winter coats and high boots began saying to the passersby, "Come on now, let's be clearing the sidewalk!" And the passersby hurriedly stepped down into the roadway.

At six o'clock, when the November dark had set in, a car pulled up outside the orphanage. Two figures—a woman and a very short man in a light autumn coat—walked up to the main entrance. The director himself opened the door to them.

The short man breathed in the slightly sour, milky smell, gave a little cough, and said to the woman, "It's probably best not to smoke in here." Then he rubbed his cold hands together.

The woman smiled apologetically and returned her cigarette to her handbag. She had a sweet face, with quite a large nose. She looked tired and a little pale.

The director led the visitors to the cot between the two windows, then stood back. It was quiet; the infants were all asleep after their evening feeding. The director gestured to the nurse to leave the room.

The woman and her companion, who was wearing a badly fitting jacket from the Moscow Tailoring Combine, looked into the face of the sleeping baby girl. Appearing to sense their gaze, the child smiled, with her eyes still closed, then frowned, as if remembering something sad.

Her five-month-old memory had been unable to hold on to the way cars had kept hooting in the fog or how her mother had held her in her arms on the platform of a London railway station while a woman in a hat said mournfully, "And now what are we going to do at the embassy? Who's going to sing for us when we have our staff family evenings?" And yet, without the girl knowing it, all these sounds and images—the railway station, the London fog, the splash of waves in the English Channel, the cry of gulls, the sleeping-car compartment, the faces of her mother and father bending down over her as the express approached Negoreloye Station—had managed to hide themselves away somewhere in her little head. And decades later, when she was a gray-haired old woman, certain images would, for no obvious reason, suddenly appear to her: autumn aspen trees, her mother's warm hands, slender rosy fingers with unmanicured nails, and two gray eyes gazing at the broad spaces of the Russian Motherland.

The little girl opened her eyes, clicked her tongue, and went back to sleep.

The short man, who seemed rather timid, looked at the woman. The woman wiped a tear away with her handkerchief and said, "Yes, yes, I've made up my mind. It's strange, it's quite extraordinary. Look—she's got your eyes."

Soon they were walking out of the main entrance. A nurse was walking behind them, carrying a baby girl wrapped in a blanket.

The short man sat down next to the driver and said in a quiet voice, "Back home!"

The woman clumsily took the little girl in her arms and said to the nurse, "Thank you, comrade!" Then she said sadly, "I'm not just afraid of holding her. I'm even afraid of looking at her. I keep thinking I'll do something wrong."

And within only a minute the huge black car had moved off, the junior officers reading newspapers had disappeared from the lobby, and the young men in winter coats and high boots keeping guard out on the street seemed to have vanished into thin air.

At the Spassky Gate there was a ringing of bells and a flashing of lights—and the black car, the huge black car of Nikolay Ivanovich Yezhov, general commissar for State Security and loyal comrade-in-arms to the great Stalin, sped like a whirlwind past the guards and into the Kremlin.

And in the little streets beyond the Moscow River everyone was talking about how this "closed" orphanage had been declared a quarantine zone. In this high-security orphanage there had been a sudden outbreak—so the rumor went—of either anthrax or plague.

2.

She lived in a bright and spacious room. If she had a stomachache or a sore throat, her nanny, Marfa Domityevna, would be joined by a special nurse from the Kremlin hospital. And a doctor would visit twice a day.

And once, when she caught a serious cold, an old doctor with warm, kind, trembling hands came to listen to her chest with his stethoscope. Two women doctors accompanied him.

She saw Mama every day, but Mama never stayed with her for long. When Nadya sat down to her breakfast porridge, Mama would say, "Eat, my little one, eat. Eat up your porridge—but I must be off to the office now."

In the evening Mama's friends would come around. Father's

guests came a little less often. Nanny—Nyanya—would put on a starched kerchief, and from the dining room would come the sound of voices and the clatter of forks. Father would slowly pronounce the words, "Well then, we should drink to that!"

Now and again one of Father's guests would come to have a look at little Nadya. Sometimes she would lie still in her cot and pretend she was asleep. Knowing that little Nadyusha was only pretending, Mama would laugh and say, "Shush!" The man would bend down over her and she would smell wine. Mama would say, "Sleep, my little girl, sleep!" Then she would kiss Nadya on the forehead and Nadya would once again smell wine, this time more faintly.

Marfa Domityevna was taller than all of Father's guests. Father himself looked tiny beside her. Everyone was afraid of her. The guests were afraid of her; Mama was afraid of her; and Father—more than anyone—was afraid of her. Father was so afraid of her that he tried to spend less time at home.

Nadya was not afraid of Nyanya. Sometimes Nyanya would pick her up in her arms and say in a singsong voice, "My darling, my poor unhappy little darling."

Even if Nadya had understood what these words meant, she would still have had no idea why Nyanya might think she was poor or unfortunate. After all, she had lots of toys; she lived in a sun-filled room; Mama sometimes took her out for a drive, and men in handsome red-and-blue caps leaped out of sentry booths to fling open the dacha gates as their car approached.

Nevertheless, Nyanya's quiet, caressing voice troubled the little girl's heart. She wanted to shed sweet, sweet tears; she wanted to hide away like a little mouse in the embrace of Nyanya's large arms.

She knew who were Mama's best friends and who were Father's most important guests. She knew that if Father's guests were visiting, there were never any of Mama's friends.

There was a redheaded woman; she was called "a friend from childhood." Mama used to sit with her beside Nadya's cot and say, "Madness, madness." There was a bald man in glasses, with a smile that used to make Nadya smile too, and Nadya did not know who he was—whether he was a friend or a guest. He looked like a guest, but it was Mama and her women friends whom he came to see. When he came in, Mama used to answer his smile with a smile of her own and say, "Babel's come to see us!"

Once Nadya put the palm of her little hand to his high, bald forehead. His forehead was warm and kind; touching it was like touching Mama or Nyanya on the cheek.

There were Father's guests. There was one who kept giving a little laugh; he had a guttural voice and a nose that was always trying to sniff something. There was a man who smelled of wine, with a loud voice and broad shoulders. There was a thin little man with dark eyes; he usually came early, with a briefcase, and left before they'd sat down to supper. There was a dark-skinned man with a potbelly and moist red lips; one evening he took Nadya in his arms and sang her a little song.

Once she saw a guest with a pink face and gray hair, in military uniform. He drank some wine, then sang. Once she saw a guest who appeared to make Mama feel timid; he had small glasses and a large forehead and he stuttered. Unlike the others, who wore military jackets of one kind or another, he wore an ordinary jacket and a tie. He told Nadya in an affectionate voice that he had a little daughter too.

Marfa Domityevna could not remember which was Beria and which was Betal Kalmykov, and she kept forgetting that the thin man with a briefcase was Malenkov. Kaganovich, Molotov, and Voroshilov, on the other hand, she recognized from the many pictures she had seen of them.

Nadya did not know any of the guests by name. But she knew the words: *Mama*, *Nyanya*, *Papa*.

One day there was a new guest. What made him seem special to Nadya was not the way everyone seemed so agitated while they were waiting for him to arrive. Nor was it the way Nyanya made the sign of the cross when Father himself went to open the front door to him; nor was it anything to do with his clever pockmarked face and his dark gray-streaked mustache and his soft fluid movements; nor was it that this guest walked more silently than any person could walk—anyone except the black cat with green eyes that lived at their dacha.

Everyone Nadya knew had the same look in their eyes. There was the same look in Mama's brown eyes, and in Father's gray-green eyes, and in the yellow eyes of the cook, and in the eyes of every one of Father's guests, and in the eyes of the guards who opened the dacha gates, and in the eyes of the old doctor.

But these new eyes, these new eyes that looked at Nadya for several seconds, slowly and without curiosity, were entirely calm. There was no madness in them, no anxiety or tension, nothing except slow calm.

In the home of Nikolay Yezhov there was no one with calm eyes except Marfa Domityevna.

Marfa Domityevna saw, and understood, a great deal.

No longer was the voice of jovial, broad-shouldered Betal Kalmykov to be heard in their home. The mistress of the house took to wandering about from room to room in the night. She stood over Nadya as she lay asleep, whispered, clinked vials of medicine in the dark, turned on all the chandeliers, and went back to Nadya again, still whispering and whispering—either praying or repeating lines of poetry to herself. In the morning Nikolay Ivanovich Yezhov would come home looking thin and pinched. He would take off his coat, light a cigarette while he was still in the hall, and say irritably, "I don't want anything to eat, and I don't want any tea." Once his wife asked him something, then gave a frightened cry—and never again did her childhood friend with the red hair come to see her, nor did the two women ever speak again on the telephone.

Once Nikolay Ivanovich went up to Nadya and smiled. She looked into his eyes and screamed.

"Is she ill?" he asked.

"Something frightened her," said Marfa Domityevna.

"What?"

"Lord knows—she's only a child."

When Marfa Domityevna and Nadya came back from their

walks, the guard now looked straight at the little girl, straight into her little face, and Marfa Domityevna would try to prevent her from seeing his stare, which was as sharp as the filthy, bloodstained talon of a bird of prey.

It is possible that Marfa Domityevna was the only person in the entire world who felt pity for Nikolay Ivanovich; even his wife now feared him. Marfa Domityevna noticed the fear she showed at the sound of his car—and when the pale, gray-faced Nikolay Ivanovich, along with two or three other pale, gray-faced men, came in and walked through to his study.

Marfa Domityevna, however, remembered calm, pockmarked comrade Stalin, master of all and everyone—and felt pity for Nikolay Ivanovich. She thought his eyes looked confused, pathetic, lost.

It was as if she did not know that the country lay frozen in horror, that Yezhov's gaze had frozen all of vast Russia.

Day and night the interrogations went on in the Lubyanka, in Lefortovo, and in the Butyrka. Day and night trains transported prisoners to Komi, to Kolyma, to Norilsk, to Magadan and the Bay of Nogayevo. Every dawn the bodies of those shot during the night in prison basements were taken away in trucks.

Did Marfa Domityevna realize that the fate of a young adviser at the Soviet embassy in London, that the fate of his pretty wife, arrested while she was still breast-feeding her little daughter, before she had even completed her singing course at the conservatory—did Marfa Domityevna realize that these fates had been determined by the signature, at the foot of a long column of names, of a former Petersburg factory worker by the name of Nikolay Ivanovich Yezhov? He was still signing list after list, dozens and dozens of these enormous lists of enemies of the people, and the black smoke was still pushing its way up from the crematoria of Moscow.

3.

One day, as the cook was lighting a cigarette, Marfa Domityevna heard her muttering behind their mistress's back, "And that's the end of *your* days as tsaritsa!"

Evidently the cook knew something that the nanny did not.

What Marfa Domityevna would remember from these last days was the silence that entered the house. The telephone no longer rang. There were no guests. In the mornings, Nikolay Ivanovich did not summon his deputies, secretaries, assistants, adjutants, and messengers. His wife no longer went out to work; she lay on a sofa in her dressing gown, yawning, thinking, reading a book, and sometimes smiling a little, walking from room to room in silent night-time slippers.

The only person to make a noise in their home was little Nadyusha. She cried, laughed, and clattered her toys about.

One morning an old woman visited the mistress of the house. Not a sound came from the room where the two women sat together; it was as if neither were saying a word. The cook walked up to the door and put her ear to the keyhole.

Then the two women went to see Nadya. The visitor's clothes were all patched and worn—and she seemed too frightened even to look around her, let alone to open her mouth.

"Marfa Domityevna," said the mistress of the house, "let me introduce you. This is my mama."

Three days after this, Nadya's mother told Marfa Domityevna that she was going to the Kremlin hospital for an operation. She spoke quickly, in a loud, somehow false voice. She said goodbye to little Nadyusha, looking at her distractedly and giving her a perfunctory kiss. Standing in the doorway, she glanced quickly toward the kitchen, put her arms around Marfa Domityevna, and whispered in her ear, "Remember—if anything happens to me, dearest Nyanya, you're the only family she has. She has no one else in the whole wide world."

As if she knew they were talking about her, the little girl sat quietly on her little chair, looking at them with her gray eyes.

Nikolay Ivanovich did not take his wife to the hospital himself. Instead, she was taken by one of his adjutants, a stout general carrying a bouquet of red roses. They were accompanied by Nikolay Ivanovich's personal bodyguard.

Not until the following morning did Nikolay Ivanovich come home. Without even looking in on Nadya, he sat in his study for a while, writing and smoking. Then he called for his car and left.

After this came a great number of events that shook, and eventually shattered, the life of the household, and in Marfa Domityevna's memory these events all got muddled together.

First, Nadyusha's mother, the wife of Nikolay Ivanovich, died in the hospital. She was not bad or unkind, and she cared about the little girl; nevertheless, she was a strange person. That day Nikolay Ivanovich came home very early. He asked Marfa Domityevna to bring Nadya to his study. Father and daughter gave some tea to her plastic piglet and put her little doll and the bear to bed. Then Nikolay Ivanovich paced about his study until morning.

And then came a day when this short man with gray-green eyes, Nikolay Ivanovich Yezhov, did not come home at all.

The cook sat on her late mistress's bed, then went to Nikolay Ivanovich's study and made a long telephone call, smoking her master's cigarettes.

Men came, some in uniform and some in plain clothes. They walked about in their coats, treading their dirty boots and galoshes all over the rugs and the bright-colored runner that led to the room of little orphaned Nadyusha.

That night Marfa Domityevna sat beside the little girl and did not take her eyes off her. She had decided to take Nadya back home with her and she kept thinking about how, after getting off the train at Yelets, they would find a cart going to her home village. Then her brother would come to greet them and Nadya would cry out in delight at the sight of the geese, the calf, and the cockerel.

"I'll see to it she gets enough food, I'll see she has proper lessons," thought Marfa Domityevna, and a sense of motherliness filled and brightened her virgin's soul.

The NKVD men were busy all night long, noisily searching the apartment, sending books, linen, and cutlery flying to the floor.

These new people had the same tense, crazed eyes that had by then begun to seem normal to Marfa Domityevna.

Only little Nadyusha, yawning sleepily as she got up for a wee, seemed quiet and peaceful. And Stalin looked down from the portrait in his usual calm way, without curiosity, keeping his slightly narrowed eyes focused on what had to be done, on what was indeed being done at that very moment.

In the morning a man with a red face arrived. He was stout, like a child's top, and the cook called him "Major." He went through to the nursery. Wearing a starched apron embroidered with a red cockerel, Nadya was slowly and seriously eating her oatmeal porridge. "Put some warm clothes on the girl," he ordered, "and pack her things."

Trying not to show her agitation, Marfa Domityevna asked slowly, "Why? Where is she going?"

"We're placing the child in an orphanage. And you must get ready to leave too. You will receive the rest of your pay, along with a train ticket, and you will return to your village."

"But where's my mama?" Nadya asked suddenly. She stopped eating and pushed away her little bowl with the blue border.

But no one answered her—neither Marfa Domityevna nor the major.

4.

Exemplary cleanliness was observed throughout the rooms, corridors, and toilets of the hostel for the State radio factory's female workers. The bed linen was starched, there were covers on all the pillows, and the windows were hung with lace curtains. The girls had clubbed together and bought them with their own money.

On top of many of the bedside lockers stood little vases with beautiful artificial flowers—roses, tulips, and poppies.

In the evenings the girls read books and newspapers in the Red Corner, sang in the choir or went to the dance group, or watched

films and amateur theatricals in the Palace of Culture. Some girls
went to evening classes in dressmaking or did courses to prepare
them for entrance to an institute of higher education; others were
studying in the evening faculty of the electromechanical school.

The girls seldom spent their annual leave in the town. The secretary of the factory Party committee rewarded outstanding workers
with a free holiday in one of the trade-union houses of recreation.
Other girls went back to their home villages and stayed with their
families.

It was said that some girls had been behaving too freely in the
houses of recreation, staying out late at night and failing to take due
care of their own well-being, and that the young men had been
gambling and getting drunk, and getting up to no good during the
rest hour after lunch.

Apparently some boys on holiday from the mechanical factory
had broken into a kiosk and made off with a crate of beer and six
bottles of vodka. They had downed all this in the music room and
used foul language when the head doctor hurried in to see what the
singing and shouting was about. The boys were expelled from the
house of recreation and the factory Party committee was informed
of their bad conduct. A criminal case was brought against the three
ringleaders and they were each sentenced to two months of forced
labor in the workplace.

Never did anything like this happen in the radio factory hostel.

Ulyana Petrovna, the hostel commandant, was known for her
strictness. There was one occasion when a girl brought a boy into
her room and, with the agreement of her roommates, let him stay
the night.

Ulyana Petrovna hauled the girl over the coals in public and had
her thrown out of the hostel the following day.

But Ulyana Petrovna was not only strict; she could also show
kindness. The girls turned to her for advice as if she were a close
relative. They knew they could trust her; it was not for nothing that
she had been chosen several times as a deputy to the district soviet.
With her in charge of the hostel, there was no drunkenness, no

debauchery, no late-night singing to the accompaniment of an accordion.

After the rough, harsh ways of the orphanage, radio-fitter Nadya Yezhova was very happy to be living in this exemplary hostel.

Her years in orphanages had been the hardest years of her life. The worst time of all had been during the war, in an orphanage in Penza; even the other children, who had not led the spoiled life that she had led, found it hard to swallow down the soup made from rotten maize flour that was served day after day for both lunch and supper. They were only seldom issued with clean clothes or bed linen—there was not enough of either, and there was too little soap and too little firewood to do laundering at all regularly. The town soviet had ruled that the orphanage children were to wash twice a month in one of the bathhouses, but this ruling was not observed. The two main bathhouses were usually occupied by soldiers from reserve units and there were silent, surly lines outside the old, small bathhouse beyond the railway station from dawn until late in the evening. And no one, in any case, much liked washing in this bathhouse; chilly winds blew through cracks in the walls, the damp firewood gave off more smoke than heat, and the water was barely warm.

In Penza Nadya had felt cold almost all the time—in the dormitory at night and in the classroom, where they had lessons and where they made shirts for soldiers. She even felt cold in the kitchen, where she sometimes helped the cook remove worms from the maize flour. And the harshness of the staff, the malice and spite of the other children, and the constant thieving that went on in the dormitories were as unbearable as the cold and hunger. A moment's inattention—and anything from bread rations to pencils, underpants, or kerchiefs would vanish into thin air. One girl was sent a parcel; she locked it up in her little bedside cupboard and went off to her lessons. When she returned, the lock looked the same as ever, but her parcel was gone.

Some of the boys went to food shops and bus stops and picked people's pockets. One of these boys, Zhenya Pankratov, even took part in an armed attack on a cash collector.

Life in the orphanage did, of course, improve after the war. Nevertheless, when Nadya finished her seven years of compulsory schooling and was sent to work in a factory, she felt she had arrived in paradise.

Nadya now found it hard to believe that she could have cried all night long after hearing that the orphanage authorities were going to send her to this factory. It was because of her singing teacher that she had got so upset. Her singing teacher had said to her several times, "With a voice like yours you should go to the conservatory—you could be a concert singer!" At first the authorities truly had intended to send Nadya to a music college, but then some kind of additional clarification had unexpectedly arrived from Moscow—and Nadya had been sent to the radio factory.

She had wept during her last night at the orphanage. No one, she had thought, could be more unhappy than her. Not once had she lived in a Moscow or Leningrad orphanage; she had always been sent to the most out-of-the-way places. Many of the girls received letters and parcels from relatives. But in all her life Nadya had never received a single letter; nor had anyone, even just once, sent her apples or shortbread.

All this had made her grow silent and sullen, and the other children had teased her and said she was mute.

Now, in this exemplary hostel, she began to understand that she was not so unfortunate as she had thought.

She had a good job. It was clean, relatively light work, and it was well paid; and the Komsomol committee had promised to send her on a course to improve her qualifications. She had a good winter coat and several beautiful dresses. She even had a crepe satin dress that had been specially made for her in the fashion atelier; Ulyana Petrovna had signed the authorization form herself. The girls on the shop floor and in the hostel respected her, seeing her as steady and self-reliant. Along with other girls from the hostel she went to the cinema and to dance nights at the club. There was a boy called Misha whom she liked; she was always glad when he asked her to dance. He was as quiet as she was; when he escorted her back to the hostel, they usually walked all the way in silence. He lived some way off, on the far side of the goods station, and he worked as a goods-wagon mechanic in the depot.

And her life of long ago was now something she could barely remember. The gleaming black car, the luxuriant flower beds at the dacha, her walks through the Kremlin with Nyanya, Mama's affectionate absentminded face, the voices and laughter of Father's guests—it was as if all these things, rather than having a place in her memory in their own right, were only recollections of some other, more distant recollection. It was as if they were echoes that had been repeated many times and were now dying away in the mist.

This current year was going especially well for Nadya Yezhova. She had been accepted as an evening student in the electromechanical school, and she had been given a prize of six weeks' pay for over-fulfilling the work plan. Misha's boss at the depot had promised him a room in a new building being constructed by the Ministry of Transport and Communications, and Nadya and Misha had decided to marry. Nadya dearly wanted to have a child and she was happy that she was going to be a mother.

Once, a few days before she was due to go to the house of recreation for her holiday, Nadya had a dream. Some woman—not Mama, someone quite different—was holding in her arms a little child who might have been Nadya but who might not have been Nadya. The woman was trying to protect the child from the wind. There was a lot of noise round about. Waves were splashing; the sun was sparkling on the water, then fading away behind quick, low clouds. White birds were flying in different directions and crying out in piercing, catlike voices.

All day long, on the shop floor, in the workers' canteen, and when she was in the factory Party committee office, filling in forms for the house of recreation, Nadya kept seeing this woman's sweet, sad face as she hugged her little child. Then Nadya realized why she had had this dream.

Once the director of the Penza orphanage had taken the children to see a film about a young mother traveling somewhere by sea. And this half-forgotten image had come back to her in a dream, at a time when she was full of thoughts about her future motherhood.

LIVING SPACE

ANNA BORISOVNA Lomova, an old woman, had been allocated a room by the Dzerzhinsky district soviet; when she moved in, her complete lack of furniture, pots, pans, dishes, clothes, and even bedding was a source of amusement to the other tenants of the communal apartment. She did not live in her room for long. A week after being granted her living space, as she was walking down the corridor, she gave a sudden cry and fell to the floor.

One of the other women phoned for help. A doctor came. She gave the old woman an injection, said that everything would be all right, and went on her way. But in the evening Anna Borisovna began to feel a great deal worse. After a brief discussion, the other tenants phoned for an ambulance. The ambulance from the Sklifosovsky Institute came very quickly, only six minutes after being called, but the old woman had already died. The doctor checked the pupils of the newly deceased, gave a sigh for the sake of decency, and left.

During the few days that Anna Borisovna had spent in this room of hers in the southwest of Moscow, the other tenants had managed to find out a little about her. As a young woman, she had evidently taken part in the Civil War; it seemed she had been the commissar of an armored train. Then she had lived in Persia, in Tehran. And then she had done some very important job in Moscow; she might even have worked in the Kremlin. In a conversation with Svetlana Kolotyrkina, a young girl, about how Soviet literature was being taught in schools, she had said, "I was once a friend of Furmanov and Mayakovsky." And she had told Svetlana's mother, who had worked as a technical inspector at a midget-car factory, that she had been arrested in 1936 and spent nineteen years in prisons and camps. Not long ago the Supreme Court had reviewed her case, rehabilitated her, and acknowledged her to be entirely innocent. And so she had been granted a Moscow residence permit and living space.

During her long years in the Gulag, after being transferred so many times from camp to camp, she had evidently lost contact with all her friends and family. And she had not yet had time to get to know anyone in Moscow. Nobody attended her cremation. Right after her death her room was given to a trolley-car driver by the name of Zhuchkov, an extremely irritable man with a wife and child.

The other tenants were all astonishingly quick to forget that, for a few days, a rehabilitated old woman had shared their apartment.

One Sunday morning, when they were all playing cards after breakfast, the postwoman came in with the mail: the newspapers *Moscow Pravda*, *Soviet Russia*, and *Lenin's Path*; the magazines *Soviet Woman* and *Health*; the television and radio programs; and a letter addressed to Anna Borisovna Lomova.

"We don't have anyone here with that name," declared a number of male and female voices. And Zhuchkov the trolley-car driver, ushering the postwoman toward the door, said, "No, there's no one here with that name—and there never has been."

At this point Svetlana Kolotyrkina suddenly said, "How can you say such a thing? You're living in Anna Borisovna's room!"

And all at once everyone remembered Anna Borisovna Lomova and felt astonished how quickly they had forgotten her.

After a little discussion, the envelope was opened and the typewritten letter was read out loud:

"In view of circumstances that have recently come to light, in accordance with the ruling made on May 8, 1960, by the Military Board of the Supreme Court of the USSR, your husband, Terenty Georgievich Ardashelia, who died in confinement on July 6, 1938, has been posthumously rehabilitated. The sentence pronounced by the Military Board of the Supreme Court on September 3, 1937, has been overturned, and the case has been closed due to the absence of a body of evidence."

"So what do we do with this letter now?"

"Send it back. What else can we do with it?"

"I think it's our duty to hand it in to the house management committee, given that the woman was fully registered at this address."

"You're right. But it's Sunday. There won't be anyone there."

"Anyway, what's the great hurry?"

"*I* can take it. I can hand it in when I go to see about the broken taps."

For a little while, everyone was silent, and then a male voice said, "Why are we all just sitting here? Whose deal is it?"

"Whose do you think? Whoever lost the last round."

THE ROAD

No living being in Italy remained untouched by the war.

Giu, a young mule who worked in the munitions train of an artillery regiment, sensed many changes on June 22, 1941, even though he did not, of course, know that the Führer had persuaded Il Duce to declare war on the Soviet Union.

People would have been astonished how many things the mule noticed that day: music everywhere, the radio blaring away without a break, the stable doors left wide open, crowds of women and children by the barracks, flags fluttering above the barracks, the smell of wine coming from people who did not usually smell of wine, the trembling hands of his driver, Niccolo, when he came to Giu's stall, led him outside, and put on his breastband . . .

Niccolo did not like Giu; he always put him on the left, to make it easier to whip him with his right hand. And he whipped him not on his thick-skinned hindquarters but on the belly. And he had a heavy hand. It was dark brown, with twisted fingernails—the hand of a peasant.

Giu had no particular feelings about his workmate. This other mule was big and strong, morose and hardworking; the hair had been worn off his breast and flanks by the breastband and traces, and the gray, greasy patches of exposed hide had a metallic gleam to them.

There was a cloudy blue film over this other mule's eyes; his teeth were yellow and worn down, and there was the same look of sleepy indifference on his face whether they were going uphill over asphalt softened by the sun or resting at midday under some trees. Nothing

mattered to him. Even when he was standing at the top of a mountain pass, looking down at orchards, vineyards, and the winding
gray ribbon of the asphalt they had already passed along; even when
the sea was gleaming in the distance and the air smelled of flowers,
iodine, and—at one and the same time—of the cool of the mountains and the dry hot dust of the road, even then, his eyes would
remain as cloudy and indifferent as ever. A long transparent string
of saliva would be hanging from his slightly protruding lower lip
and his nostrils would not even be quivering. Now and again, if he
heard Niccolo's footsteps, he would prick up one ear. When the
guns fired during an exercise, however, he seemed not even to do
that; it was as if he were asleep.

Once Giu tried giving his companion a playful push, but in
answer the old mule just kicked Giu, calmly and without anger,
and turned away. Sometimes Giu would stop pulling on the traces;
he would watch his workmate out of the corner of one eye, but the
old mule did not bare his teeth or lay back his ears. Instead, he
would just puff, toss his head up and down, and pull for all he was
worth.

The two mules had ceased to notice each other, even though they
went on drinking from the same bucket of water and hauling the
same cart laden with crates of shells, even though, night after night,
Giu heard the old mule breathing heavily in the next stall.

Giu felt no slavish devotion toward his driver; nothing about
him—neither his wishes nor his commands, neither his whip nor
his boots nor his rasping voice—made any impression on Giu.

The old mule walked on the right; the cart rumbled behind; the
driver shouted now and again; and ahead of them lay the road.
Sometimes the driver seemed merely part of the cart; at other times
the driver was what mattered, and it was the cart that seemed an
appendage. As for the whip—well, flies bit the tips of Giu's ears until they bled, but they were still only flies. And the whip was only a
whip. And the driver—only a driver.

When Giu was first put in a harness, he felt quietly furious at the
senselessness of the long strip of asphalt; you could neither chew it

nor drink it, while on either side grew leafy and grassy food, and there was water in ponds and puddles.

Yes, at first his main enemy seemed to be the asphalt, but with time Giu grew to feel more resentment toward the reins, the driver's voice, and the weight of the cart. Giu made his peace with the road, and sometimes he even fancied it would free him from the cart and the driver.

The road climbed uphill, weaving through orange groves, while the leather breastband pressed against his chest and the cart rumbled relentlessly and monotonously behind him. The enforced, pointless labor made Giu want to kick out at the cart and tear at the traces with his teeth; he no longer hoped for anything from the road and he had no wish to go on treading it. Mirages arose in the empty space of his head: misty, disturbing visions, the tastes and smells of different foods, the juicy sweetness of leaves, or the smell of young mares, or the warmth of the sun after a cold night, or the cool of evening after the heat of a Sicilian day.

In the morning he would put his head into the breastband held out by the driver and feel against his chest the habitual chill of the dead, shiny leather. No longer any different from the old mule who was his workmate, he did all this without emotion, without throwing his head back or baring his teeth. The polished breastband, the cart, and the road had become part of his life.

Everything had become habitual and therefore right. Everything had joined together to form a life that was right and natural: hard labor, the asphalt, drinking troughs, the smell of axle grease, the thunder of the stinking long-barreled guns, the smell of tobacco and leather from the driver's fingers, the evening bucket of maize, the bundle of prickly hay.

Sometimes there were breaks in the monotony. Giu knew terror when ropes were wound around him and a crane lifted him off the shore and onto a ship. He felt nauseous; the wooden earth kept slipping away from under his hooves and he was unable to eat. And then came heat that was fiercer than Italian heat, and a straw hat was placed on Giu's head. There was the stubborn steepness of the stony red roads of Abyssinia; there were palms with leaves his lips could not reach. One day he was astonished by a monkey in a tree and then scared by a large snake on the ground. The houses were edible; sometimes he ate their reed walls and grassy roofs. The big guns kept shooting and there were outbreaks of fire. When the munitions train halted on the dark fringe of a forest, Giu heard all kinds of rustlings and strange sounds; some of these night sounds filled him with terror and made him tremble and snort.

Then came nausea again, and wooden ground slipping away from under his hooves, and a pale blue plain all around him. And then, somehow or other, even though he had barely taken a step, he was back in a stable again, with his workmate breathing heavily in the next stall.

After the day of the flags and music, the day of the women and children and Niccolo's trembling hands, the stable disappeared. In its place came more wooden ground, repeated knocks and jolts, continual banging and grinding—and then the cramped dark of this juddering and grinding stall was in turn replaced by the space of an endless plain.

Over the plain hung a soft gray dust that was neither Italian nor African; along the road trucks, tractors, and long- and short-barreled guns were moving continually toward where the sun rose, while whole columns of drivers marched along on foot.

Life became more difficult than ever; life turned into nothing but movement. The cart was always fully laden, and the breathing of Giu's workmate became still more labored; for all the noise that hung over the gray, dusty road it was clearly audible.

Defeated by the vastness of space, animals began to die of murrain. Dead mules were dragged to the side of the road. They lay there with swollen bellies and splayed legs that would never tread the road again. People treated them with boundless indifference. The still-living mules also appeared not to notice. They went on tossing their heads and pulling away on their traces; nevertheless, they were aware of their dead.

The food on this flat plain was remarkably tasty. Never had Giu eaten such tender, juicy grass; never had he eaten such tender, fragrant hay. The water on this plain was also tasty and sweet, and from the trees' young branches came shoots that were almost without bitterness.

The warm wind of the plain did not burn like African and Sicilian winds, and the sun warmed his hide gently; it was not like the merciless sun of Africa.

And even the fine gray dust that hung in the air day and night seemed tender and silky compared with the stinging red dust of the desert.

What was not gentle or tender, however, was the sheer expanse of this plain; its endless expanse was cruel. No matter how far the mules trotted, twitching their ears, the plain was always stronger than they were. The mules walked at a fast pace in sunlight, in moonlight—but the plain went on and on. The mules trotted again, their hooves beating against the asphalt or raising clouds of dust on dirt roads—but the plain went on and on. There was no way out of the plain, not in sunlight, nor in moonlight, nor by the light of the stars. It did not give birth to any sea or mountains.

Giu did not notice the start of the rainy season; it set in gradually. But the cold rains poured down, and life changed from monotonous weariness to acute suffering and profound exhaustion.

Every part of Giu's life became harder. The earth turned sticky and squelchy; it belched; it talked. The road turned slithery; a single stride now cost the mules as much effort as a dozen ordinary strides. The cart grew unbearably stubborn; Giu and his workmate seemed to be dragging behind them not one cart but a dozen carts. The driver was now shouting at them nonstop, whipping them painfully and more and more often; it was as if there were not one driver up on the cart but a dozen. And there were any number of whips—and they were all sharp-tongued, spiteful, at once cold and burning, stinging, penetrating.

Pulling the cart over asphalt was now a sweeter pleasure than eating grass or hay, but Giu's hooves did not know asphalt for days on end.

The mules got to know cold, and the way their hides shivered after being soaked by the autumn drizzle. Mules coughed and caught pneumonia. Mules for whom the road had ended and movement had stopped were more and more often being dragged to the side of the road.

The plain grew broader. The mules now sensed its vastness not so much with their eyes as with their hooves. Their hooves sank deeper and deeper into the soft ground. Sticky clods dragged at their legs. Now heavy with rain, vaster and more powerful than ever, the plain continued to stretch out, to expand, to broaden.

The mule's large, spacious brain, used to conceiving vague images of smells, of form, and of color, was now conceiving an image of something very different, an image of a concept created by philosophers and mathematicians, an image of infinity itself—of the misty Russian plain and cold autumn rain pouring down over it without end.

And then dark, turbid, and heavy was replaced by dry, white, and powdery, by something that burned lips and scorched nostrils.

Winter had devoured autumn, but this brought no relief. Heaviness had turned into superheaviness. A less cruel predator had been devoured by a crueler, more voracious predator.

Along with the bodies of mules, there were now dead people lying by the side of the road; the cold had taken their lives.

Labor beyond labor, a chest rubbed raw by the breastband, bleeding sores on his withers, constant pain in his legs, worn and crumbling hooves, frostbitten ears, aching eyes, stabbing stomach cramps from the icy food and water—all this had worn Giu down; it had exhausted both his inner strength and the strength of his muscles.

Giu was being attacked by something vast and indifferent. An indifferent, enormous world had calmly brought all its weight to bear on him. This world had exhausted even the spite of Giu's driver. Niccolo just slumped on his seat, no longer using his whip and no longer kicking Giu on the sensitive little bone on his front leg.

Slowly, inescapably, war and winter were crushing the mule. A vast, indifferent force was on the point of annihilating him; Giu countered this attack with an indifference of his own that was no less vast.

He became a shadow of himself—and this living, ashen shadow could no longer sense either its own warmth or the pleasure that comes from food and rest. It was all the same to the mule whether he was standing still with his head hanging down or walking along the icy road, mechanically moving one leg after another.

He took no joy in the hay he chewed so indifferently, and he bore hunger, thirst, and the cutting winter wind with equal indifference. His eyes ached from the whiteness of the snow, but he felt no happier in twilight or darkness; he neither wanted them nor welcomed them.

It was impossible now to tell him apart from the old mule walking beside him, and the indifference each felt toward the other was equaled only by the indifference each felt toward himself.

This indifference toward himself was his last rebellion.

To be or not to be—to Giu this was a matter of indifference. The mule had resolved Hamlet's dilemma.

Having become submissively indifferent to both existence and nonexistence, he lost the sensation of time. Day and night no longer meant anything; frosty sunlight and moonless dark were all the same to him.

When the Russian offensive began, the cold was not particularly severe.

Giu did not panic during the crushing artillery barrage. He did not shy or tear at his traces when bursting shells lit up the cloudy sky, when the ground shook and the air, rent by screaming and roaring metal, grew thick with fire and smoke, with snow and clay.

The rout that followed did not sweep Giu away. He stood there without moving, his head drooping as low as his tail, while men ran past, while men fell to the ground, leaped up again, and went on running, while men crawled by, while tractors crawled by, while blunt-nosed trucks sped past him.

His workmate gave a strange, almost human cry, fell to the

ground, thrashed his legs about, and went still. The snow around him turned red.

The whip was lying on the snow and Niccolo, the driver, was also lying on the snow. Giu could no longer hear the creak of his boots; he could no longer sense his characteristic smell of tobacco, wine, and rawhide.

Giu stood there, blankly indifferent to what fate had in store for him. His old fate and his new fate mattered equally little.

Twilight set in. It grew quiet. The mule stood there, his head drooping, his tail limp. He neither looked at anything nor listened to anything. The artillery fire had long ago gone silent, but it was still rumbling on in the deserted and indifferent space of his head. From time to time he shifted his weight from one foot to another, then stood still once again.

All around lay the bodies of men and animals, along with trucks that had been overturned or smashed to pieces. Here and there rose lazy columns of smoke.

And beyond, without beginning or end, lay the misty, twilit, snow-covered plain.

The plain had swallowed up all his past life: the southern heat, the steepness of red roads, the smell of young mares, the noise of streams. Giu could now barely be distinguished from the stillness all around him; he was merging with it, becoming one with the misty plain.

But when the silence was violated by tanks, Giu heard them. Their iron sound filled the air; this sound entered the dead ears of both people and animals, and it penetrated the ears of the sad, living mule.

And when the plain's great stillness was violated, when machines with guns and clanking, grinding caterpillar treads appeared, moving from north to south over the fresh snow, Giu saw them. The machines were reflected in the windscreens and mirrors of abandoned vehicles, and they entered the eyes of the mule standing stock-still beside an overturned cart.

Yet he did not start; he did not step to one side even when the treads passed close beside him, giving off a bitter warmth and a smell of burned oil.

White human figures detached themselves from the white plain. They moved quickly and silently, more like predatory hunters than like people. Then they melted away and vanished, swallowed by the stillness of fresh fallen snow.

Next, also from the north, came a noisy torrent of people, trucks, guns, and creaking carts.

At first this torrent kept to the road, and the mule did not so much as turn his head to look at it, and the movement went on past him. Soon, however, the movement grew so vast that it flowed over onto the shoulder.

And then a man with a whip came up to Giu. He looked Giu over, and Giu smelled a smell of tobacco and rawhide.

Just like Niccolo, this man prodded Giu in the teeth, on his cheekbones, on his flanks.

The man pulled on Giu's bridle and said a few words in a rasping voice. Involuntarily, Giu looked at Niccolo where he lay on the snow, but Niccolo said nothing.

The man pulled on the bridle a second time, but the mule did not move.

Then the man shouted and brandished his whip, and his threats were neither more nor less threatening than Niccolo's threats; the only difference was in the sounds that conveyed these threats.

And then the man kicked the mule on the front leg. This hurt. It was the same sensitive bone that Niccolo used to kick.

Giu followed this new driver. They came to some carts. There a whole group of drivers gathered around them, laughing and flinging their arms about, clapping Giu on his back and his sides. He was given some hay, and he ate a little. Harnessed to the carts in pairs were horses with short ears and vicious eyes. There were no mules any longer.

The driver led Giu up to a cart with only one mare in the shafts.

The mare was small and dark, shorter than the tall mule. She glanced at him. She laid her ears back and pricked them up again.

She tossed her head. Then she turned away and, ready to kick, lifted a back leg.

She was skinny and when she breathed in, her ribs moved like a wave beneath her hide. There were bleeding sores on her hide, the same as on Giu's.

Giu stood there, hanging his head, as indifferent as before to the question of whether to be or not to be, calmly indifferent to the world because the world, this flat world of the plains, was indifferently, unconcernedly destroying him.

Just as he had done hundreds of times before, Giu thrust his head into the breastband. It was not made of leather, but that made no difference to how it felt against his worn, weary chest. It had a strange, unaccustomed smell, a smell of horse. But that made no difference to the mule.

The mare stood beside him, but the warmth from her hollow flank meant nothing to him.

She laid her ears back almost flat against her head, and her face looked vicious and predatory, not like that of a herbivore at all. She rolled her eyes, curled her upper lip, and bared her teeth, ready to bite; in his deep indifference, Giu did nothing to protect his cheek and neck. And when the mare began to edge around, pulling on the harness, wanting to turn her rump to him and give him a good, hard kick, he was not in the least concerned. He went on standing there, hanging his head, just as he had stood beside the smashed-up cart, his dead workmate, dead Niccolo, and the whip lying flat on the snow. But the driver gave a shout and struck the mare with his whip. Next he struck the mule with this whip—a twin brother to the whip left lying on the snow. The driver probably felt annoyed by the mule's dejected bearing and, like Niccolo, he had the heavy hand of a peasant.

And Giu looked sideways at the mare, and the mare looked at Giu.

Soon the train of carts set off. The cart creaked in the usual way, and the road stretched out ahead of Giu, and there was a heavy weight behind him, and a driver, and a whip. But Giu knew that the road would not help him to escape from this weight; he trotted slowly along, and there was no beginning or end to the snowy plain.

But strangely, as he moved in his usual way through this world of indifference, he felt that the mare trotting beside him did not feel indifferent toward him.

She flicked Giu with her tail. Her silky, slippery tail was not in the least like either the driver's whip or his old workmate's tail; it slid caressingly over his hide.

After a while, the mare gave another flick of her tail, even though there were certainly no flies, gadflies, or mosquitoes anywhere on this snow-covered plain.

And Giu looked out of the corner of one eye at the mare trotting beside him, and she glanced at him at the same moment. Now there was no viciousness at all in her eye; it was just a little sly.

In the blank wall of the world's indifference there had appeared a tiny snakelike fissure.

As they moved, their bodies got warmer. Giu could smell the mare's sweat, and the mare's breath, imbued with moisture and the sweetness of hay, was affecting him more and more deeply.

Not knowing why he was doing it, Giu began to pull harder on the traces. The bones of his rib cage sensed the weight and the pressure, while the mare's breastband slackened and the cart grew lighter for her.

So they trotted on for a long time. Then the mare whinnied. It was a quiet little whinny, too quiet for the driver or anything around them to hear.

It was a very quiet whinny, because she wanted only the mule trotting beside her to hear it.

Giu did not answer, but it was clear from the way he flared his nostrils that he had heard.

They trotted on for a long, long time, until it was time to stop for the night. They trotted beside each other, their nostrils flared, and their two smells, the smells of a mule and a mare pulling the same cart, merged into a single smell.

The train of carts stopped. The driver unharnessed the mule and the mare, and they ate together and drank water from the same bucket. The mare went up to the mule and laid her head on his neck. Her soft, gently moving lips touched his ear and he looked trustfully into the sad eyes of this collective-farm mare, and his breath mingled with her breath, which felt warm and kind.

In this good, kind warmth all that had gone to sleep awoke again. All that had long been dead came back to life: milk from his mother, the sweet milk that a newborn being so loves; his very first blade of grass; the cruel red stone of the mountain roads of Abyssinia; fierce summer heat in the vineyards; moonlit nights in orange groves; and the terrible labor, the labor beyond labor that seemed to have destroyed him with its indifferent weight but which, in the end, evidently had not quite destroyed him.

Through their warm breath and their weary eyes, Giu the mule and the mare from Vologda spoke clearly to each other of their life and fate, and there was something charming and wonderful about these trustful, affectionate beings standing beside each other on the wartime plain, under the gray winter sky.

"The donkey, I mean the mule, seems to have turned quite Russian," one of the drivers said with a laugh.

"No, look—they're both of them weeping," said another driver.

And it was true; they were weeping.

THE DOG

I.

HER CHILDHOOD was hungry and homeless; nevertheless, childhood is the happiest time of life.

Her first May—those spring days on the edge of town—was especially good. The smell of earth and young grass filled her soul with happiness. She felt a piercing, almost unbearable sense of elation; sometimes she was too happy even to feel like eating. All day long there was a warm green mist in her head and her eyes. She would drop down on her front paws in front of a dandelion and let out happy, angry, childish, staccato yelps; she was asking the flower to join in and run about with her, and the stillness of its stout little green leg surprised her and made her cross.

And then all of a sudden she would be frenziedly digging a hole; clods of earth would fly out from under her little belly, and her pink-and-black paws would get almost burned by the stony earth. Her little face would take on a troubled look—she seemed not to be playing a game; she seemed to be digging a refuge, digging for dear life.

She had a plump, pink belly and her paws were broad, even though she ate little during that good time of her life. It was as if she were growing plump from happiness, from the joy of being alive.

And then those easy childhood days came to an end. The world filled with October and November, with hostility and indifference, with icy rain and sleet, with dirt, with revolting slimy leftovers, the smell of which was nauseating even to a hungry dog.

But even in her homeless life there were good things: a compassionate human face, a night spent close to an underground hot-water pipe, a sweet bone. There was room in her dog's life for passion, and dog love, and the light of motherhood.

She was a small bandy-legged mongrel living out on the streets. But she got the better of all hostile forces because she loved life and was very clever. She knew from which side trouble might creep up on her. She knew that death did not make a lot of noise or raise its hand threateningly, that it did not throw stones or stamp about in boots; no, death drew near with an ingratiating smile, holding out a scrap of bread and with a piece of net sacking hidden behind its back.

She knew the murderous power of cars and trucks and had a precise knowledge of their different speeds; she knew how to wait patiently while the traffic went by, how to rush across the road when the cars were stopped by a red light. She knew the forward-sweeping, all-destroying force of electric trains and their childish helplessness: as long as it was a few inches away from the track, even a mouse was safe from them. She knew the roars, whistles, and rumbles of jet and propeller planes, as well as the racket of helicopters. She knew the smell of gas pipes; she knew where she might find the warmth given off by hot-water pipes running under the ground. She knew the work rhythm of the town's garbage trucks; she knew how to get inside garbage containers of all kinds and could immediately recognize the cellophane wrapping around meat products and the waxed paper around cod, rockfish, and ice cream.

A black electric cable sticking up out of the earth was more horrifying to her than a viper; once she had put a damp paw on a cable with a broken insulating jacket.

This dog probably knew more about technology than an intelligent, well-informed person from three centuries before her.

It was not merely that she was clever; she was also educated. Had she failed to learn about mid-twentieth-century technology, she would have died. After all, dogs that wandered into the city from some village or other often lasted only a few hours.

But technological knowledge and experience were not enough; no less crucial for her struggle was an understanding of the essence of life. She could not have survived without worldly wisdom.

This clever, nameless mongrel knew that the foundation stone of her life was vagrancy—perpetual change.

Now and again some tenderhearted person would show pity to the four-legged wanderer. They would give her scraps of food and find her somewhere to sleep on the back stairs. But if she were to betray her vagrant ways, she would have to pay with her life. Were she to settle down, the dog would make herself dependent on one kindhearted person and a hundred unkind people. And then death would creep up on her, with a scrap of bread in one hand and a piece of net sacking in the other. A hundred unkind hearts have more power than one kind heart.

People thought that the canine wanderer was incapable of devotion, that vagrancy had corrupted her.

They were wrong. It was not that her difficult life had hardened the heart of the wandering dog; it was simply that no one needed the good that lived in this heart.

2.

She was caught at night, while she was asleep. Instead of being killed, she was taken to a scientific institute. She was bathed in some warm, stinking liquid; after this, she had no more trouble from fleas. For several days she lived in a basement, in a cage. She was fed well, but she did not feel like eating. She missed her freedom, and she was haunted by a sense of imminent death. Only here, in this cage with warm bedding, with tasty food in a clean bowl, did she first truly value the happiness of her days of freedom.

She felt irritated by the stupid barking of her neighbors. People in white gowns examined her at length. One of them, a thin man with bright eyes, flicked her on the nose and patted her on the head. Then she was taken to another, quieter room.

She was about to be introduced to the most advanced technology of the twentieth century; she was about to be prepared for something momentous.

She was given the name Pestrushka: "Speckles."

Probably not even sick emperors or prime ministers had ever undergone so many medical tests. Thin, bright-eyed Aleksey Georgievich learned everything there was to know about Pestrushka's heart, lungs, liver, pulmonary gas exchange, blood composition, nervous reflexes, and digestive juices.

Pestrushka realized that neither the cleaners, nor the laboratory assistants, nor the generals covered in medals were the masters of her life and death, of her freedom, of her last agony.

She understood this, and her heart gave all its still-unspent love to Aleksey Georgievich, and no horror from her past or present could do anything to harden her against him.

She understood that everything—the injections and abdominal taps, the dizzying and nauseating journeys in centrifuges and vibration chambers, the aching sense of weightlessness that suddenly poured into her consciousness, into her front paws and her tail, into her chest and her back paws—she understood that all of this was the doing of her master, Aleksey Georgievich.

But this understanding made no difference. She was always waiting for the master she had found; she pined when he was not there; she was overjoyed to hear his footsteps; and when he went away in the evening her brown eyes seemed to moisten with tears.

After an especially difficult morning training session Aleksey Georgievich usually visited Pestrushka's living quarters. Panting, her tongue hanging out, her large head resting on her front paws, Pestrushka would look meekly up at him.

In some strange and incomprehensible way this man who had become the master of her life and fate was mixed up with her sense of that green spring mist, with the sensation of freedom.

She looked at the man who had doomed her to imprisonment and suffering, and what sprang up in her heart was hope.

Aleksey Georgievich took some time to realize that he felt pity and tenderness toward Pestrushka, that he was not simply taking his usual interest in a project's practical details.

Once, looking at a laboratory dog, he had thought how crazy and absurd it was that people who rear animals—millions of them, all over the world—should feel devoted love for the pigs and chickens they were preparing for execution. Now he felt that these kind eyes, this damp nose pressed trustfully into the hand of a murderer, were no less crazy and absurd.

Time passed; soon it would be the day of Pestrushka's journey. She was now undergoing experiments in the space capsule itself. A four-legged creature was preparing the way for man; her journey into the far distance was a rehearsal for man's farthest and longest flight.

Aleksey Georgievich was disliked by all his subordinates. Some were extremely frightened of him; he was short-tempered, and he often treated his laboratory assistants harshly. His superiors also disliked him—because of his rancor and his fondness for protracted disputes.

Nor was he easy to get on with at home; often he had severe headaches and would feel irritated by the slightest noise. He also suffered from heartburn and he believed that his wife did not give him the right diet, that instead of taking proper care of her husband she was secretly doing all she could for her countless relatives.

His friendships were no easier; he was always losing his temper, suspecting friends of envy and indifference. He would quarrel with them, feel upset, and then have to struggle to make peace with them again.

Aleksey Georgievich was no less harsh with regard to himself. Sometimes he would mutter sourly, "Yes, everybody's fed up with me, and there's nobody more fed up with me than I am myself."

The bandy-legged mongrel took no part in laboratory intrigues, could not be accused of failing to look after Aleksey Georgievich properly, and seemed free of envy.

Like Christ, she returned good for evil, paying him back with love for the suffering he caused her.

He examined electrocardiograms, or analyses of blood pressure or reflexes, and the dog's brown eyes gazed at him devotedly. Once he began explaining out loud to her that people went through the same training and that they found it difficult too. It was true, he went on, that the risks she was being exposed to were greater than the risks to which a human being would be exposed; nevertheless, she was infinitely better off than poor Laika, whose death in space had been a foregone conclusion.

Once he said to Pestrushka that she would be the first creature, since life had begun on earth, to glimpse the true depth of the cosmos. A wonderful fate had befallen her. She was about to penetrate cosmic space—the first envoy of free reason to be sent out into the universe.

The dog seemed to understand him.

She was unusually clever—in her canine way, of course. The laboratory assistants and cleaning staff used to joke: "Our Pestrushka must have completed elementary technology!" Life amid scientific apparatus was not difficult for her; it was as if she understood the principles behind the various appliances and therefore had no trouble finding her bearings in a world of clamps, screens, electron tubes, and automatic feeders.

More than anyone, Aleksey Georgievich had the ability to summon up a complete picture of the vital functions of an organism flying through empty space, thousands of miles from any terrestrial laboratory.

He was one of the founders of a new science: cosmic biology. This time, however, he was not just entranced by the complexity of the project; bandy-legged Pestrushka had somehow made everything a little different.

He would look into the dog's eyes. These kind eyes, not the eyes of Niels Bohr, would be the first to look into the cosmos, to see cosmic space that was not limited by the earth's horizon. A space with no wind and only weak gravitational forces, a space where there was no rain, no clouds, no swallows, a space of photons and electromagnetic waves.

And it seemed to Aleksey Georgievich that Pestrushka's eyes would be able to tell him what they had seen. And he would read and understand that most arcane of cardiograms, the secret cardiogram of the universe.

The dog seemed to understand by instinct that this man was allowing her to take part in the greatest event in earth's history, that he was allowing her the leading role in a drama of unparalleled importance.

Everyone who knew Aleksey Georgievich—superiors and subordinates, family and friends—everyone was aware of strange changes in him; never had he been so easy, so gentle, so sad.

This new experiment was special. It was not merely that the capsule, disdaining the ease of orbit, would pierce deep into space and leave the earth a hundred thousand kilometers behind. No, what was special was the presence of a living being, penetrating the cosmos with her psyche. Or rather the other way around—the cosmos would penetrate the psyche of a living being. This was what mattered—not just questions of overload, vibrations, the sensation of weightlessness.

Before these very eyes the earth's flat surface would begin to curve; the eyes of an animal would confirm the truth of Copernicus's vision. A globe! A geoid! And more, much more. A younger sun, throwing off the weight of two billion years, would rise up out of black space before the eyes of a small, bandy-legged bitch. Earth's horizon would slip away—in orange, lilac, and violet flame. That miraculous globe covered in snow and burning sand, full of wonderful, restless life, would not only slip away from under the dog's feet—it would slip right out of her field of sensual awareness. Then the stars would acquire body; they would grow thermonuclear flesh—brilliant, burning substance.

The psyche of a living creature would be penetrated by another kingdom—a kingdom not covered by the warmth of the earth, by soft cumulus clouds, by the damp power of phlogiston. Living eyes would see for the first time the airless abyss, the space of Kant, the space of Einstein, the space of philosophers, astronomers, and mathematicians; they would see this space not through speculation, not in the guise of a formula, but as it truly is—without mountains or trees, without skyscrapers or village huts.

No one around Aleksey Georgievich could understand what was happening to him.

To Aleksey Georgievich it seemed that he was discovering a new form of knowledge, higher than the knowledge derived from differential equations and the testimony of instruments. This new knowledge was transferred from soul to soul, from living eyes to living eyes. And everything that disturbed or angered him, that aroused his suspicion or spite, had somehow ceased to matter.

It seemed to him that a new quality was about to enter the life of terrestrial beings, enriching this life and elevating it—and that this new quality would bring with it forgiveness and justification for Aleksey Georgievich himself.

3.

The spaceship took off.

As if through a hole in the ice, an animal plunged into space. The windows and screens were arranged in such a way that, wherever it turned its head, the animal saw only space, losing all sense of what was earthly and familiar. The universe was penetrating the brain of a dog, of a young bitch.

Aleksey Georgievich was convinced that his connection with Pestrushka remained unbroken; he could feel this connection even when the capsule was a hundred thousand kilometers from earth. And this had nothing to do with the automatic radio signals telling him about Pestrushka's racing pulse and the sudden jumps in her blood pressure.

The following morning, laboratory assistant Apresyan said to him, "She was howling. She was howling for a long time." He added quietly: "It's scary—a solitary dog, alone in the universe, howling."

The instruments all worked with total, unbelievable accuracy.

The grain of sand that had gone out into space found its way back to the earth, to the grain of sand that had given birth to it. The braking systems worked flawlessly; the capsule landed on the chosen point of the earth's surface.

Apresyan smiled and said to Aleksey Georgievich, "The impact of certain cosmic particles will have restructured Pestrushka's genes and she'll have puppies with outstanding creative ability for everything in the realm of higher algebra and symphonic music. The grandsons of our Pestrushka will compose sonatas as good as Beethoven's. They'll construct cybernetic machines that will be new Fausts."

Aleksey Georgievich did not reply to this joker.

Aleksey Georgievich himself traveled to where the capsule had landed. He had to be the first to see Pestrushka; this time no deputy or assistant could go in his place.

Their meeting was everything Aleksey Georgievich had hoped it would be.

She rushed at him, shyly wagging the tip of her lowered tail.

For a long time he was unable to see the eyes that had taken in the universe. The dog kept licking his hands as a sign of obedience, a sign of her eternal renunciation of the life of a free wanderer, a sign of her acceptance of everything that was and will be.

Eventually, however, he saw her eyes—the misty, impenetrable eyes of a poor, beggarly creature with an agitated mind and an obedient, loving heart.

IN KISLOVODSK

NIKOLAY Viktorovich had removed his gown and was about to set off back home when Anna Aristarkhovna, who was famous for growing the best strawberries in town, said to him breathlessly, "Nikolay Viktorovich, a colonel's just driven up outside."

"Well," said Nikolay Viktorovich, "I suppose that's what colonels do." And he began pulling his gown back on.

Anna Aristarkhovna's admiring gaze was, he knew, a tribute to his air of sleepy calm. Really, however, the colonel's arrival alarmed him every bit as much as it alarmed Anna Aristarkhovna. And he and his wife were planning to go to the theater in the evening; this might make him late.

Nikolay Viktorovich was someone who felt compelled to appear better in the eyes of women than he was in reality. Women had always liked him, and his innate gallantry—as well as a certain protectiveness he could not help feeling with regard to his halo—prevented him from revealing the many ways in which he differed from his persona.

Even though his hair had gone gray, he was still a handsome figure—slim, tall, graceful, always tastefully dressed. His fine, distinguished face wore the expression portrait painters aspire to bestow on the good and the great, on those whose vocation is to adorn this world.

Women fell in love with him and never imagined that he was not in the least as he appeared; that really Nikolay Viktorovich was a very ordinary man, someone who did not care about world problems, someone who knew nothing about literature or music, someone who adored comfort, elegant clothes, and massive saffron-yellow rings set with large precious stones. No, it never entered their heads that he had no special love for his work as a doctor and that what he really enjoyed was dining in good restaurants, traveling first class when he went on holiday to Moscow, being seen with his dear Yelena Petrovna—who was as tall, graceful, and handsome as he himself—in the most expensive seats of a theater and intercepting admiring glances, glances that said, "What a handsome couple!"

He was too worldly, too much in love with elegance and high society, to work in a university clinic; instead, he had become head physician of the splendid government sanatorium in Kislovodsk. He never, of course, carried out any research, but it was really very pleasant indeed to stroll through the sanatorium with his entourage, to walk through marble-columned halls and exchange casually respectful greetings with acquaintances who happened to be masters of the Soviet state...

His hero was Athos from *The Three Musketeers*. "That book is my bible," he would say to his friends.

As a young man, he had played poker for high stakes and been considered a connoisseur of racehorses. On visits to Moscow, he would sometimes telephone important figures who at one time or another had been his patients, men whose names had a place in the history of the Party and whose photographs appeared in *Pravda*; their warm responses never failed to gratify him.

And it was the love he felt for his comfortable Morocco-leather armchair, his love for all his comfortable and luxurious furniture and his fear of bleak goods wagons with their tin teapots and small smoking stoves—it was this love of comfort and terror of bleakness that prompted his decision not to allow himself to be evacuated when the first mechanized and mountain light-infantry units of the German Wehrmacht began to approach Kislovodsk.

Yelena Petrovna, who liked the Germans no more than her husband did, went along with this decision. She too loved antique tables with precious inlays, and mahogany settees, and porcelain, and crystal, and fine carpets.

Yelena Petrovna also loved clothes from abroad—and especially those that provoked the envy of certain other women she knew, the wives of politicians and public figures. And as she put on dresses the like of which none of these important ladies had ever seen, her face would take on the modest, weary expression of a woman indifferent to vanity and frippery.

When Nikolay Viktorovich first saw a German motorized reconnaissance patrol pass by on the street, he felt dismayed and frightened. The faces of the German soldiers, the horned silhouettes of their submachine guns, the swastikas on their helmets, seemed unbearable, loathsome.

For perhaps the first time in his life he spent a sleepless night. What, in the end, did a Turkoman carpet or a writing desk from the reign of Paul I really matter? He had evidently acted frivolously, staying behind in a town that was about to be occupied.

All that night he kept thinking about his friend from childhood, Volodya Gladetsky, who had volunteered to fight in the Red Army during the Civil War.

Gaunt, his cheeks pale and sunken, wearing an old belted coat, Gladetsky had gone limping down the street toward the station, leaving behind him everything he loved: his home, his wife, and his sons. Years went by without the two men seeing each other, but from time to time Nikolay Viktorovich had word of Gladetsky and of the course that his life had taken.

That first night of the occupation it was as if he saw two paths: his own and Gladetsky's. How different they were!

Back in the days of the tsar, Gladetsky had been expelled during his last year of high school; he had been exiled to Siberia, then confined to the town where he was born. When war began in 1914, he had been conscripted; after being wounded toward the end of 1915, he had returned home. And always his Bolshevik soul had proved stronger than anything else he held dear, and everything harshest and bloodiest in the life of his country and people had somehow become his own life and fate.

Nikolay Viktorovich, on the other hand, had never been a member of the Bolshevik underground or been pursued by the tsarist police; he had not led a battalion against Kolchak's forces during the Civil War; he had not, like Gladetsky, been the commissar in charge of food rationing for an entire province during the famine of 1921; nor, during Party meetings, had he forced himself to denounce friends from his student days who had joined the Left and Right Oppositions; nor had he spent days and nights without sleep on the vast construction sites of the Urals; nor had he hurried through the dark to report to a man in a Kremlin office flooded with white electrical light...

Help from various acquaintances had led to Nikolay Viktorovich being exempted from service in the First Cavalry Army. He studied in the faculty of medicine; he lost his head over the beautiful Yelena, who subsequently became his wife; he journeyed to different villages, trading his family's coats and furs, along with his father's hunting boots, for supplies of flour, fatback, and honey—and with these supplies he had managed to keep his mother and his old aunt alive. During the storm and romance of the Revolution he had lived far from romantically—although he had, admittedly, sometimes come back from the countryside not only with fatback and honey but also with supplies of home-distilled vodka, and then, during evenings lit only by small oil lamps, there had been parties; they had danced, played charades, and exchanged kisses in frosty kitchens and dark corridors while from outside, from the other side of windows hung with blankets, came the sounds of shots and the tramping of heavy boots.

The country had lived out its fate, but Nikolay Viktorovich's own fate had been free of storms, calamities, hard labor, or war. And there had been times of great Socialist victories, on battlefields or construction sites, when he had been overwhelmed by despair—because a woman had rejected him...Or when what had been a harsh and terrible year for the Russian people had for him been a year of light and love...

And now here he was, standing by the dark window of his room, listening to the noise of war—to the grinding of the treads of tanks and the guttural shouting of commands. The small points of light he could see were flashlights—flashlights held by German noncommissioned officers.

A year before the war Nikolay Viktorovich had seen a man being admitted to the sanatorium—a gray-haired man with a lined face and olive-colored bags beneath his eyes—and had realized that this was his old school friend, Volodya Gladetsky.

It had been a strange meeting. The two men had been simultaneously overjoyed and wary; they had felt drawn to each other and repelled; they had wanted to talk openly and been afraid to talk openly; their former trust had suddenly been reborn, as if their days of whispering in the boys' toilet about schoolboy pranks had come around again—and yet, between the two men, between Nikolay Viktorovich and the seriously ill Party official, there lay an abyss.

Each season of the year, as a rule, someone famous came to the sanatorium for treatment. Moscow informed the doctors well in advance; a luxurious room was prepared for the visitor; and for years afterward the staff would say things like "That was when we had Budyonny staying with us..." At the time that Gladetsky arrived, they had had a well-known Old Bolshevik staying with them, a full member of the Soviet Academy of Sciences who had been a friend of Lenin. As a young man sentenced to years in a tsarist jail, this Savva Feofilovich had composed a well-known revolutionary song.

Savva Feofilovich and Gladetsky had seen quite a lot of each other. They had gone for walks and spent evenings together, and sometimes, if the old man was feeling poorly, they had had supper together in Savva Feofilovich's room.

Once Nikolay Viktorovich had chanced upon the two men as they were walking in the park. They had all sat down for a while on a bench under some laurels. Nikolay Viktorovich had felt a feeling that was familiar yet strange, sweet yet painful, an emotion compounded of a sense of power—the power of the senior doctor who, without formalities, can enter any sick grandee's heart—and a sense of astonishment that he, Nikolay Viktorovich, should be sitting beside this thickset old man who had a large head with thin gray hair and whose broad white hand had often shaken the hand of Vladimir Ilyich Lenin.

Gladetsky said, "Nikolay Viktorovich and I were at school together. And I can remember one story, Savva Feofilovich, in which you yourself play a role."

The old man expressed surprise, and Gladetsky then recounted an incident that Nikolay Viktorovich had forgotten. One day long before, when they were both still at school, Gladetsky had invited Nikolay Viktorovich to a meeting of a revolutionary circle; they were going to learn revolutionary songs. Asked afterward why he had not turned up, Nikolay Viktorovich said he had also been invited to the name-day party of a girl he knew, a student at the same school. And that, it seemed, had marked the end of his career as a conspirator.

One of the songs the students sang that evening was the famous song that Savva Feofilovich had composed in jail.

The old man laughed good-naturedly and said, "Two years before the war, you say? That was when I was a prisoner in the Warsaw citadel."

During the course of a routine medical examination Nikolay Viktorovich once said to Gladetsky, "I can't believe it. Savva Feofilovich's heart is in better shape than the hearts of men half his age. It sounds so young and strong!"

And with suddenly renewed trust, with a surge of feeling, Gladetsky replied, "But he's a superman, he has the strength of a superman! And believe me—I'm not saying this because he survived the Oryol prison, or the Warsaw citadel, or years in the underground with hardly anything to eat, or exile in Yakutsk, or life as an émigré with only the clothes on his back. No, I'm saying this because he had the strength to denounce Bukharin in the name of the Revolution. Yes, he had the strength to demand that a man he knew to be innocent should be sentenced to death; he had the strength to expel talented young scientists from a research institute merely because their names were on certain blacklists. Do you think it's easy for a friend of Lenin to do such things? Do you think it's easy to destroy the lives of children, women, and old men, to feel pity for them in the depths of your soul as you carry out acts of terrible cruelty in the name of the Revolution? I know only too well what it's like—believe me! Yes, there's no truer test of strength or weakness of soul."

All this came back to Nikolay Viktorovich the night the Germans arrived. Ashamed of his own pathetic lack of resolve, he said to his ever-young and astonishingly beautiful Yelena Petrovna, "Lena, what have we gone and done? Now we're going to have to live with the Germans."

In a serious voice she replied, "It's nothing to feel good about, I know. But it doesn't matter, Kolya. Whoever we end up having to live with—whether it's Germans, Italians, or Romanians—there's one thing that will save us. We've always wanted to stay the people we are, but that doesn't mean we wish anyone else ill. We'll survive all right."

"But it's awful. The Germans are here. And if we're still here too, it's only, really, because of all our clutter."

What Nikolay Viktorovich did not tell his wife was how Gladetsky had laughed as he told an old comrade of Lenin's about a name-day party Nikolay Viktorovich had chosen to go to when he could have gone to a meeting of a student revolutionary circle. It had been the name-day party of a high-school girl called Yelena Petrovna Ksenofontova.

Yelena Petrovna replied sharply, "Why call it clutter? This clutter is years of our life. Our porcelain, our tulip-shaped crystal glasses, our pink ocean shells, our carpet—you said yourself that it smells of spring, that it's woven from the colors of April. It's who we are. It's the way we've lived our lives, and it's the way we'll go on living our lives. What else can we do except go on loving what we've loved all along?" She struck the table several times with her long, narrow, and very white hand and repeated obstinately, in time with the blows of her hand, "Yes, yes, yes, yes. It's who we are and there's nothing we can do about it. It's who we are."

"You're very wise," he said. They seldom spoke seriously about their life, and her words had comforted him.

And they went on living, and life was livable. Nikolay Viktorovich was called to the commandant's office and asked to work as a doctor in a hospital for wounded Red Army soldiers. He was given a good ration card, Yelena Petrovna was given a somewhat less good ration card, and they were able to obtain bread, sugar, and dried peas. At home they had stores of honey, condensed milk, and clarified butter; supplementing the German rations from her own supplies, Yelena Petrovna was able to prepare meals that were ample and even quite tasty. In the mornings they went on drinking the coffee they had grown used to over the years. It would be a long time before they ran out of coffee, and the milkmaid went on bringing good milk, and it was not even any more expensive than it had been before; the only difference was that the money they handed the milkmaid was no longer Russian money.

And at the market there were people selling good-quality chickens, and fresh eggs, and early vegetables, and at prices that were not really that bad at all. And when they wanted something special, they ate bread with pressed caviar—during the period of chaos while the Germans were approaching, Nikolay Viktorovich had brought home two large jars of caviar from the sanatorium storeroom.

Cafés were opened. German films were shown in the cinema. There were unbearably tedious films about the National Socialist Party and its success in reeducating unprincipled, dissipated good-for-nothings and turning them into strong-willed, politically conscious young militants. But there were good films as well; Nikolay Viktorovich and Yelena Petrovna particularly liked one called *Rembrandt*. A Russian-language theater opened; the company included some excellent actors—and the famous Blumenthal-Tamarin was outstanding. At first, the company's only production was Schiller's *Intrigue and Love*, but then they began putting on Ibsen, Hauptmann, and Chekhov—all in all, it was possible to have quite a tolerable evening there. And there were, it turned out, some cultivated people left in the town—doctors, actors, and singers, and one very charming and erudite man, a scene painter from Leningrad—and so life carried on with its little excitements, and, just as before the war, Nikolay Viktorovich's house was often full of people who understood the exquisite design of Persian carpets, people who could appreciate the supple lines of antique furniture and the charm of fine porcelain and crystal; and it turned out that these people preferred to keep their distance from the commandant and the town authorities, from the colonels and generals of Army Group B headquarters, and that they were happy rather than disappointed if they failed to receive an invitation to a reception presided over by General List, the master of the Caucasus. But if they did receive an invitation, it goes without saying that they put on their very best clothes and fretted about whether or not their wives were dressed fashionably enough or whether they looked absurd and provincial.

There were three small wards in Nikolay Viktorovich's hospital, and he had two nurses and two assistant nurses.

There were enough provisions in the storeroom to feed the wounded quite decently, and there was a supply of drugs and dressings, and so Nikolay Viktorovich's main concern was simply not to do anything that might attract the attention of the German authorities; afraid that the less seriously wounded might be transferred to a camp, he kept them in bed.

His little building in the depths of the sanatorium park had evidently been entirely forgotten by the Germans. The stronger patients played cards, flirted with the elderly nurses, and worshipped Nikolay Viktorovich, and it seemed to them that they owed their quiet, paradisical life to him alone.

When Nikolay Viktorovich came home from the hospital, his wife would ask, "Well, how are our boys today?"

They had no children, and so that is how the two of them referred to the wounded young soldiers. And Nikolay Viktorovich would laugh as he told his wife amusing stories about life in the little hospital.

But the Germans had not entirely forgotten about the little building in the depths of the park. One day Nikolay Viktorovich was called to the town council medical department and asked to supply a list of all the wounded under his supervision. He felt anxious as he compiled the list, but the official on duty did not even read it. He threw it carelessly into a file; evidently it was no more than a bureaucratic formality.

The Germans continued to advance; the military bulletins in the newspapers sounded more triumphant than ever, and Nikolay Viktorovich tried not to read them.

There were rumors that the Kislovodsk sanatoriums would soon be reopening, and that they would be receiving not only colonels and generals but also eminent members of the Reich's intelligentsia.

It appeared that there were some people who had had well-educated Germans billeted on them, Germans who seemed to be afraid of Hitler and Himmler and who seemed to disapprove of the horrors reported by people living near the Gestapo headquarters. All in all, then, life was not really so very different from the life they had known before. Once again, Nikolay Viktorovich found himself delighting in the comfort of his house and the beauty and charm of his wife; once again, he was confident he had been right to prefer Yelena Petrovna Ksenofontova's name-day party to the meeting of the revolutionary circle.

And now, just as Nikolay Viktorovich was about to go home, intending to relax for a while and then have something to eat before going with his wife to see a performance of Gerhart Hauptmann's *The Sunken Bell*, a car crunched over the gravel and up to the little building in the depths of the park. Out of it stepped a stout man with high cheekbones, a snub nose, gray eyes, and fair hair; he could have been a Soviet district agronomist, or the manager of a shop, or someone giving a talk on social insurance at a meeting of a domestic workers' Party committee.

It was clear, however, from the peaked cap, the belt, the armband, the shoulder straps on his gray uniform, and the swastika and Iron Cross on his chest that he was a Gestapo officer, equal in rank to a Wehrmacht colonel.

As always, Nikolay Viktorovich looked tall and sleek; his face had a handsome glow, his hair was an elegant shade of silver, and his eyes were almost indecently expressive. Beside this runt of a potbellied German, a man who looked as if he had been put together out of some kind of waste matter, Nikolay Viktorovich could have been a distinguished landowner whom Fortune smiled on; he could have been taken for an important Russian aristocrat or perhaps a foreign duke.

But it was not like that at all.

"*Sie sprechen Deutsch?*"

"*Jawohl,*" Nikolay Viktorovich replied. When he was a boy, he had learned German from a governess called Augusta Karlovna.

"Heavens!" he said to himself, realizing what grace, what coquettish eagerness, what a passionate desire to seem polite, pleasant, and obedient he had infused into his cooing *Jawohl*.

And the German, hearing the voice of the gray-haired aristocrat and quickly appraising him through almost divinely omniscient eyes—the eyes of a being who existed on some exalted height, decreeing who should live and who should die—immediately understood what kind of man he was talking to.

The stout, stocky Gestapo officer had been given the task of destroying vast mountains of human flesh.

There were thousands of human spirits that he had had to break—to cleave or shatter, to bend or fragment: there were Catholics and Orthodox, there were fighter pilots, princes who were passionate monarchists, Party functionaries, inspired poets who had trampled over every convention, nuns whose spiritual frenzy had led them to renounce the world. When life is under threat, everything cracks and splits apart, everything turns upside down, sometimes slowly, sometimes resisting obstinately, sometimes yielding with an ease that makes you want to laugh. But the result is always the same, and the exceptions only proved the rule. Like children in front of a Christmas tree, people had pushed and shoved as they reached out to grab the simple, crude little toy that a Gestapo Grandfather Frost now offered, now snatched away...Yes, everyone wants to live—Schmulik from the ghetto no less than Johann Wolfgang von Goethe.

It was not a complicated matter, and the Gestapo bureaucrat explained everything concisely and clearly, without a single coarse or cynical word, and he even came out with a few sentences that were not strictly necessary—about how civilized people all understand that, when it comes to matters of worldwide historical importance, there can be only one morality: the morality of state expediency. In Germany, doctors had understood this long ago.

Nikolay Viktorovich listened, nodding quickly and obediently, and the look in his eyes was that of an attentive pupil, a pupil determined to memorize as accurately and conscientiously as possible everything that his teacher says. Or perhaps it could better be described as a look of servility, of servile devotion to power.

Examining this sanatorium doctor, this well-groomed aristocrat, the Gestapo bureaucrat thought good-naturedly that he did not really have the right to laugh at him after all. This man had been exposed to overwhelming temptation; he had been enslaved by his many years of sweet living in the wonderful climate of a spa town, surrounded by flower beds and bubbling, purling, health-giving Russian water. No doubt, he had many well-tailored Russian suits and an apartment full of expensive antique furniture. And no doubt this apartment was well stocked with delicacies; no doubt he regularly ate Russian caviar that he had stolen from the sanatorium stores. No doubt he collected fine crystal, or amber cigarette holders, or walking sticks with ivory handles . . . And there was no doubt at all that he would have a beautiful wife.

The stocky, thick-necked German, this man who looked as if he had been molded out of some kind of waste matter, was by no means simpleminded. His work had to do with the human soul, that mystery of mysteries; when it came to clarity of vision, and one or two other things, this man could vie with God.

The men left the hospital together and Nikolay Viktorovich saw two German sentries standing beside the doors; no longer were people free to enter or leave the hospital as they chose.

The Gestapo bureaucrat offered to drive Nikolay Viktorovich home. Sitting in silence on the hard seats of the staff car, they looked out at the friendly streets and comfortable houses of the world-famous spa town.

Before saying goodbye to Nikolay Viktorovich, the German quickly went through everything once again: "A car will come for you in the morning. The hospital staff will have to leave the building for a brief period while you attend to the medical side of proceedings. Once the covered trucks have left the hospital, it must be explained to the staff that the chronically ill and seriously wounded have been transferred, on instructions from higher authorities, to a special hospital outside the town. It is, of course, crucial that you should exercise discretion; there is probably no one to whom it matters more that this operation should not become public knowledge."

Nikolay Viktorovich recounted all this to Yelena Petrovna and said, "Forgive me." After a minute or two of silence, she said, "And I'd got everything ready for the theater. I've taken your suit out and ironed my dress."

He did not answer. She went on: "You're right. There's nothing else you can do."

"I've just had a thought, you know," said Nikolay Viktorovich. "In twenty years I've never once been to the theater without you."

"I'm going with you this time too. This is one more theater we'll be going to together."

"You're out of your mind!" he shouted. "Why?"

"*You* can't stay here. So how can *I*?"

He began kissing her hands. She put her arms around his neck and kissed him on the lips; she kissed his gray hair.

"My handsome one," she said. "What a lot of orphans we're going to leave behind."

"My poor boys—but there's nothing I can do for them, only this."

"It wasn't them I meant. I meant our own orphans."

They behaved very vulgarly. They put on the clothes she had got ready for their evening at the theater and she doused herself with French perfume. Then they had supper. They ate pressed caviar and drank wine; he clinked glasses with her and kissed her fingers as if they were young lovers in a restaurant. Then they wound up the gramophone, danced to vulgar songs by Vertinsky, and wept because they worshipped Vertinsky. Then they said goodbye to their dear children—and this was more vulgar still. They kissed their porcelain cups goodbye; they kissed their paintings goodbye. They stroked their carpets and their mahogany furniture. He opened her wardrobe and kissed her underwear and her slippers.

Then, in a harsh voice, she said, "And now poison me, like a mad dog—and yourself too!"

PART FOUR

Three Letters

Grossman with his mother, probably 1913–14

GROSSMAN dedicated *Life and Fate* to his mother. Yekaterina Savelievna's death, Grossman's guilt, and the ensuing recriminations between him and his wife are all reflected in *Life and Fate*. Grossman evidently felt that his mother remained alive in his novel, and this sense of his mother's continued presence seems to have led him to look on *Life and Fate* almost as a living being. His letter to Khrushchev in 1961 ends, "There is no sense or truth in my present position, in my apparent freedom, while the book to which I have given my life is in prison. For I have written it, and I have not renounced it and am not renouncing it. Twelve years have passed since I began work on this book. I still believe that I have written the truth, and that I wrote this truth out of love and pity for people, out of faith in people. I ask for freedom for my book."

There is perhaps no more powerful lament for Eastern European Jewry than the chapter from *Life and Fate* now often referred to as "The Last Letter"—the letter that Anna Semyonovna, a fictional portrait of Grossman's mother, writes to her son and manages to have smuggled out of the ghetto. Though probably always intended as a chapter in *Life and Fate*, this letter is first mentioned in *For a Just Cause*, which contains a number of moving accounts of Viktor's feelings about his mother's death. The first is based on a dream that Grossman himself dreamed in September 1941, around the time of the Berdichev massacre.

During the night Viktor dreamed that he entered a room full of pillows and sheets that had been thrown onto the floor. He went up to an armchair that still seemed to preserve the warmth of someone who had recently been sitting in it. The room was empty; the people who lived there had evidently left all of a sudden in the middle of the night. He looked for a long time at the kerchief hanging over the chair and almost down to the floor—and then realized that his mother had been sleeping in this chair. Now the chair was empty, standing in an empty room.

The second passage comes later, after Viktor Shtrum has received his mother's letter and when he no longer has any doubt of her death.

Getting on the plane for Chelyabinsk, he had thought, "She's gone. And now I'm flying east, I'll be farther away from where she is lying." On the way back from Chelyabinsk, as the plane was approaching Kazan, he had thought, "And she'll never know that we're here in Kazan." In the midst of his joy and excitement at seeing his wife again, he had said to himself, "When I last saw Lyudmila, I was thinking I'd be seeing Mother again once the war is over."

The thought of his mother, like a strong taproot, entered into every event of his life, big or small. Probably it always had done, but this root that had nourished his soul since childhood had previously been transparent, elastic, and yielding, and he had not noticed it, whereas now he saw it and felt it constantly, day and night.

Now that he was no longer imbibing what he had been given by his mother's love but was giving it all back in confusion and anguish, now that his soul was no longer absorbing the salt and moisture of life but was giving it all back in the form of tears, Shtrum felt a constant, incessant pain.

When he reread his mother's last letter; when he divined between its calm, restrained lines the terror of the helpless, doomed people who had been herded behind the barbed wire; when his imagination filled in the picture of the last minutes of Anna Semyonovna's life, on the day of the mass execution that she had known was imminent, that she had guessed about from the stories of a few people from other shtetls who had miraculously survived; when he forced himself, with merciless obstinacy, to imagine the intensity of his mother's suffering as she stood in front of an SS machine gun, by the edge of a pit, among a crowd of women and children; when he did this, he was gripped by a feeling of terrifying strength. But it was impossible to alter what had happened, what had been fixed forever by death. [...]

Shtrum had no wish to show this letter to any of his family. Several times a day he would bring the palm of his hand to his chest and pass it over the jacket pocket where he kept the letter. Once, in the grip of unbearable pain, he thought, "If I kept it somewhere else, somewhere farther away, I should gradually start to feel calmer. As it is, it's like an open grave in my life—a grave that is never filled in."

But he knew that he would sooner do away with himself than part with the letter that had so miraculously found him.

———

Grossman not only wrote the farewell letter he wished he had received from his mother; he also replied to it. After his death, an envelope was found among his papers; in it were two letters he had written to his mother on September 15, 1950, and September 15, 1961, on the ninth and twentieth anniversaries of her death, along with two photographs. One photograph shows his mother with Grossman when he was a child; the other, taken by Grossman from the pocket of a dead SS officer, shows hundreds of naked dead women and girls in a large pit. We have included the first of these photographs but not the second. In both his fictional and his journalistic treatments of the Shoah, Grossman always does all he can to restore dignity to the dead and to enable the reader to see them as individuals. He does not appear to have shown this photograph to his friends and family, and it is unlikely he would have wanted to show it to his readers. Very likely he would have agreed with Claude Lanzmann, who dismissed such photographs as "images without imagination [...] inexact visual renderings that allow viewers to indulge in an unsavory and misleading spectacle at the expense of a past that could only be tapped by a strenuous effort of listening, learning and imagining."

Grossman devoted many years to precisely such a "strenuous effort of listening, learning and imagining." We include both of his letters to his mother in full.

Dearest Mama,

I learned about your death in the winter of 1944. I arrived in Berdichev, entered the house where you lived—the house that had been home to Auntie Anyuta, Uncle David, and Natasha—and understood that you were no longer among the living. But in my heart I had known this as early as September 1941. One night, at the front, I had a dream. I entered a room, knowing that it was *your* room, and saw an empty armchair, knowing that it was where *you* slept. Draped across it was the shawl you used to put over your legs. I looked at this empty armchair for a long time; when I woke from the dream, I knew that you were no more. But I did not know what a terrible death you had; I learned about this only when I came to Berdichev and questioned people about the massacre that took place on September 15, 1941. I have tried dozens, perhaps hundreds of times to imagine how you died, how you walked to your death. I have tried to imagine the man who killed you. He was the last person to see you. I know that you were thinking about me a great deal—all this time.

It is now more than nine years since I stopped writing to you, since I stopped telling you what has been going on in my life. And so much has piled up in my heart during these nine years that I have decided to write to you, to tell you about it all and, of course, to complain about things, since there is, really, no one left who cares about my sorrows. You were the only person who cared.

I shall be frank with you and tell you everything that I feel, but this will not necessarily be the whole truth about me. Not all of my feelings, after all, are true; there is probably much in my feelings that is shallow and false. But I want first of all to tell you that during these nine years I have been able to prove to myself that I really do love you. My feelings for you have not diminished by one iota; I have not forgotten you and I have not found any consolation. Time has not healed me. To me you are as alive as when we saw each other for the last time, as alive as when I was a little boy and you used to read aloud to me. And my pain is still the same as when one of your neighbors on Uchilishchnaya Street told me that you were gone and that there was no hope of finding you among the living. And it seems to me that my love and this terrible grief will never change until the end of my days.

Dearest Mama,

It is now twenty years since your death. I love you, I remember you every day of my life, and through all these twenty years this grief has been constantly with me. I wrote to you ten years ago. And ten years ago, when I wrote my first letter to you after your death, you were the same as when you were alive—my mother in my flesh and in my heart. I am you, my dearest. As long as I am alive, then you are alive too. And when I die, you will continue to live in this book, which I have dedicated to you and whose fate is similar to your own fate.

During these twenty years many people who loved you have died. You no longer live in Papa's heart, nor in Nadya's, nor in Auntie Liza's. All are gone.

And it seems to me that my love for you is all the greater, all the more responsible, now that there are so few living hearts in which you still live. I have been thinking of you almost all the time, almost all these last ten years that I have been working; the love and devotion I feel for people is central to this work, and that is why it is dedicated to you. To me you represent all that is human, and your terrible fate is the fate of humanity in an inhuman time.

All my life I have believed that everything that is good, kind, and honorable in me—everything that is love—comes from you. Everything bad in me—and there's more than enough of this—is not you. But you love me, Mama; you love me even with all that is bad in me.

Today, as I have done so often during these years, I have been rereading the few letters that still remain from among the many hundreds that I received from you. I have also reread your letters to Papa. Reading these letters, I have been crying once again. I cried over the words, "And also, Syoma, I do not expect to live a long life. I'm expecting something to sneak up on me from a dark corner. But what if I were to suffer a long and difficult illness? What would my poor boy do with me then? How terrible it would all be!"

I cry reading the passage where you, who were so lonely and who imagined life under one roof with me as a supreme joy, say to Papa, "It seems to me, weighing everything up sensibly, that, if Vasya had any extra space, you should move in with him yourself. I'm saying this a second time, since things are going all right for me. And there is no need to worry about how I'm feeling; I know how to protect my inner world from the world around me."

I cry over these letters, because you are present in them. Your kindness is there in them, and your purity, and your bitter, bitter life, and your nobility, your sense of justice, your love for me, your concern for others, and your wonderful mind.

There is nothing I fear, because your love is with me and because my love is eternally with you.

PART FIVE
Eternal Rest

"ETERNAL Rest" is a meditation on cemeteries and on the relationship between the living and the dead. Much of the first part is about the battles people often have to fight in order to arrange for a loved one to be buried in a particular cemetery. It is ironic, in the light of Grossman's delicate understanding of the feelings aroused by these battles, that there has been sharp disagreement about where he himself wished to be buried.

Olga Mikhailovna's original wish was for Grossman's ashes to be buried in the Vagankovo, the large and well-established cemetery opposite the Grossmans' apartment that he describes in "Eternal Rest." Grossman had buried his father in the Vagankovo eight years before, and she wanted Grossman to be buried beside him. Her request, however, was refused; it was considered too soon to disturb the grave of his father. Olga Mikhailovna then tried to arrange for Grossman to be buried in the Novodevichye, the most famous of all Russian cemeteries. Wanting him to be honored as a great writer, she enlisted Semyon Lipkin to battle with the Writers Union on her behalf. The authorities, however, refused to allow Grossman—a nonperson during his last years—to be buried somewhere so prestigious. Eventually Grossman's ashes were buried in the Troyekurovskoye Cemetery; this was farther from the city center, but it had been designated to become a branch of the Novodevichye. Although delays in carrying out this administrative reorganization led to a period during which the Troyekurovskoye was neglected, it is now one of Moscow's most important cemeteries.

This picture, however, is complicated by a postscript Lipkin added in January 1989 to the memoir about Grossman that he had first published in 1984. In it Lipkin accuses Olga Mikhailovna of failing to honor her husband's wishes. He claims that Grossman told both him and Yekaterina Zabolotskaya, shortly before his death, that he did not want an official ceremony in the Writers Union and that he wanted to be buried in the Vostryakovo Jewish Cemetery. It is hard to know what to make of this postscript. Neither Grossman's daughter nor his stepson have any recollection of their father expressing any such wish. According to Fyodor Guber, "Had Lipkin suggested the Vostryakovo, I think my mother would have done her best to achieve this." And Lipkin does not say so much as a word about this wish in the main body of his memoir. On the contrary, he more than once, somewhat regretfully, mentions Grossman's lack of interest in Jewish history and Jewish culture.

It is possible that Lipkin was fantasizing, that he added his postscript because his own sense of Jewishness had grown stronger in the six years since the memoir's first publication and he wanted to make out that his admired friend shared his feelings. It is possible that Grossman truly did express this wish and that Olga Mikhailovna did indeed fail to honor it, that Lipkin chose not to criticize Olga Mikhailovna while she was still alive, and that her death in 1988 freed him to speak his mind. It is also possible, however, that it was Lipkin who for some reason failed to communicate this wish and that, reluctant to admit this, he preferred to blame Olga Mikhailovna.

It seems likely that "Eternal Rest" was written within a few years of the death of Grossman's father in 1956. According to Guber, "Grossman often went for walks in the Vagankovo Cemetery, which lay very close to our apartment. After his father's death, he began going there more often still, to visit his father's grave. I think the essay was inspired by an occasion in May 1959 that he recounts in this letter to Olga Mikhailovna, who was then in the Crimea, 'Yesterday I visited Papa's grave—it was his birthday. A priest came up to me in his robes and said, "I imagine this is the grave of your father. Allow me to say a prayer for him." I replied, "My father is a

Jew." He said, "That doesn't matter. Before God, we are all equal."
And he recited a prayer of remembrance. I don't think Papa will be
angry, even though he was not a believer. I planted some pansies and
daisies. I forgot to bring a knife with me, so I dug the holes with my
fingers.'"

ETERNAL REST

I.

THE VAGANKOVO Cemetery is close to the tracks leading to the Belorussian Station. Between the trunks of the cemetery maples you can glimpse trains setting out for Warsaw and Berlin. You can see the blue Moscow–Minsk expresses and the shining windows of restaurant cars. You can hear the quiet hiss of suburban trains and the earthshaking rumble of heavy-goods trains.

The Vagankovo Cemetery is close to the main road to Zvenigorod, with its cars and vans full of clutter being transported to dachas. The Vagankovo Cemetery is also close to the Vagankovo market.

From up in the sky comes the racket of helicopters. From the station comes a resonant voice—a train controller giving clipped, precise instructions about the composition of trains.

While in the cemetery there is eternal peace, eternal rest.

On Sundays in spring it is difficult to squeeze onto the buses going in the direction of the cemetery. Coming from the Presnenskaya Gate, making their way past all the construction sites and ramshackle wooden buildings on "The Year 1905" Street, past the Radio Technical Institute and the lockers and booths of the Vagankovo market, are crowds of people carrying spades, saws, watering cans, paintbrushes, buckets of paint, and string bags full of food. It is spring; it is time to plant flowers on the graves and to repaint the little wrought-iron railings.

Just outside the cemetery the streams of people converge. This vast crowd makes it difficult for the new settlers in their funeral cars to inch their way through the gates. Everywhere there is spring sunshine and fresh green leaves. And what a lot of animated faces! What a lot of talk about the concerns of everyday life! And how very little sadness! Or so, at least, it seems.

There is the smell of paint and the knocking of hammers. There is the squeak of wheelbarrows, the creaking of little carts carrying loads of sand, turf, and cement. The cemetery is hard at work.

Men and women wearing protective canvas sleeves are laboring diligently and enthusiastically. Some are quietly humming to themselves; others are enjoying shouted exchanges with their neighbors.

While Mama paints the fence around Papa's grave, a little girl is hopping about on one foot, trying to get all the way around the grave without letting her other foot touch the ground.

"And now your whole sleeve's covered in paint—what a messy little creature you are!"

Over there, though, they have already knocked off for the day. The railings and the memorial itself have been painted some ridiculous shade of gold. A cloth has been spread out on a bench. They are having a bite to eat and, evidently, a little something to wash it all down with. Their voices are now very jolly, their honest, open faces look flushed. Suddenly there are peals of laughter. Do they then remember with a shock where they are? Do they look around in shame at the grave? No, they do not. But the deceased is not going to take offense—he is, after all, very pleased with the painting job they have done.

Working in the fresh air feels good. It's satisfying to plant some flowers and to pull out a few weeds that have come up through the earth of the grave.

It's Sunday. Where can you go? To the zoo? To Sokolniki Park? No, the cemetery's more enjoyable. You can do a little leisurely work, and you can get some fresh air at the same time.

Life is powerful. It bursts through the fence around the cemetery. And the cemetery surrenders; it becomes a part of life.

There is almost as much everyday drama here, almost as much

passionate excitement, as there is at work, or in a communal apartment, or in the great market nearby.

"Our Vagankovo, of course, isn't the Novodevichye. Still, there are some important people buried here in the Vagankovo. We've got Surikov the painter. We've got Dahl who compiled the great dictionary. We've got Professor Timiryazev the botanist. And there's the poet Sergey Yesenin. And we've got generals, and we've got important Old Bolsheviks. Bauman lies here—he gave his name to a whole district of Moscow. And we've got Kikvidze the civil war hero, the legendary divisional commander. And it wasn't just merchants who were buried here in the days of the tsars—bishops were brought here too."

It is difficult to get oneself a space in the Vagankovo Cemetery—every bit as difficult as to come to Moscow from the provinces and get oneself a residence permit.

And the arguments the families of the deceased adduce before the man with the brick-red face—the arguments this man in boots, a fur hat, and a leather jacket with a zip fastener has to listen to day after day are the very same as those that the passport-section staff have to listen to day after day.

"Comrade Director, his old mother's lying here in the Vagankovo, his elder brother's lying here in the Vagankovo. How can you even suggest such a thing? How can we possibly take him to the Vostryakovo?"

And, just as if this were indeed a Moscow police passport office, the director replies, "I can't. I've received special instructions from the Moscow city soviet. We've exhausted our quota. Anyway, we can't have the whole world coming to the Vagankovo—the Vostryakovo needs people too."

A particularly strict regime was enforced during the weeks immediately before the World Festival of Youth in 1957. It was rumored that Christians participating in the festival were going to be taken on a tour of the Vagankovo, and so the cemetery workers were run off their feet. Everything had to be in order before the festival began.

The people who suffered most were the beggars: the hunch-backed, those who sang, those who whispered, those who shook, disabled veterans from the Great Patriotic War, the blind, the re-tarded. They were taken straight from the cemetery and packed off in trucks. The police too had received special instructions.

Anyone who came into the cemetery office during this period was told, "Come back again once the festival's over."

But when the festival came to an end, the life of the newly smartened-up cemetery simply returned to its normal course.

Once again people are begging the director and his assistants for "Just some earth, just a little patch of earth!"

What is to be done? There is very little space. The deceased—in the words of one of the cemetery workers—"just keep piling in." And not one of them wants to go to the Vostryakovo.

People argue, threaten, and weep.

Some bring requests and certificates from different institutes and social organizations: the deceased was an expert who it will be impossible to replace; he was a remarkable social activist; he was awarded a special pension for achievements of significance to the entire Russian republic; he was awarded medals for his prowess dur-ing the war; he had been a Party member since before the Revolu-tion.

Others try to cheat, to pretend they have important connec-tions—and the cemetery administrators catch them out: "You stated that you wish to bury her beside her husband, but it turns out that we're talking about her first husband and that she's had two more. Have you no shame?"

A third group try to get their way through bribery, with the help of bottles of vodka or fine brandy. Some try to get around the ad-ministrators; others try to win over the men with the spades.

A fourth group just try to barge their way in—like someone who first moves into a room without authorization and only afterward sets about the long and tedious process of trying to obtain the nec-essary documents.

It has, however, been decreed that some neglected graves should be "liquidated" and new graves created in their place. This possibility excites no less passion than an area of living space inhabited by a lonely old woman who just refuses to lie down and die.

Eventually the authorization comes through: one of these sites can indeed be reused. Sometimes it is a matter of one of the old coffins being placed on top of another, while a third coffin lies still farther down. There they lie: a merchant who has now lost even his name; a no less forgotten Old Bolshevik, a true believer who showed no mercy toward the bourgeoisie, with a red ribbon—now half rotted away—still pinned to his lapel; and a director of the secret section of some government institution. Who will be the fourth person?

Why is it that so many people like to spend time in cemeteries?

It certainly is not just a matter of the large number of trees, of the pleasure people take in planting flowers and in working with planes and paintbrushes.

All that is secondary, superficial. The true reason, like most true reasons, lies hidden, deeply buried.

Worn out by grief, by sleepless nights—and often by unbearable feelings of guilt—people come to the cemetery and embark on the struggle to obtain a space there.

This struggle is painful and humiliating. Sometimes people feel resentment toward the deceased: It's all very well for *him*—but what about *us*? What about our own suffering? What about all our sleepless nights while he lay dying? The times we had to rush to the drugstore for oxygen pillows? The times we had to call for an ambulance? The medicines we had to try to get hold of? The fruit? And there's still no end to it all. It may all be over for *him*, but it certainly isn't for *us*.

Other people at the cemetery give wise advice: "Don't get upset. It'll be all right in the end. They may be bureaucrats, but they'll still have to bury him. No one stays unburied forever—it just doesn't happen."

And they were right: he was buried.

Clods of earth knock against the coffin, and a first ray of light—a sense of peace and relief—finds its way into hearts that have been feeling bitter and inflamed. There—he's in the ground now. It's all over.

This very slight, delicate sense of relief is the bud that will develop into a new relationship—a new relationship between the living and the dead. It is this thin ray of light that engenders the animated crowds passing through the cemetery gates—all the joyful labor of painting, planting flowers, and tidying up the graves.

Just how does this relationship develop?

In order to get a sense of this, in order to understand how it is that the agony of an eternal separation can be transformed into the tender joys of the cemetery, we must leave the cemetery and return for a while to the town.

Few close relationships are entirely clear and transparent; they are seldom—as it were—linear and single-story.

More often they are buildings with thick walls and deep cellars, with dark, stuffy little bedrooms, with all kinds of little outbuildings, with extra floors added on top.

And there is no knowing all that goes on in these little rooms and cellars, in these little corridors and attics. There is no end to what has been seen and heard by the walls of these incorporeal structures deep inside the human heart. They have seen clear light, merciless reproaches, eternal lust, satiety to the point of nausea, truth, the desperate wish to have done with someone once and for all, year upon year of one trivial grievance after another and the need to account for every last kopek. They have seen terrible secret hatred. They have seen fights. They have seen blood being drawn. They have seen meekness.

[...]

So here we are—a mound of earth over a grave, and a woman planting forget-me-nots. No, her husband won't be seeing any more of his other woman now. Everything is so peaceful. Her only anxiety now is whether or not she should have planted pansies instead. She has forgiven him, and this forgiveness ennobles her.

Nearby is a young couple, lovingly painting some railings. They talk to the widow, who has already learned that the old woman buried inside these railings loved cats and rubber plants and that there was nothing she would not do for her son and his sweet wife. Peace, simplicity, a blue sky and—chirping over the grave—a young sparrow whose clear voice has yet to be roughened by cold January air. Gone are the old woman's mad, grieving eyes.

And the tear-filled eyes of the paralyzed old man are gone too.

And the little mound over the poor insane boy also looks peaceful. There is an end now to the agonizing confusion felt by his parents, an end to their terror. Pansies, daisies, forget-me-nots.

"What torments the poor girl suffered!" the elderly woman says of her sister.

She has a good look at the grave. The sun shines through the new leaves; it lies bright on the ground. Everything is so quiet now, and relations with the dead are so easy, so peaceful.

"Soon I'll plant some nasturtiums. They'll do well here."

And there is no longer a wall between the loving husband and wife. Their love is no longer poisoned by jealousy and fear, by his hostility toward her daughter by that first husband of hers and the little grandson whom she loves with such passion. "Sleep in peace, dear friend whom we shall always remember."

It feels good in the cemetery. Everything confused and painful has become easy.

A loved one leads a particular kind of life here—a good, clear life—and there is real tenderness in your relationship with them.

A husband who used to come home from work feeling bored and depressed has now learned to enjoy the company of his wife; going to the cemetery on a day off has become his greatest joy. The trees and the grass and the flowers are so very beautiful. There are so many nice people who come regularly to the neighboring graves. He talks about his wife; he thinks about his wife. Remembering her, thinking about her, now feels anything but boring and depressing. Their relationship has been renewed.

Who told people that there is nothing more splendid than life? Who told them that death is terrible?

Here they come with their hammers and paintbrushes, with

their spades and their saws—crowds of people ready to construct a new and better life. Their eyes are looking straight ahead. How difficult and painful it is in the city! How bright in the cemetery!

Had there ever been a way of bridging that gulf—the gulf between the father and his contemptible but ever-so-successful children? Now, anyway, there is no such gulf. "Sleep in peace, dear teacher, father, and friend."

While they work on the grave, the children talk about their lives, their travels, their friends. He, their father, is there beside them. Everything feels so peaceful, so good. Never again will they see that anguished, pitying look on his face. Never again will he look as if he were ashamed of them.

These crowds of the living enter the cemetery, as if the city is pushing them through the gates. And when these exhausted, despairing people see the peaceful green of the graves that have become the sleeping places of husbands, mothers, fathers, wives, and children—at that moment they start to feel hope. Now they are constructing a new life, a better life than the life that had formerly been lacerating their hearts.

2.

Many gravestones bear information about the deceased—about his academic titles or military rank, about his work or number of years as a Party member.

Until 1917 it might have been stated that the deceased was a merchant of the First or Second Guild, or a Full State Councillor.

There is another category of inscription—inscriptions that speak of the feelings of those who were close to the deceased. These inscriptions, in verse or prose, are sometimes very prolix. They are often monstrously ungrammatical or unbelievably absurd, stupid, or vulgar, but this is of no importance to our discussion.

What is important is that both categories of inscriptions—those that speak of the status of the deceased and those that speak of how much he is loved by those near and dear to him—have only one purpose: to inform outsiders. They have nothing to do with the feelings that live in the depths of people's hearts.

Both categories of inscription serve a practical purpose. They are like the statements people make when they apply for a new job, when they propose marriage, when they put someone forward for some prize or medal.

These inscriptions never mention menial or everyday occupations. You never read, "Here lies a barber, a carpenter, a cleaner, a bus conductor…"

If a career is mentioned, it is usually that of professor, actor, writer, fighter pilot, doctor, or artist…

If a rank or position is mentioned, then it is usually an important one: a colonel, an admiral, a senior judge. It is seldom mentioned that someone was a lieutenant or a laboratory assistant.

What matters to the State or to society pursues us as far as the cemetery. Here too everyday human feelings do not dare to speak up.

Inscriptions of the second category—about love, eternal sorrow, tears of grief—serve the same external and self-regarding aims. Whether an inscription is touching or vulgar, whether it is a splendid poem or absurd and ungrammatical doggerel, is irrelevant.

The inscription is not really addressed to the deceased; the deceased, obviously, is unable to read it. Nor is it there for the sake of the bereft; they know what is going on in their hearts even without an inscription.

The inscription is there in order to be read. It is addressed to those who pass by.

In the cemetery a widow is mourning her husband; her lamentations can be heard a long way away. Why must she howl so loudly? The deceased, after all, cannot hear her. And the soul's anguish does not need to be howled out with such power, as if the widow were on the stage of an opera house. But the widow knows very well why she howls. She needs to be heard by the passersby. She too is making a statement; she too is providing information.

Those who repeatedly come to the cemetery in mourning clothes and sit with pious faces on the little benches by the graves are doing the same thing; they too are making statements, they too are providing information.

They are very different from those who come to construct a new life, to refashion a relationship and make it happier and wiser.

Those who go to the cemetery to make statements believe that the most important thing in life is to prove their own superiority, the superiority of their feelings, the unusual depth of their hearts. Yes, there are many reasons, many reasons indeed, why people go to a cemetery.

An NKVD official, a man who lost his mind during the terrible year 1937, is walking among the graves, shouting and waving his fist in the air. The graves remain silent, and this fills the mad investigator with despair. Nothing he can do will make the deceased speak, and he has still not concluded his investigations. There are many reasons, many reasons indeed, why people go to a cemetery.

Lovers arrange trysts in cemeteries. And people go for walks in cemeteries; they go there to get some fresh air.

3.

The cemetery lives an intense, passion-filled life.

Stonemasons, painters, gravediggers, handymen, women whose job it is to keep the cemetery tidy and clean, truck drivers delivering turf and sand, sellers of flowers and seedlings, workers in the store where you rent spades and watering cans—these are the people who determine the material aspects of life in the cemetery.

Nearly all of these jobs have their counterpart in the clandestine world of the black economy. As in the world of contemporary physics, a person or object can, it seems, exist in two different spaces at once.

The black economy has its unwritten price lists and work norms. Workers in this economy charge more than the State does, but they offer more choice and provide materials of better quality.

The cemetery is a part of the State, and it is administered according to the same hierarchical fashion as all other parts of the State.

The administration of the cemetery is centralized; power is concentrated in the hands of the director. And like most centralized systems, this system oppresses even its most senior officials. Even the director does not draw up directives himself; his task is merely to execute directives that come from above.

The Church is separate from the State.

The Church has cadres of its own. It has senior cadres, and it has subordinate cadres: those who sing in its choirs, those who sell candles or communion bread.

It is not only when someone elderly is being buried that people require the help of the Church; even deceased members of the Party are sometimes installed in the cemetery in the presence of a priest. No matter how young a man may be, no matter how contemporary his profession, no matter if he is a nuclear physicist, a designer of rockets, or a worker in a television-repair shop—if he goes and dies, it is possible that the Church will play a role in his funeral.

Here too there is a duplication or split. As well as the official patriarchy, there are dozens of "private" priests, equally separate from the State and from the Church itself. These men wear ordinary clothing, but their long hair, their good-natured puffy faces, and their magnificent red noses make it easy to recognize them as "private" priests.

The official Church has no love at all for these men. The carelessness with which they perform Church rites is positively sacrilegious, and then they are only too ready to accept the most token of payments, to carry out these rites for no more than the price of a glass of vodka—or, perhaps, of a few glasses.

Once, to the great satisfaction of the Vagankovo archpriest, the police organized a raid on the cemetery, a roundup of these "private" priests. From a distance it seemed quite funny to see these long-haired figures leaping over the boundary fence, creeping along the ground like soldiers on a reconnaissance mission, or rushing about between the graves to the accompaniment of police whistles.

If you had a closer view, however, none of this was in the least funny. There was nothing funny about the tears in their eyes, about their heavy, tormented breathing, about the look of shame and terror on their elderly faces.

4.

The cemetery shares the life of the country as a whole, of the people, of the State.

In the summer of 1941 the tracks leading to the Belorussian Station suffered particularly severe bombing. Many heavy bombs fell on the Vagankovo, which adjoins the tracks. These bombs destroyed trees and scattered clods of earth, fragments of granite, and splinters of crosses. There were times when coffins and dead bodies, torn from the ground by the force of an explosion, flew into the air.

During the hungry years of the civil war people came to the cemetery to gather sorrel and the leaves of linden trees. They broke off small branches to feed to their goats.

Even the crimes committed in a cemetery are determined by the conditions of people's lives at a given time.

During the first years after the Revolution there were stories about a cemetery watchman who sold pork: he used to fatten his pigs with human flesh, which he dug up at night from the graves. The police who discovered this were shocked by the look of the pigs; they were huge, wild, and aggressive.

During the years of the New Economic Policy there were stories of a cooperative supplying small food kiosks with spicy, garlic-flavored sausages. It was discovered that these sausages contained meat from human corpses.

During the years when Stalin declared that "life has become better, life has become merrier," grave robbers turned their attention to valuables, to gold teeth, to the suits worn by the deceased.

After the Great Patriotic War there was an influx of items from abroad. Grave robbers were now on the lookout for foreign suits, foreign shoes, anything foreign . . .

A colonel who had served in the Soviet Occupation Forces in Germany had brought back a talking doll for his little daughter. Soon after this the girl died. Since she adored this doll, her parents placed it in the coffin with her. Some time later the mother saw a woman trying to sell this doll. The mother fainted.

But these crimes are atypical, out of the ordinary.

Cemetery crime today is something altogether more petty. Today's thieves steal flowers, portrait frames, vases, iron railings.

5.

One could say, following von Clausewitz, that the cemetery is a continuation of life by other means. The graves express both the characters of individuals and the character of a particular time.

There are, of course, plenty of dull, featureless graves. But then there are plenty of dull, colorless people.

There is a great difference between the graves of important people from recent years and the graves of merchants and privy councillors from before the Revolution.

But no less instructive than this difference is a similarity—the remarkable similarity between the simple, ordinary graves of the past and the simple, ordinary graves of our century of rockets and nuclear reactors.

What staying power! A wooden cross, a mound of earth, a paper wreath ... And if you go and look at the graves in an ordinary village cemetery, this staying power becomes still more evident.

"Everything flows, everything changes," said the Greek.

But this is not evident from the little mounds with their gray crosses. If everything changes, then it changes in a manner that is barely perceptible.

And it is not simply a matter of the tenacity of burial traditions. What we see here is the tenacity of the spirit of life, of the very core of life.

What stubbornness! As if in a fairy tale, all has changed. The new order—electricity, the application of chemical and nuclear power—has brought about countless changes, and we hear about these changes every day.

But this little gray cross, so similar to the gray cross put there one hundred and fifty years ago, seems to symbolize the futility of great revolutions, of great scientific and technical changes that have proved unable to change the deeper aspects of life. The more immutable life's depths, the sharper, the more abrupt are the changes on the ocean's surface.

Storms come and go, but the ocean depths remain.

The Revolution and its storms have left traces. Amid the grass of the Vagankovo Cemetery can be found strange gravestones, bizarre monuments. A black slab of stone with an anvil on top. A cast-iron mast crowned by a hammer and sickle. A heavy ingot of cast steel. A terrestrial globe made from rough, unpolished granite, with a five-pointed star resting atop oceans and continents. New indeed!

The half-effaced revolutionary inscriptions are already harder to read than those on the polished granite gravestones of merchants, princes and factory owners.

But what incandescent passion breathes from each half-effaced word written by the hand of the Revolution! What faith, what a flame, what impassioned power!

And how few—how very few the gravestones and monuments of those who believed in a world commune! To find these monuments you need to search a long time among a dense forest of crosses and slabs of granite, among cast-iron railings and slabs of marble, among tall, wild grass:

> To a mad thought you sacrificed
> Yourselves. It seems you hoped
> Your own thin blood might melt the ice
> That blankets the eternal Pole.
> Against the glacial mass, your spilled
> Blood shone in the darkness like a flame.

Then winter breathed her iron breath—
And nothing of that hope remains.

Stalin once said that Soviet culture was Socialist in content and national in form. It proved, however, to be the other way around.

The Vagankovo Cemetery, the Armenian Cemetery, and the German Cemetery always continued to reflect the depths of life, but they do not reflect the surface of Soviet life between 1917 and the assassination of Kirov in 1934. During this period the national element had not yet emerged from the realm of mere form to become the content of Soviet life, and the Socialist element had yet to be limited once and for all to the realm of external form. This, of course, was a period when the Party was dominated by the revolutionary intelligentsia, by workers with experience in the revolutionary underground.

This period of Soviet life is reflected in the cemetery beside the Moscow crematorium. What a huge number of mixed marriages there were in those years! What wonderful equality between different nationalities! What a plethora of German, Italian, French, and English surnames! Some of the gravestones bear inscriptions in foreign languages. What a lot of Latvians, Jews, and Armenians! What militant slogans on the gravestones!

Here, in this cemetery surrounded by a red wall, it still seems possible to glimpse the flame of young Bolshevism—of a Bolshevism not yet nationalized and taken over by the State: a Bolshevism still imbued with the lyrical passions of youth, with the spirit of the "Internationale," with the sweet delirium of the Paris Commune, with the intoxicating songs of the Revolution.

6.

The living human heart is the most splendid thing in the world. There is true splendor in its ability to love and to have faith, to pardon and to sacrifice everything in the name of love. But in the earth of the cemetery even a living heart must sleep an eternal sleep.

Grand tombs, memorial inscriptions, and the flowers that grow on a grave are all equally unable to show us the soul of someone who has died; they cannot show us their love or grief. Stone, music, prayer, and the lamentations of mourners are all equally powerless to convey the mystery of a human soul.

The sanctity of the soul's holy mystery makes everything else seem contemptible. The drums and brass trumpets of the State, the wisdom of history, the stone of monuments, howls of loss, prayers of remembrance—all these seem as nothing in the presence of this mystery.

So here we are—this is death for you.

APPENDIXES

1. Grossman and "The Hell of Treblinka"

GROSSMAN wrote this long and powerful article with remarkable speed. The Red Army reached Treblinka in early August 1944; the article is dated September 1944 and was published in November 1944.

Grossman was overwhelmed by what he learned at Treblinka; we know that he suffered some kind of nervous collapse on his return to Moscow later that autumn. Nevertheless, "The Hell of Treblinka" is clear, measured, and carefully structured. The tone constantly modulates; horror gives way to irony, fury to pity, passion to mathematical logic—and even, near the end, to a moment of startling lyricism. The perspective from which Grossman writes is no less varied. Many passages are written from the perspective of those about to be gassed. Others are written from the perspective of the guards, from that of the Polish peasants living nearby, from that of a Red Army soldier, or from Grossman's own perspective.

Having established at the outset that nearly all the victims were Jews, Grossman largely gives up using the word "Jews"; instead he insistently repeats the word "people." This may be, in part, a rare instance of Grossman paying lip service to the demands of the anti-Semitic Soviet authorities. Nevertheless, the repetition of "people" is rhetorically effective. First, it is only the Jews whom Grossman refers to as "people"; he refers to the SS either simply as "the SS" or as "beasts"—a word that they, of course, used for the Jews. Second, rather than allowing the non-Jewish reader to stand outside, to imagine these horrors being inflicted only on members of some other nationality, Grossman invites us all to identify with the victims; both we, the readers, and they, the victims, are—simply—"people."

One difficulty that faces anyone writing about the Shoah is the question of "aestheticizing" the death camps. It goes without saying that few writers addressing the Shoah consciously set out to create something beautiful. Nevertheless, most writers wish to write clearly, vividly, and powerfully. If a writer succeeds in these aims, his or her work will inevitably take on a certain beauty and begin to live a life of its own. There is then a danger that the subject matter—*no matter how terrible it may be*—will somehow be transcended, that it will be left behind and forgotten. This fear of transcendence is a driving force behind much of the later work of Paul Celan.

A second difficulty arises from a sense that the only true witnesses, the only witnesses who experienced the full truth of the camps, are the dead, those who can no longer speak to us. Primo Levi voiced this concern more than once. And Aleksandr Solzhenitsyn wrote with regard to the Gulag that "all those who drank of this most deeply, who learned the meaning of it most fully, are already in the grave and will not tell us. No one will now ever tell us the *most important thing* about these camps."

Consciously or otherwise, Grossman comes as near to resolving these dilemmas as anyone is ever likely to come. Passages of near-poetry, passages that appeal vividly to all our senses, are followed by passages in what may seem like the most prosaic literary form of all: the list, the catalogue of objects. But these lists of objects, of the former belongings of former people, do more than just bring us down to earth—to what Grossman refers to as "the swaying, bottomless earth of Treblinka." They are also the truest witnesses to the lives that have been destroyed. Grossman knows that these objects say more than he can.

———

Grossman wrote "The Hell of Treblinka" in wartime and with little in the way of sources. He evidently had access to a copy of Jankiel

Wiernik's *A Year in Treblinka*, but it is unlikely that he had any other written sources. He spoke to Poles from the surrounding area. He interviewed former Treblinka inmates who had escaped during the uprising in August 1943 and who had been hiding in the forest. He was present while Soviet officers took down the testimony of former Wachmänner who had been captured. His notebooks contain facts, names, and numbers, though there is little indication of how he learned them. The manuscript takes up thirty-nine pages of lined paper; there are deletions and changes, but it is on the whole clear and neat. He also drew a small map, which broadly corresponds to maps drawn by former prisoners, and he wrote out the words of two songs that the prisoners were often made to sing: "Edelweiss" and "Lied für Arbeiter 'Treblinka.'"

Around seventy people survived Treblinka, and a number of them wrote about their experiences. The very first account is Abraham Krzepicki's "Eighteen Days in Treblinka." Krzepicki was deported to Treblinka in August 1942, but he escaped to the Warsaw ghetto. There the historian Emanuel Ringelblum asked Rachel Auerbach to record his testimony. Krzepicki was killed in April 1943, during the ghetto uprising, and the manuscript lay buried in the rubble until December 1950. It was first published, in Yiddish, in 1956.

The first account to be published was Jankiel Wiernik's *A Year in Treblinka*. Wiernik escaped from Treblinka during the uprising of August 2, 1943. His account was set in type in a clandestine printshop in Warsaw and published in Polish, in May 1944, in an edition of two thousand copies. A courier from the Polish underground took a microfilm copy to London, and later that year it was published in New York, in both Yiddish and English. It is clear from Grossman's notes that he possessed a Russian translation, and there is at least one occasion when Grossman follows Wiernik very closely indeed.

Another outstanding testimony is Samuel Willenberg's *Surviving Treblinka*. This was written in Polish in 1945 but first published, in Hebrew, only in 1986; an English translation was published in

1989. A man of extraordinary strength and courage, Willenberg fought against the Russians when they invaded eastern Poland in 1939, survived thirteen months in Treblinka, took part in both the Treblinka uprising and the 1944 Warsaw uprising, and then joined a partisan group fighting *alongside* the Russians. Willenberg is probably the only Treblinka survivor still living. His daughter, a well-known architect, is the designer of the Israeli embassy in—of all cities—Berlin.

It has taken us many decades even to begin to take in the truth about Treblinka. Richard Glazar, another survivor of the 1943 uprising, wrote a memoir in Czech immediately after the war but was unable to find a publisher. Only in 1992 did his memoir first appear, from Fischer Verlag, in Glazar's own German translation. Chil Rajchman's testimony, written in Yiddish as early as 1944, has taken still longer to surface. Rajchman seems to have chosen not to publish it during his lifetime, but he instructed his family to publish it after his death. He died in 2004; French and German translations appeared in 2009, and an English translation, titled *Treblinka*, is due in 2011. Rajchman writes without a wasted word and with absolute clarity. His account reads like a medieval vision of Hell; he records the actions of the SS as straightforwardly as a medieval priest might record the behavior of a band of demons.

Our notes also draw on the work of a number of historians, journalists, and anthologists. Rachel Auerbach (1903–76), one of the most dedicated chroniclers of the Warsaw ghetto, was one of a party of twelve (four of them Treblinka survivors) who, on the initiative of the Central State Commission for the Investigation of German Crimes in Poland, made an official inspection tour of Treblinka on November 7, 1945, probably about five or six weeks after Grossman had completed his article. Her account of this visit, "In the Fields of Treblinka" (first published in Yiddish in 1946), includes this unforgettable picture:

The Treblinka veterans [...] wanted to do something, to make some extravagant gestures, that would at least reflect their emotions, bound up as they were with this place. They wanted to gather bones. They leaped into ditches, reached their bare hands into rotted masses of corpses to show they were not repelled. They did the right thing. Now we were just like the Muslim sectarians who carried their dead along in their caravans to Mecca, considering it their sacred duty to bear the smell of death with patience and love as they went along the road. That was how we felt in these fields, where there lay the last remains of our martyrs.

Alexander Donat (1905–83) was a survivor of the Warsaw ghetto who published, among other works, *The Death Camp Treblinka*, an anthology that includes complete English versions of Krzepicki's and Wiernik's testimonies, as well as extracts from others. Yitzhak Arad, a member of both Jewish resistance and Soviet partisan groups in Nazi-occupied Lithuania, was director from 1972 to 1993 of Yad Vashem, Israel's Holocaust Remembrance Authority; his *Belzec, Sobibor, Treblinka: The Operation Reinhard Death Camps* is probably still the most complete account of these camps. Gitta Sereny's *Into that Darkness*, based on interviews conducted in a West German prison with Franz Stangl, the commandant of Treblinka, is an inquiry into how an apparently ordinary person can be capable of what might seem like inconceivable evil. Witold Chrostowski is the author of *Extermination Camp Treblinka*, a clear account that, unfortunately, often fails to name sources. I have also made use of two excellent websites: that of the U.S. Holocaust Memorial Museum at www.ushmm.org and also www.deathcamps.org/treblinka/treblinka.html.

This is the first time that "The Hell of Treblinka" has been published in English in full. Previous translators have made various omissions. In particular, they have omitted many of the references to the Battle of Stalingrad, perhaps seeing them as propagandist. These passages, however, serve a purpose. First, they help us to remember how much Grossman witnessed in the course of only a few years; he was filing reports from the right bank of Stalingrad only eighteen months before composing "The Hell of Treblinka." Second, it was indeed—as Grossman tells us—within weeks of the German defeat at Stalingrad that Himmler visited Treblinka and ordered the bodies of the dead to be dug up and burned. We tend to see the Nazi leaders as possessed by an unquestioning faith in their own rightness. This episode indicates that Himmler, at least, was quick to imagine how the world would see their crimes.

2. Natalya Khayutina and the Yezhovs

In the late 1930s, Soviet cultural life was frenziedly intense; sex, art, and power were—morbidly, dangerously, often fatally—intertwined. There were a number of cultural salons in Moscow, and the most glamorous was that of Yevgenia Solomonovna Yezhova, the wife of the head of the NKVD. While Yevgenia Solomonovna worked as deputy editor of a prestigious journal, *The USSR Under Construction*, and presided over her salon, her husband, Nikolay Yezhov, was presiding over the Great Terror. Between late September 1936 and April 1938, he was responsible for about half of the Soviet political, military, and intellectual elite being imprisoned or shot. He was also responsible for the deaths of approximately 380,000 kulaks and 250,000 members of various national minorities.

Among the members of the Soviet elite who visited Yevgenia Yezhova's salon were the Yiddish actor Solomon Mikhoels; the jazz-band leader Leonid Utyosov; the film director Sergey Eisenstein; the journalist and editor Mikhail Koltsov; the poet and translator Samuel Marshak; the Arctic explorer Otto Shmidt; and the writers Isaak Babel and Mikhail Sholokhov, with both of whom Yezhova had affairs. Babel, whose affair with Yevgenia began in Berlin in 1927, is reported to have said of her, "Just think, our girl from Odessa has become the first lady of the kingdom!" In some respects, at least, Yezhova seems to have been impressively bold; Otto Shmidt's son remembers her as being the only person who came up to speak to his father after Stalin had publicly criticized him at a Kremlin reception.

That Mikhail Sholokhov should have visited Yezhova's salon is not surprising. Sholokhov moved in powerful circles; he was a member of the Supreme Soviet from 1937, and he was admired by Stalin. He appears to have been fearless; both in 1933, during the Terror Famine, and in 1938, toward the end of the Great Terror, he wrote to Stalin with surprisingly direct criticisms of his murderous policies. Isaak Babel's presence is equally unsurprising; he was fascinated by violence and power. The writer Dmitry Furmanov records in his diary that Babel wanted to write a novel about the Cheka. And Nadezhda Mandelstam records her husband as asking Babel why he was drawn to such people as the Yezhovs: "Was it a desire to see what it was like in the exclusive store where the merchandise was death? Did he just want to touch it with his fingers? 'No,' Babel replied. 'I don't want to touch it with my fingers—I just like to have a sniff and see what it smells like.'"

Whether Grossman ever visited the Yezhovs is impossible to establish with certainty. We know only that he was on friendly terms with at least two of the regular visitors to the salon, Babel and Mikhoels, and that in 1938 he wrote to Nikolay Yezhov asking him to release his wife, Olga Mikhailovna, from prison. We also know that in 1960, more than twenty years after the death of both Nikolay Yezhov and his wife, Grossman wrote a story based on the life of a girl from an orphanage whom the Yezhovs had adopted. Grossman changes the girl's name—he calls her Nadya, a name that means "hope"—and he has the Yezhovs adopt Nadya in 1936 or 1937, although they may well have adopted the real Natalya as early as 1933. In most respects, however, Grossman is factually accurate; he evidently knew a great deal both about Natalya's life and about the life of her adoptive parents.

Natalya—who is still alive as I write—has tried to trace her true parents, but to no avail; other researchers have had no more success. The first page of Grossman's story, set in London, hints at the possibility that Natalya was Yevgenia Yezhova's daughter by her previous husband, the journalist and diplomat Aleksandr Gladun. In late 1926 and early 1927 Yevgenia and Aleksandr lived in London; she herself was employed in the Soviet embassy as a typist. In May

1927, as a result of Britain breaking off diplomatic relations with the Soviet Union, they were both expelled. Aleksandr returned to Moscow, but Yevgenia went first to work in the Soviet embassy in Berlin; it was during the several months that she spent there that she began her relationship with Babel. Soon after her return to the Soviet Union, she and Yezhov met in Sukhumi, a resort on the Black Sea. Yezhov fell in love with her; Yevgenia and Aleksandr divorced; and, in the summer of 1930, Yevgenia and Nikolay Yezhov were married.

Toward the end of the first section of "Mama," however, Yezhova says to her husband that the baby girl they are about to adopt has the same eyes as he does. This hints at a very different possibility: that the girl was Yezhov's illegitimate daughter—a claim made by Yezhov's sister. Grossman, however, merely hints at these two possibilities; he does not insist on either.

Russians often refer to the Great Terror as the *Yezhovshchina*. Five feet tall, Yezhov was known as "the bloody dwarf." A well-known pun on his name was *yezhovye rukavitsy*—"rod of iron" or, more literally, "hedgehog skin gauntlets." Grossman's irony with regard to Yezhov is subtle and penetrating; his suggestion that this terrifying figure was himself terrified of his little daughter's nanny—the only person in the apartment with eyes that are free of madness, anxiety, and tension—is as convincing as it is unexpected.

The real Natalya, however, remembers Yezhov with love. She has said in an interview, "He spent a lot of time with me, more even than my mother did. He made tennis rackets for me. He made skates and skis. He made everything for me himself." And the authors of the first English-language biography of Yezhov write, "At the dacha, Yezhov taught her to play tennis, skate, and ride a bicycle. He is remembered as a gentle, loving father, showering her with presents and playing with her in the evenings after returning from the Lubyanka."

Grossman's portrayal is in keeping with Natalya's. Even the "plastic piglet" to which father and daughter give a drink of tea is evidently based on a real prototype. Only once, as Yezhov is already beginning to fall from power, does Grossman puncture this idyll. Nadya looks into Yezhov's eyes and suddenly, for no apparent reason, screams. Yezhov asks if she is ill, and the nanny replies, "Something frightened her." Yezhov asks, "What?," and the nanny replies, "Lord knows—she's only a child." Here, as elsewhere in the story, Grossman has chosen to hint at something rather than to state it explicitly. In his first version this hint was more heavy-handed; Yezhov's "What?" was followed by the sentence, "She wanted to reply but, instead of replying as she wanted, she said, 'Lord knows—she's only a child.'"

Neither version offers any serious explanation for the girl's sudden terror. She may have glimpsed Yezhov's own terror or she may somehow, uncomprehendingly, have glimpsed the terror to which Yezhov has subjected the country. It is possible that this episode is a distillation of an incident that Natalya herself recounted in an interview more than sixty years later. During a game of hide-and-seek Natalya apparently once slipped into her father's study and hid on the windowsill, behind the blinds. There she opened a photograph album and found it to be full of neatly arranged photographs of dead children. In her horror, she was barely able to sleep for several days. Eventually she told her mother what had happened—and from then on Yezhov took care to lock his study securely. Natalya, however, remained frightened even to go past the door; to her it seemed that the dead children were not in a photograph album but there behind the door.

This account has the quality of a nightmare. It is possible it really was a nightmare—perhaps a nightmare that Natalya had some years later and that she remembered as real. There is, however, no doubt as to the reality of Yezhov's macabre ways. The NKVD captain who searched Yezhov's Kremlin apartment shortly after his arrest in April 1939 found four used revolver bullets in a drawer of his desk. In his report the captain wrote, "Each bullet was wrapped in paper with the words *Zinoviev*, *Kamenev* and *Smirnov* written on each in pencil, with the paper saying *Smirnov* wrapped around two bullets. Apparently, these bullets were sent to Yezhov after the exe-

cutions of Zinoviev, Kamenev and the other. I have taken possession of this package." Whatever she saw in reality, and whatever she
saw with her inner eye, Natalya came to a true understanding of
something very dark. A number of interviews with her have been
published during the last ten years, and she mentions this story
about the dead children only in one of them. For the main part, she
is unremittingly positive in her portrayal of Yezhov; this story seems
to have slipped out almost in spite of herself.

The apparent peak of Yezhov's career was on December 20, 1937,
when the Party held a huge gala at the Bolshoy Theatre to celebrate
the twentieth anniversary of the NKVD; Stalin, however, pointedly
failed to toast or congratulate Yezhov. From early 1938, Stalin made
it increasingly obvious that Yezhov had fallen into disfavor. Yezhov,
who had always drunk a great deal and had many affairs with both
men and women, turned to sex and alcohol with greater despera-
tion than ever. As for Yevgenia, she became more and more emo-
tionally disturbed. In May 1938 she resigned from *The USSR Under
Construction* and moved to the family dacha. In mid-September
1938 Yezhov told her that he wanted a divorce. He may have wanted
to disown her because he was afraid that, having lived in both London and Berlin, she was vulnerable to accusations of espionage, or
he may simply have been jealous with regard to her recent affair
with Sholokhov. As head of the NKVD, Yezhov had been monitor-
ing Sholokhov, and he had recently received an all-too-detailed report of a visit by Yevgenia to Sholokhov's hotel room. Not only was
Yevgenia being unfaithful; not only was Yezhov being forced to notice an infidelity he might have preferred to overlook; worst of all,
Yevgenia was being unfaithful with one of her husband's most fearless critics. During a recent audience with both Stalin and Yezhov,
Sholokhov had criticized Yezhov and begged Stalin to put an end to
the Purges.

Yezhov abandoned divorce proceedings, but, in late October
1938, Yevgenia was hospitalized for depression. On November 19, at
the age of thirty-four, she died from an overdose of sleeping tablets;
it was Yezhov who had supplied her with these tablets, and it is

probable that the couple had agreed that she should commit suicide rather than allow herself to be arrested. Yezhov's rival, Lavrenty Beria, had already arrested nearly everyone close to her. According to Yezhov's friend and lover, Vladimir Konstantinov, Yezhov later said, "I had to sacrifice her to save myself." On November 25, 1938, long after he had lost all effective power, Yezhov was formally succeeded by Beria. In April 1939 Yezhov was arrested. Accused of plotting against Stalin's life, he was shot during the night of February 3–4, 1940.

After Yevgenia's death, Natalya was taken care of by her nanny, Marfa Grigoryevna. After Yezhov's arrest, however, when Natalya was six years old, she was taken to an orphanage in Penza, a city about seven hundred kilometers southeast of Moscow. The woman who accompanied her during the journey tried to teach her that her surname was now "Khayutina" (the authorities, unsure what to do with this girl and generally embarrassed by her existence, had given her the surname of her adoptive mother's first husband, Lazar Khayutin—Gladun was Yevgenia's second husband, and Yezhov was her third). When Natalya, unable even to pronounce this name, insisted that she was not "Khayutina" but "Yezhova," her companion hit her on the mouth until her lips bled. In the orphanage, as during the whole of her adult life, Natalya refused to disown her father. She has described the price she paid for her loyalty: "They called me a traitor and an enemy of the people. There was nothing they didn't call me."

After seven years of schooling, Natalya attended a trade school, to which she gained admittance only with difficulty. She was badly bullied. Once she tried to hang herself from a tree, but the branch broke. Then she worked for several years in a watch factory. Finally she was able to go to music school and study the accordion. In 1958 she voluntarily settled in the Russian Far East, in Kolyma, a region six times the size of France that had, in effect, been a single vast camp—an almost autonomous State run by the NKVD. She worked as a music teacher in schools and local Houses of Culture. Though never married, she had a daughter and several grandchildren.

As a child, at a time when it was standard practice to obliterate all images of "enemies of the people" and to tear out their photographs from books, Natalya doggedly tried to save photographs of Yezhov, to hide them from the ever-watchful eye of the orphanage director. As an adult, she petitioned several times, both in the 1960s and more recently, for the official rehabilitation of Yezhov, arguing that his guilt is no greater than that of any of the other prominent figures around Stalin, and that she and Yezhov alike are *victims* of the "repressions" of Stalin's day. The awareness that Yezhov is one of the last century's most terrible mass murderers seems—not surprisingly—to be more than she can live with. She herself claims that she went to Kolyma in order to get away from KGB supervision, to escape to a world where she would no longer be labeled "the daughter of the Iron Commissar." This, however, makes little sense; nowhere in the Soviet Union would she have been more likely to encounter people who had suffered because of her father. She has also, in some interviews, suggested that she was hoping to find her father in Kolyma.

Natalya never—except, possibly, as a small child—had any contact with Grossman, and she has no idea what sources he used; she has written to Grossman's daughter, Yekaterina Korotkova, asking if Grossman's papers contain any more information about her life story. As we have seen, Grossman knew a considerable amount about her life in the orphanage. The passage in "Mama" about Nadya's disappointment at being denied the chance to study at music school accords precisely with Natalya's real story. The authorities, afraid that Natalya might become well known and thus attract attention not only to herself but also to a "father" who had been erased from the history books, initially denied her the opportunity to study either at a music school or at a sports academy. Eventually, however, Zinaida Ordzhonikidze, the widow of a prominent Soviet politician and a close friend of Yevgenia Yezhova, intervened on Natalya's behalf—and Natalya was allowed to enter a music school and study the accordion.

It is possible that Grossman's informant was Natalya's former nanny, Marfa Grigoryevna. Even though the authorities repeatedly refused to give her any information, Marfa Grigoryevna managed to find out Natalya's whereabouts, and she visited her in the orphanage soon after World War II, when Natalya was fourteen. Her intention was to adopt Natalya, but Natalya—wounded by her repeated experience of being abandoned—treated her with extreme aggression, and Marfa Grigoryevna gave up the idea. Natalya and Marfa Grigoryevna do, however, seem to have met at least once more, in Moscow, around 1949. We also know that Natalya met Zinaida Ordzhonikidze in Moscow in 1957. It is possible that Grossman could have heard about this meeting, and he could have met Marfa Grigoryevna any time between 1946 and 1960, when he wrote "Mama."

Grossman, however, was not simply observing the world of the Yezhovs from a distance; he was more personally involved than is immediately apparent. When Boris Guber, Ivan Kataev, and Nikolay Zarudin (all of them former members of the literary group known as Pereval and all of them friends of Grossman) were arrested in 1937, two main accusations were leveled at them. They were accused not only of a failed plot against Stalin's life in 1933 but also of attempting, in late 1934, to organize a plot against Yezhov's life. They intended—according to a scenario constructed by the NKVD with their characteristic blend of unbridled fantasy and careful attention to detail—to take part in one of the literary evenings presided over by Yevgenia Yezhova and then attack Yezhov when he came home late at night. Among the other writers expected—according to this scenario—to be taking part in the literary evening, though not in the "conspiracy," were Babel, Grossman, and Boris Pilnyak. A woman by the name of Faina Shkol'nikova—a friend of Yevgenia Yezhova, and also of Grossman, Guber, and Kataev—was supposed to have provided the conspirators with information about the layout of the apartment and the running of the household.

Guber, Kataev, and Zarudin were shot in 1937; Pilnyak in 1938; and Babel in 1940. As on several other occasions in his life, Grossman seems to have been extraordinarily—almost miraculously—fortunate to survive.

The only other survivor among those implicated, however peripherally, in this "conspiracy," was Faina Shkol'nikova. She too was arrested but, rather than being shot, she was sent to the Gulag. After returning to Moscow in 1954, she became one of the several camp survivors who paid regular visits to Grossman. Conversations with her—about the Yezhov family, about this imaginary "conspiracy"—may well have been at least part of the inspiration for "Mama."

It is not difficult to imagine the impact of such conversations on Grossman. The "conspiracy," which he was almost certainly learning about for the first time, could easily have led to his own execution—and most of those implicated in the "conspiracy" were people who had played a crucial role in his life. Babel was one of the writers he most admired; Guber, Kataev, and Zarudin were his main sponsors at the beginning of his literary career; and Guber was the ex-husband of his second wife and the father of two boys he brought up as his own sons.

Part of the power of "Mama" derives from a tangible sense that there is much that Grossman does not tell us. He writes laconically and with tact and decorum. This is evident in his decision not to incorporate the personal material discussed above—which could easily have overloaded the story. It is still more evident in his matter-of-fact and nonjudgmental portrayal of Yezhov. As if considering it dangerous to look for too long and too directly at Yezhov and his world, Grossman shows them to us, for the main part, through a protective prism of innocence—through the eyes of a child and the eyes of a peasant nanny with something of a child's wisdom.

Both Grossman's "Mama" and Natalya Khayutina's true story encapsulate much of the lasting suffering inflicted on Russia by Stalin. Grossman's version, however, is gentler. He describes only the general physical misery of the orphanage in Penza, saying nothing about the emotional torment Natalya underwent there. He says nothing about her fierce loyalty to the disgraced Yezhov. And as if wanting to find a way out for her, to give her at least the possibility of a better future, he ends the story on a note of quiet hope—in accord with the name he has given her.

Grossman assigns a greater place to Natalya's birth parents, whereas she herself assigns the determining role in her life to Yezhov. Grossman's Nadya remembers seagulls and the splashing of waves; the real Natalya remembers nothing further back than her kind, loving, adoptive father. Central to both stories, however, is a sense of rupture—and a sense of the power of that from which we have been cut off, of recollections of still more distant recollections, of "echoes that had been repeated many times and were now dying away in the mist."

AFTERWORD

by Fyodor Guber

IN LATE 1937 or early 1938, my mother was arrested. My brother and I were still living, along with my nanny, Natalya Ivanovna Darenskaya, in the room on Spaso-Peskovsky Street where we had lived with my father before his arrest on June 20, 1937. Our mother was living with Vasily Grossman, whom she had married a year earlier in May 1936. She was arrested on one of her regular visits to us. The NKVD had evidently been too busy to spend time looking for her; instead, they must have asked a neighbor to phone when she appeared at what was still her official address.

Since Misha and I now had neither father nor mother, the authorities must have been intending to send us to a special orphanage—or, more likely, orphanages. But Vasily Grossman insisted on looking after us himself. He was recovering from a severe attack of asthma, but he made sure that we were brought to him immediately. And so we were taken at night to Herzen Street, where Grossman had recently obtained two rooms in a communal apartment. My brother, who was five years older than me, had witnessed Mama's arrest, but I myself had been sound asleep and I had no idea what was happening. All I remember is streets covered in snow and the uniformed men in the car. We drove into a yard and stopped beside a two-story building. One of the NKVD officers rang, and Grossman opened the main entrance door. Disturbed by our arrival, other tenants were looking out of their windows. The following morning—I was to learn later—Grossman went to the People's Education Department and began the process of having himself appointed our legal guardian.

Anyone who remembers those years will appreciate the remarkable strength of character he showed in taking it upon himself to
bring up the children of an "enemy of the people." There was no realistic hope of my mother's release. It was with regard to these
months that Grossman once said to his friend Semyon Lipkin, "You
can have no idea what life is like for a man trying to look after small
children while his wife is in prison." Nevertheless, Grossman's determination, and the letters he wrote to Nikolay Yezhov and
Mikhail Kalinin and many other important people, brought about
a miracle. On April 1, 1938, my mother was released; she remembered the date all the more clearly because fellow inmates had
thought that she was making an April Fools' Day joke when she
told them her news. One morning I woke up and saw Mama's dressing gown hanging on the door between our two rooms. Misha and
I rushed into the other room. There she was—our Mama. Misha at
once understood that she had been released from prison. I, on the
other hand, had been told that Mama had gone to see her parents in
Siberia. Now I believed that she had, at last, come back. Only in
1944 did she tell me the truth—in response to my saying, "But
Mama, you went to see grandmama and grandpapa in 1938!"

From the moment we moved in with him until the end of his
life, I called Vasily Grossman "Papa." Misha, however, always addressed him more formally, as "Vasily Semyonovich." The fact that
Misha was eleven when our father was arrested, while I was only six,
was very apparent. Grossman looked on both of us as his sons; if he
did not adopt us formally, this was only to avoid creating the impression that he was asking us to betray our father.

We continued to live in the apartment on the corner of Herzen
Street and Bryusov Lane until 1947. It was in a two-story building
said to have been built in the reign of Catherine the Great. It was
now surrounded by eight-story buildings, and we shared it with
three other families. Our two rooms must have once been one large
room. Standing in what was the left-hand corner of our room and
the right-hand corner of the room that served as Grossman's study,
bedroom, living room, and dining room was a large, snow-white

Russian stove. In the shared kitchen there were tables with the small paraffin and Primus stoves that we used in those days for cooking. There was no bath in the apartment. We went regularly to the bathhouse, but we also greatly enjoyed going to my aunt Marusya's or to the apartment of one of Grossman's friends, Ruvim Fraerman, for what we called a "real bath."

Grossman tried several times before the war to move to a self-contained apartment, but without success. The communal apartment was, of course, a considerable improvement on "nomadic" existence—on living in the corners of rooms belonging to friends and acquaintances, as he had done since the arrest of Nadya Almaz in 1933. Nevertheless, life in a communal apartment was far from conducive to literary creativity.

And yet it was in this building on the corner of Herzen, with its six-foot-thick walls, that Grossman wrote his second novel, *Stepan Kolchugin*, and a great number of stories. It was from here that he set out, in a jeep provided by *Red Star*, to work as a war correspondent. And it was in this building, immediately after the war, that he wrote a large part of *For a Just Cause*—the prequel to *Life and Fate*.

When I was a child, Grossman spent a lot of time reading poetry to me. He sang songs and even arias from operas, although he did not have a musical ear. He especially loved Tchaikovsky's *The Queen of Spades*. He told me stories from his own childhood and youth, and fairy tales that he made up as he went along. He retold Jack London's *Star Rover* and Charles de Coster's novel about the adventures of Till Eulenspiegel—, and all for my benefit alone. He did not carry on reading poetry aloud after I had grown up.

The poet he read to me most often was Nikolay Nekrasov, the great "civic" poet of the second half of the nineteenth century. He also read Eduard Bagritsky's "The Lay of Opanas," a long poem, in the style of a folk epic, about the Russian civil war. Opanas is a simple Ukrainian peasant caught up in the complex struggle between the Reds (Communists), the Whites (anti-Communists), and the Greens (peasant anarchists). Grossman knew the whole of this poem by heart, and often quoted his favorite lines from it. He also read me more modernist poems that were far from standard fare at the time: Sergey Yesenin, Innokenty Annensky, and Osip Mandelstam—and even Ivan Bunin and Vladislav Khodasevich, both of whom had emigrated.

Grossman often told me about the Museum of New Western Art, the fine museum of impressionist and early-twentieth-century art based on the collections built up before the Revolution by Sergey Shchukin and Ivan Morozov. This museum was closed after the Second World War; the paintings were divided between the Hermitage and the Pushkin Museum, but many were not exhibited for several decades. He told me about Gauguin, Monet, and Matisse, about Picasso's Blue Period and Rose Period, and about Matisse's friend Albert Marquet. I was able to imagine these paintings vividly from his descriptions of them.

I often saw Grossman reading his black volumes of Tolstoy and his red volumes of Dostoevsky, but the writer he loved most of all was Chekhov. The small Marx Publishing House volumes were always on his writing desk. He also very much admired Ibsen and Knut Hamsun. Before the war I saw him read and heard him talk about many other writers and works of literature: Homer, Aristotle, Longus's *Daphnis and Chloe*, Catullus (whom he often quoted), Machiavelli, Eckermann's *Conversations of Goethe*, Shakespeare ...

Grossman often reread the work of Isaak Babel—both *Red Cavalry* and the Odessa stories. He more than once read his favorite stories aloud to us, and there were particular sentences that remained with him throughout his life. He always spoke with passionate enthusiasm about the work of his friend Andrey Platonov. He knew not only the published work but also the unpublished stories and novels.

He admired the first two volumes of Mikhail Sholokhov's *The Quiet Don*, but he had a low opinion of Sholokhov's later work.

He read Rider Haggard with real interest. He read and reread

Sherlock Holmes. And there was a series—*Geografgiz*—of popular-science books about animals that he greatly enjoyed. One book from this series, about a man-eating black panther, was in his hospital room during his last days. I read to him from it one evening, and the following morning he said to me, "I dreamed of the panther. I felt real terror."

In 1938 Mama exchanged the room in which we had lived with my father on Spaso-Peskovsky Street for rooms in a two-story wooden house in Lianozovo, a dacha village not far from Moscow. The house had a large garden, with bushes and thickets big enough to hide in. Part of the garden was turned over to flower and vegetable beds. My mother grew a variety of vegetables, including cucumbers and tomatoes. She also grew flowers. For some reason I particularly remember her snapdragons and tobacco plants.

There was also a parking place for an M-1 looked after by one of our neighbors, a professional driver; he would sometimes lie on the grass beneath it and carry out repairs. I thought the smell of gasoline and leather was quite wonderful.

Above us lived the family of an artillery commander. After the Soviet occupation of the Baltic States and western Ukraine in 1939, he was posted somewhere close to the Soviet frontier. His son used to visit him there and come back with wonderful toys; we all felt envious. Once, in 1940, Grossman was sent to one of the Baltic states with Aleksandr Tvardovsky to write an article about one of the Soviet divisions there, and he brought me back similar toys—a little tank, and a toy pistol that flashed and let out puffs of smoke.

Grossman's mother, Yekaterina Savelievna, spent two summers with us in Lianozovo, and his daughter, Katya, also stayed with us sometimes; I remember her as tall and thin. Many of Grossman's friends also used to visit us there.

Somewhere on the outskirts of Lianozovo was a dacha belonging to Marshal Voroshilov, the People's Commissar for Defense. When we went for walks in the forest, serious-looking figures in plain clothes would sometimes make us turn back just as we reached some particularly picturesque spot.

The path from the railway station to our house led through dense forest, and we often picked mushrooms on the way. We would cut hazel branches and use them to hold back the long grass and bushes so we could see the mushrooms more easily. Grossman had a Swiss penknife with a red handle and a red leather case; I think he had been given it by his mother. He often used to decorate our hazel sticks, carving little circles and squares on them. We would collect pieces of bark and he would make them into little boats or other small toys for me. As well as spending our summers in Lianozovo, we sometimes went there in winter to ski.

In summer Grossman used to wear a *tyubeteika* (a central Asian skull cap), a white shirt, white tussah-silk trousers, and sandals on bare feet. Before the war he was stout, and he walked with a stick. He looked older than his thirty-five years. The young women used to address him as "Uncle," even though he was only slightly older than they were—young enough to have been one of their admirers.

Grossman and my mother never said a word to us about their fears, or about any of the terrible experiences they had gone through. I remember those years before the war as a happy time, the happiest time of my life. But my brother was almost certainly less happy.

———

Grossman had a touching love for the animal world. For many years we had fish in small aquariums. At one time we kept a very aggressive squirrel, and we had a number of cats and dogs over the years. Grossman was especially fond of a white poodle named Lyubka, who lived with us for about twelve years. During her last days she could hardly move, and we used to carry her out in our arms "for a walk." We buried her opposite our apartment.

Grossman loved going to the zoo; he went several times a year.

Once he spotted a porcupine quill lying on the ground. He climbed over the fence of the porcupine's little enclosure and picked it up. I just stood and watched. To this day the porcupine quill lies on his writing desk in my daughter's apartment in Moscow, along with his inkwell and penholder—Grossman often wrote not with a fountain pen but with a simple dipping pen.

———

Grossman was not—as has sometimes been said—gloomy and unsociable. It is simply that his last years brought him little to celebrate. He did, nevertheless, greatly enjoy convivial meals, and one or another of his friends would call on him almost every day. They would tell jokes and sometimes they would sing together. He would read aloud his stories, or extracts from his longer works.

Friends and relatives would come around every Sunday. Most often, at least from the mid-1950s, we would see two of Grossman's oldest friends, Faina Abramovna Shkol'nikova and Yefim Abramovich Kugel (described with great warmth in Grossman's autobiographical story "Phosphorus"), along with Nikolay Mikhailovich Sochevets (my maternal uncle, on whom Grossman based the hero of *Everything Flows*). We would all do a crossword together. Yefim Abramovich would say, "A four-letter word beginning with K," "A seven-letter word beginning with N," and so on. Uncle Kolya would be standing by the bookshelf leafing through a book, or working on one of the remarkably lifelike little animals he used to mold from clay. His eyesight was extremely poor and he was usually looking somewhere else, "seeing" the clay not with his eyes but with his hands. Faina Abramovna would always be smoking; Grossman would be making jokes or teasing us. When it was time for our main meal, we would have vodka and wine, and I would often be sent out to buy ice cream.

There were three other old friends Grossman saw a great deal: Semyon Tumarkin, Aleksandr Nitochkin, and Vyacheslav Loboda, who preserved the original manuscript of *Life and Fate*. And there was the poet Semyon Lipkin, who wrote an important memoir about Grossman. He and Grossman used to meet several times a week, and they often went out for walks lasting several hours.

Translated by Robert Chandler, with the author

CHRONOLOGY

1881   Alexander II assassinated by members of The People's Will (Narodnaya Volya) terrorist organization.

1891   Beginning of construction of Trans-Siberian Railway.

1905   The wave of mass political unrest known as the 1905 Revolution leads to the establishment of the Duma (a parliament) and a limited constitutional monarchy. Birth of Vasily Semyonovich Grossman.

1910–12   Grossman and his mother live in Geneva.

1914–19   Grossman attends secondary school in Kiev.

1917   Tsar Nicholas II abdicates after the February Revolution. Workers' soviets (councils) are set up in Petrograd and Moscow. Lenin and his Bolshevik Party seize power in the October Revolution.

1918–20   Russian Civil War, accompanied by the draconian economic policies known as War Communism. Although there were many different factions, the two main forces were the Red Army (Communists) and the Whites (anti-Communists). Foreign powers also intervened, to little effect. Millions perished before the Red Army, led by Leon Trotsky, defeated the Whites in 1920. Smaller battles continued for several years.

1921   After an uprising in March 1921 by sailors at the naval base of Kronstadt, Lenin made a tactical retreat, introducing the at-least-relatively liberal New Economic Policy (NEP), which lasted until 1928. Many of the more idealistic Communists saw this as a step backward. The NEP was not, however, accompanied by any political liberalization.

1924   Death of Lenin. Petrograd is renamed Leningrad. Stalin begins to take power.

1928–37   The first and second of Stalin's Five-Year Plans bring about increased production of coal, iron, and steel.

1928	Grossman marries Anna (usually known as Galya) Matsuk and publishes his first newspaper articles.
1929	Collectivization of agriculture begins. Grossman graduates from Moscow State University and starts work as an engineer in the Donbass region.
1930	Birth of Grossman's daughter, Yekaterina Vasilievna (Katya).
1931	Grossman returns to Moscow, where he works in a pencil factory. Grossman and Galya are divorced.
1932–33	Between three and five million peasants die in the Terror Famine in Ukraine.
1933	Hitler comes to power in Germany. Grossman's cousin Nadya Almaz is arrested in Moscow.
1934	First Congress of the Union of Soviet Writers. Grossman publishes "In the Town of Berdichev" and the novel *Glyukauf*, about the life of the Donbass miners.
1935	Mussolini invades Ethiopia. Grossman's mule (the hero of "The Road") takes part in the campaign.
1936	Grossman marries his second wife, Olga Mikhailovna Guber.
1936–38	Approximately half the members of the Soviet political, military, and intellectual elite are imprisoned or shot. Roughly 380,000 supposed kulaks and 250,000 members of various national minorities are killed. The period from September 1936 until November 1938 is known as the Great Terror, or Yezhovshchina—after Nikolay Yezhov, then head of the NKVD (the Soviet secret police).
1937	Grossman is admitted to the Union of Soviet Writers.
1937–40	Publication, in installments, of Grossman's second novel, *Stepan Kolchugin*.
1939	Molotov-Ribbentrop Pact is signed. Beginning of Second World War.
1939–41	Death of 70,000 mentally handicapped Germans in the Nazis' euthanasia program.
1941	Hitler invades the Soviet Union. Leningrad is blockaded and Moscow under threat. Grossman starts work as a war correspondent for *Red Star* (*Krasnaya zvezda*), the Red Army newspaper.
1941–42	An estimated two million Jews are shot in western areas of the Soviet Union. Grossman's mother is one of approximately 12,000 Jews killed in a single day at the airport outside Berdichev.

1941–44   Two and a half million Polish Jews are gassed in Chelmno, Majdanek, Bełzec, Sobibor, Treblinka, and Auschwitz.

1942   Publication of Grossman's novel *The People Immortal*.

1942–43   The Battle of Stalingrad was the first important German land defeat of the war. Grossman spends nearly three months in the thick of the fighting.

1944   Between April and June, 436,000 Hungarian Jews are gassed at Auschwitz, in only fifty-six days.

1945   End of Second World War.

1946   Nuremberg Trial of the Nazi leadership. In the Soviet Union, Andrey Zhdanov tightens control over the arts. Grossman's play *If You Believe the Pythagoreans* is fiercely criticized.

1948   Destruction of the plates for the Soviet edition of *The Black Book*, a documentary account of the Shoah in the Soviet Union and Poland, compiled by Ilya Ehrenburg and Vasily Grossman between 1943 and 1946.

1951   Death of Andrey Platonov. Grossman gives the main speech at his funeral.

1952   Secret trial of members of the Jewish Anti-Fascist Committee. Publication in *Novy mir* of Grossman's novel *For a Just Cause*.

1953   Publication of article in *Pravda* in January about the Jewish "Killer Doctors." Preparations continue for a purge of Soviet Jews. *For a Just Cause* is attacked in *Pravda* and elsewhere. Death of Stalin on March 5. On April 4, official acknowledgment that the case against the "Killer Doctors" was fabricated.

1954   *For a Just Cause* is published as a book.

1955   Grossman sees Raphael's *Sistine Madonna* on exhibit in Moscow before it is returned to the Dresden Art Gallery.

1956   Millions of prisoners are released from the camps. Khrushchev's denunciation of Stalin at the Twentieth Party Congress marks a high point in the more liberal period known as the "Thaw."

1957   A Russian dog, Laika (her name means "Barker"), travels into space on *Sputnik 2*.

1958   Publication abroad of *Doctor Zhivago*. Under pressure from the Soviet authorities, Pasternak declines the Nobel Prize.

1961   The KGB confiscates the manuscript of *Life and Fate*.

1962   Publication of Solzhenitsyn's *One Day in the Life of Ivan Denisovich*.

1964 Fall of Khrushchev. Grossman dies on September 14, of lung cancer.

1970 Publication in Frankfurt of an incomplete Russian edition of *Everything Flows*.

1974 Solzhenitsyn deported after publication in the West of *The Gulag Archipelago*.

1980 *Life and Fate* is published in Russian, for the first time, in Lausanne.

1985 Mikhail Gorbachev comes to power. Beginning of the period of liberal reforms known as perestroika; the next few years see the first publication in Russia of Grossman's *Life and Fate* and *Everything Flows*, and of important works by Krzhizhanovsky, Platonov, Shalamov, Solzhenitsyn, and many others.

1991 Collapse of the Soviet Union.

NOTES

PART ONE: THE 1930S

5   *abroad to study*: John and Carol Garrard, *The Bones of Berdichev*
     (New York: The Free Press, 1996), 31 and 376.

6   *an uprising in Sebastopol*: Fyodor Guber, *Pamyat' i pis'ma* (Moscow:
     Probel, 2007), 7. The Garrards suggest that Grossman's father,
     Semyon Osipovich, was active in the Jewish Labor Bund, but this is
     no more than a supposition, based on the fact that Geneva was, at the
     time, a center for Bund activities.

6   *lost his interest in science*: He was quick, a decade later, to grasp the
     importance of nuclear physics; one of his notebooks for 1944 includes
     a diagram of a nuclear chain reaction [Guber, 39]. It is not for nothing
     that Grossman chose to make Viktor Shtrum, the central figure of
     Life and Fate and in many respects a self-portrait, into a physicist.

7   *found in her possession*: See Garrard, 109. Serge had been arrested for a
     second time two months before this, in February 1933. He may have
     been the first person to refer to the USSR as a "totalitarian" state.

7   *in Astrakhan*: After spending three years in exile in Astrakhan,
     Nadya was given another three-year sentence, this time in a labor
     camp in the far north. She returned to Moscow in 1939. See Guber,
     20; and Garrard, 112 and 129–30.

8   *Glyukauf*: this is derived from the German *Glück auf* ("Luck up!" or
     "Good luck!"), a phrase used to greet a miner just brought up to the
     surface.

8   *Literaturnaya gazeta*: See A. Bocharov, *Vasily Grossman* (Moscow:
     Sovetsky pisatel', 1990), 11. This excellent monograph is an expanded
     version of a study first published in 1970.

8   *and Boris Pilnyak*: See Semyon Lipkin, *Kvadriga* (Moscow: Knizhny
     Sad, 1997), 516. Babel apparently said, "Our Yid capital has been seen

through new eyes." Lipkin then quotes Bulgakov as saying, "Don't say it's really been possible to publish something worthwhile!" This has been understood to mean that he too admired the story, but it was probably no more than a polite response on Bulgakov's part. An English translation of "In the Town of Berdichev" was included in John Lehmann's *New Writing* 2 (Autumn 1936): 131–45. Five Soviet writers were represented in the first two issues of this journal: Grossman, Pasternak, and Sholokhov, and the now-lesser-known Ognev and Tikhonov.

9   *in danger himself*: Grossman's friends proved remarkably loyal. According to Fyodor Guber, who obtained access to his father's NKVD file, "When questioned by the investigator about Vasily Grossman, my father replied, 'Nothing compromising is known about Grossman.' The other former members of Pereval gave similar answers." [Gruber, 32.]

9   *the NKVD*: The Soviet security service was renamed many times; the most important of its names and acronyms, in chronological order, are the Cheka, the OGPU, the NKVD, and the KGB.

9   *chief executioner*: See Lipkin, 518. Tzvetan Todorov has written that "Grossman is the only example, or at least the most significant, of an established and leading Soviet writer changing his spots completely. The slave in him died, and a free man arose." [Tzvetan Todorov, *Hope and Memory* (London: Atlantic Books, 2005), 50.] Impressive though this may sound, Todorov is mistaken: Grossman showed great courage and independence throughout his life.

9   *Olga Mikhailovna was released*: For Grossman's astutely phrased letter to Yezhov, see Garrard, 122–25 and 347–48. See also Guber's afterword to the present volume.

9   *in the Ukraine in 1932–33*: In August 1931, when the hunger was only just beginning, he had written a coded (his own word is "Aesopian") letter about this to his father [Garrard, 93–95].

9   *the Soviet government*: Ibid., 348.

10   *I wish to triumph?*: Lipkin, 516.

11   *then rejects again*: A study of Grossman's manuscripts suggests that he was aware of the delicacy of the ideological balancing act he was performing. The story ends with Vavilova abandoning her baby and rushing out to join some Red Army cadets as they march suicidally toward the advancing Poles. Magazanik and his wife, Beila, in whose home

Vavilova has been lodging, are watching. The published version ends as follows:

> Not taking his eyes off Vavilova, Magazanik said, "Once there were people like that in the Bund. Real human beings, Beila. Call us human beings? No, we're just manure."
>
> Alyosha had woken up. He was crying and kicking, trying to get out of his swaddling clothes. Coming back to herself, Beila said to her husband, "Listen, the baby's woken up. You'd better light the Primus—we must heat up some milk."
>
> The cadets disappeared around a turn in the road.

In the manuscript, however, there is one more sentence: "Beila sighed and said loudly, "A Tatar, an ignorant Tatar!" (The Russian is simply "Nu, Tatarin!"—a phrase that is oddly difficult to translate. In English we say "He/she is a real Tatar" of someone we see as fiercely disciplinarian; we do not use the phrase simply to indicate savagery. Adding the word "ignorant" seemed the only way to make the words sound plausible on both occasions.) Beila has already, once before, called her husband a Tatar—and so her words carry weight. As well as criticizing Vavilova for having abandoned her baby, Beila is criticizing her husband for appearing to condone Vavilova's behavior. Evidently either Grossman or his editors decided that this ending was too dangerous. Grossman's uncertainty about the story's conclusion is still more clearly shown by the changes he introduced when, at some time between 1934 and 1939, he wrote a film script based on the story [RGALI, fond 1710, opis' 1, ed. khr., 95]. In the published story Vavilova is a fanatic; in the script she is a devoted mother who has little choice but to leave her baby *for a short time*. In the story—and only in the story—Grossman poses an important question with shocking sharpness. Soviet literature of the 1920s and '30s contains many examples of people sacrificing a husband, wife, or parent, but only Grossman asked whether it is right for a mother to abandon her newborn child for the good of the cause. Contemporary critics were evidently ill at ease with this question. Even though the story was praised in Soviet journals, there was almost no serious discussion of the dilemma it poses.

Grossman's script was never made into a film; it is not to be confused with Aleksandr Askol'dov's *The Commissar*, based on the same story. Made in 1967, *The Commissar* was banned for two decades but won two international prizes on its release in 1988. Curiously, just as

Life and Fate was more thoroughly banned than any other Soviet book, so *The Commissar* may have been more thoroughly banned than almost any other Soviet film. Askol'dov was told that the only copy had been destroyed. In the Gorbachev era, however, it was discovered that workers in a film archive had preserved a copy. What made *The Commissar* so unacceptable was, no doubt, its final sequence (not, of course, corresponding to anything in Grossman's original story) about the Shoah.

All the above—the importance of the repetition of "Nu, Tatarin!," the differences between story and script, the reaction of contemporary critics—is summarized from an article by Yury Bit-Yunan to be published in 2010 by *Voprosy literatury*.

12   *his professional career*: At one point in "A Tale About Love," a long story written in 1937, a film director and a scriptwriter talk about their joint project. They agree that Chekhov's "The Steppe"—a story in which almost nothing appears to happen—is "real art." In the context of Soviet literature from the 1930s, this discussion is startling.

"IN THE TOWN OF BERDICHEV"
Written in 1934; first published in Literaturnaya gazeta *(April 2, 1934).*

16   *pointed Budyonny helmet*: Semyon Budyonny (1883–1973) was a hero of the Russian civil war. His name was given to a helmet worn by Red Army soldiers between 1918 and 1921.

17   *voluntary working Saturdays*: There was a Soviet tradition of voluntary working Saturdays (*subbotniki*). Lenin himself participated in the first all-Russian *subbotnik* (May 1, 1920), helping to clear building rubble from the Kremlin. These days soon ceased to be voluntary—if ever they were.

19   *the Jewish nation*: Yury Bit-Yunan suggests that Grossman is alluding to a story told by Grushenka in *The Brothers Karamazov*: a wicked woman is cast, after her death, into a lake of fire. Her guardian angel remembers that she once gave a spring onion to a beggar. God tells the angel to try pulling her out of the lake with that onion. The angel almost succeeds, but the woman realizes that other sinners have caught hold of her and are hoping to be pulled out themselves. She kicks out and yells, "It's my onion, not yours!" The stem of the onion breaks, and the woman falls back into the lake.

22 *the July days*: This refers to a period during July 1917 when soldiers and industrial workers spontaneously demonstrated against the Provisional Government. The Bolsheviks eventually tried to provide leadership, but the demonstrations were repressed. Kerensky was appointed prime minister and the Bolsheviks temporarily lost much of their influence.

22 *footcloths*: Lengths of cloth wound around the foot and ankle—more common in Russia, until the middle of the twentieth century, than socks or stockings. By the 1950s, however, they had largely disappeared—except in labor camps and the army.

27 *Bald Hill*: Hills with this name—and there are many Bald Hills in Russia and Ukraine—were associated with witches and their sabbaths.

31 *the same story each time*: Simon Petlyura (1879–1926) was the leader of a Ukrainian nationalist movement that was at its most powerful during 1918 and 1919. Anton Denikin (1872–1947) commanded the White armies in the south of Russia during the Civil War. And there were many other bands of anarchists, criminals, lawless peasants, etc.

32 *the Bund*: The Jewish Labor Bund was a secular Jewish Socialist party in the Russian empire, active between 1897 and 1920.

"A SMALL LIFE"
Written in 1936; first published in Dobro vam! *(Moscow: Sovetsky pisatel', 1967).*

35 *Central Rubber Office*: Vera Ignatyevna works at Rezinosbyt, which was responsible for the distribution of rubber products throughout the Soviet Union.

35 *Air-Chem Defense Society*: The Society for the Promotion of Defense, Aviation, and Chemistry (Osoviakhim or Obshchestvo sodeistviya oborone i aviatsionno-khimicheskomu stroitel'stvu) was a "voluntary" civil-defense organization, described by Stalin as vital to "keeping the entire population in a state of mobilized readiness against the danger of military attack, so that no 'accident' and no tricks of our external enemies can catch us unawares." Founded in 1927, it sponsored clubs and contests throughout the USSR; by the early 1930s it had around twelve million members.

38 *Mostorg Department Store*: A portmanteau word, derived from the words for "Moscow" and "trade."

"A YOUNG WOMAN AND AN OLD WOMAN"

According to one Russian edition, this was written 1938–40; another edition gives 1940–62. It is one of four stories that Grossman entrusted in 1961 to his friend Anna Berzer, the fiction editor at Novy mir. *Berzer managed to publish it in the September 1964 issue of the journal* Moskva; *Korotkova remembers Berzer showing Grossman the proofs in the hospital, hoping this might cheer him up. How much of the story Grossman wrote in the late 1930s and how much in the early 1960s is unclear. Most of his stories, however, are based on recent experience, and during the 1930s Grossman spent several summer vacations in elite government houses of recreation similar to the one described here. It seems likely that he began the story in the 1930s, realized that the subject matter made it unpublishable, and so waited until the time of Khrushchev's "Thaw" before completing and attempting to publish it.*

41 *All-Union People's Commissariat*: "People's Commissariat" was the term used between 1918 and 1946 for a government ministry. There were People's Commissariats for each constituent republic and also for the Soviet Union as a whole; the latter were known as All-Union People's Commissariats.

41 *Kuntsevo*: This village on the bank of the Moscow River first became a summer resort for Muscovites during the nineteenth century. In the 1930s Stalin and other members of the political elite had dachas there.

41 *long ZIS's—beige, green, or black*: The M-1 was, at the time, a new model. ZIS is an acronym for Zavod imeni Stalina (Factory named after Stalin).

45 *thorn apple*: *Datura stramonium*—a powerful narcotic, usually considered too poisonous to eat.

45 *our wheat's all burning!*: Compare: "And while they were still transporting the grain, there was dust wherever you went. It was like clouds of smoke—over the village, over the fields, over the face of the moon at night. I remember one man going out of his mind. 'We're on fire!' he kept screaming. 'The sky is burning! The earth is burning!'" [Vasily Grossman, *Everything Flows* (New York: NYRB Classics, 2009), 125.]

46 *Nevraev*: His name means "not a liar."

48 *"try to get their hands on our Motherland!" said Gagareva*: In 1939 Ja-

pan and the Soviet Union fought a brief, undeclared war. Japan was defeated at the Battle of Khalkhin Gol. This is probably why Japan later chose not to ally with Nazi Germany against the Soviet Union.

52 *twenty-one minutes late*: During the 1930s workers were penalized harshly for absenteeism or for being more than twenty minutes late for work.

PART TWO: THE WAR, THE SHOAH

64 *an ancient and peaceful town*: Vasily Grossman, *Sobranie sochinenii*, (Moscow: Vagrius, 1998) vol. 3, p. 203.

64 *defenders of Stalingrad*: A. Bocharov, *Vasily Grossman* (Moscow: Sovetsky pisatel', 1990), 112.

64 *one of their comrades in arms*: John and Carol Garrard, *The Bones of Berdichev* (New York: The Free Press, 1996), 162. See also Yekaterina Korotkova, "Yanvarskiye kanikuly," *Raduga* (May–June 2009): 142.

64 *until they were in tatters*: Frank Ellis, *Vasiliy Grossman* (Oxford: Berg, 1994), 48. There are similar accounts by people who first read Grossman's articles in Leningrad during the Siege [Bocharov, 132].

65 *his own experience of the battle*: E-mail from Jochen Hellbeck, May 5, 2008.

65 *whom we had nicknamed Zhuchka*: Korotkova, 144. Zhuchka is a name given to dogs—and to women seen as garrulous or bad-tempered.

65 *ready to talk to him*: See David Ortenberg, *Letopistsy pobedy* (Moscow: Politizdat, 1990), 42–55, especially 51–53.

65 *the required article*: see Yekaterina Korotkova, "O moyom ottse," *Sel'skaya molodyozh'* (March 1993): 49.

66 *in September 1941*: The genocide of European Jews began when the Germans invaded the Soviet Union. Four special SS formations known as Einsatzgruppen (a typically Nazi euphemism meaning "special task force") advanced with the forward units of the Wehrmacht. Their task was to combat what Hitler called "Judaeo-Bolshevism" by murdering Jews, Communist Party officials, and Red Army political commissars. Along with local collaborators, the Einsatzgruppen rounded up Jews, drove them to nearby ravines, swamps, and forests, and shot them dead. There were two main waves of these massacres: August to December 1941, and the summer of 1942. Approximately two million Jews were murdered. Mordecai Altshuler writes that "the

Nazi authorities viewed the annihilation of the Jews within the USSR's original boundaries with particular urgency, since they regarded them as the mainstay of the Bolshevik regime." [Mordecai Altshuler, "The Unique Features of the Holocaust in the Soviet Union," in *Jews and Jewish Life in Russia and the Soviet Union*, Yaacov Ro'i, ed. (Ilford, UK: Frank Cass, 1995), 175.]

67 *unpublished until 1988*: The original text was first published in the journal *Vek* (Riga, 1990), no 4, pp. 1–8; until then the only Russian text available was a back-translation from Yiddish of the portion—a little less than half—that had been published in *Eynikayt*.

68 *long after Grossman's death*: The Russian text was first published in the 1980 (Jerusalem) edition of *The Black Book*. Much of the article is included, in English translation, in *A Writer at War*. Earlier historians have unwittingly exaggerated the number of Jews shot outside Berdichev. Dieter Pohl, in "The Murder of Ukraine's Jews under German Military Administration and in the Reich Commissariat Ukraine," states that 4,144 Jews were murdered, mostly in Berdichev, on September 4, and that, in the early hours of September 15, around 12,000 Jews from the Berdichev ghetto were shot at the airport outside the town [in Ray Brandon and Wendy Lower, eds., *The Shoah in Ukraine* (Bloomington: Indiana University Press, 2008), 35].

68 *a very small hardback book*: A copy of this may have been given to the Soviet prosecutor at the Nuremberg Trials. Bocharov states that a very small number of copies of *The Black Book* (which includes "The Hell of Treblinka") were in fact printed, and that it was one of these that was given to the Soviet prosecutor, but we have been unable to find confirmation for this [Bocharov, 162].

68 *not to be published*: See Yitzhak Arad, *The Holocaust in the Soviet Union* (Lincoln and Jerusalem: University of Nebraska Press and Yad Vashem, 2009), 543. The complete Russian text of *The Black Book* was published in Israel in 1980, in Kiev in 1991, and in Vilnius in 1993. A separate volume, *The Unknown Black Book* (*Neizvestnaya chornaya kniga*), containing not only material from *The Black Book* but also material previously rejected for censorship reasons, was published in Moscow in 1993 and in the United States in 2008.

69 *to render my novel safe*: Fyodor Guber, *Pamyat'i pis'ma* (Moscow: Probel, 2007), 64. "Render safe" is our translation of *obezopasit'*. Grossman's reply was *"Boris Nikolaevich, ya ne khochu obezopasit' svoi roman."*

70 *he should give Einstein*: Semyon Lipkin, *Kvadriga* (Moscow: Knizhny Sad, 1997), 533.

70 "*... through Publishing Houses*": A fifteen-page document in which Grossman, evidently anticipating difficulties from the beginning, records all his official conversations, letters, and meetings to do with the novel [RGALI, fond 1710, opis' 2, ed. khr., 1].

71 *instigation of Stalin himself*: Bocharov, 84. Korotkova remembers her father saying, "Stalin has a very particular attitude toward me. He does not send me to the camps, but he never awards me prizes." That Grossman's two previous novels should have incurred Stalin's disapproval is not surprising. *Stepan Kolchugin* is largely about the generation of Old Bolsheviks that Stalin was to destroy in the Purges of 1937, and Grossman had publicly announced his intention to devote much of the novel's (never-written) fourth volume to the Comintern, the internationalist organization that Stalin marginalized in the late 1930s and finally dissolved in 1943. According to Lipkin, Stalin referred to this novel about a young revolutionary as "Menshevik" [Lipkin, 520]; Lipkin does not explain how he knew Stalin's opinion, but he might have heard it secondhand, perhaps from a writer such as Fadeyev who moved in higher circles. Grossman's earlier *The People Immortal* is about the encirclement of a Soviet military unit. There were many such encirclements during the first months of the war, some involving the death or capture of hundreds of thousands of Soviet soldiers. In 1942 it was possible to write about such catastrophes; after the Soviet victories of early 1943, however, they became a taboo subject.

71 *anything else I have written*: Guber, 67; and RGALI, fond 1710, opis' 2, ed. khr., 8.

71 *in October 1951*: Guber, 67.

71 *new suggestions for the title*: These included "On the Volga," "Soviet People," and "During a People's War" [RGALI, fond 1710, opis' 2, ed. khr., 1]. The earlier title "Stalingrad" had been abandoned after Sholokhov's indignant, and anti-Semitic, response to Tvardovsky when the latter tried to enlist his support: "*Whom* have you entrusted to write about Stalingrad? Are you in your right mind?" [Lipkin, 534.]

71 *in Literaturnaya gazeta*: Natalya Gromova, *Raspad* (Moscow: Ellis Lak, 2009), 337.

71 *for a Stalin Prize*: Anna Berzer, *Proshchanie* (Moscow: Kniga, 1990), 151.

72 *he was feeling badly sick*: Lipkin, 543–44; see also Gromova, 346–50.

73 *one timid gesture of protest*: Vasily Grossman, *Life and Fate* (London: Vintage, 2006), 656.

73 *anti-Soviet essence of the book*: In late 1952 *For a Just Cause* was also accepted by Sovetsky pisatel', the publishing house which, in 1956, brought out what, according to Lipkin, Grossman considered the most complete version of the novel [Lipkin, 153 and 164]. Guber, however, has said that Grossman did further revisions for the edition published by Sovetsky pisatel' in 1964 (and republished in 1989). The State Military Publishing House (Gosudarstvennoe voennoe izdatel'stvo) was often referred to either as Voenizdat or Voengiz.

74 *from Russian villagers*: Bocharov, 107.

75 *a number of European languages*: "The Hell of Treblinka" was translated into English, French, German, Hebrew, Hungarian, Romanian, and Yiddish in 1945, and into Polish and Slovenian in 1946. There may have been other translations. Grossman's article was also published in tandem with other accounts: with Simonov's report on Majdanek, in German, in 1945; and with Jankiel Wiernik's testimony, in Yiddish, in Buenos Aries in 1946.

"THE OLD MAN"
First published in Red Star *(February 8, 1942).*

79 *Kamyshevakha!*: Velika Kamyshevakha (Great Kamyshevakha) is a large village in the province of Kharkov.

80 *makhorka*: The very coarsest, strongest tobacco.

81 *Poltava*: Peter the Great's victory over Sweden at the Battle of Poltava (1709) marked Russia's emergence as a great power.

"THE OLD TEACHER"
Written in 1943; first published in Znamya *(July and August 1943).*

89 *the Black Hundreds*: A nationalist—and violently anti-Semitic—movement in early-twentieth-century Russia.

93 *Zhitomir*: A town in western Ukraine, sixteen miles from Berdichev. On September 19, 1941, 3,145 Jews were shot just outside the town [Pohl, 35].

95 *Vinnitsa*: An industrial town in central Ukraine. About half the pop-

ulation of 60,000 were Jews. The police chief might have been supervising preparations for a bunker being built there for Hitler's
easternmost headquarters, Werwolf, and he might have been playing
a role in massacres of Jews. Around 15,000 Jews were massacred in
Vinnitsa on September 19–20, 1941 [Pohl, 37], and there was a second
massacre in April 1942. Hitler first flew to Werwolf in mid-July 1942
and remained there until October; he was also there during February
and March 1943. In early summer 1943, the SS invited international
forensic experts to observe as they exhumed 9,432 victims of NKVD
Purges from 1937 and 1938. Whether Grossman was aware of this is
unknown. The exhumation took place around the time that he was
writing "The Old Teacher," though the story is set a year earlier, in the
summer of 1942.

95   *Was? Was?*: "What? What?"

95   *aber er ist Jud*: "Here, a good doctor—but he is a Jew."

98   *block warden*: In most of the Reich and the occupied territories, a
block warden was a low-level Nazi Party organizer. Here Grossman
imagines the Germans as making do with whatever collaborators
they could find.

100   *my campfire shines*: A popular Russian song about friendship. The
words are by the poet Arkady Polonsky (1819–98).

100   *to nach Haus or for to spazier*: Going home or going for a walk.

110   *when it comes down to it, are essential*: Becker is, of course, referring to
the use of gas. Mobile vans were first used to gas large numbers of Jews
in the Polish town of Chelmno, where at least 150,000 Jews were murdered between December 1941 and the summer of 1944. Nazi officials
of every rank employed similar euphemisms with regard to the Shoah;
transportation to the death camps, for example, was referred to as "re-
settlement." The Final Solution is, of course, itself a euphemism.
Claude Lanzmann has observed that the extermination of the Jews
was "a nameless crime, which the Nazi assassins themselves dared not
name, as if by doing so they would have made it impossible to enact."
[Claude Lanzmann, *Shoah* (Eureka, 1985), page 53 of the booklet accompanying the 2007 DVD of the film.]

111   *greatly slows down the work*: Probably an inaccuracy. According to
Altshuler, "Most of the mass killing of the Jews in the Soviet Union
was accomplished by machine gun...The Einsatzgruppen units,
trained and prepared for this type of assignment, almost always took

charge of the mass killings." Altshuler continues, "Apparently, the re-action of most of the local population to the mass killings varied from joy at their fate, through indifference, to passive identification with the victims. All these feelings, contradictory as they might be, could be experienced by the same people in different situations and at dif-ferent times." [Altshuler, 176–77.]

112 *ten percent always drop out*: Christopher Browning [*Ordinary Men* (London: Penguin, 2001)], gives a similar figure, stating that around 10 to 20 percent of the members of a German police battalion in-volved in shootings and deportations to Treblinka accepted offers to be transferred to other work. Often, however, the composition of kill-ing squads was arbitrary; soldiers were chosen at random, and they could not refuse.

112 *nervous strain*: There was concern among the higher echelons of both the Wehrmacht and the SS about the effect of the massacres on those who carried them out. It was this, in part, that lay behind the decision to move to the use of gas chambers. In late summer 1941, an SS Ober-gruppenführer (a rank equivalent to lieutenant general) said to Him-mler, after they had watched a hundred Jews being shot on the outskirts of Minsk, "*Reichsführer*, those were only a hundred ... Look at the eyes of the men in this commando, how deeply shaken they are. These men are finished [*fertig*] for the rest of their lives. What kind of followers are we training here? Either neurotics or savages?" [Raul Hilberg, *The Destruction of the European Jews* (Chicago: Quadrangle, 1967), 218–19 and 646.]

112 *at such a sad moment*: There were, of course, unabashed sadists among the Gestapo and the SS, but there were also officers who liked to phi-losophize about what they were accomplishing on behalf of humanity.

113 *running up from one side*: After the war Grossman adapted this story for the stage. In the play, Kulish resists with still greater determina-tion, his son becomes a partisan, and he himself joins Voronenko in throwing grenades at the commandant's office [Bocharov, 153]. In 1947 Grossman's play was turned down by the Vakhtangov Theatre. Grossman then hoped that it could be produced in Yiddish. The fa-mous Yiddish actor Solomon Mikhoels agreed to play Rosenthal, but the production was canceled. In 1948 Mikhoels was murdered, at Sta-lin's instigation, while on a visit to Minsk. His death was disguised as an accident. Mikhoels had said to Grossman and Lipkin, who had

accompanied him to the Belorussian Station, "I'm certain I'll play the part of the teacher. It'll be my last role." Lipkin's account continues, "And so he never played his last role. Or rather he did play it, but not on the stage. Like the hero of Grossman's play, he was killed by murderers. He was knocked down by a lorry on a dark Minsk night. He was killed by the same forces that killed Rosenthal." [Lipkin, 592–93.]

"THE HELL OF TREBLINKA"
Written in September 1944; first published in Znamya *(November 1944).*

117 *Bełzec, and Auschwitz*: The *Dictionnaire de la Shoah* gives an estimate of 900,000 deaths. Timothy Snyder [*Bloodlands* (New York: Basic Books, 2010), 408] gives a figure of 780,863 for the total number of Jews murdered at Treblinka. This is taken from a study by Peter Witte and Stephen Tyas ["A New Document on the Deportation and Murder of Jews during 'Einsatz Reinhard' 1942," *Holocaust and Genocide Studies* 15, 3 (2001): 468–86]. Hershl Polyanker, a lesser-known Soviet journalist, gives the same mistaken estimate of three million deaths in an article written, like Grossman's, in September 1944. His "Treblinka—Hell on Earth," probably originally written in Yiddish, was translated into Spanish and sent by the Jewish Anti-Fascist Committee to newspapers in Cuba, Mexico, and Uruguay [GARF, fond 8114, opis' 1, delo 346, 162–72].

118 *the General Government*: Since 1939 a large area of Poland, renamed the Generalgouvernement, had been under German civil administration. Some parts of the country, however, had been incorporated into the German Reich.

118 *passed through its gates*: It is likely that about 10,000 prisoners passed through the camp, and that about 2,000 prisoners were kept there at any one time [Ilya Ehrenburg and Vasily Grossman, *The Complete Black Book of Russian Jewry*, David Patterson, trans. and ed. (New Brunswick, NJ: Transaction Publishers, 2002), 555, note 9].

118 *the Wachmänner*: An additional security force was formed to assist the SS in running the camps; it was composed mainly of former Soviet POWs who had initially volunteered to serve as policemen in the occupied territories of the Soviet Union. These volunteers usually referred to themselves as Wachmänner (guards); the Germans referred to them as Hilfswillige (auxiliaries) or as Trawniki men, since they

had been trained at a camp near Lublin called Trawniki; the camp inmates and the local Poles simply called them "the Ukrainians." The subject of collaboration with the Nazis on the part of Soviet citizens was taboo. Grossman was obliged to use the term Wachmänner and say as little as possible about who these men were. Most were indeed Ukrainian; the Germans correctly considered Ukrainians especially likely to be hostile to Soviet rule—and in any case, the Ukraine, unlike Russia, had been occupied in its entirety. There were, however, representatives of other Soviet nationalities, including Russians and at least one half-Jew [Snyder, 256ff; Arad, 20–22].

119 *"Broad Is My Motherland!"*: A popular Soviet song.

119 *Panie Wachman*: *Panie* is a standard Polish form of address. The boy's first two words could be translated as "Mister Guard."

121 *a thousand workers involved*: The number of workers employed at any one time was, in fact, four hundred to five hundred [Witold Chrostowski, *Extermination Camp Treblinka* (London: Vallentine Mitchell, 2004), 26].

121 *Unteroffizier*: A noncommissioned officer.

122 *other Belorussian cities*: Łomza, Białystok, and Grodno are now part of Poland. In 1939 they were incorporated into the Soviet Union in accordance with the Molotov-Ribbentrop Pact.

122 *Bessarabia*: A name more commonly used before 1917; it corresponds, approximately, to the area now occupied by the Republic of Moldova.

122 *return to this figure*: Many of Grossman's estimates—the number of prisoners in each wagon, the number of wagons in each train—are accurate. His most serious error lay in accepting the peasants' mistaken reports that transports arrived every day. From June 23, 1942, until mid-December 1942, and from mid-January 1943 until the end of May 1943, there was probably an average of two new transports each day. During other periods, however, there was, on average, only one new transport each week [Chrostowski, 99].

123 *act with impunity*: It is now generally agreed that this decision was made between late August and mid-December 1941.

124 *extermination of the Jews*: By March 1941, as many as 445,000 Jews were living in the Warsaw ghetto, but this number was soon reduced by illness and starvation. In the summer of 1942 around 300,000 Jews were deported, most of them to Treblinka; nearly all were killed in

the gas chambers. Around 7,000 Jews died in the Ghetto Uprising in April 1943, and another 7,000 were deported immediately afterward to Treblinka. The remaining Jews, approximately 42,000, were deported to forced-labor camps; most were murdered in November 1943. [Figures from U.S. Holocaust Memorial Museum, available at www.ushmm.org/wlc/en/article.php?ModuleId=10005413.]

125 *those with weak hearts would die*: "Thousands of Jews died en route to the death camps during that summer from thirst, suffocation and lack of minimum sanitary facilities in the crowded freight cars. The trip from Warsaw and other ghettos to Bełzec, Sobibor and Treblinka, which should have lasted a few hours, sometimes lasted a day or two." [Arad, 65.]

125 *a large number of people were wounded*: Arad quotes the testimony of a Pole from Treblinka village: "I saw how guards, who were always drunk, would open the freight-car doors at night and demand money and valuables. Then they would close the doors and fire into the cars." [Arad, 67.] Gitta Sereny quotes from the diary of an Austrian soldier on his way to the front in a troop train, who chanced to observe a transport of Jews: "When we reach Treblinka station the train is next to us again—there is such an awful smell of decomposing corpses in the station, some of us vomit. The begging for water continues, the indiscriminate shooting by the guards continues..." [Gitta Sereny, *Into that Darkness* (London: Pimlico, 1995), 250.]

125 *for the necessary visas*: This paragraph is confirmed by other sources. Around 95 percent of those murdered at Treblinka, however, were Jews from Poland [Chrostowski, 107].

125 *when the war broke out*: There was no such train, though there were indeed cases of "enemy alien" Jews being used as hostages.

126 *the number of people on it*: Sereny comments on the "astuteness" with which the Nazis "recognized the capacity of the Western Jews individually to grasp the monstrous truth and individually to resist it, and therefore ordered that great pains be taken to mislead and calm them until, naked, in rows of five and running under the whiplash, they had been made incapable of resistance. By the same token they recognized that these precautions were unnecessary with the Eastern Jews." [Sereny, 199.]

126 *TO WOŁKOWICE, etc.*: Ticket windows and various timetables and arrows were painted on the façade of the barracks used for sorting

clothes and valuables. There was also a clock with numerals permanently indicating six o'clock.

126 *Warsaw, and Wołkowice?*: Arad cites an anonymous account: "We held one another's hands and jumped down into the sand…Everyone went toward the wall of crowded pine trees. Suddenly I had a strange thought. Those trees aren't growing, they're dead. They had made a fence, a tight fence that looked like a forest, made out of trees that were cut down. I looked at the fence and saw something else— barbed wire between the branches. I thought—concentration camp." [Arad, 83.]

127 *the entrance to a slaughterhouse*: Richard Rhodes has written: "One place Holocaust historians seem not to have looked for models of the killing process is the history and anthropology of the slaughtering of animals for food. The parallels are compelling." [Richard Rhodes, *Masters of Death: The Einsatzgruppen and the Invention of the Holocaust* (New York: Vintage, 2003), 280–82.] Rhodes points out that the aim of the industrialization of slaughter—whether of animals or of people—was not only to improve efficiency but also to absolve individuals of responsibility. Grossman, however, was well aware of this parallel, and he develops it in "Tiergarten" (1955).

127 *were considered quiet*: According to Chrostowski, the maximum number to arrive in a single day was probably around 16,000, but this was unusual. Even during busy periods, it was more often around 6,000 or 7,000 [Chrostowski, 99–100].

128 *threaded with branches*: Trees planted around the perimeter and branches woven into barbed-wire fences served as camouflage, blocking any view into the camp from outside, as well as between different parts of the camp.

129 *and so is New York*: This sentence was omitted from the published versions, as well as from that prepared for *The Black Book*. Grossman's criticism, however, is justified: both British and American governments had received reliable reports of the exterminations as early as August 1942.

129 *removing straps from bedrolls*: Most of the camp work was performed by 700 to 800 Jewish prisoners, organized into special squads (*Sonderkommandos*). The blue squad was responsible for unloading the train, cleaning out the wagons, and clearing the platform and the station square. The red squad supervised the prisoners as they un

dressed and then took their clothes to the storerooms. The *Geldjuden* (money Jews) were in charge of handling money and jewelry, melting down gold teeth, etc. The *Totenjuden* (Jews of death), of whom there were about 200, lived in a barrack in the extermination area; their job was to carry the dead from the gas chambers to the grave pits. Later they had to dig up the corpses, carry them to the grill pits to be burned, sift through their ashes, grind up recognizable parts, and then bury these ashes. Other groups took care of the general maintenance of the camp. New workers (usually the young and strong) were selected from transports and pressed into these various *kommandos*. The guards repeatedly whipped and beat them. Most were shot after a few days and replaced by new arrivals. From the spring of 1943, however, when fewer new transports were arriving, members of these squads survived longer. This made it possible to organize the August 1943 uprising.

129 *children's toy building blocks*: According to Korotkova, Grossman kept on his writing desk a child's building block from Treblinka. It was covered in scratches, and the pictures were almost erased. [See www.lechaim.ru/ARHIV/193/LKL.htm.]

129 *sent to Germany*: In her article "In the Fields of Treblinka," Rachel Auerbach writes: "We must remember that *the killing of Jews was primarily a crime of robbery with murder*. The utilization of gold and valuables...was organized in a first-rate manner." She quotes a Treblinka survivor, Alexander Kudlik: "From the sorting of garments, we proceeded to the sorting of gold pens. I spent about six months going through gold pens—ten hours a day, for six months, just sorting pens." Auerbach also quotes notes recorded by three of the prisoners: "The following items were shipped out: about 25 carloads of hair packed in bales, 248 carloads of men's suits, about 100 carloads of shoes, 22 carloads of ready-made textile goods...Over 40 carloads of medicines, medical equipment and dentists' metal were sent off. Twelve carloads of artisans' tools, 260 carloads of bedding, feathers, down, quilts, blankets. In addition, about 400 carloads of miscellaneous items, such as dishes, baby carriages, ladies' handbags, valises, pens, eyeglasses, shaving gear, toilet articles and other small items. Several hundred carloads of various types of clothing, underwear, and other used textile items." [In Alexander Donat, ed., *The Death Camp Treblinka* (New York: Holocaust Library, 1979), 68 and 56–67.]

Sereny, on the other hand, points out that the sum of DM 178,745,960 netted by the three Aktion Reinhard camps is—in the context of a large nation's income and expenditure—"a trivial sum" [Sereny, 101]. She argues convincingly that the Nazis were motivated primarily by ideology, not by financial considerations.

130 *allowed to wash with it*: Workers who looked weak or unhealthy were likely to be shot. It was essential to appear well and strong. The Treblinka survivor Abraham Krzepicki writes: "We would get up every morning before reveille and wash and make ourselves look as youthful and vigorous as possible ... Everybody shaved every morning and washed their faces with cologne taken from packages abandoned by the Jewish prisoners. Some even put on powder or rouge." [In Donat, 100.]

130 *shot before her eyes*: Wachmänner with rifles and machine guns were stationed on the roofs of the barracks.

131 *the Scharführer*: An SS rank equivalent to that of staff sergeant.

131 *"Achtung! Achtung!"*: In his manuscript Grossman writes these words with particular emphasis. Each letter is two or three times its usual size. His exclamation marks are thick vertical wedges.

132 *saddles for the cavalry*: The hair was used for a variety of purposes: in the uniforms of soldiers and railway workers, in carpets and mattresses, in ropes and cords on ships, and in socks and gloves for submariners.

133 *"on transport duty"*: Another mistake with regard to numbers. There were only between 20 and 35 SS men working in the death camp as a whole. And since there were only 90 to 120 Wachmänner in the entire camp, there could not have been so many "on transport duty" at any one time.

134 *trampled beneath their boots*: An elaboration of Jankiel Wiernik's thoughts in "A Year in Treblinka": "Everything the Jews left behind had its value and its place. Only the Jews themselves were regarded as worthless." [In Donat, 168.]

134 *"Schneller! Schneller!"*: "Hands up! March! Quicker! Quicker!" Like *"Achtung,"* these words are written in huge letters in Grossman's manuscript, and they are followed by still bigger, wedge-shaped exclamation marks.

134 *Faster into nonexistence!*: Most accounts of Nazi camps mention the guards' constant demands that the prisoners—both the workers and the condemned—should do everything *"schneller."*

135 *the Hell that was Treblinka*: Grossman has underestimated the Nazis' orderliness. There was a special squad whose duty was to clean the path and sprinkle fresh sand on it after the passage of each batch of victims [Chil Rajchman, *Treblinka: A Survivor's Memory* (London: MacLehose Press, 2011)].

135 *"The Road of No Return"*: They more often called it Himmelfahrt-strasse or Himmelweg ("The Road to Heaven"). The alley was also known as *der Schlauch* (the tube); branches were intertwined with the two-meter-high barbed wire so as to make it impossible to see in or out.

135 *the name of Suchomel*: Unterscharführer Franz Suchomel's main job at Treblinka was, in fact, the collection and processing of money and valuables. Lanzmann interviews him at length in the film *Shoah* (Eureka, 1985). Most survivors consider Suchomel to have been one of the less vicious of the guards. One of ten Treblinka personnel tried in 1965, he was sentenced to six years in prison—a relatively light sentence.

136 *what I had heard was true*: Joseph Hirtreiter (nicknamed "Sepp") was tried in Frankfurt in 1951 and sentenced to life imprisonment. Among the crimes of which he was found guilty was "killing many young children ages one and one-half to two, during the unloading of the transports, by seizing them by the feet and smashing their heads against the boxcars." [In Donat, 277.]

137 *flowers in large pots*: Above the door were a Star of David and a Hebrew inscription: "Through this gate only the righteous pass." [Chrostowski, 61.] The building—razed to the ground thirteen months before the Red Army reached Treblinka—was in fact made of brick. It would have been difficult to achieve a hermetic seal with stone.

137 *in charge of the complex*: Arad confirms that Scharführer Fritz Schmidt was in charge of the gas-chamber engines [Arad, 121]. Schmidt was arrested in Saxony. Sentenced in December 1949 to nine years in prison, he escaped to West Germany and was never retried.

137 *a strong dose of quinacrine*: An anti-malarial drug.

138 *holding a saber*: It was, in fact, the shorter man, Nikolaj Marchenko, who tortured people with a thick pipe, and the taller man, Ivan Demjanjuk, who hacked at people with his saber. In 1986 Demjanjuk, known as "Ivan the Terrible" was deported from the United States to

Israel. Two years later, he was sentenced to death for crimes against humanity. In 1993, however, Israel's highest court overturned the sentence, finding "reasonable doubt" as to whether Demjanjuk truly was "Ivan the Terrible." He was returned to the United States. On April 2, 2009, it was announced that he would be deported to Germany to face trial on charges of accessory to 29,000 counts of murder in Sobibor, where he had served as a guard before being transferred to Treblinka. On May 11, 2009, he was deported by plane to Germany. His trial, in Munich, began on November 30, 2009.

138 *something of a theoretician*: Kurt Franz's rank was the equivalent of second lieutenant. Although officially deputy to Hauptsturmführer Franz Stangl (camp commandant from September 1942 to August 1943), Franz was effectively in charge of the day-to-day running of the camp. Young and handsome, with a round, almost babyish face, he was nicknamed Lalke (Yiddish for "doll"). He was, however, a sadist, and many accounts of Treblinka mention his vicious dog. According to Rajchman, Franz would order Barry, "Man, bite that dog!" [Rajchman] In 1959, in Düsseldorf, Franz was arrested. During a search of his apartment, police found a photograph album labeled "The Best Years of My Life" (*Die schönsten Jahre meines Lebens*), which contained pictures of the camp, of Stangl, of Barry, of the excavator, etc. [Chrostowski, 103]. In 1965, in Düsseldorf, Franz was sentenced to life imprisonment. He died in an old people's home in Wuppertal on July 4, 1998.

138 *of spectators*: Henry Noel Brailsford was a left-wing British journalist and the author of *Our Settlement with Germany* (1944). He was in no sense a defender of Hitler. He had, however, been one of the relatively few left-wing writers in Britain to criticize the Soviet show trials—and this had made him unpopular with the Soviet authorities. Grossman seldom repeats Soviet propaganda so unthinkingly.

138 *the entire staff of his Vatican*: The intensity of Grossman's venom may seem startling. Recent research, however, suggests that his criticism of the pope is justified. Susan Zuccotti has established that, during the Holocaust, Pope Pius XII and the Vatican knew what the Nazis were doing yet chose to keep silent [Susan Zuccotti, *Under His Very Windows: The Vatican and the Holocaust in Italy* (New Haven, CT: Yale University Press, 2000)]. Sereny also discusses the culpability of the pope and the Vatican [Sereny, 64–77, 140–42, and 277–86].

139 *stabbing an SS officer*: On September 10 or 11, 1942, Meir Berliner, a citizen of Argentina, jumped out from the ranks of the prisoners and stabbed Max Bialas with a knife. Berliner and at least ten other prisoners were shot on the spot; Bialas died en route to the military hospital, and another 160 prisoners were shot in reprisal. The Wachmänner's barracks were then named the Max Bialas Barracks.

140 *no one can honor it*: These stories are exaggerated, but some parts, at least, are confirmed by other sources. [For example, see Samuel Willenberg, *Surviving Treblinka* (Oxford: Basil Blackwell, 1989), 127; and Wiernik, in Donat, 172.] Rajchman records that, on November 10, 1942, a transport of Jews from Ostrowiec was—unusually—forced to enter the gas chambers at night. A group of thirty or forty men resisted. Naked, they fought with their fists before being brought down by automatic rifles.

141 *Majdanek, Sobibor, and Belzec*: Christian Wirth, the gassing expert, had aimed at the destruction of 25,000 people a day, but this proved impossible [Donald James Wheal and Warren Shaw, *Dictionary of the Third Reich* (London: Penguin, 2002), 288]. Aktion Reinhard was evidently imbued with a sense of manic urgency at every level—from that of strategic planning to that of the day-to-day running of the camps. According to Mark Mazower, "A sense of excitement and urgency coursed among those charged with the secret killing, and they felt under constant pressure to accelerate it and finish before the news leaked out. Globocnik believed that 'the whole Jewish action should be carried out as quickly as possible to avoid the danger of one day finding ourselves stuck in the middle of it in the event of difficulties forcing us to halt the action.' Victor Brack, a leading figure in the programme, noted that Himmler himself wanted them to 'work as fast as possible if only for reasons of concealment.'" [Mark Mazower, *Hitler's Empire* (London: Penguin, 2008), 386.] Himmler told Wirth that he expected him and his men to be "inhuman to a superhuman degree" (*Ich mute ihnen Übermenschlich-Unmenschliches zu*). [In Donat, 273.]

142 *with the help of straps*: There was indeed a period during which the bodies were taken to the grave pits by trolleys pushed along a narrow-gauge track. This system, however, proved impractical; the *Totenjuden* went back to carrying the corpses on stretchers. [This information available at www. deathcamps.org/treblinka/treblinka.html.]

144 *on an industrial scale*: There are no other accounts of the use of steam

or pumps to remove the air from the chambers. According to Rajchman, however, "On days when they had been warned by the Extermination High Command in Lublin that there would be no transport arriving the following day, the executioners, out of pure sadism, left people shut in the gas chambers until they died from suffocation, simply from lack of air." [Rajchman.]

144 *a single human being*: Arad writes: "When the doors were opened, all the corpses were standing; because of the crowding and the way the victims grasped one another, they were like a single block of flesh." [Arad, 86.] Rajchman, himself one of the *Totenjuden*, writes, "This compression results from people being terrorized and pressed against one another when they are forced to enter the gas chamber. They hold their breath in order to squeeze in. After suffocation and the death agony, the bodies swell up and so the corpses form a single mass." [Rajchman.]

145 *breathing for longest*: In Auschwitz, at least, where the Germans used Zyklon B rather than carbon monoxide, children and weaker people fell to the ground, while those who were stronger climbed over them, trampling and crushing them as they tried instinctively to claw their way to the more breathable air up above.

146 *important Gestapo officials*: Himmler visited Aktion Reinhard headquarters and the death camps of Sobibor and Treblinka in late February or early March 1943. By this time, nearly all the Jews of Poland had been exterminated, and Auschwitz-Birkenau had, in any case, greatly increased its killing capacity. Sobibor and Treblinka had fulfilled their purpose.

147 *far away on the Volga*: It seems that Himmler had always intended the corpses to be cremated and that, during this visit, he merely reiterated a previous order that the camp command had failed to carry out [Arad, 167]. Grossman may, however, be right in a broader sense. Arad writes: "In January 1944, the question of hiding his crimes began to bother Globocnik, whereas a year and a half earlier, in August 1942, when asked by visiting SS officers whether it would not be better, for reasons of secrecy, to cremate rather than to bury the corpses . . . Globocnik had answered, 'We ought, on the contrary, to bury bronze tablets stating that it was we who had the courage to carry out this gigantic task.'" [Ibid., 376.] It has been suggested that it was the German discovery of the mass graves of Katyn that made Himmler de-

cide to cover up traces of Nazi crimes. (In 1940 the Soviet NKVD had shot about 22,000 Polish officers and other members of the country's elite. The Wehrmacht found the mass graves in 1943 and tried to exploit this discovery for anti-Soviet propaganda.) This hypothesis, however, is untenable: Himmler visited Treblinka in mid-March 1943, and the Katyn massacre was discovered only in April 1943.

148 *cremation of millions of human corpses*: Mazower writes that "*Standartenführer* Paul Blobel, who had ... been responsible for the SS death squad which organized the Babi Yar massacres outside Kiev, was the man Himmler chose for the job. Starting with Auschwitz and Chelmno, Blobel ordered that the huge burial pits be uncovered and their remains burned, either in special crematoria or on huge bonfires. He issued similar instructions for Bełzec, Sobibor and Treblinka, and his underlings visited the camps to make sure the burning of the hundreds of thousands of bodies proceeded according to instructions." [Mazower, 410.] Grossman may, however, have been thinking of one of these "underlings," Scharführer Herbert Floss, who served successively at Bełzec, Sobibor, and Treblinka as the cremation "expert" [Arad, 173].

148 *the pine forest that surrounded the camp*: Compare the words of Richard Glazar, a Czech Jew who survived Treblinka: "Suddenly ... flames shot up. Very high. In a flash, the whole countryside, the whole camp, seemed ablaze ... We knew that night that the dead would no longer be buried, they'd be burned." [Claude Lanzmann, *Shoah: The Complete Text* (New York: Da Capo, 1995), 9–10.]

149 *burning the bodies*: As noted, there were in fact around two hundred *Totenjuden*.

149 *from Bulgaria*: No Jews were deported from Bulgaria proper. It is possible that these were Greek Jews from Thrace. Thrace was occupied by Bulgaria, and Jews were deported from there. My thanks to Jeanmarc Dreyfus for this suggestion.

149 *including white bread*: In *Shoah*, Richard Glazar describes how, after a period during which there had been few transports and, as a result, very little food in the camp, transports began to arrive from the Balkans: "These were rich people; the passenger cars bulged with possessions. Then an awful feeling gripped us, all of us ... a feeling of helplessness, of shame. For we threw ourselves on their food ... The trainloads from the Balkans brought us to a terrible realization: we

were the workers in the Treblinka factory, and our lives depended on the whole manufacturing process, that is, the slaughtering process at Treblinka." [Lanzmann, 137; also Sereny, 212–14.]

150 *his favorite word*: Grossman has misunderstood the German word *tadellos*. This does not mean "blame-free" in the sense of "innocent" but "blameless" in the sense of "beyond reproach" or, more colloquially, "first-class." Auerbach notes that one German official document stated: "The burning of corpses received the proper incentive only after an instructor had come down from Auschwitz." She goes on to say that the Jews nicknamed this instructor Tadellos, since that was his favorite expression: " 'Thank God, now the fire's perfect [*tadellos*],' he used to say when ... the pile of corpses finally burst into flame." [In Donat, 38.]

151 *Das unser Schiksal ist*: "For us today there is only Treblinka. This is our Fate."

151 *Geliebte Mädelein*: "I picked the little flower and gave it to the most beautiful and beloved maiden." Grossman has misspelled several words in these lines quoted from songs. These may simply be mistakes on his part or he may have been trying to reproduce the words as he heard them pronounced.

151 *orders for them to be killed*: Grossman is not the only person to have made this allegation, but Sereny argues convincingly that it is false [Sereny, 259].

152 *destroy the gravestones*: Grossman seems to have added this paragraph later. Though not in the manuscript, nor in any Soviet publications, it is included in the Russian text of *The Black Book* [available at http://jhistory.nfurman.com/shoa/grossman005.htm]. Grossman's account is confirmed by Willenberg: "Kurt Franz ordered the foremen to go to the storeroom and procure two rabbinical black suits and a couple of black hats with pompoms on them. Two prisoners were equipped with whips and ordered to don this get-up ... alarm clocks dangled from their necks on strings. They were called the *Scheisskommando*—the Shit Detail." [Willenberg, 117.]

153 *vile beasts, SS beasts*: Compare: "The great majority of Germans among the Treblinka personnel were young men aged 26–30, mostly married and with small children. They considered themselves special human beings, who had been given a difficult and responsible mission by the *Führer*. SS men debated with Engineer Galewski, the 'camp

elder'... about the superiority of the German race... about their so-
phisticated culture and the coming new order in Europe. They forced
prisoners to organize choirs and orchestras, to dance, play football
and box. Their commanders felt compassion for them in their hard
service and they often sent them to Germany on leave. The German
camp staff were concerned about their own well-being, and constantly worked on improving their living conditions. They tried to
keep their barracks looking nice, by planting and tending flower gardens." [Chrostowski, 41; see also Willenberg, 114–15.]

153 *like a timid complaint*: Auerbach describes the road as being surfaced
with "a weird mixture of coals and ashes from the pyres where the
corpses of the inmates were cremated." [In Donat, 70.] Auerbach may
be mistaken about the coal, which is not mentioned in any other account.

154 *120 to 130 kilos of ash*: A large part of the ashes was returned to the
grave pits. Alternate layers of sand and ashes were covered by a two-
meter layer of sand [Rajchman].

154 *flash by in a single moment*: As noted, the *Totenjuden*—the Jews
working and living in the extermination area—in fact numbered
about 200. The "little happiness" they were supposed to hope for was
a bullet in the back of the head—a quick death.

154 *for an uprising*: The camp was divided into three zones: the living area
(*Wohnlager*), the reception area (*Auffanglager*), and the extermination area (*Totenlager*). The living and reception areas were known as
the Lower Camp, the extermination area as the Upper Camp. An organizing committee was formed in the Lower Camp in late February
or early March 1943; an organizing committee was formed by the *Totenjuden* in the Upper Camp in late May or early June.

155 *hid them in secret places*: Most of the various sources for the history of
the uprising indicate that the armory was opened with the help of a
key that the prisoners had copied. It also seems that the weapons were
probably taken from the storeroom only on the afternoon of the uprising.

155 *to provide the escapees with money*: The prisoners whose job it was to
sort through the clothes and belongings of the dead often found
money and valuables. It was not difficult to hide some of this away.

156 *the secret remained a secret*: All the slightly different versions of this
story agree that the Scharführer entered the barrack unexpectedly,

taking Doctor Chorazycki by surprise, that Chorazycki took poison, and that Kurt Franz was enraged by the failure of another prisoner-doctor to save Chorazycki's life.

156 *with a revolver shot*: The uprising began thirty minutes earlier than intended. Afraid that the commander of the Lower Camp had gotten wind of their plans, one of the conspirators shot him. The uprising thus began before the conspirators had finished removing weapons from the armory and distributing them.

156 *the moment of revenge*: Much of this, sadly, is exaggerated. For all their heroism—Sereny justly refers to the uprising as "one of the most heroic efforts of the war-time years in East or West" [Sereny, 236]—the rebels failed to capture any watchtowers. Nor did they kill any SS, although they did kill twelve to fifteen Wachmänner. Several barracks were burned down, but the camp received three more transports that month. The last of these—the last of all the transports to Treblinka—arrived on August 19. Around three hundred prisoners escaped during the uprising, but two-thirds of these were quickly recaptured or killed.

157 *Sashko Pechersky*: On being first taken to Sobibor, Pechersky said, "How many circles of hell were there in Dante's *Inferno*? It seems there were nine. How many have already passed? Being surrounded, being captured, camps in Vyazma, Smolensk, Borisov, Minsk ... And finally I am here. What's next?" [*Argumenty i fakty* (August 10, 2008).] For more than a year after escaping from Sobibor, Pechersky fought as a partisan. But when the Red Army liberated Belorussia, he and his fellow partisans—like most Red Army soldiers ever taken prisoner by the Germans—were conscripted into the special penal battalions for suspected traitors that were used as cannon fodder and for clearing minefields. Pechersky survived this too, was promoted to the rank of captain, and even received a medal for bravery. Appalled by Pechersky's account of Sobibor, his battalion commander risked his own life, contravening regulations by sending Pechersky to Moscow to testify to the Jewish Anti-Fascist Committee. "Uprising in Sobibor," compiled by Pavel Antokolsky and Venyamin Kaverin on the basis of Pechersky's testimony, was published in *Znamya* in April 1945; it was also included in the unpublished *Black Book*. In 1948, Pechersky was dismissed from his job as a theater administrator and arrested; only after Stalin's death in 1953 and mounting international pressure on

his behalf was he released. Pechersky died in 1990, never having received any medal or award for his heroism at Sobibor. In 2007 a small memorial plaque was placed on the side of the building where he had lived.

157 *the blood of the innocent*: As if unable to believe how few SS there were in the camps, Grossman again exaggerates the numbers.

157 *farewell to the ashes of their fellows*: In "A Year in Treblinka," Wiernik writes that, during the minutes just before the uprising, "We silently bade farewell to the spot where the ashes of our brethren were buried." [In Donat, 187.]

157 *with guns in their hands*: These last two sentences are present in the manuscript but omitted from all published versions.

157 *it too was burned down*: The Ukrainian's surname was Strebel [Arad, 373].

159 *earth as unsteady as the sea*: Franz Suchomel has said that when he first came to Treblinka in August 1942, "The ground undulated like waves because of the gas ... Bear in mind, the graves were maybe eighteen, twenty feet deep, all crammed with bodies! A thin layer of sand, and the heat. You see?" [Lanzmann, 46.] Grossman, however, was in Treblinka in September 1944, more than a year after the corpses had been burned. The instability he describes may have had other causes. The ground was sandy, and the vast grave pits may not have been packed down firmly enough. We also know that local peasants had been digging up the ground in search of valuables that the Germans had failed to recover.

160 *any human being can endure*: It is clear from the manuscript that this is the original conclusion, and that the remaining paragraphs were added later.

162 *any uncommon expenditure*: Sereny quotes Glazar: "This is something, you know, the world has never understood; how perfect the machine was. It was only lack of transport because of the Germans' war requirements that prevented them from dealing with far vaster numbers than they did; Treblinka alone could have dealt with the 6,000,000 Jews and more besides. Given adequate rail transport, the German extermination camps in Poland could have killed all the Poles, Russians and other East Europeans the Nazis planned eventually to kill." [Sereny, 214.]

162 *entire population of the earth*: The previous three and a half paragraphs,

from "to commit mass murder" to "entire population of the earth," were omitted from all published versions of this article. It is not known who was responsible for this omission.

"THE SISTINE MADONNA"
Written in 1955; first published in Znamya *(May 1989).*

167 *the Kishinyov pogrom*: This pogrom in April 1903, in the city now known as Chişinău (the capital of Moldova), was instrumental in convincing tens of thousands of Russian Jews to emigrate.

168 *Przemyśl and Verdun*: In 1914–15, the Russians besieged Austrian forces in the fortress of Przemyśl (now in southeastern Poland) for 133 days; a soldier in *Stepan Kolchugin* says to a comrade that the shell holes there have become lakes of blood because no more blood can be absorbed by the earth. The battle of Verdun, fought between the French and German armies, lasted for most of 1916 and resulted in more than 250,000 deaths.

170 *The Sistine Chapel*: Raphael's painting is known as *The Sistine Madonna* not because it ever hung in the Sistine Chapel but because it includes a portrayal of Pope Sixtus II, who was martyred in AD 258. This error does not, of course, invalidate Grossman's juxtaposition of one of the most sublime, and one of the most infernal, moments of Western civilization. Pope Sixtus's robe is decorated with the stations of the cross; this, perhaps, led Grossman to see the baby Jesus as going forward "to meet his fate."

170 *the Horst Wessel song*: A marching song written by Hans-Horst Wessel (1907–30), a Nazi activist killed during a brawl with a group of Communists. This song became the Nazi Party's anthem.

170 *Moabit prison*: The Gestapo used this Berlin prison as a detention center.

171 *to the sands of Kazakhstan*: The mother and son have evidently been arrested as kulaks (supposedly exploitative peasants) and are now being deported.

171 *in Konotop, at the station*: Konotop is a city in northern Ukraine. Grossman was seeing his mother off on a train to Odessa. He described this incident in 1930, in a letter to his father.

172 *one place of exile to another*: Stalin was exiled to eastern Siberia several times. In 1903 he was sent to the village of Novaya Uda, in the prov-

ince of Irkutsk. He arrived there on November 17, 1903, but escaped on January 5, 1903. In July 1913 he was exiled to Turukhansk, and in early March 1914 he was transferred to the small village of Kureika, north of the Arctic Circle.

PART THREE: LATE STORIES

179 *usually considered his masterpiece*: The relationship between the two novels is hard to define. *Life and Fate* has been referred to as "a sequel" or "a semi-sequel" to *For a Just Cause*; it is also sometimes called the second half of a dilogy.

179 *growing into a deeper feeling*: Nikita Zabolotsky, *The Life of Zabolotsky* (Cardiff: University of Wales Press, 1994), 321; see also 323–24 and 336.

180 *the text he submitted*: Fyodor Guber, *Pamyat' i pis'ma* (Moscow: Probel, 2007), 99.

180 *Lyolya Klestova*: Most published sources refer to this woman as Lyolya Dominikina. Korotkova has explained the origin of this confusion: she remembers Lyolya Klestova as one of the four people— along with herself, Zabolotskaya, and Grossman—who attended the funeral of Grossman's father in 1956. Some time after Grossman's death, Zabolotskaya told Korotkova that it was Klestova who had preserved the manuscript of *Life and Fate* in a locked suitcase under her bed in a communal apartment. Critics and journalists writing about Grossman knew from Zabolotskaya and Korotkova that the manuscript had been preserved by a woman called "Lyolya" but they confused this Lyolya with another Lyolya, the niece (or possibly daughter from a previous marriage) of a family friend by the name of Dominika, who had at one time been married to Grossman's father. In his letters, however, Grossman refers to this other Lyolya not as "Lyolya Dominikina" but as "Dominika's Lyolya" (*Dominikina Lyolya*). No one by the name of Lyolya Dominikina ever existed. Symbolically, however, it seems appropriate that the preservation of Grossman's manuscript should be ascribed to a mythical figure. See also Yekaterina Korotkova, "O moyom ottse," *Sel'skaya molodyozh'* (March 1993): 48.

181 *ever considered so dangerous*: The OGPU confiscated two copies of the manuscript of *The Heart of a Dog* from Mikhail Bulgakov's flat in

May 1926; two years later, however, these were returned. A comparison of the authorities' treatment of *Life and Fate* with their treatment of *Doctor Zhivago* is revealing. Pasternak showed *Doctor Zhivago* to friends and editors and even trusted the manuscript to the Soviet postal service; his offense lay not in writing the novel but in publishing it abroad.

181 *with Lipkin and Klestova*: Before his death Grossman arranged for Klestova to give her copy to another old friend, Vyacheslav Loboda, who lived in a town about 150 kilometers from Moscow. In 1988 Loboda's widow gave this copy to Guber and it was used to correct textual lacunae before the republication in Moscow of the text established by Yefim Etkind and Shimon Markish.

181 *his vegetable garden*: Tatiana Menaker, "Posvyashchayetsya Vasiliyu Grossmanu," *Narod moy* 18, 30 (September 2007).

182 *His walk became a shuffle*: Semyon Lipkin, *Kvadriga* (Moscow: Knizhny Sad, 1997), 582.

182 *They strangled me in a dark corner*: Ibid., 575.

182 *Even the cat reports to the OGPU*: In Russian: *Koshka sluzhit v GPU*.

182 *"frozen in time"*: E-mail from Tatiana Menaker. Korotkova suggests that Menaker's sense of Grossman's tension and sadness can, at least in part, be accounted for by a tension (which Korotkova learned about only long after Grossman's death) between Grossman and Sherentsis. Her own memories of her father are very different.

182 *to visit a urologist*: Lipkin, 615.

182 *several months in the hospital*: According to Korotkova, John and Carol Garrard are mistaken in ascribing Grossman's death to stomach cancer.

183 *reaching out for more work*: Ibid., 189.

184 *I want to write about him*: Guber, 41. Grossman continued, probably to the end of his life, to revere Zhelyabov and The People's Will. In 1961, in a letter to his old friend Yevgenia Taratuta, he wrote: "I'm growing old now, my hair is going white, but my feelings toward the members of The People's Will are not aging. My feelings about them are the same as when I was sixteen. There is something divine and holy about them, even though they were engaged in work that was bloody and terrible." [A. Bocharov, *Vasily Grossman* (Moscow: Sovetsky pisatel', 1990), 318.]

184 *theme in Grossman's work*: In his posthumously published "Thoughts

and Stories About Animals and People" ["Mysli i rasskazy o zhivot-nykh i lyudyakh," *Raduga* (October 1988): 122–23], Grossman attacks hunting, fishing, and our treatment of domestic pets. He had a deep love of animals. According to Korotkova, "There were always cats and dogs in his home, and [my father] had a wonderfully funny way of talking to them. I was always entranced when I overheard him chatting to the cat called Misha." [Korotkova, "O moyom ottse," 48–50.]

186 *it's a terrible phenomenon*: Lipkin, 589.

186 *avid to know*: RGALI, fond 1710, opis' 3, ed. khr., 23.

186 *even in the orphanage*: In Grossman's manuscript there is, in fact, mention of one more mother. [See note for *This is my mama* on page 358.)

187 *the warming breath of motherly love*: Yekaterina Korotkova-Grossman, "Neozhidanny Grossman," *Al'manakh* 7–8, 1 [available at http://almanah-dialog.ru/archive/archive_7-8_1/pr13].

187 *Grossman admired wholeheartedly*: Guber, Korotkova, and Lipkin have all written about the close friendship between the two writers and their admiration of each other's work.

187 *"without any settled position"*: David Ortenberg, "Andrey Platonov—Frontovoy Korespondent," in *Andrey Platonov: Vospominaniya sovremennikov,* N. V. Kornienko and E.D. Shubina, eds. (Moscow: Sovremenny pisatel', 1994), 105.

187 *material relating to the Minsk ghetto*: Platonov is not usually listed among the contributors to *The Black Book*. Nina Malygina, however, has discovered a document from the archives of the Jewish Anti-Fascist Committee confirming the transmission to Platonov of a variety of materials relating to the Minsk ghetto. Malygina transcribes this document [GARF, fond 8114, opis' 1, delo 945, 164] in her article "Yevreiskaya tema v tvorchestve Andreya Platonova," in *Semanticheskaya poetika russkoi literatury. K yubileyu professora Nauma Lazarevicha Leidermana* (Yekaterinburg: 2008), 128–39. See also Shimon Redlich, *War, Holocaust and Stalinism* (Luxembourg: Harwood Academic Publishers, 1995), 353–54.

187 *Grossman visited him almost daily*: Lipkin, 527. Platonov's daughter-in-law, Tamara Grigorievna Platonova, has confirmed this in conversation with Malygina [e-mail from Malygina].

187 *said in Russia about Platonov*: Lipkin, 528.

188 *known only to them*: Bocharov, 323.

188 *like the life of a plant*: Lipkin, 527.

188 *part of a splendid person*: Guber writes that Grossman "was ecstatic (*byl v vostorge*) about his friend's work and knew all its subterranean [that is, unpublished] parts." [Guber, 41.] And Lipkin heard Platonov read aloud from *Soul* (*Dzhan*), which was first published only fifteen years after Platonov's death [Lipkin, 524]. There are, however, no accounts of Platonov showing, or reading, *Happy Moscow* to anyone. It is not impossible that Grossman knew this passage about Sartorius, but it is unlikely.

189 *life in all its manifestations*: Lipkin, 526.

189 *the Russia that was sent to the camps*: Lydia Chukovskaya, *Zapiski ob Anne Akhmatovoy*, vol. 2 (Moscow: 1997), 190.

190 *allow themselves to be fooled*: Bocharov, 336.

190 *dominates Grossman's thoughts*: "The Avalanche" (1963) can be read as an expression of Grossman's anxiety about what would happen to his own legacy. An old woman has just died. Her children and grandchildren have difficulty dividing up her belongings; some are rude and grabbing, others hypocritical. The story ends on a note of unexpected grace: Irina, the youngest of the grandchildren, is walking down the street early on a sunny morning. Someone on the other side of the street is whistling the Toreador's aria from *Carmen*; a man walking beside Irina joins in, awkwardly humming the same aria. The two men glance at each other. Irina thinks, "Bizet's inheritance seems so easy to share!" Like Irina, Grossman can be understood to feel both envy and wonder with regard to Bizet. A composer, at least in some respects, is more fortunate than a novelist. A long, complex, and subversive novel cannot, after all, be passed from person to person across a street.

191 *Viktor Shklovsky*: Ilya Ehrenburg and Vasily Grossman, *The Complete Black Book of Russian Jewry*, David Patterson, trans. and ed. (New Brunswick, NJ: Transaction Publishers, 2002), 219–22.

192 *I didn't betray anyone, did I?*: Anna Berzer, *Proshchanie* (Moscow: Kniga, 1990), 251.

"THE ELK"

This was first published in Moskva *(January 1963), but there has been disagreement about when it was written. Some Russian editions give 1938–40.*

The four-volume collected works, however, gives 1960–62; Guber broadly agrees. Korotkova recalls her father showing her the story during one of the January holidays she spent with him, probably in 1954 or 1955. This recollection is confirmed by Bocharov, who cites a letter indicating that Grossman sent "The Elk" to a Moscow literary journal in 1956 [Bocharov, 177]. Guber states that the hero is at least partly based on the figure of Pyotr Vavrisevich (the husband of Grossman's wife's elder sister, Maria Mikhailovna), who was housebound for many years. The head of an elk he had once shot hung on the wall of his room. Guber remembers Pyotr Vavrisevich being disabled as far back as the late 1930s—so this does not help us to date the story. Yury Bit-Yunan, however, has found that Grossman's handwriting in the manuscript of this story is much closer to his handwriting in "Mama" than to his handwriting in "A Small Life" or "In the Town of Berdichev." This confirms the view held by both Guber and Korotkova that it is indeed a late work.

194 *The People's Will*: The most important of these figures are Andrey Zhelyabov (1851–81); his wife, Sofya Perovskaya (1853–81); and Nikolay Kibalchich (1853–81). All three were members of The People's Will, and all three were executed for their part in the assassination, on March 1, 1881, of Tsar Alexander II. Sofya Perovskaya was the first woman to be executed in Russia for political reasons. Nikolay Kibalchich, the organization's explosives expert, is a distant relative of the writer Viktor Kibalchich (better known by his pseudonym of Victor Serge). Nikolay Ishutin (1840–79), one of the first Russian utopian Socialists, was arrested in April 1866 in connection with an earlier attempt to assassinate Tsar Alexander II. The Chaikovtsy was a populist organization that flourished in Petersburg from 1869 to 1874; many of their members later joined The People's Will. The Black Repartition was a short-lived populist organization opposed to the use of terror. [See also note for *I want to write about him* on page 352.]

195 *Lizogub of The People's Will*: Sinegub and Lizogub are both historical figures, but Dmitry Petrovich's confusion is nonetheless comical. "Sinegub" means "blue lips"; "Lizogub" means "lick lips."

199 *nitroglycerine*: Nitroglycerine, which has the effect of widening the blood vessels, has been used since the late nineteenth century to treat angina.

202 *DDT on the elk's head*: The insecticidal properties of DDT were discovered in 1939. It was most widely used in agriculture between 1950

and 1980, though in the United States it was banned as early as 1972. Reference to it in this story, which appears to be set in the mid- or late 1930s, seems to be a slip on Grossman's part.

"MAMA"
Written in 1960; first published in Znamya *(May 1989).*

205 *an army commissar, second grade*: An army commissar was the commissar responsible for the moral and political education of an entire army, just as a battalion commissar was responsible for the moral and political education of a battalion. Grossman's middle-aged NKVD officer is equivalent in rank to a general; the only higher rank was army commissar, first grade.

206 *Moscow Tailoring Combine*: Clothes produced by this factory were notoriously ugly. A sketch by the Soviet satirists Ilf and Petrov describes a young man and woman who fancy each other when they meet on a beach, then put on their Moscow Tailoring Combine clothes and run away from each other in horror, each shocked at the ugliness of the other.

206 *Negoreloye Station*: From 1921 until 1939 the small town of Negoreloye, fifty kilometers west of Minsk, lay on the Polish-Soviet frontier. During the Great Terror there were many instances of Soviet citizens being recalled from foreign capitals only to be taken off the train at Negoreloye and shot by the NKVD. By having Nadya's parents bend down over her, perhaps saying their last goodbyes, Grossman suggests they may have foreseen their fate. His first draft includes the more explicit description: "her mother's pale face with eyes wet from tears, and the gloomy face of her father, who already knew his implacable fate." [RGALI, fond 1710, opis′ 3, ed. khr., 23.]

207 *Marfa Domityevna*: We have slightly changed the nanny's patronymic. In reality, the name of the little girl's nanny was Marfa Grigoryevna, but Grossman calls her Marfa Dementyevna. The Russian name "Dementii" is derived from the Latin name "Domitianus," which is related to the participle *domitus*, meaning "having been tamed." We have chosen to emphasize this etymology rather than risk the reader being misled by the apparent link between "Dementyevna" and "demented."

209 *and sang her a little song*: The man with the guttural voice and the

laugh is Vyacheslav Molotov, chairman of the Council of People's Commissars (the equivalent of prime minister) from 1930 to 1941. The other three men, in order of appearance, are Betal Kalmykov, the Party boss in Karbardino-Balkaria, an autonomous republic in the North Caucasus; Georgy Malenkov, the Central Committee's personnel officer; and Lazar Kaganovich ("Iron Lazar"), the People's Commissar for Transport.

209 *he had a little daughter too*: These two "guests" are Kliment Voroshilov, a marshal of the Soviet Union, and Lavrenty Beria, who in November 1938 was to replace Yezhov as head of the NKVD.

209 *pictures she had seen of them*: Stalin's three most loyal henchmen.

209 *Mama, Nyanya, Papa*: "Mama, Nanny, Daddy"—all three words are stressed on the first syllable.

210 *and understood, a great deal*: In both manuscript and typescript this is followed by two sentences that Grossman later deleted [RGALI, fond 1710, opis 3, ed. khr., 23]:

> Marfa Domityevna understood that she must never, through word or look, show how much she had seen and understood— neither to the cleaner, nor to the yellow-eyed cook, nor to the guards who opened the door to her.
>
> Her calm, just, and straightforward mind noticed many things that the perceptive and sensitive Isaak Babel, whom she thought the kindest of Nikolay Ivanovich's guests, would have been avid to know.

210 *to be heard in their home*: Kalmykov remained in his post as Communist Party First Secretary of the Kabardino-Balkar Autonomous Soviet Socialist Republic until November 1938. In 1940, on Beria's orders, he was tortured and shot.

210 *speak again on the telephone*: The childhood friend is Zinaida Glikina, who went to school with Yevgenia in Gomel. Glikina was arrested on November 15, 1937. Yevgenia and her husband would have understood that Beria was responsible both for this arrest and for that of another close friend of Yevgenia's [Marc Jansen and Nikita Petrov, *Stalin's Loyal Executioner: People's Commissar Nikolai Ezhov 1895–1940* (Stanford, CA: Hoover Institution Press, 2002), 123, 168, and 191; see also Vitaly Shentalinsky, *Donos na Sokrata* (Moscow: Formika–S, 2001), 418].

211 *and in the Butyrka*: Three of Moscow's most notorious prisons. Feliks

Dzerzhinsky (founder of the Cheka) and the poet Vladimir Maya-kovsky were both imprisoned in the Butyrka under the tsarist regime; Isaak Babel and Aleksandr Solzhenitsyn were two of the many writers imprisoned there under the Soviet regime.

211 *Bay of Nogayevo*: Towns and regions associated with important labor camps.

212 *This is my mama*: Another passage that Grossman chose to shorten [RGALI, fond 1710, opis′ 3, ed. khr., 23]. Both the manuscript and the first version of the typescript read:

"Marfa Domityevna," said the mistress of the house. "Let me introduce you, this is my mama." And Marfa Domityevna immediately thought that the mother and daughter had similar noses and eyes.

Marfa Domityevna could see that the old woman felt timid both before her and before Nadya, that she was afraid of touching Nadya's toys, that she was afraid of the cook.

The old woman was looking at her daughter with love and pity. When Marfa Domityevna was just a little village girl, when people had just called her "Marfutka," her own mother had used to look at her in the same way.

213 *a strange person*: The manuscript contains a more direct criticism: "She was not bad or unkind, and she cared about her little girl; nevertheless, she was somehow strange, lacking in character (*strannaya, nesostoyatel′naya*)." It is unclear whether this is the narrator's criticism or Marfa Domityevna's [RGALI, fond 1710, opis′ 3, ed. khr., 23].

214 *the Red Corner*: The Russian word *krasny* means both "red" and "beautiful." The "red corner" was originally the corner of a room where icons were hung, on the diagonal. During the Soviet period, a "red corner" was an area in a factory, hostel, or other public building that was set aside for quiet reading. Discussions could be held there and notices could be posted on the walls.

216 *a cash collector*: A man whose job was to collect cash from shops or other institutions and deliver it to a bank. There was no check-clearing system in the Soviet Union; checks could be used only to withdraw money from one's own account.

"LIVING SPACE"

Written in 1960; first published in Znamya *(May 1989).*

220 *Furmanov and Mayakovsky*: Dmitry Furmanov (1891–1926) was a Bolshevik commissar during the Russian Civil War. His novel *Chapaev* was made into a well-known film. Vladimir Mayakovsky (1893–1930) was a futurist poet and playwright. Unhappy in love and disillusioned with the Revolution, he shot himself in 1930.

"THE ROAD"

Written in 1961–62; first published in Novy mir *(June 1962).*

231 *more like predatory hunters than like people*: These were probably Russian scouts and snipers. The mule is witnessing the beginning of the Soviet offensive at Stalingrad. This follows a standard pattern: an artillery barrage, a reconnaissance, the advance of the tanks, and lastly the advance of the infantry.

"THE DOG"

Written in 1960–61; first published in Literaturnaya Rossiya *(1966). The downbeat final sentence was omitted in this first publication; an editor, or censor, was evidently trying to make the story sound more optimistic. This sentence has also been omitted in at least one recent Russian publication of the story, but there is no doubt that Grossman intended it to remain. See Bocharov, 314.*

240 *a foregone conclusion*: Laika (the word means "Barker"), the first living creature to enter orbit, was launched into space on *Sputnik 2* on November 3, 1957; she died earlier than expected. During the 1950s and 1960s Soviet research scientists subjected a number of dogs to suborbital and orbital flights. Most were stray bitches from the streets of Moscow; it was thought that strays would be better able to tolerate the stresses of flight. Bitches were chosen because they were considered more patient and because they did not need to cock a leg to urinate. The dogs' "training" included having to stand still for long periods, wearing space suits, riding in centrifuges that simulated the acceleration of a rocket launch, and being kept in progressively smaller cages to prepare them for confinement in a space capsule. Dogs that flew in orbit were fed a nutritious gel.

241 *phlogiston*: According to a once widely held scientific theory, disproved by Lavoisier in the eighteenth century, all flammable materials contain phlogiston (the word is derived from the Greek *phlogistos*, meaning "flammable"), a substance without color, odor, taste, or weight that is liberated in burning.

"IN KISLOVODSK"

Written in 1962–63; first published in a bowdlerized version in Literaturnaya gazeta *(1967) and in a complete version in* Nedelya *(1988).*

245 *The Three Musketeers*: This novel by Alexandre Dumas was first published in 1844. Athos, the eldest of the musketeers, is noble, handsome, intriguingly melancholy, and a fine swordsman—a Byronic figure. According to Korotkova, Grossman especially valued *The Three Musketeers* because there are "so few books about true male friendship."

247 *Kolchak's forces*: Aleksandr Kolchak (1874–1920), commander of the White forces in Siberia and the Urals during the Civil War, was executed in 1920.

247 *the Left and Right Oppositions*: The Left Opposition was a Communist Party faction opposed to Stalin and led, from 1923 to 1927, by Leon Trotsky. The Right Opposition was a Communist Party faction opposed to Stalin in the late 1920s; its most important figures were Nikolay Bukharin and Aleksey Rykov.

248 *Budyonny staying with us*: Marshal Semyon Budyonny was a Russian Civil War hero.

249 *Warsaw citadel*: A fortress built by Tsar Nicholas I. During the late nineteenth and early twentieth centuries many important revolutionaries were imprisoned there.

249 *Oryol prison*: An infamous prison, with a high death rate. Political prisoners were kept together with criminal convicts. Feliks Dzerzhinsky, the first head of the Cheka, served two terms there.

251 *Blumenthal-Tamarin*: A Russian actor, notorious for collaborating with the Nazis during the war.

251 *Hauptmann*: Gerhart Hauptmann (1862–1946) was once well known for his plays of social protest. In 1912 he was awarded the Nobel Prize for Literature.

257 *they worshipped Vertinsky*: Born in 1889, Aleksandr Vertinsky emi-

grated after the Revolution but returned to the Soviet Union in 1943. He remained the object of official disapproval until his death in 1957. His first legal vinyl record was released in the Soviet Union only in 1976.

PART FOUR: THREE LETTERS

261 *I ask for freedom for my book*: Fyodor Guber, *Pamyat' i pis'ma* (Moscow: Probel, 2007), 102.

262 *standing in an empty room*: Vasily Grossman, *Sobranie sochinenii*, (Moscow: Vagrius, 1998) vol. 1, p. 133.

263 *so miraculously found him*: Ibid., 413.

264 *listening, learning and imagining*: Claude Lanzmann, *Shoah* (Eureka, 1985), page 76 of the booklet accompanying the 2007 DVD of the film.

Letter of September 15, 1950

265 *Auntie Anyuta, Uncle David, and Natasha*: David and Anyuta Sherentsis, Grossman's maternal uncle and his wife, supported him throughout his childhood. David Sherentsis was a wealthy doctor, entrepreneur, and philanthropist, and Grossman and his mother lived in his and Anyuta's house for many years. Anyuta died of natural causes in the mid-1930s. David Sherentsis was arrested in 1938, as a "speculator"; it is likely that he died or was executed during the following year. Natasha (a mentally retarded young relative who lived with David and Anyuta) was, along with Grossman's mother, among the 12,000 Berdichev Jews shot by the Nazis on September 15, 1941; in *Life and Fate* she is portrayed as Natasha Karasik.

Letter of September 15, 1961

267 *nor in Auntie Liza's*: Grossman's father, Semyon Osipovich, died in 1956. Auntie Liza was another of Grossman's maternal aunts. For the importance in Grossman's life of her daughter Nadya Almaz, see page 7.

268 *Syoma*: An affectionate form of Semyon—Grossman's father's first name.

268 *my love is eternally with you*: For the Russian text of both letters, see Guber, 78–79.

PART FIVE: ETERNAL REST

273 *describes in "Eternal Rest"*: Here we follow the account given by
Fyodor Guber. Semyon Lipkin, however, remembers Novodevichye
as being Olga Mikhailovna's first choice: "Grossman's relatives, Zabolotskaya, and I wanted to bury the urn with Grossman's ashes in the
Vagankovo Cemetery, beside the grave of Grossman's father...But
Olga Mikhailovna insisted—obstinately—on the Novodevichye—
the country's most prestigious cemetery." [Fyodor Guber, *Pamyat' i
pis'ma* (Moscow: Probel, 2007), 624.] It is unclear which of Grossman's relatives Lipkin has in mind here. Guber insists that the
Vagankovo was Olga Mikhailovna's first choice; he suggests that Lipkin may have heard of her wish to have the ashes buried in the Novodevichye only after she had already failed with regard to the
Vagankovo.

274 *the Vostryakovo Jewish Cemetery*: Semyon Lipkin, *Kvadriga* (Moscow: Knizhny Sad, 1997), 632. John and Carol Garrard [*The Bones of
Berdichev* (New York: The Free Press, 1996), 305–08] expand on Lipkin's account, suggesting that Grossman wanted to lie in Jewish
ground in order to be united, at least symbolically, with his mother
and other victims of the Shoah. Olga Mikhailovna's behavior was—
they believe—motivated in part by a love of prestige and in part by a
desire to be buried beside her husband. Seemingly unaware that the
main Moscow cemeteries were administered by secular authorities,
the Garrards mistakenly assume that, had Grossman been buried in
the Vostryakovo Jewish Cemetery, it would have been impossible for
Olga Mikhailovna, a non-Jew, to be buried beside him. Grossman has
often been compared to Tolstoy; Olga Mikhailovna's role in his life
seems oddly similar, at least in some ways, to Sofya Andreyevna's role
in Tolstoy's life. Not only did Olga Mikhailovna run the household
but she also, at least after 1945, typed and retyped *all* her husband's
manuscripts—even the chapters in *Life and Fate* about Viktor Shtrum
and his love affair with Maria Sokolova. According to Guber, she retyped *For a Just Cause*; *Life and Fate*; *Good Wishes*; *Everything Flows*;
all Grossman's postwar stories; the articles "The Murder of the Jews
in Berdichev," "The Sistine Madonna," and "Eternal Rest"; and Grossman's letter to Khrushchev. Together with Korotkova, she also typed
out his wartime notebooks, which Grossman read aloud. And, like

Sofya Andreyevna, Olga Mikhailovna is often cast in the role of trivial-minded wife, unworthy of her husband.

275 *I dug the holes with my fingers*: Guber, 154; and e-mail from Guber, March 30, 2010.

"ETERNAL REST"

Written in 1957–60; first published in Znamya *(May 1989). The article seems almost to have been lost forever, although Guber is certain that Olga Mikhailovna prepared it for publication. Yekaterina Korotkova, however, writes, "As I was going through my father's files, I came across a large envelope that seemed, at first glance, to have nothing in it but rubbish: scraps of newspaper, and other bits of torn-up paper covered in handwriting. I noticed a few pages—squared pages from a school exercise book—that had been crumpled but not torn up. I read one page and found it interesting. I read more pages— and began to feel upset that notes like this should have been lost. But then I went through the envelope more carefully—and I found still more pages. From these I was able to piece together the sketch: 'Eternal Rest.' I do not know what happened to the final manuscript; my father never spoke of it. Nor do I know why he threw away this rough draft—something he did not normally do."*

281 *oxygen pillows*: These bags made from rubberized cloth—small oxygen reservoirs with a tap and a connecting pipe—are still used in Russia by people with breathing difficulties. Once emptied, they can be taken to a chemist's and refilled.

282 *They have seen meekness* [...]: Here we have taken a liberty we have not allowed ourselves elsewhere—that of abridgment. We have omitted the next three pages, which are taken up by some rather dull, excessively generalized accounts of a variety of unhappy family relationships.

284 *First or Second Guild*: The First Guild comprised very wealthy merchants; the Second Guild, less wealthy merchants; and the Third Guild, artisans and small tradesmen.

288 *life has become merrier*: That is, it is the mid-1930s.

289 *life by other means*: In "On War" Carl von Clausewitz wrote, "It is clear that war is not a mere act of policy but a true political instrument, a continuation of political activity by other means."

289 *said the Greek*: "Everything flows" (Πάντα ῥεῖ—*panta rhei*), the aphorism used by Grossman as the title of his last novel, has conventionally

been attributed to Heraclitus, a pre-Socratic philosopher who lived circa 535–475 BC.

291 *And nothing of that hope remains*: From "14 December 1825," Fyodor Tyutchev's skeptical response to the Decembrist Rebellion.

291 *and the German Cemetery*: In 1918 all three cemeteries were secularized and began to accept the dead of all nationalities and creeds. The German Cemetery (Vvedenskoye) was, from the early 1770s until 1918, the main burial ground for Catholics and Protestants. The Armenian Cemetery, established in 1804, is close to the Vagankovo Cemetery.

291 *the assassination of Kirov in 1934*: Sergey Kirov (1886–1934), an Old Bolshevik who enjoyed considerable popularity, was assassinated in 1934. It is possible that Stalin was himself responsible. Stalin exploited the assassination as a justification for the Great Terror, during which he arrested or executed most of the remaining Old Bolsheviks.

APPENDIXES

1. Grossman and "The Hell of Treblinka"

295 *later that autumn*: See Vasily Grossman, *A Writer at War*, Antony Beevor and Luba Vinogradova, eds. and trans. (London: Pimlico, 2006), 306.

296 *about these camps*: Aleksandr Solzhenitsyn, *Sobranie sochinenii v deviati tomakh* (Moscow: Terra, 2000), vol. 5, page 9.

297–298 *published in 1989*: The original text can be found in the Jewish Historical Institute in Warsaw (record number 247); much is omitted from both the Hebrew and the English editions [e-mail from Timothy Snyder].

299 *the last remains of our martyrs*: Rachel Auerbach, "In the Fields of Treblinka" in Alexander Donat, ed., *The Death Camp Treblinka* (New York: Holocaust Library, 1979), 73.

300 *how the world would see their crimes*: See also note for *Majdanek, Sobibor, and Bełzec* on page 343, and note for *far away on the Volga* on page 344.

2. Natalya Khayutina and the Yezhovs

301 *first lady of the kingdom!*: See Simon Sebag Montefiore, *Stalin: The Court of the Red Tsar* (London: Orion, 2004), 273. Babel, for his part,

was one of the stars of Yevgenia's salon. According to Babel's wife, Antonina Pirozhkova, "If you invited people 'for Babel,' they all came." [Ibid., 272.]

301 *at a Kremlin reception*: See http://www.seagullmag.com/article.php?id=1297.

302 *a novel about the Cheka*: According to Furmanov, Babel continued, "I don't know, though, if I can manage it—my view of Cheka is just too one-sided. The reason is that the Chekists that I know, they are, well, they are simply holy people, even those who did the shooting with their own hands...And I fear [the book] may come out too saccharine." [Gregory Freidin, *The Enigma of Isaac Babel* (Stanford, CA: Stanford University Press, 2009), 229, note 65.] It is unlikely that Babel said this without irony.

302 *see what it smells like*: Nadezhda Mandelstam, *Hope Against Hope* (London: Penguin, 1975), 385.

302 *as early as 1933*: The date of Natalya Khayutina's birth and the date of her adoption are both unclear. According to her birth certificate, she was born on May 1, 1936, but she considers this a fiction of Yezhov's; one of the reasons she gives is that May 1 was Yezhov's own birthday. [Erik Shur, "Reabilitiruyut li Yezhova?," available at www.sovsekretno.ru/magazines/article/166.]

302 *her adoptive parents*: The most complete account of the life of the real Natalya Khayutina is by G. Zhavoronkov, in the journal *Sintaksis* 32 (1992). All unreferenced information about her life is taken from this, from Shur, or from http://www.ntv.ru/novosti/31837.

303 *Yezhov's sister*: Natalya grew up believing that the Yezhovs were her real parents. Only when she met Yezhov's sister in the 1960s did she learn that she had been adopted. She has continued, however, at least intermittently, to cling to the idea that Yezhov was her biological father [Zhavoronkov, 47; see also N. Zen'kovich, *Elita: entsiklopediya biografii: samye sekretnye rodstvenniki* (Moscow: Olma Medis Group, 2005), 125–26].

303 *"hedgehog skin gauntlets"*: Stalin, however, used to call him by the affectionate name of Yezhevichka, or "Little Blackberry," and Lavrenty Beria, taking his cue from this, sometimes referred to him as Yozhik or "Little Hedgehog."

303 *after returning from the Lubyanka*: Marc Jansen and Nikita Petrov,

Stalin's Loyal Executioner: People's Commissar Nikolai Ezhov 1895–1940 (Stanford, CA: Hoover Institution Press, 2002), 121.

303 *a real prototype*: See www.moscvichka.ru/article/035/32-04.htm.

304 *that she remembered as real*: My thanks to Leigh Kimmel for suggesting this, and for showing me a draft of "The Hedgehog's Daughter"—her fictional treatment of the life of Natalya Khayutina [available at www.leighkimmel.com].

305 *taken possession of this package*: See http://skoblin.blogspot.com/2009/03/yezhov-file-iv.html.

305 *an end to the Purges*: Donald Rayfield, *Stalin and His Hangmen* (London: Penguin, 2005), 322.

306 *to save myself*: For the circumstances leading up to Yevgenia's death, see Rayfield, 327; Montefiore, 289; and Jansen and Petrov, 166–71.

307 *find her father in Kolyma*: In 1959, after giving birth to a daughter, Yevgenia, Natalya returned to Penza, but she settled permanently in Kolyma a few years after this.

307 *study the accordion*: Zhavoronkov, 59. Zinaida's husband, Sergo Ordzhonikidze, died in 1937—possibly from a heart attack, though it is more likely that he committed suicide.

308 *Marfa Grigoryevna gave up the idea*: Zhavoronkov, 55–57; see also Jansen and Petrov, 189–90 and 258, note 67.

308 *the running of the household*: Fyodor Guber, *Pamyat' i pis'ma* (Moscow: Probel, 2007), 32. See also Vitaly Shentalinsky's discussion of the Pereval "conspiracy" in "Rasstrel'nye nochi," *Zvezda* 5 (2007).

309 *learning about for the first time*: On February 25, 1938, Grossman was interrogated in the Lubyanka in connection with Olga Mikhailovna's arrest. The NKVD records of this interrogation contain no mention of anything pertaining to this "conspiracy" [John and Carol Garrard, *The Bones of Berdichev* (New York: The Free Press, 1996), 123–24].

309 *nonjudgmental portrayal of Yezhov*: In the manuscript version of the first section, Grossman five times refers to Yezhov as *chelovechek* ("a little man"). This use of the diminutive sounds condescending, and the first mention of Yezhov—*malen'kii, shchuplyi chelovechek* ("a small, puny little runt")—is positively contemptuous. In the typescript and in the final version, however, Grossman refers to Yezhov simply as *chelovek* ("a man," "a person").

AFTERWORD

311 *or, more likely, orphanages*: The Soviet authorities usually sent the children of "enemies of the people" to orphanages rather than allowing them to be brought up by relatives who might imbue them with a sense of grievance against the regime. Siblings were usually separated.

FURTHER READING

Ilya Altman and Joshua Rubenstein. *The Unknown Black Book*. Bloomington: Indiana University Press, 2008.

Anne Applebaum. *Gulag: A History of the Soviet Camps*. New York: Doubleday, 2003.

Yitzhak Arad. *Belzec, Sobibor, Treblinka: The Operation Reinhard Death Camps*. Bloomington: Indiana University Press, 1999.

Jonathan Brent and Vladimir P. Naumov. *Stalin's Last Crime: The Plot Against the Jewish Doctors, 1948–1953*. New York: HarperCollins, 2004.

Witold Chrostowski. *Extermination Camp Treblinka*. London: Vallentine Mitchell, 2004.

Alexander Donat, ed. *The Death Camp Treblinka*. New York: Holocaust Library, 1979.

Ilya Ehrenburg and Vasily Grossman. *The Complete Black Book of Russian Jewry*. David Patterson, trans. and ed. New Brunswick, NJ: Transaction Publishers, 2002.

Orlando Figes. *The Whisperers*. London: Penguin, 2008.

Sheila Fitzpatrick. *Everyday Stalinism*. New York: Oxford University Press, 1999.

John and Carol Garrard. *The Bones of Berdichev*. New York: The Free Press, 1996.

J. Arch Getty and Oleg Naumov. *Yezhov: The Rise of Stalin's "Iron Fist."* New Haven, CT: Yale University Press, 2008.

Richard Glazar. *Trap with a Green Fence*. Evanston, IL: Northwestern University Press, 1992.

Vasily Grossman. *Everything Flows*. Robert and Elizabeth Chandler with Anna Aslanyan, trans. New York: New York Review Books, 2009.

———. *Life and Fate*. Robert Chandler, trans. New York: New York Review Books, 2006.

———. *A Writer at War*. Antony Beevor and Luba Vinogradova, eds. and trans. New York: Pantheon, 2005.

Marc Jansen and Nikita Petrov. *Stalin's Loyal Executioner: People's Commissar Nikolai Ezhov 1895–1940*. Stanford, CA: Hoover Institution Press, 2002.

Mark Mazower. *Hitler's Empire*. London: Penguin, 2008.

Catherine Merridale. *Night of Stone*. London: Granta, 2001.

Simon Sebag Montefiore. *Stalin: The Court of the Red Tsar*. London: Orion, 2004.

Rachel Polonsky. *Molotov's Magic Lantern: A Journey in Russian History*. London: Faber, 2010.

Donald Rayfield. *Stalin and His Hangmen*. London: Penguin, 2005.

Richard Rhodes. *Masters of Death: The Einsatzgruppen and the Invention of the Holocaust*. New York: Vintage, 2003.

Gitta Sereny. *Into that Darkness*. London: Pimlico, 1995.

Timothy Snyder. *Bloodlands*. New York: Basic Books, 2010.

Arkady Vaksberg, *Stalin Against the Jews*. New York: Knopf, 1994.

Samuel Willenberg. *Surviving Treblinka*. Oxford: Basil Blackwell, 1989.

ACKNOWLEDGMENTS

I AM ESPECIALLY grateful to Vasily Grossman's daughter, Yekaterina Korotkova, and his stepson Fyodor Guber, both of whom have been patient and generous in answering my many questions. All quotations or references without endnotes are from personal correspondence. I also thank Fyodor Guber and his daughter Elena Guber for allowing us to reproduce a number of photographs from their fine collection.

It has been a joy, as always, to collaborate with my wife, Elizabeth, and a great pleasure to collaborate for the first time with Yury Bit-Yunan and Olga Mukovnikova. Olga Meerson has, as always, provided brilliant insights, especially into "In the Town of Berdichev," and Vadim Altskan has sent me copies of important material from the archives of the U.S. Holocaust Memorial Museum.

I also wish to thank Lily Alexander, Antony Beevor, Karel Berkhoff, Michael Berry, David Black, Emily Van Buskirk, Inna Caron, Frederick Choate, Elizabeth Cook, Jane Costlow, Vivian Curran, Martin Dewhirst, Masha Dmitrovskaya, Irina Dolgova, Jean-Marc Dreyfus, David Fel'dman, Jennifer Foray, John and Carol Garrard, Andrew Glikin-Gusinsky, Igor Golomstock, Elena Fyodorovna Guber, Gasan Gusejnov, Jochen Hellbeck, Jeremy Hicks, Gerard Jacobs, Elana Jakel, Mike Jones, Martha Kapos, Leigh Kimmel, Giovanni Maddalena, Nina Malygina, Irina Mashinski, Tatiana Menaker, Mark Miller, Polina Morozova, Nina Murray, Anna Muza, Elena Ostrovskaya, Katarina Peitlova, Anne Pitt, John Puckett, Donald Rayfield, Joe Roeber, Margo Rosen, Karen Rosneck, Tim Sergay, Nina Shevchuk, Jekaterina Shulga, Robert Smith, Tim Snyder, Pietro Tosco, Val Vinokur, Yevgeny Yablokov, Sarah Young, and the many members of my translation classes at Queen Mary, University of London, and of the SEELANGS e-mail discussion group who have contributed to these translations.

—R. C.

CONTRIBUTORS

YURY BIT-YUNAN was born in western Russia, in the city of Bryansk. He graduated from the Russian State University for the Humanities in Moscow, where he now lectures in literary criticism. He is writing his doctorate on Vasily Grossman.

ELIZABETH CHANDLER is a co-translator, with her husband, of Alexander Pushkin's *The Captain's Daughter*, of Vasily Grossman's *Everything Flows*, and of several volumes of Andrey Platonov: *The Return*, *The Portable Platonov*, *Happy Moscow*, and *Soul*.

ROBERT CHANDLER is the editor of *Russian Short Stories from Pushkin to Buida* and the author of *Alexander Pushkin* (in the Hesperus Brief Lives series). His translations of Sappho and Guillaume Apollinaire are published in the series Everyman's Poetry. His translations from Russian include Vasily Grossman's *Life and Fate* and *Everything Flows*, Nikolai Leskov's *Lady Macbeth of Mtsensk*, and Alexander Pushkin's *The Captain's Daughter* and *Dubrovsky*. Along with Olga Meerson and his wife, Elizabeth, he has translated a number of works by Andrey Platonov. One of these, *Soul*, won the American Association of Teachers of Slavonic and East European Languages (AATSEEL) Prize for 2004. His translation of Hamid Ismailov's *The Railway* won the AATSEEL prize for 2007 and received a special commendation from the judges of the 2007 Rossica Translation Prize.

FYODOR GUBER is the son of the writer Boris Guber, who was arrested and shot in 1937, and of Olga Mikhailovna, Vasily Grossman's second wife. From 1937 Vasily Grossman was Fyodor's official guardian and substitute father. Fyodor Guber is the author of a number of scientific papers about polymer mechanics, several articles about Vasily Grossman, and a selection of Grossman's letters and biographical material titled *Pamyat' i pis'ma* (Memory and Letters).

OLGA MUKOVNIKOVA is a freelance translator and a member of the Chartered Institute of Linguists. She graduated from Oryol State University in 1998, where she read English and history. Since 2004 Mukovnikova has worked as a translator and translation reviser for Amnesty International. She lives and works in the United Kingdom.

OTHER NEW YORK REVIEW CLASSICS

For a complete list of titles, visit www.nyrb.com.